D1093557

The Brides of Bellenmore

AND

Falcon's Shadow

The Brides of Bellenmore
AND
Falcon's Shadow

ANNE MAYBURY

NELSON DOUBLEDAY, INC.
Garden City, New York

All names, characters and events in this book are fictional and any resemblance which may seem to exist to real persons is purely coincidental.

PRINTED IN THE UNITED STATES OF AMERICA

The Brides of Bellenmore

I

My FEET made no sound as I came down the great staircase of Glanmory. Below me, in the hall, the clock struck. Vaguely I counted the strokes, my gaze upon the bland, bronze dial.

All my life I would remember that morning in a house I was never to see again. For two things happened: one insignificant, one shocking. The first was that the clock, pointing to ten, struck eleven booming, reverberating chimes. The other that, as the last stroke died away, I heard a man's voice from the partly-open double doors of Lady Harriet Remfrey's drawing room. The words he spoke were clear and unmistakable.

"Oh, a lot of foolish gentry visit Mark Bellenmore for his so-called treatment. But it is well-accepted by the more discerning that he is a charlatan."

"I believe a stone was thrown through his window the other day and tied round it was a piece of paper on which was written one word, 'Quack!'." Lady Harriet's voice had the avidity of the born gossip. "And by the way, did you ever hear the truth about his wife's death? They said Helen died from a fall down the stairs, but—" and then she laughed.

The man spoke again, but I did not hear it. All senses stopped suddenly in me. I was no longer aware of myself, Elizabeth Bellenmore; I no longer felt the cool carved wood of the banister under my groping hand nor smelt the acrid scent of age which always seemed to pervade Glanmory.

After the first moment of shock, my anger leapt so swiftly that I was shaking with it. They had dared to call Mark a charlatan; they had questioned the manner of his wife, Helen's death.

I finished my journey down the stairs in a headlong rush, ran across the hall, with its palms in their shining brass pots, to the drawing room. I put out both hands to the half-open double doors and pushed them wide.

The room was empty. The French windows leading to the lawn were open. I crossed and looked out over the parkland. Lady Harriet and her guest were nowhere in sight. My train went in half an hour so that there was no time to seek them out and demand an explanation of the outrageous snatch of conversation I had overheard.

Defeated, I turned to the door. My heart hammered with indignation and shock; tears of anger stung my eyes, anger for Mark who had been so slandered.

I ran across the hall to the waiting carriage.

Nobody stood on the steps of the house to wave me good-bye. The inquisitive little face of Nancy, the parlormaid, closing the double doors firmly before I had even stepped into the drive, was the last thing I saw.

The coachman looked at me with interest.

"You be goin' a long way, Miss!"

"To London," I said.

"Back to your own people?"

"Yes."

I sat in the corner of the carriage, my hands clasped tightly inside my muff; I looked up at the house with its tall windows, its cold stone. After all, why should anyone there bother to see me off, or even to remember me once I had gone? I had merely been for four months, companion to Lady Remfrey while she convalesced after the difficult birth of her son.

The coachman flicked his whip; the horses fresh in the vigorous autumn morning, pranced up the great drive.

Back to your own people the coachman had said. Yet, sitting there in the darkness of the carriage, I felt only an overwhelming sense of loneliness. For, although I *was* going to my own people, I scarcely knew them. I was going, as the poorest relation, into a beautiful and lordly house. To my grandmother Bellenmore, Aunt Geraldine, James and Armorel, his wife, and little Kenny, their son. And Mark, of whom strange rumors had spread as far as Dorset.

I leaned my head back, closing my eyes. A gleam of common sense began to seep through my anger. I had met Mark only four times in my life. What was my devotion to him, therefore, but the blind adoration of an image created by a small, lonely girl? I doubted if he ever gave me a thought!

My mother had died bearing, stillborn, the young brother I had so longed for. Before my father, who was a sea captain, sailed again, he had brought a buxom Irishwoman, Rosie O'Greer, to the house to look after me. For fourteen years she had been mother to me and I had loved her dearly.

My father used to be away from home for months at a time. I had learned not to cry when he left, but I loved it when his ship was in port. I would board the *Empress Cristabell* and play on those decks smelling strongly of wet rope and sea salt.

Father had made one concession to my education. I had been sent to Belgium for my final schooling. During the first difficult months I nearly broke my heart with homesickness and to hide it, behaved in my most rebellious and recalcitrant way. Gradually, however, I settled down to enjoy school. It was pleasant to have pretty and charming companions, to learn to play the piano, to speak French, to dance.

But I was never entirely one of them. I had not their everlasting dreams of rich marriages. Nor could I ever bring myself to call my father by the more genteel name of 'Papa.'

My father, a giant of a man with a constitution to match his physique, had never bothered to make provision for me. I think he believed himself to be immortal. But then, just over a year ago, in an alley in Alexandria, he had been killed in a fight with an Arab who had tried to steal his purse.

Immediately she heard of the tragedy, Aunt Geraldine had come to Dover with the intention of taking me back to London with her. I was nineteen. Still suffering from shock and unable to think clearly, I clung to some wild idea that I must be independent.

Aunt Geraldine could not understand my determination to earn my own living. Strength of purpose, however, was never one of her characteristics and she accepted my refusal to accompany her to London sadly enough, but with no real effort to override me.

In the end she even helped me, obtaining for me a post as governess with a family in Dulwich. She herself came to fetch me and took me to their house.

I would always remember that last morning in Dover. Rosie, inconsolable, wept as she kissed me good-bye. She was returning to live with her family in Hythe. With my trunks piled on to the carriage, I looked my last on the gray stone house by the Dover cliffs. I even picked a small bunch of flowers from my father's beloved raggle-taggle garden and climbed into the carriage by Aunt Geraldine's side.

When the Dulwich family left to live in Rome, Aunt Geraldine again found me the temporary post with Lady Harriet Remfrey. Now this, too, was over and I had at last been persuaded to go to London.

"Your grandmama views these posts of yours unfavorably, Elizabeth." Aunt Geraldine had pleaded in a letter. "She is old and it would please her so if you would come to live with us."

Because a Bellenmore did not take employment where she was only once removed from the servants' hall!

On my rare visits to my grandmother's house in Manchester Square, I had never been at my ease. It was all so splendid and spacious.

I had been shy, too, in front of James and Mark whom Aunt Geraldine had adopted when they were both very small. James, three years older than Mark and six years older than myself, was the son of parents who had both died in a cholera epidemic in India. Mark had been left behind when his young and practically penniless parents had gone to America to seek a living in the New World. The idea had been, I was told, that they would send for him to come over later. But no word had been heard of them from the day they sailed.

My first sight of my grandmother, after whom I had been named, had filled me with alarm. She was like an ancient, awe-inspiring goddess. At the end of each visit to Manchester Square, I returned with relief to Dover, holding only two things from my visits to that great house tenderly in my memory. The warmest was Aunt Geraldine's plump enfolding arms hushing me to sleep in the big four-poster bed where I slept alone, and the other, Mark's kindness. It was he who joined in my childish games while James merely tolerated me.

I sat, aware of a wave of quickening excitement. I felt different; I *was* different! I no longer wore my subdued gray merino dress, but had put on the dark green cloth with a matching fur-edged cape. My bonnet had a little posy of moss roses on the crown and was tied with pink ribbons.

After tonight, I would no longer be in that stateless place between the gentry and the servants. I would be Elizabeth Bellenmore. I would know for certain that Mark was no charlatan . . . and I would learn, at last, how Helen had died.

II

THE TRAIN journey which, when I had taken it some weeks ago traveling to Glanmory, had been so exciting, was proving on my return to London to be dull and interminable.

I stared out of the window and tried to enjoy my last sight of the Purbeck Hills lying under the scudding clouds.

When, at last, I arrived at Waterloo Station, I found to my great relief that Aunt Geraldine's brougham had been sent to collect me.

I sat, staring at London in the misty autumn twilight, craning my neck for a glimpse of the glitter in the jeweler's window, a last sight of a little sable jacket on a young woman with a bonnet of cowslips.

When the brougham turned into Manchester Square, I saw the house—four storied, wide-fronted, with a wrought-iron balcony running the length of the tall windows of the first floor. I could even see the glimmer of green brocade curtains.

What would they say to me? What would *I* say to them, these relatives who were almost strangers?

The carriage stopped and the coachman helped me down; the front door of the house opened. I went up the path between the dark evergreens, mounted the steps, holding my gown carefully from the damp stones, and saw Mrs. Vine's broad, smiling face.

"Welcome, Miss Elizabeth."

"It's nice to see you again, Mrs. Vine," I said a little shyly to the friendly housekeeper. "How are you?"

"With a doctor living in the house, what else could I be but well?" She spoke proudly, but I saw a little gleam of mischief in her eye.

Then I heard someone call my name and I was swept up into Aunt Geraldine's plump, pretty arms. She kissed my cheek and looking at her, I wanted desperately to believe that I was really welcome here.

"You look tired, child. You have had a long journey." Aunt Geraldine held me away from her. "But you can rest before dinner."

I did not want to rest and I said so, laughingly but firmly. Glancing around the big, square hall, I saw that nothing was changed. There were the same tall Italian chairs, the refectory table on which Mark, as a little boy of seven, had carved his initials with Mrs. Vine's kitchen knife.

Then I looked up at the great crystal chandelier. It was pyramid of sparkling crystal and all the candles had been lit. I stood for a moment watching it sway very gently. As though it were yesterday, I felt again my old fear that it would fall on me, crushing me under a mountain of brilliant, broken prisms. I moved quickly from underneath it.

Two people came out of the room to the right of the door. Although I had not seen James for some years, I recognized him immediately.

He was very tall and broad and as handsome as he had been as a boy, with thick chestnut hair and fine dark eyes. His manner, as he held out his hand to me, had more warmth than in the old days.

"It is wonderful to see you again, Elizabeth. I hope you will be very happy here with us!"

"I'm sure I shall!" I told him, glancing about me with frank pleasure. "How could I not be? And by the way, James, I have heard of your success as a doctor. The news, you see, has traveled even as far as Dorset."

He looked pleased and his eyes deepened and darkened upon mine. Then he turned to the young woman by his side.

"You have never met Armorel, have you?"

"Indeed I have! On my last visit here six years ago." I turned my attention to James's wife. "I was only fourteen at the time, but

I have never forgotten seeing you come down the stairs on your way to a ball. You wore white satin and crimson roses on your bodice."

Her face softened a little at the implied compliment. She was very beautiful. Her smooth, fair hair was parted in the middle and drawn down on each side of her perfectly oval face. She had a pretty, slightly petulant mouth and fine deep blue eyes. Tonight she wore a claret-colored gown and the Bellenmore diamond star at her throat.

I hoped Armorel was going to like another young person in the house with her, but something deep inside me doubted it.

"You will want to go to your room," Aunt Geraldine said. "The fire has been lit and I will tell Susannah to bring up hot water to you. Armorel, will you take Elizabeth upstairs, please?"

I had wished that Aunt Geraldine herself would show me to my room, but she bustled toward the back of the house. I paused for a moment and looked up at the staircase that curved in gracious arcs up to the top of the house. It was immensely wide, the stairs were shallow and the banister was of wrought-iron delicately worked.

"Shall we go?"

I turned and smiled at Armorel and together we climbed up, past the half-landing with its stained-glass window in an alcove, past the drawing room and then up to the room on the second floor which was to be mine. It was not very large, but it was prettily furnished with muslin flounces frothing around the dressing table, a sofa and a rosewood writing table.

The fire burned brightly and I was grateful to it for I was very cold after my journey. I crossed to the bed and stroked the patchwork quilt.

Armorel wandered round the room, checked the coal in the scuttle, the towels on the rail of the marble topped wash-hand stand.

"You will, I hope, be comfortable here."

"Yes. Oh yes!" I cried and secretly contrasted it with my dull and rather dreary room at Glanmory.

As though she read my thoughts, Armorel asked, "How did you like working for Lady Remfrey?"

"Well enough," I said guardedly.

She laughed. "You do not have to be cautious with me, Elizabeth! I have met Harriet Remfrey once or twice and I cannot believe that you enjoyed yourself in her employ!"

"I would not like to live in that isolated place for the rest of my life!" I said evasively. "Here, it is different. I am going to be so happy."

"Are you?" she asked unsmilingly.

"But of course!"

She gave me a long, strange look as she moved toward the door. Her dress rustled and the jewel on her bodice sparkled. She was glancing down the passage.

"Here is Susannah with hot water for you. When you have changed, you will come to the drawing room. And I should not be too long. Grandmama does not like to be kept waiting."

When the furniture in the Dover cottage had been sold, Aunt Geraldine had told me to send to her for storage of my own small, precious possessions.

"You will not wish to be lumbered with very much," she had said kindly, "and there is plenty of room in our attic for the things you may not need until you have a home of your own." And here, in a corner of the room I saw the trunk that contained my most valued possessions standing ready to be unpacked. I felt in my reticule for the key of the trunk and then hesitated, recalling Armorel's departing words: "Grandmama does not like to be kept waiting."

I would leave unpacking the trunk until the morning.

I washed in the bowl with the rose garlands on it and changed into a dress of green silk with bands of bronze velvet. It was not particularly fashionable, but I put it on with a gesture of gaiety at my release from Glanmory, where I had had to wear my dull brown merino dresses. I felt now like tossing them to the first beggar I saw. I leaned forward to look at myself in the mirror.

My hair was nearly black, yet the lamp gave it curious tinges of gold. I put up my hand and pulled out the pins, letting the long strands fall about my shoulders. Then I ran my fingers through it, shaking it free.

I did not have a fashionable face. My eyes were not round and large and luminous; they were tilted slightly at the corners and

Rosie used to laugh and say that they were the same color as Malou's. Malou was my little gray cat. She had died through running out under horses' feet only a few days before we had heard of my father's own death. My mouth was large, deeply curved and, as I had been told often at that school, rebellious.

I paused to warm my hands at the fire before I went downstairs to greet my grandmother. Why had Armorel looked at me so strangely when I had spoken about my pleasure at being here? Why had she even questioned that I would be happy?

I wished that Mark still lived here. My gaze moved to the window. I crossed the room and drew the curtains aside. Aunt Geraldine had told me that he had become so successful that he had bought his own house immediately opposite, on the far side of the Square.

Which house? As the wind parted the branches of the trees, I peered through the lamplight. But all I could see was the terrace of tall, fine houses, and all I could hear were the dry leaves whipped into flurries by the wind.

III

In black silk and Valenciennes lace, grandmother Elizabeth Bellenmore sat in the carved chair with the lion's claw feet.

As I entered the room I had a feeling that she had not moved from that chair for all these years. The same thick opossum rug covered it, keeping her short, straight back and thin legs from draughts. Although she was over eighty her iron-gray hair was still thick, her small dark eyes could still snap fire, her thin hands were heavily ringed.

It was at them that I looked longest.

Far back, on my first visit to the house when I was barely seven, I remembered that her hands were seldom still. She would sit, silent or talking, her fingers playing with some small treasured possession much as my father had told me the Chinese mandarins would play with a piece of jade. Sometimes she would be handling a heart-shaped piece of amber, sometimes it was the fan which she now held and which fascinated me. It was made of thick black lace mounted on mother-of-pearl. There were two eyeholes in the lace which, I learned, enabled the fans to be used in olden times for peering at some rather risqué play.

"Well, child, must you stand staring at me?"

"I am sorry, grandmother," I said contritely and crossed the room, bending to kiss the dry, thin flesh of her cheek. Then I raised myself and smiled. I reached out and touched the fan.

"I remember when I was a little girl, you used to tell me wonderful stories about your fans." Immediately I knew that I had pleased her, for she was very vain.

"You have charm as well as boldness." She tilted her head to look at me. "You must develop the one and conquer the other!"

"Elizabeth looks tired," James said, "I think a little port wine will bring back the color to her cheeks. It has been a cold day for such a long journey."

"We will all have wine," said my grandmother.

Aunt Geraldine entered the room, walking lightly on small, plump feet, smiling at me.

"Elizabeth has grown into a very pretty young lady, has she not, Mama?"

"Pretty? No!" The black eyes scrutined me. "You misuse words, Geraldine! Elizabeth is very like her father."

"I am glad," I said quietly. "I loved my father very much and I like to think I resemble him in looks!"

As I knew he was the scapegrace among the Bellenmores, a man who had laughed in the face of society, I sought quickly to change the subject. If my grandmother made some disparaging remark about my father, I would feel bound to challenge it and I did not want to cross swords with her on my first evening.

"If it is not too late," I said sipping my wine, "I would like to see Kenny. Just a peep."

"He is longing to see you too, Elizabeth, although of course, he doesn't remember you," Aunt Geraldine said eagerly.

I glanced at the gilt clock under its glass dome. "It is late, I suppose! If you think he might be asleep—"

"Drink your wine first," my grandmother said, "and come nearer the fire."

I went obediently to a chair she indicated and suffered her

small, shrewd eyes upon me while she questioned me about my post at Glanmory.

While I answered questions, another part of me was aware that nothing had changed in this handsomely furnished room. Grandfather Nicholas Bellenmore still watched me through shallow black eyes from the portrait over the fireplace.

I was relieved when my grandmother's questioning and scrutiny were over and I was being taken to see Kenny.

"I heard, of course, about his accident," I said, walking down the stairs at Aunt Geraldine's side.

"He was climbing the garden wall to look for his ball which had become lodged in the creeper. His spine is injured, Elizabeth, and Doctor Rowlins who is attending him, says that complete rest is the only hope of a cure."

"You mean," I cried aghast, for I had not realized the seriousness of his accident, "that he is still unable to walk?"

"I'm afraid so."

"But four months in bed to a growing boy must seem like a lifetime!"

"James has great faith in Doctor Rowlins." A little flush touched Aunt Geraldine's cheeks. "He is old, I know, but he has a very rich practice and his patients love him." She turned to me, her eyes appealing as though for corroboration of the status of someone I did not even know. I was silent and troubled as we crossed the hall.

Kenny's room was on the ground floor, on the left hand side of the wide hall. Aunt Geraldine paused with her hand on the door handle.

"Sometimes I wonder—" she began.

At that moment a peal of mingled laughter from inside the room, a man's and a child's, cut her short.

"Mark is with him!" Aunt Geraldine said in surprise. "He must have arrived while we were in the drawing room! Although he no longer lives here, he has a key—" Again her voice trailed off into nothingness. I remembered so well from the past how Aunt Geraldine never seemed to be quite certain of what she wanted to say.

Gas light cast a yellow glow over the pleasant room we entered. Kenny lay propped up in his bed, which stood near the window. He had a quantity of black and white paper and some scissors on the counterpane and I saw that he had been making silhouettes.

A man rose from the bedside and I looked straight into Mark's light, laughing gray eyes.

"Elizabeth!" He greeted me with warmth, taking my hands in his, bending his dark head a little to look deeply at me. "I was wondering how soon we would meet!"

I withdrew my hands as discreetly as I could and lowered my eyes from that luminous, searching gaze.

"I am glad that you recognized me after all these years," I smiled.

"Had I not known that you were coming, I would have been waiting for an introduction! You have changed very much; you have grown beautiful!"

"Flattery!" Aunt Geraldine tut-tutted at him but she was smiling.

"There isn't a woman alive who does not like to know the pleasant truth about herself!" Mark said.

I turned my attention to the little boy in the bed.

"Kenny doesn't know me," I said and sat down by his side and took his hand. It was limp and cautious. His big, burning eyes were wary in his thin face. "But I saw you years ago when you were a very little boy," I continued, "so little, in fact, that you scarcely came up to grandmother's footstool."

His eyes lost their wariness and he chuckled. "You are Miss Elizabeth!"

"I think," I said gently, "that we could dispense with that formality, Kenny. I would like you to call me Aunt Elizabeth. Will you?"

He nodded.

"You were having a wonderful joke with Uncle Mark when I came in," I said.

"We were playing a game and it's my turn." He curved his fingers, put them up to his eye and with the other hand pulled the curtain back from the window.

"'I spy with my little eye, something beginning with 'Y'."

"You're cheating!" Mark accused. "You can't see anything out there. It's dark."

"But it *was* there and it had horses and I often see it. Guess, Uncle Mark!"

"Not now Kenny!" Aunt Geraldine said quickly. "You have had your supper, but the gong will be sounding at any moment for our dinner." She bent and kissed him. "Goodnight, darling."

At the door, she looked back and fluttered her hand at him. Kenny, however, was watching Mark.

"Guess just this one, Uncle Mark. It begins with 'Y'. It's two words," he pleaded.

"Keep it for tomorrow," Mark said and bent over him.

I watched the strong hands gentle with the little boy as he settled him on his pillows.

Kenny made a face. "I don't want to lie down!" The dark brows drew together into a scowl, the mouth drooped. "I hate my bed!"

"When you're well and can run about you'll find that it's sometimes a good place to be!" Mark observed matter-of-factly.

"I *will* get better, won't I?"

"Of course."

"Mamma said you'd make me well, but you haven't. Mamma said—"

Mark stopped the plaintive sing-song by ruffling the tousled hair.

"One of these days, if you're patient, you and I will go riding together over the hills. You like horses, don't you?"

Kenny said doubtfully that he did.

I bent and kissed him. "I'll come and see you tomorrow morning and you can show me your silhouettes." I glanced down at the black and white paper on the bed. "Shall I put them on the table by your side?"

"No thank you," he said a little sulkily. Then, as Mark and I went to the door, Kenny scooped back one of the window curtains and chanted loudly, wildly defiant: "I spy, with my little eye, something beginning with 'Y'. You can't guess, can you?" He was doing his utmost to keep us there with him. "You *can't!*" He was shouting now. "It's a yellow carriage! *You* know, Uncle Mark, a yellow—"

"Go to sleep," said Mark and closed the door firmly.

I walked through the hall and up the stairs wishing I could have stayed with Kenny a little longer. I had a feeling that nobody wanted to play his game with him!

I paused on the landing which was between the two flights of stairs leading to the drawing room. Mark was immediately behind me. Leaning over the baluster, I looked down into the hall.

"When I was a little girl," I said, "I used to imagine that the chandelier would fall on me and crush me. I was terrified of it. What makes it sometimes swing?"

"Footsteps. It is immediately under the landing," he reminded me. "It used to be a game of James's and mine when we were young."

"A game?"

"Guessing, by the swing, who was walking there. A small movement for Aunt Geraldine; barely a quiver for grandmother. It swings most strongly for James, but then he is a big man."

"And it won't fall?" I asked doubtfully.

"It has survived fifty years and it has always had a slight movement. You do not need to be afraid."

I looked up and met his light gray gaze. "I am not afraid."

But as I moved towards the short second flight of stairs that led to the drawing room, I shivered suddenly and without reason for I was not cold.

A door opened below us. I glanced down and saw that Armorel had come to the foot of the stairs.

"Oh Mark! I must speak to you."

"Later."

"Now! Now, please! It is urgent!"

I did not intend to stand watching them, but in the moment's hesitation before Mark turned to go back down the stairs, I saw a look pass between them. I could not interpret it, yet it disturbed me for it was more full of some vibrant meaning than any speech. I turned quickly and continued my way to the drawing room.

My grandmother watched me enter. "You walk well, Elizabeth."

I said smiling, "It is one of the attributes they taught me in the Brussels school to which my father sent me."

"I am glad," she snapped, "that he had that much sense!"

Again I steered the conversation from its dangerous topic. "I have seen Mark," I said. "I hear he now has his own house. He must have become very successful. His profession—"

"Profession!" My grandmother shot a black gaze at me. " 'Charlatanism' is the more correct word. What he is doing is something which all the great medical men deplore. But, so long as there are foolish people, and women in particular, so men like Mark will flourish!"

"But if he does good, relieves people of pain—" I began.

"And how do you know that Mark relieves pain?" my grandmother demanded. "These people who pay him well to twist their joints and crack their bones would not admit afterwards publicly that he had fooled them. It would be too great an affront to their dignity."

"Oh Mamma, please," Aunt Geraldine had entered the room. "Do not let us have this argument on Elizabeth's first evening among us."

"She will have to face the possibility that Mark will one day run into terrible trouble," my grandmother said. "You brought him into the family, Geraldine, and one day you may live to regret it!"

"I shall *never* regret what I did!" There was a sudden, unusual authority in Aunt Geraldine's voice. "I wanted children to bring up as my own and I have done so! Whatever happens, I have had those years and nothing can take them away from me."

I looked away, sensing an old antagonism. I knew that Aunt Geraldine had money of her own, inherited from a rich uncle and she had spent much of it on her two adopted sons.

At that moment, to my relief, James appeared. He carried decanter and glasses on a silver tray and as he set them down on a rosewood table, Armorel joined us. She looked, I thought, a little flushed and her eyes were over-bright although I could not tell whether it was from pleasure or anger.

"How is Kenny tonight?" my grandmother asked her.

"Restless." She hitched her shoulders irritably. "I do not believe Doctor Rowlins knows in the least how to treat him." She swung round on James, who had just handed me my wine glass. "Both you and he must see that Kenny is no better, yet all you say is: 'Rest, he must have rest'!"

"No one can do more for Kenny than Doctor Rowlins."

"He is old-fashioned," Armorel cried. "Surely you must see that! Why cannot we call in someone else?"

"Because there is no one who can cure a spine irreparably injured in a fall."

"I don't believe it! He is my son and—"

"You seem to forget, Armorel," James said quietly, "that he is my son, too! Are you setting yourself up to be more qualified a judge than we who have studied medicine? Do you want me to quote again what Dr. Hutton wrote in his great book? 'Rest is the proper treatment for all conditions that give rise to pain'."

"And perhaps, since your remarkable Dr. Hutton uttered that announcement, others have come along with different ideas!" She looked toward the door and color burned in her cheeks.

I followed her gaze. Mark stood cool and at ease, watching Armorel. There was a faint smile around his mouth.

"I have just looked in on Kenny. He is already half-asleep."

"And nobody solved his guessing game!" I said sadly. "He was saying: 'I spy with my little eye, something beginning with 'Y'. He was so anxious for us to guess that he said there were horses and—"

My voice trailed away, the laughter went from my face. No one spoke; no one even looked at me. But I could feel a strange crawling sense of tension pulling and tightening among the people in that room. I did not dare ask what was the matter.

But it was something to do with 'Y'.

IV

I soon became used to the routine at my new home and found that there were things I could do to help in the house.

James and Armorel had the main ground floor rooms. Behind were the kitchen quarters. The basement consisted of the laundry where Mrs. Bell came three times a week to wash and clear-starch the family's laces, and the store rooms.

My grandmother and Aunt Geraldine lived on the first floor. Then the staircase swept in another graceful arc to the guest rooms and up again to the two large attics where the two servants slept.

Sometimes, hearing footsteps across the floor above me, I would remember that when I had first stayed here as a little girl, I had heard of a strange dwarf-like creature called Ibbet who had once been my grandmother's servant. Nobody had ever talked much about her and she had been pensioned off long before my first visit to the house. The young maid, Susannah, now occupied the room which Ibbet must once have had.

It was, however, a large house and there was much I could take off Aunt Geraldine's shoulders. I helped mend the linen and when it was discovered that I was not clumsy with my hands, I was allowed to wash the beautiful old china and glass which was on display in the cabinets.

I spent part of every day with Kenny. He was a quaint little boy, in some ways so much older than his age, in others such a child. He was given to outbursts of temper and I realized early that I must not appear to pity him.

At the end of the month the first fog descended over London. I had never before experienced the thick choking saffron-colored cloud that hung for days at a time over our Square. I hated having to go out in it to grope my way to shops, to stumble over a step, collide with strangers and feel myself imprisoned.

Then on the fourth day a strong west wind blew the fog away and I was delighted when Aunt Geraldine asked me to go to a shop in Marylebone Lane to match some embroidery silks.

As I came down the stairs fastening my squirrel collar around my throat, Armorel called me from the Blue Room, which she and James had as their sitting room. It was the first time I had set foot in it since I was a child and I thought how pretty it looked with autumn sun pouring in through the French windows. This suite of rooms which James and Armorel occupied had been completely refurnished with great taste, mostly with French Empire furniture.

"You are going out?" Armorel was watching me with faint amusement as I glanced about the room. "I wonder if you would do a little errand for me?"

"But of course." I glanced down at the envelope she held in her hand.

"Will you deliver this at Number 174?" she asked. "Knock and hand it to the housekeeper and tell her that it is very important."

"But that is Mark's house," I exclaimed.

"Exactly." Her deep sapphire eyes hardened, defying questions. I held out my hand for the envelope and she gave it to me, her manner relaxing, her mouth smiling.

"You are a good girl, Elizabeth." She patted my shoulder lightly as though I were a little lap dog. "I am sure that we shall none of us regret that we have given you a home here."

My face flamed at the patronizing words. "I am not a child, Armorel. I am a young lady and . . . *and* a relative. I am not—" I was going to say "a servant" but stopped myself for fear that her biting tongue would out-match my own indignation.

"Of course you are one of us, my dear. Do you think I have forgotten that for a moment? And you are a young lady. In fact, you will soon be thinking of marriage. Have you anyone in whom you are interested?"

I said with as much dignity as I could manage, that I had not.

She laughed. "You must not be offended at such questions. It is natural at your age—twenty is it not?—to think of marriage. James and I must arrange some meetings for you with eligible friends."

"Thank you, but—"

"But of course! It is our duty!" she said and with her hand on my arm piloted me gently but firmly from the room.

At the door, however, she laid her hand over the letter in my hand. "Put that in you muff. It is not necessary to let everyone know that you are on a little errand for me."

I slid the letter between the folds of my squirrel muff, protesting, "There is no one around to see, even if it should matter."

"Kenny," she said shortly, "sees everything! And he is incapable of keeping quiet!"

Her words troubled me as I went out of the house and across the Square. Why should a note sent by Armorel to her brother-in-law have to be secret?

I went through the gate and up the few steps to Mark's front door. I was about to knock when it opened and there was Mark. He wore his outdoor coat and carried his hat. He looked pleased to see me.

"Why, Elizabeth! What is this, a friendly call or do you want my professional advice?"

"Neither," I said with some asperity to hide my shyness at being caught mounting the steps of his house uninvited. "I came to deliver this." I felt for the letter and held it out to him.

He looked at the envelope and frowned. "Armorel sent you?"

"I was about to go shopping and she asked me to hand this in."

He slipped the letter into his pocket without a word.

"It is urgent," I said.

"But not so urgent as my appointment!" he smiled. "I have to visit a bedridden patient whom the doctors cannot cure." There was mockery in his voice.

"And you think that *you* can?"

"Of course! Come." He closed the door after him and took my arm. "I am going your way so I will walk with you and tell you how clever I am!"

"But you do not know which way I am going!"

"I can guess." His smile was warm and quiet. "Aunt Geraldine wants some silks. Am I right? You see, I can even read thoughts! *That* is how clever I am!"

The sunlight, cool with autumn, poured on our faces and the wind was keen. I guessed that he was checking his own long stride to fit my smaller steps. I am not tall and came merely to just above his shoulder.

"Why did you not study medicine like James?" I asked him.

He glanced sideways at me in surprise. "But surely, they told you."

"You forget, except for a few visits some years ago, I am almost a stranger to you all."

"Never to me, I have too good a memory! You were an odd little scrap, Elizabeth!"

"Thank you!" I said loftily.

He laughed. "But I liked you, even then. I had always admired your father's freedom in his way of life and you had that same wild independence." I felt him glance down at my upturned face. "You ask me why I am not qualified. You must have heard that I went abroad."

"For a long time. Yes."

"I didn't want to go to University like James. I wanted to see the world. First I went East, working my passage. Then the desire to find my own family nagged at me and I went to America. Not that I would have left Aunt Geraldine for them since they had deserted me, but curiosity drove me to go West. I traced them as far as St. Louis and then I lost their trail."

"So it was all in vain!"

"Oh no, I wouldn't have missed my experiences for anything in the world! Do you know, Elizabeth, that I learned the rudiments of my work from a man I met out there? They thought him a kind of healer; one day I went to him with an injured shoulder—I had fallen while carrying a pile of logs. The man manipulated the joint and then he looked at my hands. He told me that I could have the same power as he." He lifted his right hand and held it out to me. "There is nothing fine-boned about that is there? But then slim, so-called sensitive hands are not those that heal. They must be strong and full of vitality."

"It is a very new treatment," I began.

"As old as medicine itself!" he laughed. "Hippocrates in the fifth century B.C. instructed his pupils in manipulation."

We had come to the corner of Marylebone Lane and Mark stopped.

"That, Elizabeth, is just a little of my story," he said and his voice was so gentle that I searched his face for the hinted sadness behind his words.

"And then," I said, "you came back to England and set up a practice and married Helen."

I do not know what induced me to speak of her; in fact I was scarcely aware that I had done so until I saw a closed look come over his face.

"Oh Mark," I cried, "it must have been terrible for you when she died!"

"A fatal accident to someone in full and vivid life is always cruel," he said in a curious impersonal voice, his eyes looking away over my head.

I put my hand up to my bonnet as a sudden wayward wind swirled around us.

"I must leave you here," Mark said in a light, changed voice. "Go and buy your silks." He half turned from me and then paused, asking, "Do you like the theater?"

"I think I would like it very much," I said. "I do not know."

"Then one of these days I shall take you to see *Trial by Jury*. It is by two men, Gilbert and Sullivan, and all London is talking about it. Aunt Geraldine shall come, too."

He had turned the conversation away from tragedy into a channel that would please me. "That will be lovely, Mark," I said and smiled.

But as I walked on towards the Marylebone shops, I felt disturbed.

I matched the rose-red and green embroidery silks for Aunt Geraldine and then bought a book for Kenny.

I was turning out of Marylebone Lane when a child stopped me. She had a small basket with two pathetic bunches of wilting violets in it. She picked one up and held it out to me.

"Buy my sweet flowers, Missie."

I smiled at her and began to shake my head; beggars were everywhere here in London, I thought sadly, and one could not give money to them all. Suddenly she thrust the flowers into my muff.

"Take them, Miss. And good luck be with you! You'll be needing it! Indeed, indeed, you will!"

Surprised by the vehemence of her tone, I looked hard into that strange little face. Then I realized with a small shock, that this was no child but a dwarf woman, and in the elongated black eyes was a strange penetrating look that was part cunning, part curious, ancient wisdom. She was, after all, just an itinerant fortune-teller. I felt in my purse for a silver coin. I would toss it into her basket and be on my way quickly. But as my fingers struggled to find a sixpence, she leaned forward conspiratorially.

"I warn you about your luck because I know who you are . . . Miss Elizabeth Bellenmore!"

I caught my breath sharply. "You know my name!"

Her fingers clung to my arm. "And much about the Bellenmores!" Her little painted, none-too-clean face was thrust up to mine. "Get away, Miss, right away! Quick, while you are still living and unharmed. There has been death already in that house and it will come again."

Before I could collect myself after the shock of her words, she had slipped away. I ran after her, calling, "Wait! Whoever you are, wait, please!"

But she had already dived in front of a carriage and was on the other side of the street. I stood on the pavement, shaken by the odd encounter.

Who was she? Why had she made this special effort to speak to me? And I was quite certain that, for all its brevity, it had been no chance meeting. What had she to gain by warning me? I felt the violet leaves cold to my touch.

Slowly, I turned and made my way home. And, puzzling over the disturbing and slightly frightening incident, I remembered that grandmother's old servant had been a midget, too. Ibbet! Ibbet, now pensioned off and living with relatives in Wales. This woman I had seen therefore, could be a relative. Now I came to think of it, there *had* been a Welsh lilt to her voice! What did she know about my family? Why was she hovering here, so near the house? Questions and no answers were my companions all the way home.

When I arrived there, Armorel let me in. It was almost as though she had been watching from the window for my return. She glanced quickly about her and then took my arm and almost dragged me into her sitting-room.

"You spoke to Mark!"

"Yes," I said in surprise. "I did. You saw us?"

"I was in Kenny's room. I could not help but see Mark walk with you through the Square. What did he say when you gave him my letter?"

"He said—" I tried to recollect. "He said 'Thank you'."

She was looking particularly beautiful, but her movements were tense. She went to a table and fidgeted with a thin volume that lay there.

I undid the velvet ribbons of my bonnet and moved to the door, saying, "It is lovely out, Armorel, after the fog! So keen and the air is as clear as in the country."

"I am quite sure you enjoyed your walk!" There was a hint of something so malicious in her tone that I turned to her in surprise.

"Yes," I said. "I did. I enjoyed meeting Mark, too! Even when I was a little girl, it was always easy to talk to him. He is kind."

"Mark's kindness is like one of the wonders in that book by Mr. Lewis Carroll, *Through the Looking Glass*," she snapped.

"What do you mean?"

She turned and looked me up and down. "Surely you have read the book! It is full of unreality! But then you wouldn't understand my meaning. You have led such a sheltered life!"

"Sheltered!" I broke in derisively. "When I lost my home and became a governess at nineteen and then a companion?"

"What I mean is," she explained, "you do not understand the world. You have not had experience."

"And to what particular experience, pray, are you referring?" I asked haughtily.

"You have not yet learnt how to distinguish the good from the bad. You read people at face value. They smile, so they are good. They frown, so they are bad. You are still but a child, Elizabeth!"

I felt my face flush angrily. "I am quite certain," I said steadily, "that I would never love the bad. You misjudge me if you think me that much of a simpleton!"

"Oh, you are no simpleton! That I know!" She gave a short laugh. "But—"

"But what?" I waited.

Again she picked up the book and began playing with it, leafing through it absently. Then she raised her head and looked very directly at me.

"I want you to understand that I feel only kindness toward you, Elizabeth. You are a young girl, I am a married woman. I want to help you."

"Thank you," I said drily. "But I was not aware that I needed it!"

"I want to give you some advice." She dropped the book with a little plop on to the table and came toward me. Her eyes, like dark sapphires, were brilliant and intense upon me. "You must be careful of Mark."

I think I had known all along the eventual trend of her conversation. I heard myself laugh.

"Be careful of Mark? But Armorel, I have known him ever since I was a little girl, although slightly," I added honestly. "He is . . . he is like a dear relative, a brother almost!"

"But he is *not* a brother! And nor is James. They are your aunt's adopted children and no blood relations."

"So?"

My gaze seemed to disconcert her and I saw color suffuse her throat and cheeks.

"You may have stayed here in the past, Elizabeth. But your visits were brief; you do not know what I know."

"Really, Armorel!" I laughed again, with a little less conviction. "You make it all sound sinister!"

Suddenly something in me lost patience. I was considerably smaller than Armorel, but I drew myself up to my full height. "You have been hinting long enough! Can we now have the facts? Why are you warning me against Mark?"

She went to the French windows and stood with her back to me looking out over the gold and russet of the autumn garden.

"I am the only one in this house," Armorel said at last without turning round, "who will tell you frankly what has been happening here these past few years. Grandmama is too proud; Aunt Geraldine too doting and James," she gave a short laugh, "too . . . dignified. I am none of these things!"

I waited. There was silence all around me except for the ticking of the painted enamel clock on the mantelpiece and the soft thudding of the flames licking the coal.

"Well," I whispered at last. "What do you want to tell me, Armorel?"

She turned and faced me.

"When Mark first set up a practice here no one would go near him. No one trusted him. His claim to cure pain, to straighten limbs by manipulating bones was, they said, quackery. He had taken a suite of rooms on the far side of the Square, in the house he has now been able to buy, and all he could do to keep his hands in practice was to go around treating any poor person who would trust him. He did that for nothing."

"Mark was always good," I said, "to those less fortunate than himself."

She shot me another of her brilliant mocking looks.

"Then one day he happened to pass the Lyceum Theater just as Lucia Emsworth was coming out of the stage door. She was being besieged by admirers and, getting into her famous yellow carriage, she slipped. Mark went to her aid. At first she refused to allow him to touch her but she was weeping and in such pain that Mark just took command. He found that a small bone had been displaced in her foot, or so he says. He took her back into the theater and in her dressing room manipulated the injured foot. From that night Mark had no lack of patients. Everything Lucia Emsworth does, everything that happens to her, is the talk of London. So, this incident was most certainly Mark's stroke of luck."

"Then why does Grandmama call him a charlatan?" I cried.

"A great many people do! He has no acknowledged qualification and he is a constant source of embarrassment to James." She gave a short, sharp laugh.

"But Mark cures pain!" I cried. "People would not go to him to pay him good money to be further harmed!"

She shrugged her shoulders.

I demanded, "Do you think he's a charlatan?"

"I think," she said, "he has acquired some knowledge that the doctors do not yet understand. And when you do not understand a thing, you mistrust it."

"So you believe in Mark!" I insisted.

"Yes," she said. "I do."

"And all that warning to me of not trusting him—"

"You little dunce!" Her mood changed. "I trust Mark's work. The man is quite a different matter!"

"How?" My voice was so low that I did not think she heard me.

"Sometimes I wish I could hate him! But—" she broke off as though she had remembered, after momentarily forgetting, that she had a listener. But I had seen, before she turned her head away, the flash of some inner fire sweep across her features.

Although I knew that she did not trust him, Armorel was in love with Mark.

I knew then why she had watched us walk along the Square together, why she had been at such pains to warn me against him. She was jealous of any woman who had contact with him. I was so shocked that I wanted immediately to escape that room. I turned without a word. There was a communicating door between this and Kenny's room and I heard him singing tunelessly.

Kenny . . . Kenny, who had been playing 'I spy' on my first evening here.

I spy, with my little eye,
something beginning with 'Y'.

And then shouting at Mark to guess, giving him clues.

I turned suddenly and looked at Armorel. She was again at the window with her back to me.

"I believe I have seen Mrs. Emsworth's yellow brougham in the Square," I said deliberately. "It is very elegant."

"Look long enough and you will see it a hundred times! It is always outside Mark's house!" She glanced over her shoulder at me.

"Well, they have become good friends!" I said as matter-of-factly as I could.

"Lucia Emsworth does not become friends with men, my dear Elizabeth! Don't you know that she is an actress and a divorcée? In another strata of society she would be called . . . well, never mind!" Still half turned away from me, she watched me from under half-closed lids. "But I'd better warn you not to mention Lucia Emsworth in this house! You see, when Helen died, people talked. Since then, the yellow carriage is never mentioned."

"Helen was alive at the time Mark treated Mrs. Emsworth?"

Armorel swung around upon me so swiftly that she knocked over a footstool. She kicked it to one side.

"It was just a year ago that Mark met Mrs. Emsworth." Her voice was bitter and brittle. "But don't expect your calculations to come out too easily when you add up two and two! Nothing in this house is as obvious as it seems!" She thrust open the French window and stepped outside.

I moved my hand and as I did so, the little crushed bunch of violets fell from my muff to the floor.

"Armorel!" I called.

But she didn't hear me. I picked up the flowers and went slowly out of the room. In the pantry, I filled a tiny Venetian glass vase with water and put the flowers into it to try and revive them. I must tell someone about that morning's meeting with the dwarf woman. But who? Not Armorel, not my grandmother. Aunt Geraldine? But I didn't want to distress her.

Now that I was home, the brief incident lost its impact. All that had happened was that some mischievous creature had waylaid me and amused herself by trying to frighten me. The more I thought about it, the more certain I was that the woman had been a relative of old Ibbet. She must obviously be someone with an ancient grudge, either of her own or on Ibbet's part. It had all been slightly macabre, the meeting, the warning words, the woman herself. I would be wise to forget that it ever happened. When the violets died, it would be easy enough.

Carrying the small Venetian vase, I went into the hall and glanced up at the chandelier. The sunlight through the fan window over the great double doors shafted on to every chain of crystal, every sconce, so that it was like a living, breathing thing swaying gently, so very gently.

I had a sudden realization that I was clutching the iron baluster as though I were afraid of falling. It was absurd, of course! All that was happening was that James was walking across the landing above me and shaking the ceiling with his heavy tread.

I was out of breath when I reached my room. I wandered to the window and looked on to the Square. Through the trees I could see something yellow like a gigantic chrysanthemum. But I knew quite well what it was. It was the yellow brougham again . . . and it had stopped outside Mark's house.

V

From the moment I met her, I knew that Miss Stanhope was not the ideal governess for a little invalid boy. In spite of her excellent academic qualifications, she was nondescript to the point of being depressing and she had no sense of humor.

When Kenny was angry, he could protest as loudly as a child with twice his strength and passing his room one morning on my way from the kitchen, I heard him shouting, "I will! I *will!* I *will!*" the last becoming a bellow.

I knew that James was in his consulting room with a patient and so I went quickly in to see if I could stop the commotion.

Kenny was sitting up, white-faced and furious, hammering with his fist on the bedclothes. Miss Stanhope was, on the other hand, standing very red-faced and very still.

"Kenny!" I said pretending to be shocked. "I thought there was a little street urchin in here!"

He glanced at me and I sat down on his bed and tried to take one of his hands. He snatched it away. I looked questioningly at Miss Stanhope.

She was gathering her things together, her mouth prim, her dark brown skirt rustling angrily round her thick ankles. I felt sorry for them both. The governess was past her prime, and yet was condemned to teach children, difficult, pampered and often mulish, for the rest of her life. I was sorry too, for Kenny, lying there, his face pink with fury, pounding the bedclothes, denied normal outlet for his energies.

"We'll have to buy you a drum to beat," I said drily, "and then you can play at being leader of the band." The small fist ceased beating on the crumpled sheet. He looked at me suspiciously.

"I'm afraid Kenny is a very naughty little boy!"

I looked at Miss Stanhope's pursed-up lips and then at Kenny, gathering himself for another outburst.

"Don't you like your lessons?" I asked.

"Not when I have to learn about silly kings and queens!" He picked up a book on his bed and flung it to the floor.

"I have been telling Kenny what happens to little boys who do not tell the truth," Miss Stanhope said, lips still pursed.

"I do tell the truth! I *do!*"

I took his hand quite firmly in mine and he stopped shouting. His hazel eyes framed by dark lashes, surveyed me doubtfully.

"I only said I saw Mama go into Uncle Mark's house last night. She wore her red cloak and she ran all the way across the Square."

"And *I* have told him," Miss Stanhope's voice was high with indignation, "that he could not possibly see all that way and that his Mama was upstairs in the drawing room with you all."

I rose from the bed. "And is that what all this fuss is about, Kenny? Why," I managed a laugh, "Grandmama probably wanted to see Uncle Mark and your Mama went to fetch him."

I saw the little boy's face clear. He shot a triumphant look at Miss Stanhope.

"You have very good eyesight, Kenny!" I continued. "Miss Stanhope and I could not possibly have seen all that distance!" I smiled at her but she refused to meet my eyes.

She had collected her things and set her bonnet on her head, smoothing a strand of lank, sandy hair beneath it. Her cape, I thought, was much too thin for this raw day and wished I had money of my own so that I could have given her a thicker one. Perhaps I could talk to Aunt Geraldine.

Mrs. Vine, entering with Kenny's lunch, broke my thoughts. I watched her set the plate of delicious Irish stew upon the invalid tray. When Armorel was not around, it was Mrs. Vine who stayed with Kenny while he ate his meals.

I left the room with Miss Stanhope and in the hall she paused. "I hope you won't tell Mrs. Bellenmore of this episode."

"Don't worry, I have no intention of doing such a thing. It is really quite unimportant, anyway!"

To my horror, I saw that tears were welling up in her small, anxious-looking eyes. "Miss Stanhope, please!" I laid my hand on her arm. "You must not be troubled about such a trivial incident. Kenny is not a normal child, he cannot possibly be in the circumstances. He is bright and intelligent and his only contact with the outside world is through his window."

"I know all that, Miss Bellenmore. But he sees so much—*too* much!"

"At least," I replied, "to be able to watch the comings and goings of the people in the Square keeps him occupied."

"Wrongly so!" she cried. "Miss Bellenmore, can you please suggest that he is found a room on the other side of the house, looking out over the garden? It would be so very much better for him."

"But he would be so lonely!"

"Indeed he would be better employed!" she cried. "I could, perhaps, teach him the names of the birds that come to be fed; we might even tame a robin for him to amuse him."

"Charming as they are," I said drily, "I do not think one small robin could hold a lively child's interest all through a winter!"

I saw her gloved hand go to her face. She was in such genuine distress that I said, "You really love Kenny don't you, Miss Stanhope?"

She nodded. "When he is good he is the dearest little boy. But he is too observant."

I drew her a little nearer the door, away from James's surgery, because I was not certain if he were still there.

"Suppose you tell me what you are afraid he might see . . . or know."

Fear touched her face. She drew away from my hand on her arm.

"Oh no!" she said. "I cannot say anything!" Then she added doubtfully, "Only I do not want any more harm to come to him!

When evil touches a group of people, it is the innocent who can suffer most!"

With a swift gesture she opened the door and was gone. I knew by her nervous, backward glance from the gate, that she already regretted her outburst.

I went slowly upstairs and the sunlight shining into the conservatory leading off the drawing room, drew me to it. It had been built quite recently on the flat roof of the Blue Room. Palms and ferns and exotic Indian azaleas stood in pots on the black and white tiles and on shelves. At the far end were two little papier-maché chairs, from which one could sit and look down upon the gardens of the houses. Below me I could hear Susannah's high laugh from the kitchen. Apart from that, the house was very still.

Who, or what, engendered the air of unease which seemed to surround me here? I shivered slightly and sat down in one of the fragile chairs.

All old houses must hold the memory of some tragedy within their walls. Here, Helen had died.

"I hope," said a voice behind me, "that you feel like company!"

I started and, turning, saw Mark.

"It seems that I am to have it," I replied equally lightly. He pulled the second chair round at right angles to mine and made a slight grimace at it.

"These chairs are not meant to carry a man's weight!" he said ruefully. Then he asked, "Are you happy here, Elizabeth?"

His question was so unexpected that I started. My fingers were busy twisting my coral necklace.

"How could I be otherwise?" I asked. "I have a home at last and everyone is so kind to me."

"Aunt Geraldine is very happy to have you," he said kindly. "She will miss you when you go."

"Go?" His words shook me. My mouth fell a little open as I stared at him.

"Of course." He smiled and touched my hand. "One day, Elizabeth, you will leave us all. You will get married. That's every woman's dream, isn't it?"

I turned my head away quickly and reached nervously again to my throat, catching at the necklace. The string broke and little chips of pink coral scattered on the black and white checkerboard marble. Mark and I moved simultaneously groping together over the floor.

"Whatever your dream," he said laughing, "I can imagine your occupation tonight will be concerned with threading your necklace!"

I reached for a coral piece that had rolled under one of the chairs. Mark saw it too. We reached and collided. "Oh!" I said, and we sat back on our heels and laughed, our hands full of coral pieces.

Suddenly I felt impelled to look over my shoulder. My grandmother was standing in the drawing room watching us through the glass door. Immediately I was aware of my undignified position. I scrambled to my feet, brushing my dress.

"I think we have picked up all the pieces. Here you are." Mark tumbled the coral into my hand. I thanked him and murmured that I must go and put them safely away in a bowl in my room.

"And tonight," he said softly as he followed me down the conservatory between the damp-smelling greenery, "as I told you, I shall think of you sitting under the lamplight threading your beads!" I made no comment.

Near the drawing room fire my grandmother stood leaning on her silver-headed stick and the large garnet brooch on her black silk bodice glowed in the dancing firelight.

I held out my cupped hands to her. "My necklace has broken," I said laughing. "And Mark and I have had such a business picking up all the pieces."

"So I observed!" she said crisply and looked beyond me. "Good morning, Mark. Are you intending to lunch with us? Geraldine did not tell me."

"I had an hour to spare and I looked in to see Kenny. Then I came up here for a chat with anyone I could find." He looked at the clock. "I have stayed longer than I meant and I have a patient in a few minutes' time."

"A patient!" She snapped the word out.

"Or a dupe for a charlatan!" He laughed and crossed to the door.

I glanced from his erect, disappearing back to my grandmother. She sat down heavily in her chair with the opossum rug draped over it and leaned back. Her ebony stick slid to the floor and I bent and picked it up. She scarcely thanked me.

"Do not be angry with Mark," I said gently. "I really believe he does help people, in his way."

She began shaking her head slowly from side to side. Her old eyes stared into the flickering fire. "One day the events of the past will catch up with us; the sins of the fathers— Oh dear God, help us all!" Her voice was soft as though she mumbled in a dream.

Involuntarily I shuddered, but she did not even notice me. The sins of the fathers! Mark's father? Oh, don't let it be Mark! Helen did not die because Mark had met Lucia Emsworth; the yellow carriage had no place in the tragedy. It must not! Mark was wild, but he must not be bad, for he had a part of my heart.

There was a stir behind us. "Your Honitan lace cuffs have washed well, Mama, but Mrs. Bell has pointed out a few places where the threads have gone. I will mend them for you."

I could have laughed with relief at Aunt Geraldine's pleasant, matter-of-fact words as she pattered across the room to set the lace down on the table near her own special chair. She gave a quick look at my grandmother when she did not answer, then she smiled at me.

"Ah, Elizabeth! I believe I heard James come in a few minutes ago. Will you ask him if he will be lunching with us? He told me that he was to join some friends who were entertaining that brilliant Mr. Lister some time this week, but I forget the day." There was pride in her voice.

I went down to James's consulting room and paused listening before I knocked on the door in case he should have a patient. But he was alone. He sat at his desk, his head in his hands and for a moment I thought he was ill.

"Why, James!" I went quickly to him, and he gave me an uncertain smile. Clouds, scudding across the sun, made patches of shadow in the room with its tall windows and a sudden shaft of light poured on to his untidy desk.

James waved his hand at the litter of papers. "It is one thing to be a busy doctor, but quite another to have to attend to all this!" He pushed some letters and reports aside impatiently.

"I would like to help you," I heard myself say impulsively. "I could write letters to your dictation and keep your papers in order."

As I waited for his answer, my suggestion became both important and exciting. Here was an answer to my longing for more useful work. I did not take my eyes from his face while he stood there, half turned away from me. At last, I could bear his silence no longer.

"I would not be in your way," I pleaded. "I would not obtrude!"

He looked at me then, and laughed. "Dearest Elizabeth, you would never obtrude!"

"Then I may help you?"

"I wonder if it would be wise?"

"Wise?" I asked, puzzled. "But how could it not be? You obviously need help here and I want something to do that would be worth while. So, you see, we would be helping one another." I broke off as the clock on the mantelpiece struck the half-hour after twelve. "Oh, I almost forgot! Aunt Geraldine sent me to ask if you were lunching with us."

He nodded.

"Yes. I've told Mrs. Vine. I believe Armorel is with Kenny. I'll call her." I looked round the room, anxious not to break completely the trend of our previous conversation.

"Your desk is a disgrace, James! I wonder you can ever find records of anything in that muddle!"

He lifted his hands in mock surrender. "Very well! You've won your point! Miss Bellenmore," he bowed with laughing mockery, "you are employed by me as from such date as shall be arranged between us."

"Tomorrow!" I said, eagerly.

"Have you never learned patience, Elizabeth?"

"Yes," I said. "But I find it a distinctly frustrating virtue and therefore I intend to unlearn it!"

He threw back his head and laughed. It was the most happily spontaneous act I had ever seen James make.

"You are ahead of your time, Elizabeth," he said with amusement. "And I am not certain that I should encourage you in your feminism! But we shall see what you can make out of this chaos."

With an unthinking impulsiveness I took his hand. "James—"

I began. Then I stopped abruptly as I saw his eyes go past me to the door.

I swung round. Armorel stood there.

I had forgotten that I had not closed the door when I came in since all I had intended to do was to ask if James were joining us for lunch. She looked at each of us in turn, her face impassive.

Quickly, before she should misunderstand, I explained, "James is allowing me to do some work for him, tidying his papers and writing his business letters. I have so longed to be able to be of use to someone!"

"You seem to have made yourself very useful already in this house!" There was a faintly sullen smile on Armorel's face. "But I suppose it must be difficult, after the kind of life you have led, at the beck and call of your employers, to accustom yourself to the gentility of leisure!"

I chose to ignore her deliberate insolence. I was more interested in the meaning glance she exchanged with James. With a sense of shock I realized that these two, bound not only by the church and the law, but also by the strict Bellenmore code that forbade scandal, had a deep dislike of one another.

For two days I could not get the dwarf woman's words out of my mind. They lurked, like a sibilant whisper, through every quiet moment. I kept telling myself that strange things happened in London. Riffraff, lured by money, bright lights and vice, wandered the West-end streets. Why should I think it strange that the woman had known my name? There were any number of ways in which she could have learned it. And some burning envy of my physical normality as compared with her tiny, stunted body might have impelled her to speak to me, to try to frighten me with her terrible warning.

Then the violets died and, magically, the memory faded.

Up in my room a week later, I was curled up on the rug by the fire. I had slipped up here after dinner because there were times when the formal drawing room with grandmother playing cards and Aunt Geraldine embroidering, became oppressive. Outside, the wind howled and moaned, rattled the windows and died away into occasional deathly silence. I thought how uncannily the wind could rise to a sound like a human scream.

I lifted my head, listening, and heard it again. But it *was* a human scream, harsh, shattering! Then I heard another sound, the squeak of the gate which Aunt Geraldine had told Mrs. Vine to oil that morning.

I jumped to my feet and went to the window. I could see nothing. In that moment not even the trees stirred. But something . . . someone was there, enclosed in darkness, terrified. I ran down the stairs, pausing at the drawing room. There was no one there, nor was anyone in the hall. The house had a breathless, deserted air. Yet someone had closed the gate not two minutes ago!

Suddenly a dog began to howl. Then there were running footsteps and voices. Something was happening outside in the street.

I dragged open the front door. A little crowd had gathered at the gate leading to the Square gardens. As I glanced into the windy street, a man detached himself from the group and came quickly across, demanding, "Is Dr. Bellenmore at home? A woman has been hurt."

I went to the study door, knocking, calling, "James! There has been an accident."

The study door opened so quickly that I felt he had been on the point of coming out.

"I'm wanted?"

"Yes. An accident," said the man behind me.

James reached for his Gladstone bag and followed the man across the street.

I hesitated. There was just a chance that I could help. I went to the cupboard under the stairs and seized an old cape that hung there. Swinging it round my shoulders, I ran through the gate to the gardens. The little dog still yelped with excitement. I pushed through the people to try to get to James's side.

Someone said, "You keep away, Missie! It's not a sight for your eyes!"

An arm thrust me back and the few people closed in again, murmuring, craning their necks. But a lamp, held high, shone on to the face of the woman they were lifting from the ground.

I could not help the small, swift cry, the grip of my shocked fingers upon the arm of the man next to me.

The woman whose face I beheld before they covered her with

reverence to the dead, was the dwarf who had sold me violets. I fled back to the house without knowing how I got there.

When James came back, he found me huddled in a chair in the hall, the old cloak still around me.

"Poor woman! Poor woman!" he murmured.

"What . . . happened?" I asked faintly.

"She was attacked—hit on the head with some heavy object. She must have died at once; her skull was abnormally thin. No one seems to have seen what happened."

"Who . . . is . . . she?"

"The policeman said she might be attached to the traveling fair that is in London at the moment. They aren't sure, yet, of course. They go on the fact that she is a midget and such people are usually employed by fairs." He looked at me more closely. "I'm sorry you had to see it all, Elizabeth! It is not a sight for women. Come into the study and let me give you a little wine to warm you."

"James," I made no effort to move, "I . . . I talked to her . . . only a few days ago."

"She was begging?"

"Not . . . not really. She had some violets to sell and—"

"Yes?"

"She told my fortune. At least she . . . she warned me."

"What about?"

"She didn't say specifically," I said shakenly. "She was probably wanting me to cross her hand with silver or whatever it is these people demand."

"I hope you sent her packing!"

I nodded vaguely as he helped me to my feet. I knew, suddenly, that I did not want to tell him the whole story. Not yet, anyway!

"It's strange no one else in the house heard," I said through teeth that still chattered.

"Grandmother and Aunt Geraldine are probably in their rooms at the back of the house; Kenny will, I hope, be tucked up with his dreams. Armorel—" he shrugged. "I suppose she's in the Blue Room."

But someone had shut the gate seconds after the scream, someone who must have seen, or heard, the little dwarf's screams.

"Had you ever seen the woman before, James?"

He looked utterly surprised by my question. "Why on earth do you ask? Of course I haven't! I don't gather she would have stopped a man to try and tell his fortune! She'd know he would send her packing!"

His gaze was so bland, so open, that I had to believe him. After all, why should a small, nagging suspicion haunt me that the dead woman had any connection with Ibbet, a pensioned-off servant?

Two days passed before, glancing through a copy of the morning paper, I came across an account of the murder in the Square. It was a short paragraph, merely reporting the woman's death. She was, it explained, attached to a traveling fair and the search for her killer centered round the fairground people. The caravans had now left London and were on their way to Colchester, but the police were with them, investigating. It gave on the last line, the dead woman's name.

It was Morag Nanog.

The name rang a bell in my mind; it was sufficiently unusual to be unique. Ibbet's surname had been Nanog and I had heard, long ago, that she had had a child.

I felt very cold. Eleven o'clock struck as I laid the newspaper down. I was sure that Grandmother and Aunt Geraldine had already seen the paragraph. We had talked only last night of the dreadful thing that had happened in our Square. Grandmother had passed it off with a characteristic cool comment, "Riffraff are singularly insensitive as to where they commit their crimes!" she had said.

The whole thing had been dismissed as sordid and tragic. It was a slice of life outside our world. But now, surely, it was different if the dead woman was Ibbet's daughter.

I waited in the study for James to return from his morning rounds. When at last he came, I showed him the paragraph.

"Ibbet had a daughter, didn't she?" I asked. "James, was her name Morag?"

He nodded, frowning. "But the similarity of names must be purely coincidental!"

"Do you really think that?"

He met my disbelieving gaze with surprise. "Of course I do!" His eyes, however, quickly averting, told me that he hadn't!

"Why can't you treat me like an adult instead of a child who must know nothing?" My quick temper flared at him. "A midget woman called Morag Nanog! *Could* there be two? You know there couldn't! James, why was she here, near this house for the second time within a week or so?"

"How do I know?" he demanded. "Perhaps it amused her to walk in the Square where her mother once lived and worked."

"Or perhaps she came here, to this very house, to see someone. Did you ever see her here?"

"I've told you, I've never seen her before. And that is the truth."

"But she *could* have come here?"

"Why are you so insistent? Do you think she was killed on her way to or from this house the other night?"

"Yes." I startled myself. To my amazement, James agreed with me.

"She could have been coming here." He lifted his shoulders in a kind of resignation. "Very well, Elizabeth, you may as well know one thing. Although I never met her, I do know that in the past Morag has been to this house to see grandmother. Whenever the fair came to London, she would call and demand money. I think it happened about three times. Then grandmother threatened that she would call the police if she came again. I think that was about a year ago."

"And then . . . she *did* come again!"

"And was followed by someone from the fairground, probably. That's what grandmother thinks."

"So you've discussed it!"

He nodded. "And we've decided not to tell the police that we even know her name. Nothing can be gained by bringing the family into it. She hadn't called here. It is not our problem, anyway. It is best that she is dead, Elizabeth. Her life on show in a fairground, stared at, laughed at, cannot have been a happy one."

I sat, feeling an overwhelming pity for her. And curiosity. Why had she come here for money? I heard myself ask James.

He shook his head. "I gather she doesn't think grandmother is giving Ibbet a fair pension. But I happen to know that she receives twenty pounds a year from us and that is more than fair." He came and stood over me and touched my cheek lightly. "Forget the whole terrible incident, Elizabeth. It is over!"

"Who . . . killed her?"

His eyes were stern. "You are not the police. It is not your problem. Be quite certain they will find out. And now, it is over and done with. And you must not dwell on such things."

It was all over, I thought, turning from James. I crossed to Kenny's room to play with him for a little while before lunch. Morag's death had made no more stir than the lightest current of air in this house where her mother had worked. And yet I knew that the shadow of the girl with the tired bunches of violets would lie, not just in the Square, but in this house . . . for me, at least. And I would ask myself the question I dared not ask anyone else. Why did she come here for money?

VI

THERE WERE TIMES when it did not seem to me that Armorel was quite the devoted mother she should be to a little boy tied to his bed. True, she was always at pains to see that he was neat and tidy, that he was well supplied with such amusements as he could use. But it was Mrs. Vine and Aunt Geraldine and myself who gave him most companionship.

After a few weeks in the house, Armorel and I, the nearest in age, were no closer to one another. I knew she had a great many friends, mostly among the young Society. They would come to tea, stepping carefully from their carriages over the mud and wet of the winter street, wrapped in furs, their high, sweet voices filling the hall with chattering.

My feeling that Armorel did not spend enough time with Kenny was the reason why, when I went to his room one morning, I was delighted to hear her voice.

I had brought some colored chalks for him and turning the handle of the door, I heard her say,

"So you see, everything will be all right, darling! You will get better. Mama promises you!"

As I hesitated uncertainly, my fingers still on the brass doorknob, I heard Kenny protesting, "Papa never tells me I'll get better. You just say it to me, don't you, to make me happy? But—"

"Listen, Kenny. I'm going to tell you a secret. But you must promise to say nothing to Papa. Do you hear? Promise!"

"Yes, Mama."

"Well, then. I've been talking to Uncle Mark and he says he can make you walk again."

I dropped my hand quickly from the handle of the door but as I turned, I heard Armorel call loudly, "Who is there?"

I pushed the door open.

"Oh, it's you, Elizabeth!"

"I've brought some chalks for Kenny."

"Well, come along in."

They made a charming picture in the bright room, the little boy, his eyes large and excited in his pale face, and Armorel in her silver-gray dress with frills at her throat.

I laid the box of chalks on the bed and touched Kenny's cheek. He opened the box and began picking them up, but I could see that his delight was for something more than my simple gift.

"Thank you, Aunt Elizabeth," he said politely. Then he looked up at me and his eyes were brilliant. "I've got a secret. I'm going to walk again. Uncle—"

"*Kenny!*" Armorel almost shouted at him, her eyes narrowing angrily.

He gave a little adult sigh of exasperation. "All right, Mama! But I did think we could tell Aunt Elizabeth!"

"Nothing's a secret if you tell people, is it?" I asked lightly. Then I turned to Armorel. "Miss Stanhope is late this morning."

"She is!" Armorel agreed icily and took the box of chalks from Kenny. "You can play with those after your lessons."

I took my cue and murmuring that I had to go out and shop for Aunt Geraldine, I escaped from the room.

At intervals during the stormy, windy day, however, I continually remembered that snatch of conversation. I could interpret it only in the obvious way. Armorel was going to ask Mark to treat Kenny. I knew she had faith in him but I dreaded James's reaction. And how could Mark treat a child in his own home without everyone there knowing? For one thing, was it possible that a small boy would keep such an exciting secret? And if, by a miracle, the secret *were* kept, suppose Mark failed!

Standing at my bedroom window I watched the globules of rain on the window.

A spinal injury such as Kenny's was far more serious than the bone displacements on which Mark usually worked.

I shivered a little and reached for a shawl.

It was unthinkable that a man should use a little boy for an experiment which, if it succeeded, would give him supremacy over James, but which, if it failed, might further injure Kenny for the whole of his life. Would a man take such a risk? Not Mark, surely!

After dinner that night, we sat in the drawing room, grandmother gazing into the fire, Aunt Geraldine and I working at our embroidery and Armorel at the piano. She was an accomplished musician and her singing voice was particularly charming, being rich in tone and with a sweetness at variance with her slightly hard speaking voice. Presently she stopped playing and sat at the piano, saying, "I have been thinking, now that Kenny is older, he should have more lessons. I think he should learn French and perhaps he could study Shakespeare's plays with me. I shall give him an hour each afternoon after his rest."

"Oh poor little boy!" Distress was in Aunt Geraldine's wide blue eyes. "Must you labor him with so much study? Cannot he be allowed more leisure than other children?"

"He will be happier with something more serious to occupy his time," Armorel said. Under her long lashes, her eyes watched the people in the room. My grandmother was nodding her head.

"The more he learns, the more he will be able to converse when he is older. It is an excellent idea."

"But Mama—" Aunt Geraldine began. And then, as her gaze met that of my grandmother, her voice faded. She began to stitch agitatedly again at the beautiful linen tablecloth she was mending.

I saw a faint smile of triumph curve Armorel's lips. And then I bent my head over my embroidery. I heard the rustle of silk as she passed my chair, saying, "I am going downstairs to look through my volumes of Shakespeare."

But, I thought, as she went out of the room, would that hour in the afternoon really be for learning? Or for the secret they had talked about? I looked up and saw my grandmother's eyes upon me.

"You look troubled, Elizabeth."

"I am not doing very well with these rose petals," I said vaguely, "I fear I shall never be a needlewoman."

"You are restless, child. This house has been quiet too long. We are out of mourning now and we must arrange for you to meet people. Geraldine, we will hold some soirées!"

"Armorel will sing and play for us, and Lady Van Quorn has a beautiful voice. We will ask her." Aunt Geraldine's eyes were bright. She was like a child at the thought of a party.

"When I was young," my grandmother began, "I heard Jenny Lind sing." She glanced at the portrait on the wall. "Your grandfather, Elizabeth, was enamored of her. But then he was enamored of anyone behind the footlights."

"Mama!" Aunt Geraldine's blue eyes gave a shocked look in my direction.

My grandmother, however, was not so squeamish. "A certain type of man will always be fascinated by actresses."

I knew, in the silence that followed her remark, that we were all thinking of the same man. Of Mark.

I raised my eyes to my grandfather's portrait on the far wall. In my imagination, I was sure that his left eye, under the tousled black hair, closed in a wink. But it was, of course, only the play of flickering firelight thrown upon that dark and dissolute face.

Armorel and James entered the room. I thought what a handsome pair they made—Armorel in her rustling silks and her beautiful golden head, and James, handsome and looking tired.

Aunt Geraldine asked if Kenny were asleep.

"So deeply that he did not stir when I bent over him and took a piece of red chalk from his hand. He had gone to sleep clutching it and it has made large red slashes all over his pillow."

"I hear you gave the chalks to him, Elizabeth," James said kindly. "You have made a conquest you know, and won his heart!"

It was my grandmother who spoke. "It is all very excellent that Elizabeth should win over a little boy, but it is time she began thinking about a young man's heart. How can she expect to marry and have a home of her own when she meets no one but the family? I have already said that we must start entertaining again."

"Please do not go to any trouble on my account!" I protested. "I have all the interest I need."

"It would be better if it were diverted, would it not, Elizabeth dear?" Armorel asked softly.

But I was not deceived. Bending my head to thread my needle, I knew that she would like me married and out of the house as quickly as possible.

VII

Every morning from nine o'clock until eleven I worked in the study behind James's consulting room, answering letters for him, making appointments and keeping his records up to date.

With the first week's salary James insisted on my accepting, I ordered a new bonnet with one of the fashionable ostrich feathers draped across its crown. It was delivered on a day when Aunt Geraldine was confined to her room with one of her headaches. Late that morning, after I had finished my work, I went to see her. She was lying in her pretty bedroom with the curtains drawn, unable to lift her head from the pillow. There was one thing, she whispered, that I could do for her. Would I see that the plants in the conservatory were well watered? I promised that I would do so that afternoon, put my lips to her gray, curly hair and left her in her shadowed room.

When lunch was over, Miss Mills arrived with my bonnet. I tried it on and was delighted with it. When I had paid her, I went downstairs and spent an hour with Kenny. We read and played games together and when I left him, my grandmother called from her room and asked me to go down to the basement to see if her guipure lace was ready yet to be sewn back on her gray dress. I spent a fascinating quarter-of-an-hour with Mrs. Bell among the jars of soap-jelly and the board on which the lace was fixed to be patted clean.

It was late in the afternoon, therefore, before I was able to turn my attention to the conservatory. The light was already failing. In a basket I found scissors for snipping off dead leaves, cloths for cleaning shelves and a little fork and trowel for turning the soil. I left the conservatory door open, hoping that some of the warmth from the room would penetrate. Presently, my arms began to ache and I sat down for a moment in one of the chairs. I think it must have been the airlessness of the place that made me feel drowsy. I shut my eyes.

Voices drifted into my mind, voices in a dream. I lay listening to them, feeling strangely impersonal, almost disembodied. Eyes closed, I heard a quarrel between two people. In my dream, it was inevitable that I should be pinioned in space, listening. Nor did I, in this dream, feel capable, or even wish, to break my role of eavesdropper.

James's voice floated angrily to me.

"By coming up here, you will not escape what I have to say to you."

And Armorel, also invisible, answered him coolly, "Then I shall go to my room and lock the door."

"Not until you have listened to me."

I think he barred her way for I heard her protest in an exaggeratedly bored voice, "Please let me pass! These dramatics do not amuse me."

"Then you should not have started them, should you?"

"I have done nothing."

"Nothing but fill Kenny with some wild story that he will be well again one day, that some miracle will happen and he will walk and play like other boys."

"And if I have?" Her voice vibrated with defiance.

"It is not fair to him! You know, and I know, that his injury is permanent."

"I know no such thing!" she said angrily. "I think it is time you stopped relying on your own and Doctor Rowlins' opinions."

"Doctor Rowlins has great experience."

"And a rich practice," she retorted, "from which you hope to benefit when he grows too old even to dose his patients with laudanum! He is as out of date as the barber-surgeons! Why, he still uses leeches on his patients!"

"You know quite well that I have even discussed Kenny's case with Professor Pastern at Kings College. Do you really think I would leave any stone unturned?"

"But you are afraid of new methods."

"New methods?" James demanded. "In other words, Mark's! You think I would allow him to touch my child?"

A great shiver went through me and I opened my eyes. I made an effort to rise. Before I could do so, there was a sound behind me. I turned my head sharply, glancing round the outspread palm. With a sense of shock, I saw Armorel in the drawing room standing at the fireplace, her green silk skirt lifted a little so that the warmth could play on her narrow foot resting on the heavy brass fender. James towered behind her.

The argument I had believed to be listening to in a dream was a reality; I had eavesdropped on a private quarrel.

I shook my head to clear it; I was in a dilemma! If I went into the drawing room and told them the truth, they would not believe me. James would think that I had deliberately listened and he would despise me. Armorel would dislike me more than ever.

I faced it; for all that I had been in a somnambulistic state, I *had* listened. And now all I could do was to sit quite still, willing them to go. Until they did, I was a prisoner.

"I don't know why you are in such a state!" Armorel was saying unpleasantly. "Really, James, your behavior is out of all proportion to what Kenny said to you!"

"I know he would not have spoken as he did unless the idea of his being cured had been put into his mind. He has been gradually growing used to the tragic thought that he will not walk again. And then, I hear that you have been instilling some wild hope into him! It is cruel! It is so cruel that—"

"That what?" she demanded.

"I sometimes wonder if you know how to love . . . even your own child!"

"My concern for him is surely obvious!"

"Or concern for yourself?" James asked with bitter impatience. "Have you ever done anything in your life, Armorel, that was not for your own gain?"

"Gain? But of course I would gain if Kenny were cured! Do you think I want our child to be bed-ridden for the rest of his life?"

"It is my nightmare, too!" James reminded her.

"But your pride will not allow you to give Mark his chance!"

There was a moment's silence. Then I heard a movement and a little cry, "You are hurting my wrist."

"What has Mark promised you if you will let him experiment on my son?" James's voice cut in on her protest.

I held my breath. A draught, whistling between the panes of glass, whipped like ice across my shoulders.

"You must be mad to ask such a question." Armorel's voice blazed with fury and contempt.

"On the contrary, I am too sane, my dear, too sadly sane! You see, I have not lived with Mark all these years without knowing that behind his charm there lies an overriding ambition."

"And is that a sin?"

"When it is based on quackery, yes."

"I don't agree with you."

"Of course you don't! And heaven help us all, Armorel, I know why!" He broke off and then, in a dead blank voice, he said, "You are in love with Mark."

I waited, expecting wild denial, anger. Instead, I heard Armorel laugh.

"And if I say I am, what could you do about it? And if I say I am not, would you believe me?"

Her taunt appalled me.

James said with fierce bitterness, "Do you think I am so occupied with my work that I see nothing else? Do you think I haven't noticed you watching from the window in the early evenings when a yellow carriage stops outside Mark's house far too often for your peace of mind?"

"And are you such a despot that I may not even look out of the window?" she demanded icily. "This house has been like a prison ever since Helen died! The evenings are so dull, so endless! It is nearly a year since there was music or singing here!"

"We have been in mourning."

"Oh, we have been in much more than mourning for Mark's dead wife!" she retorted. "You know as well as I that grandmama rules this house. We have been guarded and watched in case more notoriety should fall upon the Bellenmore name! It is amusing, is it not, when a family with a wild history becomes afraid of its own shadow? And you are as fearful as all the rest. Only Mark has no fear!"

"You are quite wrong! I have nothing to be afraid of!"

"Nothing?" Her voice was so soft that I scarcely distinguished the word. "Oh, but that is not true! There is always fear in a house where a tragedy has never been explained, and you are as much under its shadow as anyone else. Put yourself in my place, James. Is it any wonder that I feel caged? That I look out of the window?"

"What you say is not true! You have far more freedom than many wives. It is because you have so much that you have become reckless. You make your actions too clear! But let me warn you. If you defy me, if I find that Kenny has been subject even to an examination by Mark, I shall take great pleasure in throwing him out of the house."

"Because his methods do not agree with yours!"

"No! Because I know that wrong treatment could destroy all the good that rest is doing to Kenny. At least he is no longer in pain. In the hands of an unqualified man, heaven knows what damage could be done! If Mark touched my son and aggravated his condition, I think I would kill him."

"You tire me with your dramatics!"

"It is a dramatic thought, Armorel, that a child might be used to satisfy the vanity of two people."

"Vanity?" she flashed.

"Of course. Obviously to be allowed to treat Kenny would be Mark's greatest moment. And such is his colossal conceit that he would believe he could succeed where I failed."

I thought I heard a movement towards the conservatory and shrank back into the shadows. When James spoke again, his voice came, harsh with hatred.

"What is the price you demand for allowing Mark to treat Kenny?"

"Now I know you must be mad!" Her voice was high and sharp.

"Is it that he gives up his friendship with Mrs. Emsworth?"

If Armorel made a sound, I did not hear it.

"There are women who derive pleasure from winning a man away from another woman. You are one! And I am not in the least interested in a denial! Although you do not dare become unfaithful to me, you would use what power you could to break a friendship that is distasteful to you. You would give much to have power over Mark. Do you think I haven't learned to know you, Armorel, after all these years . . . just as Mark knew Helen?"

"Helen!" Her voice came savagely. "I knew her, too! I told you when Mark first brought her here to warn him against that laughing angel's face!"

"It would have given you the greatest pleasure, wouldn't it, to have stopped that marriage, just as it would give you pleasure now to look out of the window and know that you would never again see a yellow carriage waiting across the Square!"

"At least if the marriage had been stopped, Helen would be alive today!" she cried.

There was a long silence. Then out of that room with its golden embroideries and Chinese treasures, came a harsh and unrecognizable voice, choked with anger, with horror.

"You know, don't you, who killed her? Mark—" And there was no way in which I could tell which of them had spoken, Armorel or James.

I started to my feet without realizing that I had moved. My hand reached out to touch something and I found broken palm fronds in my hand. My heart was thudding so strongly that it almost drowned the sound of running footsteps. Had those last words been a question or a statement?

I was shivering with cold, yet I could not leave the glass conservatory because my legs would no longer support me. I sank down again in the chair and my head went forward on to my hands, the scissors falling with a little crash on to the tiled floor.

I did not know whether someone had remained in the drawing room. I did not care. I was beyond all feeling, drowning in a kind of limbo of nothingness. Never in my life before had I felt such a sense of horror and misery. The first emotion I could understand; the second I could not. For Mark was nothing to me . . . nothing! Yet although I kept repeating the word to myself, I was suffering out of all personal proportion to the dreadful thing I had overheard.

How long I remained there, I have no idea. But suddenly I felt a hand lightly on my shoulder and a shudder went through me as I heard James's voice, "Have you fallen asleep, Elizabeth?"

I moved my head from my cramped and frozen arms. "No," I said. "No! Perhaps I felt a little faint."

His arm went round me. "You must not stay here in this cold place. Come by the drawing room fire and get warm."

I let him lead me into the room and seat me in Aunt Geraldine's special chair by the fire. He poured me out a little port wine in a glass and told me to drink it.

"I would prefer to give you brandy."

"No thank you," I said quickly. "It is like drinking fire!"

"And fire would warm you."

He came and crouched by my side, taking my hands and chafing them gently.

"You must never do such a thing again in this weather or you will be ill. The wind beats against the glass and cuts through the cracks."

I looked into his troubled, handsome face, asking myself who had uttered that terrible indictment against Mark. It had been too torn with harsh, whispered horror for me to recognize the voice.

"You are shivering again! Drink up that wine, Elizabeth."

I drank obediently, forcing myself to ask if Aunt Geraldine were better.

"I have looked in on her again. I think she will be well by tomorrow."

"It must be wonderful to know that you can cure pain," I said.

"I wonder if the knowledge that you can make people happy is not greater?" he said and, taking my hand, bent and kissed my palm. As gently as I could I withdrew my hand but even as I linked my fingers in my lap, trying to steady them, I could still feel the faintest pressure where James's lips had been.

He had risen and was standing by the mantelpiece, lifting the glass dome from the gilt clock and reaching along the back for the place where the key was kept. Then, inserting it, he began to wind.

"This clock loses time," he said, so matter-of-factly that I might have imagined the previous moment when he had knelt by my side chafing my ice cold hands. Then he replaced the dome of glass and stood staring at his reflection in the mirror of the overmantel. "Time! Why cannot we put it back and change the past?" The reflection of his dark brown eyes burned through me. "Why, because we have made mistakes, do we have to suffer for the rest of our lives?"

"You have so much," I cried. "How can you speak like that? You have a very successful career."

He continued to regard me through the looking-glass and I saw him shake his head. "You are too young to understand. It is an irony, Elizabeth, that you are the one person in this house to whom I could talk and yet to whom I dare not."

"Why?"

He gave me no answer.

"But you could talk to Aunt Geraldine," I went on. "She has a big heart. If you are in any trouble—" My voice trailed off. I could not go on for I knew his trouble and I knew, too, that he could not talk about it to Aunt Geraldine. The implications were too deep . . . too shocking. She was a good woman, but she had an almost childlike simplicity. She would be distressed and hurt and frightened; but she would not understand.

Light footsteps sounded. I glanced across the room as Aunt Geraldine entered.

"My dear children, you both look so sad!" she cried.

Immediately our faces lightened and we exclaimed together with pleasure at seeing her up and around again.

"My James is a very good doctor. You see," she said with a laugh, "no more pain! Now please, no fuss!" She pushed me lightly from her. "I have things to do. James, we must make a list of the guests for the soirée. Mama is right! It is time Elizabeth met people." She touched my cheek in passing and went to her little knee-hole desk in the corner of the room by the window. I escaped and went slowly downstairs.

Outside Kenny's room, I paused and heard high, clear, gasping sobs. I crossed quickly and opened the door. The little boy's face was swollen with weeping. As I approached he cowered quickly away from me as though from a dreaded blow.

"Kenny, don't do that! I'm not going to hurt you! What is the matter? Are you in pain?"

His fist was doubled up on the sheet, wet from contact with his swimming eyes. I reached out gently and put my arm round the thin little shoulders. The scissors and his black and white cutting-out paper lay on the bed. "Have you cut yourself?"

He shook his head and his fist swept the paper to the floor. It was, I was to learn, a characteristic gesture of his when he was upset.

"That," I said drily, "isn't going to help matters, is it?" and picked up the mutilated pieces of paper and put them on the table by his bed. Then I reached over and turned up the lamp which was placed just out of his reach, yet near enough to enable him to see by.

"You haven't got enough light in here," I said. "Who lit this for you? Susannah?"

"Mama did," he murmured a little sullenly. "She was angry with me. She said that she would never let me get well if I was going to be so stupid."

"Oh no, Kenny!" I protested. "You cannot have understood her! We all want you to get well and you are not stupid. In fact, I would say you were very intelligent." I picked up a book and flicked over the pages. "I think, perhaps, you and I could read together sometimes in the afternoons. Tomorrow morning I will see what books there are in the shops and I will buy some I think you would enjoy."

He looked at me doubtfully. "In the afternoon Mama is going to stay with me for a long time and Uncle—" He stopped and his eyes grew dark with fright that he had again nearly given away a secret.

I knew everything, then! I did not let him see how shocked I was. Instead, I merely smiled and said lightly, "Very well, we'll find some other time to read together. Just before your supper, perhaps. Don't worry!" I leaned over and kissed him and tucked him in. I was arranging his pillows when the rich, deep sound of the Chinese gong beat through the house.

"That's for my dinner," I said.

Kenny gave a loud sigh intended to melt my heart. "I want you to stay here with me."

I smoothed the quilt. "I'll come back just before you go to sleep. But I must go now. I'm very, very hungry. I could eat a whole farmyard of animals!" I was gratified to hear him laugh, but my heart was heavy as I left him.

Armorel was closing the door of their sittingroom as I came into the hall. She looked anything but pleased to see me and so I forestalled any comment she might have seen fit to make.

"I went in to say goodnight to Kenny," I said calmly. "He seemed to be upset."

"He has behaved very stupidly." Her shoulders moved impatiently. "And even a bedridden child has to be disciplined!"

I think my steady gaze must have disturbed her, however, for her voice sharpened. "What did he say to you?"

"That you were angry with him. But he did not tell me why." That was, in essence, the truth.

She was at the staircase. Her hand reached down to lift the folds of her glowing gown, one foot poised on the first stair.

"I had hoped," I said clearly, "that I might read with him for a while each afternoon. It would be much more fun for him than reading by himself. I could have made the books live, explained things to him. I have had," I added, "quite a considerable experience in this with my pupils at Dulwich."

"It is kind of you, Elizabeth." The lights from the chandelier turned her hair to dark gold. "But you must not trouble yourself with Kenny. You seem to have found plenty to occupy your time, helping Aunt Geraldine and working for James." She lowered her lids and looked at me through the dusky arcs of her lashes. "I shall be spending quite a part of each afternoon from now on teaching him French and reading with him. Shakespeare," she added.

I knew that she had not told me the truth and that there would be no French and no Shakespeare during that hour while she sat with Kenny. Because Mark, too, would be there. But how dare they make such plans with James around? Indeed, how could they?

"What is it?" she asked with amusement. "You look like a young witch standing there staring into the future! Oh, a very pretty witch, of course!"

Slowly my eyes focussed on her. "I don't want to see into the future!" I cried. "It frightens me . . . it frightens me dreadfully!" I rushed past her up the stairs. Her voice followed me.

"If you feel like that why don't you leave here? Get married, Elizabeth! Make your own life, for there's nothing in this house for you!"

I ran up the remaining stairs so quickly that I was out of breath when I reached the first landing. I leaned, panting, against the sofa that stood against the wall in the alcove.

Armorel was right, of course! It would be better for me if I left here. And yet I knew that I could not.

I had not heard a key in the lock of the front door, but suddenly I knew someone had entered the house. I looked over the iron baluster and saw Mark. His glance lifted immediately and our eyes met. Voices came to me from the drawing room, but I did not heed them. Impelled by something I did not understand, I stood waiting for Mark.

"You look from a distance," he said when he reached my side, "like part of the stained glass window behind you. You stand so still, Elizabeth!" His smile openly appraised me. "Were you waiting for me?"

"That is an outrageously vain remark!" I retorted and felt the absurdly guilty blood rise to my cheeks.

He laughed. "Why? There could be many things upon which you wanted to ask my advice. You used to do so, remember, as a little girl and I am still Mark, you know!"

Yes, he was still Mark. Mark, who had killed his wife.

I studied the face bent above me, the gray, amused eyes, the strong aquiline contours, the long, firm mouth.

"How do you dare believe that you can cure Kenny?"

Aghast, I heard my own voice speaking my thoughts aloud. I reached out to touch the baluster for support.

Mark's eyes had lost their light amusement; I saw his mouth tighten.

"Will you please forget you ever asked that question, Elizabeth," he said quietly.

"There are some things that cannot be forgotten." Bravado steadied my voice. It was too late to retract.

"It depends upon how much a thing matters! Remembering or forgetting is up to you!" he said a trifle impatiently. "Now come! The bell for dinner must have sounded a long time ago and you are not changed yet! Or are you dining in brown cloth?" I guessed he did not think very much of my day dress, but I did not care.

"Mark," I said, "oh, Mark please don't do anything that would harm Kenny further!"

"From which it is obvious that you, too, consider me a charlatan!"

"I know too little about your work," I said.

"Then, as I suggested, it would be as well if we both forget this conversation, wouldn't it?"

"But I must—"

Quite suddenly he leaned forward and kissed me lightly on the mouth. I darted back and put my hand up to my face. So that was how he saw me! As a young woman to be placated by a kiss, with no more dignity than the actress, Mrs. Emsworth and Armorel. And others who came to him. The healer . . . the charlatan. My heart was racing.

"That, too," I said haughtily, "is something which it would be as well if we both forgot."

I broke away and as I did so I caught sight of Armorel down in the hall. How long she had stood there watching us, I did not know. I turned and fled up the next flight of stairs to my bedroom.

I would be late for dinner and my grandmother would be angry. I unbuttoned my dress and dragged it off; I washed from the hand basin Susannah had left for me. Then I chose a silver-gray silk dress and with it I wore my coral necklace which had taken me a whole evening to re-string.

The family were all gathered in the room waiting for me. I entered with a little rush. My grandmother stood impatiently by the fireplace, leaning on her stick. Her small black eyes watched my entry.

"The fact that you are late for dinner, Elizabeth, does not necessitate such an undignified entry. And pray why are your cheeks so flushed?"

"Perhaps, Mama, she has a temperature," Aunt Geraldine began.

"Nonsense! That is not the flush of fever!" She tapped her stick in a way she had when someone irritated her. "Believe me, I would have thought she had had a declaration of love had there been any eligible young men around her!"

I felt my cheeks burning even more hotly at her remark. I had long ago learned that she said exactly what she thought without consideration for the feelings of her particular victim.

"I have already arranged to ask some of our friends in for a soirée on Thursday week," Aunt Geraldine was saying. "The invitations will be sent out tomorrow."

"I do not wish anything to be arranged for me!" I protested heatedly. Immediately I had spoken, I was sorry, for I knew that Aunt Geraldine, who was easily hurt, had meant her little party to be a pleasure for me. But I was in a strange, edgy mood.

"If you do not wish us to do what is obviously our plain duty towards a young unmarried kinswoman, then what, may I ask, is your plan for yourself?" My grandmother's tone was cutting. "A life of spinsterhood is not exactly enviable, particularly when a young woman has already suffered from an improvident father!"

"My father died too young to make any provision!" I defended spiritedly.

"So," my grandmother proceeded undeterred, "what, I ask you again, is your plan? To become a fading governess in a house that will eventually pay you some miserable pension for your old age?"

I heard Aunt Geraldine gasp.

It was the first time since I had come to live in Manchester Square that I had been reminded so deliberately of my poverty. My quick temper rose. I was my father's daughter and, ladylike or not, no one was going to subdue my spirit!

"Even if I walked out of this house tomorrow," I said over-loudly, "I have no intention of living out my life as a governess! And if you think—"

"Elizabeth," James interrupted quietly, "will never lack a home or congenial employment while I can help it!"

My grandmother's spirit was as strong as mine. "The subject will not even be open for discussion if she allows herself to be presented, like any other reasonable young woman, to eligible men!"

There was the faintest stress on the word 'eligible' and I wondered whether she was suspicious of James's deep, vibrant gaze upon me.

Suddenly from behind me, I heard Mark laugh. "Elizabeth will choose for herself, whoever you parade before her in the marriage market! It will be interesting to see her choice!"

I forebore to retort, as I would have liked, that at this moment I felt very much 'paraded'—discussed and appraised.

It was Aunt Geraldine who came to my rescue. She rose and pulled at the long bell-cord for dinner to be served.

"Shall we go into the dining room?" she asked in her sweet, hesitant voice.

I knew perfectly well as I went into dinner, that I would never wholly please my grandmother. I was too like my father and my early free life in the Dover cottage with Rosie had not been entirely obliterated by my education at the expensive Brussels school.

I ate the excellent roast chicken Mrs. Vine had cooked and sipped the claret in my crystal glass. Always, when Mark joined us, I was aware of a faint unease at the table. I do not know whether he noticed it or if it amused him. I guessed that the reason he so often dined with us was because of his love for Aunt Geraldine and his knowledge that, whatever he did, he was her beloved son. . . .

I watched her blue eyes roam round the table, alighting on each of us in turn as though to say, *This is my family—the people I love most in the world.* I sometimes wondered whether she included Armorel in this appraisement. But, since James's wife was always at pains to make everything appear harmonious when we were all gathered together, I think Aunt Geraldine was content.

I sat by James's side and I was disconcerted once or twice during the meal to find Mark's level gray eyes upon me. The two candelabra on the table spread a soft and subtle light over the rich laurel green of Armorel's velvet gown, over Aunt Geraldine's amber silk and grandmama's black with its mass of beautiful Valenciennes lace.

To anyone who might have looked in upon our lighted room from the shadowed Square, we must have appeared a well-to-do and united family, enjoying a pleasant dinner together. Yet, sitting there, listening to the table talk, I knew that the shadows over that house were deep and disturbing.

VIII

THAT NIGHT, after dinner, Mrs. Vine washed my hair for me. It was a task she had offered to do when I first came to Manchester Square, declaring that my hair was far too long and heavy for me to manage myself. Susannah had an hour or so off, and so that Mrs. Vine should not be called upon to carry hot water upstairs, I insisted that I have it washed in the kitchen. I would sit in front of the fire, a great bowl on the table, while Mrs. Vine soaped and rubbed and afterwards toweled my hair.

I sat in an armchair near the open range, holding my hair to the blaze, running my fingers through the heavy strands to separate them. Mrs. Vine sat opposite me in her favorite rocking chair. She was crocheting a shawl in wool of a particularly ugly shade which I believe she called magenta.

We talked of Kenny who had been in an excitable mood all day. I said, "He has been talking about all the things he will do when he can walk again."

"*When,* Miss Elizabeth?" She dropped her work into her lap and looked at me quizzically.

I nodded. "I'm sure he will be cured! You see," I ran my fingers through my hair, "I believe in miracles!"

"Not in this house! Not unless 'tis the devil twists them for his own amusement."

"Mrs. Vine, what do you mean?" Her vehemence startled me. Tensely I waited, leaning forward and watching her.

She picked up her work again, dropping a stitch, picking it up, her fingers fumbling.

"Nothing! Nothing for your ears, Miss Elizabeth!" she said agitatedly. I waited, knowing that she was neither very quick-witted nor particularly circumspect. "Mrs. Vine," I urged at last, "you must explain! What does . . . the devil twist?"

"Many things! Many things! Birth, for instance. The birth of a child is a miracle, yet in this house the devil has turned it into a tragedy."

"You must not speak like that!" I cried. "A great many children have accidents. They climb and tumble, they fall under horses' feet. It is terrible, but it is no one's fault."

"I do not speak of Master Kenny."

"Then?" I stared at her uncomprehendingly.

She considered me, a strange look in her old eyes.

"They have not told you? But of course not! The less who know—"

"Know *what?*" I could not curb my irritation with her.

But she shook her head. "It is not for me to say, Miss Elizabeth. Besides, it is over. It must be forgotten."

"But it is *not* over!" I sat up straight. "Mrs. Vine, I am not a child! Something terrible happened here and the shadow of it haunts this house. *That* I know for a fact! But no one will talk to me about it. It is not right that I should come here and walk with ghosts without knowing the substance of them!"

"Your grandmama or your aunt would have told you if they had wanted you to know." She was busy again with her crochet. "It is not for me—"

Suddenly I knew that I had to force her to talk. "I suppose," I said quietly, "that you are thinking of Mrs. Helen's accident? I know about it, of course, but I sometimes wonder—" I broke off deliberately and waited.

Simple soul that she was, I had baited her!

". . . if it was a case of sleep-walking, like they said, Miss Elizabeth? Sleep-walking! Mrs. Helen! Why, she was always so calm and her nerves were as steady as rocks in spite of her seeming so fragile! She never had headaches or spasms and she did not even carry smelling salts in her reticule!"

"But if it were not an accident, then—"

"The police hinted that it could have been suicide. And that's just so much nonsense too! She, three months married and carrying her first child!"

"Carrying her first child." I echoed the words, staring at Mrs. Vine. "Then . . . then she could not have wanted to die!"

Mark's child! I shivered. I did not know why the thought produced such a shock in me.

"Mrs. Vine?" I began.

"Please don't ask me any more," she interrupted quickly, "for I know nothing!"

But she did! Only she had come to the conclusion that she had talked too much. Desperately I sought a way to break down the barrier she was trying to erect.

"This is what you meant when you said just now that the birth of a child is a miracle, but that the devil turned it here into a tragedy! Two people died then, that night, a woman and her unborn child!"

Mrs. Vine's head bent lower over her work. I sat, fighting shock. No one had told me! No one told me anything in this house of secrets.

"It's so terrible," I said at last, "that she died like that . . . all alone!"

Mrs. Vine's head went lower over the crochet. "Alone? Oh, yes . . . yes. To die alone!" she whispered, her fingers unrolling the ball of magenta wool.

She had implied a lie. Her very manner admitted it. She knew that Helen had not been alone on the stairs! Who else in this house knew it? Who had been there at the time? Or did I need to ask? A name was in my mind but I would not say it even to myself. I was quite certain that, however hard I tried, loyalty—or fear—had at last silenced Mrs. Vine and I would get nothing more out of her.

"My hair is dry now," I said and put up my hands, lifting it away from my neck.

She rose at once. "I'll get the tangles out for you." She picked up the tortoiseshell brush and began brushing with long, slow strokes. "When you were a little girl you used to cry sometimes with the weight of your hair. Now that you are a young lady, you must be very proud of it!"

"I suppose," I admitted with amusement, "I am glad I am not bald!"

"Your grandmama had such thick, black hair."

"And my grandfather too, according to his portrait," I said lightly, "*and* my father. We are a family of ravens, are we not?"

"Don't say such a thing, Miss Elizabeth!" The brush caught a tangle in my hair and jerked my head back.

"Why ever not? In fact, I was complimenting my own family, in a way." I laughed. "Ravens' wings are so lovely in the sunlight —gleaming blue-black!"

"They are unlucky birds."

I remained silent, thinking how superstitious simple people were.

"Mrs. Vine," I said, jerking my head half round, "did you know Morag?"

I sensed rather than heard the indrawn breath. When she did not reply, I prompted her a little impatiently. "Ibbet's daughter. The girl who was found murdered in the Square."

"No, Miss, I never knew her." The brush began its steady rhythm again up and down my hair. "I'd heard of her, of course."

"She came to this house sometimes."

"Oh no. You must be mistaken!"

Mrs. Vine spoke with such emphasis that I knew that either Morag had managed to avoid her whenever she had called at the house, or Mrs. Vine was lying furiously to hide the truth from me. I decided it was useless to argue on that point.

"Did they ever find out who killed Morag?" I asked. "I have seen no account in the newspaper."

"Violence is always occurring in these traveling fairs," said Mrs. Vine. "They're a vicious lot and the police turn a blind eye; they'd have their work cut out if they spent too much time probing their stabbings and their murders!"

The traveling fairs! I thought. They come and they go. And if someone is left behind to be buried in a pauper's grave, nobody remembers for long. I felt a twist of pity for Morag, born of a dwarf.

The chair in which I sat had a very high back. Mrs. Vine had finished brushing and I slumped down a little, leaning my head back.

There were scuffles and giggles outside the area door. I knew it must be Susannah with the young butcher's assistant who haunted the servants' door on her free evenings.

"She is a flaunting baggage!" Mrs. Vine said angrily, listening. "I have told her times out of number to keep her giggles to Leicester Square."

"She is young," I said, feeling at that moment, a little too old myself.

I heard the door below us open and scurrying feet ran up the back stairs, through the scullery, whipping open the kitchen door.

"Lawks!" giggled Susannah. "Mr. Mark now drives to the theater with that Mrs. Emsworth! We see'd 'em tonight going through Piccadilly in the yellow carridge. Now a decent time's gone since Mrs. Helen's—" She stopped suddenly and gave a gasp. Mrs. Vine had moved her ample person aside and Susannah must have seen my head over the top of the chair.

"And now," said Mrs. Vine, "you will get out of your things and go and see if the ladies have retired. And never let me hear that kind of gossip from you again!"

Without a word Susannah ran from the room and I heard the clatter as she took off her boots and put on her house shoes.

"I'm sorry about that, Miss Elizabeth. I shall give her a good talking to later."

But, being human, I guessed that Mrs. Vine would not stop Susannah from telling the whole of her story. If, that is, there was more to tell.

She finished brushing my hair and twisted and pinned it into its accustomed knot. I thanked her, rose and said that I would now return to the drawing room.

She regarded me. "The fire has given you quite a color and your hair shines so!" I saw love and kindness in those old eyes and on an impulse I put out my arms and embraced her.

"You would spoil me and flatter me so that I became unbearable!"

She said gravely, "I would like to see you happy."

"Oh, but I am! I can't tell you how wonderful it is to me to be living here. I have not been used to so much luxury, you know that, Mrs. Vine."

"Luxury," she said sadly, "does not make for happiness!"

"Nor does poverty!" I retorted. Then, aware that she must know that as well as I, I said more gently, "I think, if I could have chosen one gift at my christening, I would have asked for a contented mind." I kissed her cheek. "Thank you for washing my hair." I was aware that her troubled eyes followed me to the door.

Susannah was on the first floor landing. She stepped to one side. "Miss, please," she hissed, her violet eyes bold and sly, "I dursn't tell Mrs. Vine I was making that story up about Mr. Mark. But it weren't true! It really weren't! I just thought—"

"If it was not true, then it would be better if you turned your thoughts to less dangerous statements, would it not?" I said with a touch of asperity.

"Yes, Miss." She bobbed her head.

But I caught the flash of her violet eyes and guessed that behind her play at humility, she was laughing at us all.

The minx, I thought, rushing in to gossip about us! But then I remembered the house in Dulwich and Glanmory Hall. There was always gossip in servants' quarters. They had little enough excitement in their lives!

And Morag? What did they say about her down here in the kitchen? I pushed thought of her away from me, and turned back to the more immediate problem. My thoughts softened towards Susannah. I knew perfectly well that she had not lied. She had seen Mark with Mrs. Emsworth. And why not? He was a man without encumbrance: young, charming, successful. There was nothing to prevent him marrying again. Nothing. Only, perhaps, the detaining hand of a dead woman.

IX

THE HOUSE was so still! I climbed the stairs to my own room and when I had undressed, I went to the window to adjust a curtain. One of the wooden rings had got caught up with another and as I pulled it free, I glanced outside.

Mark was coming through the gate. I saw him glance briefly at my lighted window and I drew back quickly, aware of my night-dress and my unbound hair.

I knew that he came and went in this house as he liked. What, though, could be the reason for so late a call since he must know that both my grandmother and Aunt Geraldine retired fairly early?

Then I remembered that James had been called out a short while ago to visit a sick patient. Had Armorel devised some way of signalling to Mark on occasions when she was alone? A light in a window, for instance?

I knelt down by the dying fire, sufficiently puzzled to listen for voices in the drawing room below me. I heard no sound. Armorel might, of course, be waiting in the Blue Room for Mark.

I heard a clock strike the quarter after ten as I climbed into bed. But I was restless and could not sleep. Sometimes when I felt like this, a little reading soothed me. I had forgotten to bring my book, *The Channings*, by Mrs. Henry Wood, from the kitchen where I had taken it to read while my hair dried. For a few minutes I lay debating whether I should go and fetch it. In the end I lit the candle and put on my ruby-red dressing gown, pulling the hood over my hair.

I crossed the room and opened my door. Someone had turned the gaslight out in the passage. There was, however, a faint light in the hall downstairs and I knew I could feel my way without bothering to go back for a candle.

Through the stained glass window, the Hunter's Moon splashed the alcove with muted yellowish light. As I passed, I thought I heard a soft rustle as of a silk gown. But I supposed it must have been my own arm brushing the tough green leaves of the palm in the brass pot. I turned towards the last flight of stairs.

Down in the hall, a small gas jet had been left to burn but the puny light did not penetrate the shadows in the far corners. I lifted my dressing gown a little to free my feet and peered below.

I was on the second step when I heard a sound. I lifted my head, listening, "Look . . . the chandelier!"

My head shot up, impelled by urgency. In the faint gaslight from the passage, the unlit prisms swung gently.

"*Look!*" The queer unsubstantial voice came again.

My childhood terror that the chandelier might fall overcame me. I made an involuntary movement backwards and in that moment when I was off-balance, I felt a sudden violent push from behind.

My scream rent the silence. I staggered, stumbled and my foot caught in the hem of my dressing gown. I put out both hands wildly towards the iron balustrade. My hood slid to my shoulders and my long hair fell around my face, blinding me so that only sheer luck guided my groping fingers. I felt the cold iron and clung to it, checking my fall but twisting my body. I was aware of a gentle lavender smell about my newly-washed hair.

"Elizabeth!"

Running footsteps sounded along the passage. A face came out of the darkness of the landing above me; someone else appeared in the hall. I was aware of all this movement through the haze of my own terror and the thick dark screen of my hair. But I could not identify a single face.

Shaken, muscles wrenched by my frantic effort to stop my fall, I could only crouch trembling on the stairs.

"Elizabeth, my dear, what happened?" Aunt Geraldine's shaken voice came from somewhere above me. James had leapt up the stairs and was by my side, his arm around me.

"Someone . . . someone tried to . . . push me . . . down the stairs!"

"Oh no!" Aunt Geraldine came and knelt in front of me, taking my hands. "Dearest, you *are* awake, are you not?"

"Awake?" I wondered myself for a moment. "Why yes! Yes, of course. Why shouldn't I be?"

"She is perfectly wide awake now, at least!" James said gently. "Are you hurt?"

"I . . . don't think so. Though I twisted my side." I put my hand in the curve above my hip.

"Come downstairs and let me have a look at you. Aunt Geraldine, please, will you come, too?"

I walked down the stairs and I was glad of James's arm around me for my legs did not seem to belong to me. At the door of the consulting room I looked back. Armorel was coming down the stairs. She still wore her silk dress and the amethysts I had noticed and admired earlier in the evening.

"What happened? Did you feel faint?"

"I have never felt faint in my life." I was surprised at the sudden power of my voice. I had recovered sufficiently from shock to realize that I must make these people realize, too, that I had not stumbled on my own, sleepwalked, felt faint—that, in fact, I had been deliberately pushed. I must make them understand that, all of them . . . except, of course, the one who already knew. But who? It had been a loud whisper, raucous, as though it came from a hand hollowed over a mouth to disguise the tone.

James's hands were gentle, probing my side, asking me if this touch hurt, or that. He had sent Aunt Geraldine for brandy and when he had satisfied himself that I had only strained myself twisting to check my fall, he pulled my dressing gown gently round me and said, touching the hem, "This is too long for a little one like you! I think you must have caught your foot in it."

"I did not. I was holding it up."

"All right," he said soothingly. "Don't worry about it any more. Here is Aunt Geraldine."

She gave me the glass of brandy, steadying my hand while I drank it.

"You're sure you hadn't fallen asleep and were dreaming? Things like that can happen, you know. People sleepwalk."

Like Helen? I sat up straight in my chair.

My eyes went beyond Aunt Geraldine and James. Armorel was standing in the doorway.

"Is there anything I can do?" she asked.

I looked at her and suddenly realized that it was her face I had seen peering down at me from the landing above.

"You came out of the drawing room, didn't you, as I fell?" I said. "Did you see anyone?"

She shook her head. "I went in there to turn out the lights. No. I saw and heard nothing until you screamed." She looked past me to James and there was something in her expression I could not fathom. Suspicion . . . or knowledge? I was in a state where I was ready to suspect and question every movement, every look.

I tried to bring my dazed mind to find reason in what had happened. Who wanted my death . . . and why? What was I to do now? Stay? Or escape?

Tomorrow, I told myself, tomorrow would be time enough to make my decision. I would be safe enough for the next few hours; nobody would make two attempts in one night. I rose, saying that I would like to go to bed.

Aunt Geraldine, her arm round me, led me up the stairs. I thought I saw Susannah's white face high up in the shadows of the third floor staircase as I entered my room. There, Aunt Geraldine fussed round me, tucking me in, adjusting my pillow. I felt the soft, wet tears upon her cheek as she kissed me.

"Try to forget your experience, Elizabeth dear," she said gently. "You have nothing to fear! No one here would harm you. James is right. You must have tripped over your dressing gown and what seemed to you to be a push from behind was a muscle of your back being twisted as you fell."

"And the voice?"

She smiled at me.

"You have always been afraid of the chandelier, have you not? Even as a little girl."

Whatever I protested to the contrary, that is how they would explain the incident. I could not argue; I realized only too clearly how outrageous my story must sound to them. Only one other person in this house knew the truth—the one who had set the chandelier in motion.

I lay for a moment or two when Aunt Geraldine had left me, trying to exert myself sufficiently to get out of bed and lock my door. From below I heard the sharp tapping of grandmother's stick and I knew that she was lying there waiting to demand of Aunt Geraldine what all the commotion was about.

A knock on my door startled me for I had heard no footstep in the passage. I felt myself tense under the bedclothes as I bade whoever waited there to come in.

Armorel entered, carrying a glass of milk on a tray. "I thought this would help you to sleep."

"Thank you, but the brandy will do that," I said, "since I am unused to it."

She set the little tray down on my bedside table and the flickering candle glittered on her diamond and sapphire ring. Her eyes regarded me unsympathetically.

"You look quite recovered."

"Oh, I am. Except that I shall not rest until I know who attacked me."

"My dear Elizabeth, sleepwalking is far more common than you think!"

"But I had not even been to sleep and woken up! Please don't keep suggesting that, because it isn't true!" I struggled to raise myself on my pillow. Immediately she laid a detaining hand on my shoulder.

"Now don't get hysterical again!"

"I am never hysterical. Only frightened, as you would be if someone attacked you. As perhaps Helen—"

"We don't discuss Helen!" she said sharply.

"Why not? What are you afraid of?"

She looked so beautiful in the soft candlelight that at any other time she could have taken my breath away.

"I am afraid of nothing," she said softly. "But let me give you some advice. Don't ask too many questions!" Then she laughed. "What a goose you are, Elizabeth, if you think I don't guess that you were wandering round the house in the dark, listening at keyholes! Or, were you on your way downstairs to James? Perhaps, unlike me, you are allowed to disturb him when he is in his study!"

I started up in bed, my hand outstretched. I could have hit her across the face so great was my fury. But her fingers shot out and held my wrist.

"Drink your milk and go to sleep. And, as I say, don't be a little goose! Live your own life and stop probing into other people's!" She turned and went to the door, closing it softly behind her.

I jumped out of bed and turned the key in the lock. Then I picked up the glass of milk and carried it to the window. There was nothing wrong with the milk, I told myself. Even if Armorel wanted to harm me, she would not do it so blatantly. On the other hand, if I were found dead in the morning, could anyone prove that she had brought the milk to me? I doubted if anyone had seen her come to my room.

A little faint by my own bewildered thoughts, I opened the window and, shivering, poured the milk out into the night. As I did so, two thoughts struck me. If no one had been there on the landing, what had made the chandelier swing? And where was Mark when I screamed?

X

To MY SURPRISE, I slept well. When I awoke I could not see the time by the clock on the mantelpiece and there was very little light coming through the chink in the curtains.

When the tap came upon my door, I started up in fear imagining that it must still be night.

"Who is there?"

"I've brought your breakfast, Miss Elizabeth," Mrs. Vine's comfortable voice called.

I got out of bed and unlocked the door and then, because the morning had an unusual chill about it, I plunged quickly under the bedclothes again.

Mrs. Vine, neat and calm as ever, set my breakfast tray down and surveyed me. "How are you feeling this morning, after your accident?"

"Quite well thank you, Mrs. Vine," I told her guardedly.

"If you will let me have your dressing gown later on in the day," she said crossing to the window, "I will take the hem up for you. I believe Miss Dee is not coming to sew until Thursday this week and it is dangerous for you to go about in a garment that is too long for you!"

So that is what she had been told! That I tripped over my dressing gown.

"Thank you," I said quietly, "but I will shorten it myself. It is quite easy to do! Although—"

"Yes, Miss Elizabeth?" She paused with her hand on the curtain, and looked at me questioningly.

"I did not trip over my dressing gown."

"But that fall—don't you remember?"

"Too well!" I said, aware of the slight pain still nagging in my side. "Who told you about the . . . accident?"

"Why," she looked at me bewilderedly, "everyone! I mean, Doctor James and then Miss Bellenmore and—"

I nodded and reached for the teapot. I knew that I would serve no useful purpose by telling Mrs. Vine the truth.

She pulled aside the curtains and as I heard the rattle of the wooden rings, I looked up in surprise for no light entered the room.

"It's dark!" I exclaimed.

"Another London fog, Miss Elizabeth!" She glanced at the tray. "Have you everything you wish for?"

I nodded.

"And when you have had your breakfast, will you please ring? Susannah will come and light a fire for you. Madam has left word that you must lie and rest."

I said that I would not need a fire for I had no intention of staying in bed. For one thing I had a lot of work to do for James and for another, I did not want to lie and think.

Yet that was precisely what I found myself doing.

Outside the dun-yellow fog covered the Square and I could see neither the street lamps nor the trees. When I had eaten my breakfast I got out of bed, buttoned my dressing gown closely round me and went to the window.

First thing every morning Lady Dyron's orange-streaked cat would sit by the gate, his great yellow eyes fixed on nothing. If he were there today, then he was invisible to me! It was a ghost-world and with my love of sunlight, I found it macabre.

Something of its desolation swept over me. I crept back to bed and lay in my dressing gown, shivering. The house seemed very silent but behind the closed doors, away from me, they would be discussing last night. '*Elizabeth tripped over her dressing gown.*' '*Of course she heard no voice! Why, she could not even identify it!*' '*It was all her imagination! She was frightened of the chandelier even as a little girl.*'

And while in each room the whispers continued, would there be one of them, just one, who would dare to link the two accidents together? Helen had died on that staircase and, if my blind fingers had not caught the iron balustrade, I, too, might easily have hurtled to my death.

Had she heard a voice, too? Had she paused and looked up at the swinging chandelier?

I turned and hid my face in the pillow, trying to shut out my own terrible questioning. But my mind was overflowing with them. What was the connection between Helen's death and last night? And would whoever had attacked me, try again? I turned on my back and lay staring out at the dirty yellow light that was a travesty of morning.

And, as never before, I faced my own aloneness. My father's free spirit had, for his lifetime, not only alienated himself, but also his daughter. Something of Rosie's haphazard training had defied the expensive Brussels' education. These two factors made me a stranger in this house. I was nearly penniless, reliant upon Aunt Geraldine's charity and the sum James paid me for the work I did for him. But these were no reasons for someone wishing to harm me. They were free, at any moment, to tell me to pack my bags and go.

As I dressed, one thought entered my mind and would not leave me. Why had Mark come to the house late last night? And who knew he had been there?

The fog made the room so dark that Mrs. Vine had lit the gas. By its light, feebly piercing the fog, I began to do my hair. I heard grandmother's stick before I could distinguish her slow footsteps. I paused, listening, my hair about my shoulders, my brush poised.

There was a tap on the door and then, before I could bid whoever was there to enter, my grandmother walked in. In the first moment's silence while her black eyes scrutinized me, I wondered why she had risen so early.

"Good morning, Elizabeth. I hope you slept well after the commotion last night."

"Yes thank you, grandmother. I slept quite well." I shook back my hair, adding silently, 'With my door locked!'

She walked slowly to the window. In spite of the seeping coldness of the morning, I noticed that she wore black silk, although I guessed by her bulky appearance that she must have had at least four flannel petticoats beneath it.

"Your Aunt tells me that you tripped and fell on the stairs. You must be careful!"

"When my father was alive," I said steadily, "I used to climb rocks a great deal. I am very sure footed. I did not trip on the stairs, grandmother!"

She had been gazing out of the window. She turned slowly and looked at me. "Then to what, Miss, do you attribute your fall?" Her tone was autocratic, yet behind it I sensed a watchfulness in her eyes.

"Someone deliberately pushed me," I said.

"That is nonsense!" The words flashed. "Absolute nonsense! Do you hear?"

I had risen from my chair and stood looking down at her. My few inches of height gave me courage. "I hear, grandmother, but I am not convinced!"

"I suppose," she regarded me, "in the back streets of Dover you were used to witnessing scenes of violence. That is your tragedy, my dear! But here, in this house, we are civilized people. You would do well to realize that before you make such an accusation!"

"In the back streets of Dover," I said, holding desperately to my rising temper, "I found only kindness."

"I am glad to hear it!" she snapped. "Then I can only conclude that you have a very fertile imagination."

I saw that this battle of words was getting us nowhere. I moved a little so that I directly faced her.

"Grandmother, please tell me. How did Helen die?"

I saw her stiffen. The topaz locket ceased to wink in the lamplight and I guessed that she was holding her breath.

"Why do you ask that?" For a moment there was a flash of something almost like hatred as she regarded me. But I refused to be intimidated by it.

"Because Helen and I both met with accidents on that staircase."

The waxen arc of her lids drooped, guarding her eyes. "Helen fell while she was sleepwalking," she said. "It was tragic but it is over. You will not refer to it again!" But it was not over and we both knew it.

"Grandmother," I said suddenly. She had walked to the door. With her hand on the handle, she turned and looked at me. "When I started to go down the main staircase last night," I said, "the chandelier was swinging. I did not imagine *that!* So someone was about."

"Before he retires for the night," she replied, "James always checks to see that the drawing room lamps are out."

It was feasible. That was what made it so much more frightening, the ease with which they explained everything that had happened.

I heard my door close softly. I was alone. The whole house was hazy with fog. It had seeped in through every possible crack and I felt it sting and burn my eyes. The brougham came early for James that morning for he knew that it would take him longer to complete his rounds of sick patients.

When I had finished work, it was half past twelve. I knew that Miss Stanhope would be on the point of leaving and so I decided to sit a little while with Kenny. In that room, at least, there were no unexplained shadows, only innocence and laughter and a few tantrums.

Miss Stanhope was pulling her cape with its worn squirrel fur edging round her shoulders. "Ah, Miss Elizabeth!" She smiled as I entered.

I asked interestedly, "How is Kenny getting along with his arithmetic?"

The little boy made a face. "I hate it. It's silly. I don't want to know that ten eights are . . . are eighty!"

"You will," I laughed, "when you're a man and have to handle money. You will be glad that you can count your change!"

"I like reading and drawing." He addressed his governess, "And Aunt Elizabeth has taught me lots of games. I know how to make cats and mice on the wall."

"Shadow pictures," I added lightly and illustrated with my

fingers. "A cat. A mouse." The lamplight threw the shadows on the near wall.

"Can you do people?" Kenny asked.

"I don't know. Let's try, shall we?" I sat down on the bed. But he had already lost interest.

"I hate fog!" he complained. "I can't see out of the window and when Miss Stanhope goes home a tiger will jump out at her!" He made a violent, darting movement with his hands, his eyes mischievous. "She'll scream and there won't be anyone to rescue her and then I won't have to do any more arithmetic!"

"You're a very cruel little boy." Her voice was plaintive. "He has been like this all the morning," she added to me, "saying horrible things."

"Tigers," I said firmly, "prefer little boys. They're more tender."

"I'm not tender," he said and held out his thin arm for me to feel. "I don't want to be eaten up."

"Nor does Miss Stanhope," I said shortly. I had learned that this matter-of-fact approach to his short-lived ghoulish moods invariably had the best results.

"What would you do if you saw a tiger, Aunt Elizabeth?"

"Nothing," I retorted. "Since I am not living in India, it would be behind bars, anyway."

He laughed. He had a quick mind and this was the kind of answer he appreciated. Poor Miss Stanhope! She should have been governess to some nice, sentimental children who would like her to cuddle and kiss them.

There was a sound from the Blue Room and the communicating door opened. Armorel stood and looked at us each in turn. There was a brightness about her face which was excitement or anger, I did not know which.

"Oh Miss Stanhope! Will you please come in a moment?"

"Of course, Mrs. Bellenmore." Anxious to please, she hurried across the room.

"Don't forget the tiger!" Kenny called out. The door closed between them.

Kenny looked at me thoughtfully. "It can't be me this time."

"You?" I asked, puzzled.

"That's made her angry."

"Oh Kenny, your grammar!" I corrected him. Then I said, "But Mama isn't angry."

"Oh yes she is. I know. She looks as though she could burn you up when she's cross. But I haven't done anything. At least, I don't *think* I have," he added slowly. "Why is she angry, Aunt Elizabeth? And why did she cry so much last night?"

"Cry?"

"Yes."

"Everyone is unhappy sometime or other," I said evasively, "and often over small things. It doesn't last. But people become happy again."

"Like I will be when I can walk?"

I glanced at the thin, helpless little limbs making so small a mound beneath the bedclothes and my heart ached for him.

"Oh Kenny!" I said and gathered him to me, resting my cheek against his tousled hair.

"You aren't crying too, are you?" I heard the touch of healthy exasperation in his voice and hastened to reassure him.

"Goodness, no!" I put him from me and laughed down into his face.

In the momentary quiet, I could hear the murmur of voices in the next room and I was quite certain that Miss Stanhope, the least assertive of people, was protesting with violence.

I rose from the bed as Mrs. Vine entered with Kenny's dinner tray.

"Roly-poly," he said with satisfaction as I hoisted him a little higher on his pillow.

"Cooked specially in a little muslin bag just for you and so many currants you can't see the pudding for them!" Mrs. Vine smiled broadly at him. "You never lose your appetite do you, Master Kenny?"

"Only when I have to eat apples," he said. Kenny hated apples.

I left them and came face to face with Miss Stanhope in the hall. She seemed startled to see me and gave one swift, furtive glance back at the Blue Room door.

"The fog is as thick as ever," I said conversationally. "I hope you can find your way home."

"Yes, thank you." She shot across the hall to the door, opening and closing it behind her as though, I thought with exasperated amusement, I were Kenny's tiger.

"You have quite recovered from your experience last night?" I swung round and saw Armorel.

"Oh yes!"

She had a way of looking at one through her dark gold lashes like a pretty, sleepy cat.

"I suppose you have been told that you imagined the whole thing?"

Caution led me to counter-question her. "What do you mean? Why should anyone tell me that?"

"Because that is what they said before." She was watching me strangely, as though trying to read every shadow of my expression. It must have been very easy for her because I was frankly startled.

"Before . . . what?"

She drew herself up, folding her arms. The gaslight fell on the satin sleeves of her striped brown and green gown. "A year ago. When Helen died!"

I caught my breath sharply. "I don't understand!"

She looked up at the chandelier. I saw her hand go up to her slender neck in what I was sure was an involuntary gesture. But it was macabre. The staircase, the chandelier and a broken neck.

"I don't understand," I said again, more loudly.

She turned and looked at me, her blue eyes seeming darker in the film of fog that lay over the hall.

"Did no one tell you? But of course they would not! Just before Helen lost consciousness, she murmured a few words. She said, 'I had to look up at the chandelier!' But she did not live to tell us why." Armorel dropped her hand from her throat and turned away. I caught her sleeve. It slid away from my grasp.

"It is always easier when you have been forewarned!" she said. "Helen was not!"

"Armorel, you must tell me—" I burst out. But there was no point in going on. She had vanished into Kenny's room, closing the door firmly behind her.

It is always easier when you have been forewarned! Because now, if I chose to stay in this house, I would walk warily. Armorel had indeed changed her tactics since last night, I thought!

One thing I now knew. She, at least, did not think I imagined what I had heard last night and, unlike everyone else, she was unexpectedly honest enough to tell me so. Why? As I went slowly up the stairs, I believed I knew the answer. She was hoping to frighten me into leaving Manchester Square.

XI

James had enquired anxiously that morning about the pain in my side and I had assured him that it had nearly gone. At lunch he asked me if I would tidy a cupboard which was full of old copies of medical journals and reports of lectures by M. Pasteur and Mr. Lister on antiseptics. He told me that there was no hurry and I could choose my own time.

After lunch that day, I thought I heard him go out and went into his study. He was sitting at his desk in the foggy gloom, his head in his hands. He looked up and seeing me, immediately rose from his chair.

"Oh Elizabeth, I did not hear you come in!"

"I thought you had gone out. I am sorry, I should have made certain first from Armorel."

He gave a short laugh. "She would probably not have been able to tell you. She is with Kenny."

"Just she and Kenny?"

"I suppose so. She seems to think he has too much time on his hands, and I think she is right. Although I hope her lessons in Shakespeare have at least an element of accuracy!" he added drily.

I could not of course tell him what I suspected. If Mark was really intending to defy his brother, flout medical knowledge and treat Kenny secretly, it was not for me to interfere. Yet I would have given much to know what was going on in the room across the hall.

"It is strange," James said, "that you, with your black hair and dark eyes, should make me think of sunlight! But that is how it is!" He was smiling again, his face released from its weary look. I was folding a newspaper I had found on the floor, turning the pages the right way out, taking my time over them.

"I don't wonder," I said at last, laughingly, "that you are a successful doctor, James! If you can flatter your patients so, you must leave them feeling infinitely better than when you arrived!"

He shot me a half reproachful look. "Can you not accept a compliment?"

"Like any other young woman," I replied. "Only I am unaccustomed to them and so you must have patience. If you will only let me practise making charming acknowledgments of compliments, I am sure I shall one day be really adept!"

"You are laughing at me! Why is it," his voice was a little sad, "that you have never been sure enough of me to treat me as a friend?"

"But I do!"

"Oh no! It was always Mark! In the old days when you came to stay here, you and Mark would talk together."

"The old days have gone!" I said sharply. "I scarcely ever see Mark now. He has other interests."

James crossed to my side and took the folded newspaper from me and dropped it on a table. Then he took both my hands.

"On your last visit here, I used to watch you two together and I hated the way Mark could make you laugh. I used to wonder what you talked about . . . and all the time I longed for you to come to me."

For a moment I could not find an answer. "You must not speak like that!" I said at last and dragged my hands away.

"No. It's too late now!" He turned to the window. "It was always Mark, wasn't it? And yet, Elizabeth, had you shown interest in me, I would have asked you to marry me!"

My heart raced, and in spite of the fact that I did not believe I cared for him, some small twist of triumph stirred in me that, although I had not known it, someone had felt at least a measure of love for me! Yet now, all these years later, I did not know how to handle the situation and I took refuge in protest.

"I was a child!" I said. "You could not possibly have felt like that about me! I . . . I have read that it is often imagination that captures men's hearts, not . . . not love itself."

"I think," James said gravely, "that I suffer from too little imagination. I think that has always been my trouble. But when you last came here at the age of sixteen, I was only too aware that you were different from the sisters of my conventional friends. You had a freedom of spirit; you were unselfconscious. You were like a breath of fresh air."

"Dover air," I interrupted, "spiced with my father and Rosie!"

"Was it any wonder that I loved you?"

"We must not talk this way!" I cried. "It is madness!"

He shook his head. "The madness was in not waiting. Had I done so, perhaps a great deal of the tragedy of this house would have been averted!"

I could not take my eyes from his face. I made two attempts to speak before the words came, stilted, because my mind was half-dazed. "You are inferring that by my lack of interest in you when I was last here some of the blame for the tragedy lies with me, too?"

"I did not mean it that way!"

I scarcely heard his protest. My gaze did not leave his face.

"What tragedy are you talking about?" I whispered. "Helen's? Married to you, how could I have stopped her fall to her death? And . . . and could I have borne Kenny and prevented the accident that has crippled him? How can you—" My throat was so constricted by emotion that I left my sentence unfinished.

In the silence that hung so heavily between us I shut my eyes against the sight of James. Enclosed by that November fog blanket, I had a strong sensation that the walls had pressed more closely in upon us, listening.

Then, out of the silence, I heard James speak. His voice was very low and soft and I knew, although I did not open my eyes, that he was standing near me.

"If I could only put the clock back, my dear . . . my very dear, Elizabeth!"

A moment later I heard the door close and I was alone. I opened my eyes and put my hands to my burning face. If James and I could go back in time, would I have married him?

The tall gilt clock under the dome of glass gave the little gurgling chuckle it invariably made a few seconds before it struck the hour. Yet to me, in my emotional state, it was as though it had answered me by laughter.

After tea, my grandmother went down for her daily visit to Kenny. Aunt Geraldine sat at her knee-hole desk, declaring that she must clear out a lot of old papers. I sat near the fire with my sewing. I was putting narrow bands of claret velvet on my blue dress to make it look a little more fashionable.

I could hear Armorel at her piano in the Blue Room. She was singing Titania's song and her voice rose, richly and sweetly.

Aunt Geraldine sat, exclaiming over old letters, old bills. By her side was a little basket into which she dropped the torn-up paper. Some of the pieces had scattered on the carpet and she had told me to leave them, she would clear them up later.

"There's a letter from you, my dear," I heard her exclaim, "written when you were only six years old. You tell me that Mama Rose, as you called that . . . that . . . your father's housekeeper," she amended quickly, "has made you a dress of white muslin with blue trimmings. Oh dear, and you spell it *trummens!* I suppose that is how Rose pronounced the word!" She shook her head and then put the letter carefully back in her desk.

I remembered that once, when I had worn that particular dress here, the blue ribbons at my waist had become undone and Mark had seized them and galloped round the room with me, crying, "Tally-ho! Tally-ho!" and I had laughed and tossed my head and snorted like a little horse while James had sat in a chair with a book and watched us without smiling.

James and Mark. James who on my last visit had found that he loved me and Mark who had been kind to me and had married Helen.

I was so lost in my own disturbed thoughts that it took me a moment or two to realize that Aunt Geraldine was no longer tearing up papers but was sitting in a frozen silence.

Glancing up, I saw that she held in her hand a silhouette such as Kenny cut out in black and white paper. But this one was framed and I could see, even from a distance, that it had been executed by an expert hand.

"Who is that?" I asked.

She looked across at me and her fingers began wrenching and tearing the portrait from its frame.

"It is Helen!" She spoke with difficulty.

I secured my needle and flinging the dress down, ran to her side. "Let me see, please! Let me look! Oh, you are tearing it!"

I reached out and for a moment we struggled almost ludicrously, Aunt Geraldine to tear the silhouette, myself to save it and study it. Then quite suddenly she released it, crinkled and despoiled.

For the first time I looked at a likeness of Helen Bellenmore, Mark's wife. It was cut in white paper upon a black background.

I had always thought Armorel beautiful, but here was a profile so enchanting of outline that I was reminded of the angels in a Michelangelo reproduction I had once seen. It was the gravest, gentlest face with a lovely sweep of brow, a short nose and curved lips with the slight pout of extreme youth. Her hair was brushed back, falling in a mass of tumbling curls.

"How beautiful she was!" I cried.

"White upon black!" Aunt Geraldine seemed not to have heard what I said. She was staring at the portrait in my hand. "White upon black!" she repeated. "It is ironically appropriate, the face of an angel and beneath it a black heart."

"Oh no!" I cried. "No! Not with that brow, that lovely, innocent mouth."

"It was the beauty of youth," Aunt Geraldine said bitterly. "Had she lived, age would have revealed her for what she was."

"She cannot have been so wicked," I said gently. "Mark loved her!"

"My two men have stranger's blood," she said. "Yet they have one strong thing in common. They make themselves slaves to beauty." Tears streamed down her face.

I laid the portrait on the desk and knelt by her side, putting my hand on her plump knee. "You must not be sad. It is over, now!"

She shook her head, holding her handkerchief to her eyes. "It will never be over." Her pretty, gentle mouth trembled. "The dreadful thing is here with us to the end of our lives!"

"I will not believe such a thing! No one can be held responsible for what was an accident."

She shook her head. "You do not understand, Elizabeth dear! What happens in a house becomes part of it, just as every evil thought becomes part of us."

"If you feel like that," I said practically, "why not leave here?"

She lifted her head and looked at me. "I cannot," she said simply.

Because, I thought, this had been the Bellenmore house for two generations. Her roots were here.

I looked again at the silhouette of Helen.

"She was very young when this was done," I said.

"Barely twenty, but she was so dreadfully wise! She already knew wickedness."

I waited, not daring to move and break the spell of confidence.

Aunt Geraldine sat with her hands folded upon the dark gray cloth of her dress.

"Her mother was an actress. Helen was beautiful and spoiled and encouraged to live a loose life at an early age." She brushed the crumpled picture from her desk and it fell to the floor.

"And Mark . . . did not mind?"

"He was blind and willful! James had married the daughter of a great family. Mark took a rebel's delight in going to the other extreme."

"Could you, perhaps, have been a little prejudiced, Aunt Geraldine?" I asked gently. "I mean because Helen's mother was an actress?"

"I was prepared to love her and welcome her to this house. I was prepared even to accept her mother for all her notorious fast ways. I did so only to find, not so long after their marriage, that Helen had never loved Mark."

Something in me felt compelled to defend the dead girl.

I said, gazing down at the portrait, "She was so beautiful that she must have been loved by many men! She was not destined to remain a spinster. So she did not *have* to marry Mark. She was young and—"

"She had to marry someone!" Aunt Geraldine was staring at the wallpaper as though she had never in her life before seen the fleur-de-lys on the green background.

I watched her, refusing the first sharp, shameful implication as being worthy more of Rosie's conversation than Aunt Geraldine's.

"Do not tell me that at nineteen, she was afraid of becoming a spinster!"

Aunt Geraldine reached for the little gold-topped bottle of smelling salts.

"She was afraid of being left with an illegitimate child!"

The room seemed to spin round me. The face in the silhouette became something living, moving across my vision of the ornate and lovely room.

"Oh Elizabeth!" As in a dream I heard my aunt's shocked voice. "I should not have told you! Your grandmama will be very angry if she knows!"

"Do not worry." I laid a hand on her lap. "She shall never know! But tell me, please, since you have said so much. Helen married Mark without his knowing about . . . about her . . . child?"

"Mark married her believing her to be a young and innocent girl."

"And when . . . he knew?"

She shook her head.

"He has refused to discuss her. We only found out the truth after the accident. Doctor Rowlins was called to her as James was out. He said her child had been conceived five months previously, and she had been married to Mark but three."

"Perhaps she had told him and he forgave her. Perhaps he loved her so much and she . . . she loved him, after all! You do not know!"

She shook her head forlornly, her eyes still swimming. I thought how pretty and helpless she still looked.

"There were always soirées, evenings out, gay times! I saw her with other men. I am quite certain that she only married Mark because she wanted a name and honor for her child."

I sat back on my heels, staring into the fire and thought of Mark. I knew that when his temper was roused it was something to fear, just as his charm and kindness at other times was irresistible. Mark had not James's control nor James's more sanguine nature.

"This room," said a voice from the doorway, "looks like a servant's quarters!"

We turned and saw grandmother walk slowly towards us. "Is that dress half on the floor yours, Elizabeth? And what is all that paper doing on the carpet?"

"I am turning out my desk, Mama," Aunt Geraldine said, averting her gentle, tearful face.

But the sharp black eyes alighted on the silhouette lying face upward on the Turkey carpet.

"Give that to me," she ordered and held out her hand.

I bent and picked it up and then scrambled to my feet. She snatched it from me and flung it into the fire.

"That," she said, "is the place for trash!"

I picked up my dress and Aunt Geraldine hurried to help my grandmother into her chair. She shook the plump hand off her arm.

"I am perfectly capable of sitting down, thank you Geraldine." Then her gaze sharpened. "What have you been saying to Elizabeth?"

It was I who answered, I, the youngest who had less fear of her than Aunt Geraldine.

"I have just seen a letter I wrote to Aunt Geraldine when I was only six," I said and managed a laugh. "I must have been a very vain little girl for I described a new dress in detail."

I might, however, have been speaking to an empty room. My grandmother's black eyes were fastened on Aunt Geraldine's face.

"Why did you keep Helen's picture?"

"I did not do so intentionally! It must have become caught in some other papers and passed unnoticed."

"Have you been discussing her with Elizabeth?"

"I only just explained that . . . that she was not the right type of wife for Mark."

"You will never again speak of Helen! Do you hear? Never!" The gold topped ebony stick tapped twice. "It is over. You hear me?"

"Of course, Mama!"

Garnets gleamed among the laces at my grandmother's throat. I looked at my aunt. She was gazing down at her taut, folded hands, a curious expression, half of rebellion, half of submission on her face. I could not understand how any woman, having successfully brought up two boys, could be so subservient and so much in fear of her own mother.

I turned my head away and picked up my sewing. The heavy folds of the dress dragged from my lap.

"Why do you sit down here sewing by hand?" Grandmother turned her attention to me. "Do you not know how to use a sewing machine?"

I said that I did.

"Then take that dress up to the front attic. You know that it is the sewing room. And put a shawl round your shoulders; it will be cold up there."

I did not see that I was doing any harm by sewing here comfortably by the fire and quite firmly I said so. I saw a flash of anger in grandmother's eyes.

"You will do as I bid you, miss!" she said in her strong voice. "Finish that sewing in the room set out for such tasks. Embroidery is a drawing room occupation, seamstressing is not."

I rose and picked up the dress, draping it over my arm. "It seems," I said lightly, "that the greater the house, the more uncomfortable one must be for the sake of the conventions! Oh well, we have a doctor in the house, so perhaps my subsequent pneumonia will not kill me!"

I walked to the door surrounded by silence. Then,

"Elizabeth."

I turned round. "Yes, grandmother?" My voice was calm although my heart was hammering with indignation.

"You have your father's devilment in you! If you wish to earn the right to be thought a lady you will not be pert to your elders!"

"I am sorry, grandmother. I did not mean to be pert. I was merely puzzled that I am banished to an unheated room because I sew a dress! If I am ever rich, I will think first of all of the comfort of those who live under my roof, even my servants. I will give to them all as many fires as they need, and baths and good food."

"Is that intended to be another piece of impertinence?"

"No, grandmother," I said honestly. "Mrs. Vine and Susannah and the other women who come to work here are well looked after. I was thinking of other poor souls, governesses and servants, banished to candle-lit and fireless attics in great houses where lights blaze downstairs. I was making a kind of solemn vow that if ever I own a mansion, it will not be the lot of *my* servants!"

"Then you will plunge your husband into penury, Miss!" my grandmother retorted. "Now, go and do whatever you have to on that dress. The sewing machine is a wonderful invention. It should not take you long."

"I shall see to it that it does not," I said and gave her a brilliant smile.

Climbing the stairs to the attic, I knew I had been impertinent, but it had been an effort to stand up to my grandmother for Aunt Geraldine's sake more than my own. I recognized in my grandmother a desire to be obeyed, not because her command was reasonable so much as for the satisfaction of forcing complete submission.

There was no gas on this floor and I lit a brass lamp and set it by the sewing machine. For all its usefulness it was a particularly ugly structure. I sought for the cotton I needed and adjusted the shuttle. I sat for a moment or two after threading the needle, running my finger along the floral decoration on the machine.

I had just begun to turn the handle and move the treadle when I heard running footsteps and Susannah burst breathlessly into the room. Over her arm she carried a carriage rug.

"Your grandmama sent me up with this for you, Miss Elizabeth."

"Thank you, Susannah."

I managed not to laugh as I took the rug and wrapped it round me. In her tough old heart, my grandmother admired spirit when it was justified and this was her way of showing it.

I was aware of Susannah hovering round me. "You bain't nervous up here on your own, Miss?"

"No, why should I be? After all, you sleep on this floor and so does Mrs. Vine."

She nodded.

"Put her head on the pillow and she's deaf to the world. And as for me, I come from the country; my mother served in a big house where they said there was ghosts. I don't take no notice."

I laughed and looked into her dark pointed little face.

"There are no ghosts here, Susannah!"

"There be noises sometimes in the night!"

"Furniture creaking, wind in the chimney."

"Or someone lookin' for somethin'. But I don't care! If they comes into my room, I can scream louder'n anyone!"

Looking at her, I quite believed it! I reassured her that I was not in the least bit nervous. And besides, I added, it was not yet dinner time. Ghosts did not walk until midnight.

"This one do!"

"Well, next time you hear it," I said cheerfully, "you just call out and tell them it's warmer down in the drawing room. I don't think they like the human voice!"

She giggled at that and went out of the room. I heard her boots clatter loudly on the top uncarpeted staircase.

There was no earthly reason why anyone in this house should wander in the attics. Old people, I knew, were often restless at night and sometimes when their minds became hazy, they forgot where they were. But grandmother's mind was as keen as mine and if there was anything she wanted from the attic she would either come up here in the daytime to look or send a servant to fetch whatever she wanted. On the other hand, if Aunt Geraldine wandered at night, I was certain I would hear her, for her room was next to mine and I was a light sleeper.

It occurred to me that perhaps the sounds Susannah had heard had come from the attic of the house next door. I knew that Lord and Lady Dyron kept four servants and they probably slept two to a room on this floor.

The heavy carriage rug kept me fairly warm while I ground away at the handle of the sewing machine. When I had finished, I folded the dress and the rug and stood up stretching my arms. Disused attics have a certain nostalgic atmosphere and I had no thought of prying as I turned to look at an old table desk such as my father used to possess. There was nothing of interest inside, just piles of bills and a few letters from various friends to my grandfather, their edges yellowing, their ink grayish-brown.

It was not for me to read the letters and I closed the little table desk.

Beyond the lamplight, where the shadows lay, I saw two lyre-backed chairs, an ancient spinning wheel and a cedarwood chest. I went over to it. It was unlocked and I lifted the lid. A strong camphor smell seeped out from the clothes packed there. A chest full of satins and velvets was irresistible! I fetched the lamp, set it on the table and knelt down, reaching out to touch the top dress of deep white satin with flounces of cerise. I turned it over carefully and came upon a yellow silk gown, then rose velvet. These I guessed by their fashion were my grandmother's dresses worn during her young womanhood. I longed to take them out, to shake them free of their folds and study the intricacies of padded underskirts and swathed bodices.

And then, plunging more deeply, I saw a little white muslin dress. I pushed the heavy pile of clothes to one side with my shoulder and lifted it out.

It was a child's dress, flounced and trimmed with blue ribbons. There were great rents down the front of it and I supposed it had rotted with the years, but when I tested the material it seemed to hold firmly. The great tears must have been done by an accident . . . or by vicious hands.

I laid the dress back gently in the chest and smoothed the velvets and the satins over it. Something about that little torn party dress disturbed me. The tears were not the slight ones caused in play; they were long and vicious. Whose dress had it been? And why had something so spoiled and ragged been carefully preserved?

XII

MARK KEPT his promise to take Aunt Geraldine and myself to the Savoy Theater to hear *Trial by Jury*.

I wore my best gown of gentianella-colored silk with claret velvet bows and a slightly décolléte neckline. I brushed my heavy hair for so long that my arm ached. Then, instead of the usual coil at the nape of my neck, I pinned it in a soft swirl on the top of my head like a coronet. It made me look older than my years but I liked it. This was my first really grown-up occasion and I wanted to please Mark.

I clasped the garnet necklace that had been my mother's round my throat and the rich gleam of the stones in the gaslight matched the bows of my dress. I spread my arms and the excitement I had felt all day burst over me in a wave. This was living!

"Elizabeth?" Aunt Geraldine called from outside the door.

I swung round to face her as she took a few steps into the room.

"My dear! How beautiful you look!" I saw her eyes, at first so full of love and pride, shade with doubt. "But what have you done to your hair?"

"Don't you like it?"

"Of course!" she said cautiously. "But do you not think it a little . . . theatrical?"

I glanced sideways at my reflection in the mirror and laughed. "Just for once, I want to look different! Please, Aunt Geraldine." I professed to plead with her to let me keep my unusual style. But I knew perfectly well that she would make no effort to deny me if it were my pleasure. She was so kind and so without the will to say 'No!'

A gust of wind rattled the windows. She glanced at my cape lying on the bed.

"I think I can find you something much more fitting to the occasion than that." She turned and left me and I heard her hurrying down the passage.

I was standing by the chest, choosing my gloves, when she returned. She carried over her arm a most beautiful cloak of thick padded silk. The color was sapphire and the hood was lined with emerald green.

She laid the cloak about my shoulders. I stood by the mirror as she secured the buckle which fastened it at the throat.

"Oh Aunt Geraldine, how beautiful! You really mean that I may wear this tonight?"

"It suits you, Elizabeth, far better than an old woman like myself!" I saw her wistful smile. "I have not worn it for many years. But perhaps you do not think it fashionable enough?"

"Fashionable enough!" I echoed, smoothing the exquisite softness of the silk. "It is lovely beyond fashion! How can you bear not to wear it yourself?"

She put her arms around me with one of her swift, impulsive gestures.

"Dearest Elizabeth, if only you had come to live with us sooner, how the pattern of our lives might have been changed!"

I saw her hand go up to her eyes as she dropped her arms abruptly and turned away. Then, with her back to me she said briskly, "Mark is waiting for us downstairs and the carriage is at the door."

I was so delighted with my cloak and my new hair style that I play-acted my way down the graceful staircase much as a child might have done, pretending to myself that I was a queen. From the hall, Mark watched me. When I reached the bottom step, he reached out to me.

"It is not fair that a woman can so transform herself that she can render a man speechless!" he said and took my hand.

"I have never noticed that you were lost for words, my dear cousin!" I retorted.

"You persist in forgetting," he said, his voice very low, "that I am *not* your cousin! My compliment—"

"I call it flattery!" I cut in lightly.

"That is because you do not know me well enough! I praise, but I never flatter! What have you done to yourself?"

"I have dressed up," I managed to make my voice light, "for a theater—my very first theater, Mark! And I intend to enjoy every moment of the evening!"

"I wish I had taken a box so that I could have shown you off to the crowd!" he said. "This is Elizabeth Bellenmore! Look at her! When you are all fat and old she will still be beautiful!"

I met his gaze coolly and he threw back his head, laughing. "And you do not even blush!"

"I do not blush easily," I replied. "You forget that I was not brought up in circles which encouraged such ladylike reactions!"

"For which, my dear Elizabeth, I thank God!"

"If," I amended, "the fact gives rise to thanks!"

We were dueling with words again! The moments of enchantment had gone. I was no longer a child playing at being a royal lady, I was Elizabeth Bellenmore of a swashbuckling father, the Dover cottage and Rosie's big, brash heart.

A young woman's first visit to a theater is a milestone in her life. I sat in my seat as in a dream, listened to Mr. Sullivan's music and Mr. Gilbert's witty words to songs; I watched the cavorting and the flirting on the stage and heard the roars from the gallery.

As the curtain fell on the last act, I applauded until my hands ached. I saw Aunt Geraldine lean forward and smile across at Mark much as a mother might have done at the enthusiasm of her child.

Our carriage was waiting for us outside. We drove home through the crystal clear night. When we arrived, I saw a light burning in the drawing room. Mark slid the rug from his knees and was first out, ready to help Aunt Geraldine. She laid her hand on his arm and said, "It was such an enjoyable evening, dear Mark. Thank you," and hurried towards the house, hugging her furs. The door opened immediately and Susannah's queer little face peered at us.

I stepped from the carriage, pausing on the pavement. "I have so loved my first theater!" I said. "Thank you!"

He looked down at me. "You will catch cold!" he said and lifted the hood of my cloak carefully over my hair. "Run along in to bed."

"I don't want to sleep tonight! I want to lie and just remember every moment." I met his eyes and knew that mine were starry.

"Every moment of those we have spent together tonight?" He bent and kissed my temple. "I would have your memory short save for just those, Elizabeth." I felt his hand rest lightly against my heart.

I broke away, running along the path into the house where Susannah stood, wide-eyed, peering round the door, waiting for me.

Mark did not come into the house that night. As I went upstairs I heard the carriage start up and move away; the horses' hooves seemed to dance in the cold, quiet air.

In my room, the fire was still burning brightly and the gas lamps had been lit. Aunt Geraldine was waiting there to bid me goodnight.

I kissed her and unclasping the cloak, handed it to her. She pressed it back into my hands. "It is yours, dear." And as I began to protest she became a little impatient. "Such a little thing," she murmured. "When you love someone there is nothing in the world you would not do for them. *Nothing*. Take the cloak and I hope it will bring you very great happiness."

When I had undressed I went to the mirror and, unpinning my hair, let it fall about my shoulders. What a little idiot I was to find myself still glowing from the excitement of Mark's touch. His life was filled with women. Did I, myself, not know of two? Lucia Emsworth, an actress at Covent Garden and a divorcée, and Armorel, another man's wife.

And if that is not enough, remember Helen.

I stared at the reflection of my white face with my father's dark eyes, my black, tumbling hair, my unfashionably large mouth.

How many men had I known in my life? How many had looked at me with livened interest? I dismissed Lord Remfrey of Glanmory. None-too-plain young ladies in the unhappy position of belonging neither above nor below stairs were a prey, so I had heard, to the odd bright glance, the surreptitious caress from the master of the house. James and Mark were different. We were of the same world.

A gust of wind shook the windows again and I thought the gaslight dimmed. I shivered and looked over my shoulder at the shadowy, reflected room and it seemed that out of the darkness, Mark's charming, unhandsome face appeared.

Strangely, in that moment, the memory of an old German legend I had once read returned to me. The Undine story. And like her, I felt my own burning gaze looking into a faithless face.

Swiftly I put my hands to my eyes. I was merely a foolish, emotional young woman, overwhelmed by the lightest of kisses as by the touch of an enchanter's wand. Yet, even as I counseled myself, I found that my right hand rested against my temple where Mark's lips had touched it.

XIII

I HAVE NEVER seen a house look more beautiful than on the night of the soirée. Down in the hall, the chandelier had been lit; in the dining room, silver and glass glittered.

I knew that the young men had been specially invited for my benefit. Harry Stangate would be coming with his aunt and uncle, Lord and Lady Dyron, and a surgeon friend of James, Anthony Winkworth, and his sister Harriet. After that, I had lost count of the number who would fill the drawing room for the soirée.

My new emerald green dress fitted me perfectly; rich black lace billowed from under the silk folds to swing like black froth around my ankles. Again I piled my hair on the top of my head, using so many pins to secure it that I could feel them, cool and hard, pressing into my scalp. But I did not mind. I would gladly suffer a headache all tomorrow for the joy of feeling that I looked my best tonight.

I heard the first carriage draw up and pulling aside the curtain, looked out. A fog had risen stealthily since dusk.

Hastily I clasped a topaz necklace that had been my mother's round my throat and hurried downstairs.

I sat at dinner with Harry Stangate on one side of me and Anthony Winkworth on the other. Across the table, between the two candelabra, I was very aware of Mark. I was glad that I had spoken the truth to him some nights ago when I had said that I did not blush easily, for in the candlelight, his gray gaze had a brilliance and a steadiness that could have nonplussed me.

After dinner, other guests arrived and the music began.

It was in an interval between the music that I began to feel the pins in my hair tightening like a steel band and I decided to go down and ask Miss Stanhope in the ladies' retiring room, to help me ease the pressure.

She was a kindly soul and she tut-tutted as her fingers probed the heavy coils of my hair.

"How you have been able to bear all these, Miss Bellenmore, I cannot think! You do not need so many!" She pulled them out and with expert hands secured my hair with half the number.

"There!"

I thanked her gratefully, leaned across to the oval mirror and ran rice paper over my face.

When I went into the hall, I saw that the chandelier swung with the weight of so many people on the floor above. I skirted it cautiously, watching the jewelled clusters sparkle and the dip and stream of candlelight.

There was such a murmur from above that I had reached the staircase before I realized that Kenny was shouting frantically. I lifted my heavy satin skirts and ran to his room, opening the door and calling, "What is the matter?"

He pointed to the window, his face crumpled with distress. "I heard a little cat mewing," he said and his voice was a wail. "It's outside somewhere. I think it's starving. Aunt Elizabeth, please, please can someone go out and make it warm?"

"But it must belong to one of the houses round here and I'm sure it will find its way home."

"It won't! It *won't!*" His voice rose. "It was such a little mew, Aunt Elizabeth! There it is." He held up a thin, imperious hand. "Listen!"

I heard it, too—a small, plaintive, lonely whine coming out of the foggy night.

"I'll go and find him," I said comfortingly, "and if he really seems lost, I will bring him back here. Mrs. Vine shall give him some warm milk."

"And I want to see him," Kenny began.

"First let me find him!" I warned. "Now tuck down, Kenny, like a good boy!" I pulled the bedclothes up around him.

I ran to the cupboard under the stairs and reached for the cloak. Pulling up the hood, I ran to the front door. The yellow fog was like a wall through which, dimly, I could see the solitary street lights.

I searched the windowsill and the strip of garden, but no small, furry object came to my call. Shivering a little, I went into the road, leaving the door open. But the light from the chandelier was puny against the opaqueness of the fog.

Suddenly something very small shot across my path toward the gardens in the center of the Square. I ran after it, careful not to call too loudly and alarm the kitten. As I reached the center of the Square I heard it rustle the bushes. It was somewhere near, wanting food, wanting warmth, yet afraid of me. I bent down, holding out my hand, coaxingly, certain that it was watching me.

I crept along by the bushes, using the tone that used to bring my own little white cat running to me so many years ago. "Tibby! Tibby."

And then from under the foggy bushes a tiny face peered out at me. Still talking I bent down and put out my hands slowly so as not to frighten it. Soft fur rubbed against my finger and, delighted, I picked the little thing up. It was very thin and began to mew without ceasing. I guessed it was half-starving and opening the cloak, I tucked the kitten inside, holding it against the warmth of my flesh.

I heard the sound of hooves and waited until the looming shadow of horse and cab should pass.

Suddenly, from somewhere behind me, I felt a violent blow between my shoulders. Such force was used that I lost my balance at the edge of the step and pitched forward.

The sound of the hansom cab became a roar. I was aware of a

horse's head rearing in front of me, giant-size to my terrified eyes. I heard a man's voice shouting and tiny talons inside the cloak clawed my shoulder. I think I screamed as I half fell, flinging myself backwards as I did so.

"You should look where you're going, lady, in the fog!" I heard a rough voice call through my swirling fear.

I stumbled up from my knees, unable to speak. The horse had been reined to a stop but it was fretting and stamping and the harness rattled angrily.

"You all right, lady?" the cabby called and I knew he could not quite see what had happened.

In my panic, there was no time even to answer him. Directly I had managed to scramble to my feet, I darted into the fog right in front of the horse. My only thought was that I had to reach the safety of the house while someone, even a stranger, watched.

I do not know what miracle prevented my shaken legs from giving way under me. As I ran, I heard the driver whip up his horse and suddenly I was alone and in complete darkness.

The fog made tall, inanimate ghosts of the houses and I did not know which was mine. There was no light to guide me.

But I had left the door open!

Inside my cloak, the little cat fought in fear and I knew it had drawn blood on my shoulder. I tried to murmur soothing words to it, but it could not possibly have heard my breathless whisper. I was nearly speechless and preoccupied with fear. I knew my attacker must be somewhere behind me. At any moment I would feel his hands again at my back.

I ran along by the railings of the houses, terrified that if I had to retrace my steps I would come face to face with my attacker. I peered at numbers and saw that I was many houses too far along the Square. I braced myself and turned, my eyes raking the thick sulphur blanket overlying the night.

No one confronted me. In fact there seemed to be not another living soul walking in Manchester Square.

I realized, as I searched for the house, how easily one could lose one's sense of direction in a fog. Then, clutching the little fighting, mewing cat, alert to the faintest sound I found the house. I dashed through the gate and pulled the big iron bell. While I waited, I leaned shakenly against the door and stared into the fog. A place in my back, between my shoulderblades seemed to burn with the violence of that lunge at me. Someone had tried to throw me under the horse's hooves. But who? And why?

I rang again, frantically, my shaking fingers fighting with the protesting kitten. At last the door opened. Mrs. Vine stared at me.

"Miss Elizabeth!"

I pushed past her into the hall. "Take . . . this," I gasped and opened the cloak.

"Why! The poor little thing!"

"Take it," I insisted breathlessly, "into the kitchen and give it milk. I will explain later to Aunt Geraldine. And . . . and tell Master Kenny . . . that I have found his little cat."

"You are ill, Miss Elizabeth! What has happened?"

I shook my head. "No! No! I am all right."

I slid the cloak from my shoulders and on my way to the kitchen, hung it on the peg in the cupboard. Mrs. Vine saw the livid marks on my bare shoulder.

"You must let me bathe those scratches for you. They look angry."

Because they were painful, I let her settle me in the armchair by the kitchen range. We put the kitten on the rug and sent Susannah for milk.

"Warm it a little," I said and pointed to the large black kettle on the hob.

While Mrs. Vine bathed my shoulder, I tried to collect my thoughts, to tell myself that some pick-pocket had seen me come out of the house and had thought to rob me, hoping maybe that I wore jewels.

But surely it was too great a coincidence that a thief should be passing at that moment! Besides, he would not have called attention to his presence by trying to thrust me under a horse's hooves! He would have snatched at what he saw and disappeared.

Mrs. Vine was putting a little soothing powder on the red slashes on my shoulder while the little cat lapped up the milk. I could hear the hired servants talking and laughing together in the pantry.

Who had watched me leave the house, had stalked me? Had

it been the same person who had attacked Morag Nanog? And why? Who was our enemy, a midget's and mine?

From this house I called my home, who had escaped into the fog as I had stumbled and righted myself? Someone rushing across the street, not waiting to see if I had been killed, closing the door I had left firmly opened. Because, should a young woman have been found later, lying trampled to death by a horse, Number 243 Manchester Square would be as ignorant of it all as any other house closed and cloistered by night.

XIV

I HAD TO talk to someone! But whom could I trust? As I left the kitchen, the sense of malevolence and aloneness that surrounded me was like the fog itself.

I was too shaken to look in on Kenny. Mrs. Vine would see that he quietened now that the fate of the little cat was settled for one night at least.

I could hear someone singing as I passed the drawing room door on my way to my room. I wanted to fetch something with which to cover the livid scratches on my shoulder.

I stood in my room for a full five minutes, a gray velvet cape over my shoulders. I knew I had to return to the drawing room, to behave as though nothing had happened. I must not spoil the party, and in any case it was too late now to find my attacker. The fog had been on his, or her, side.

Harry Stangate watched me come in and crossed quietly to my side.

"You are cold, Miss Bellenmore?" he asked in surprise. His own face, I noticed, was very pink.

"Not any more," I managed to whisper and drew the cape more closely round my shoulders.

Mrs. Eyre was singing a song I loved, "Greensleeves." But the summer-light music had no place in this house!

I glanced around the room. Had someone here followed me into the night?

James was sitting with Lady Dyron and Aunt Geraldine. My

grandmother sat with her eyes closed, her hands playing with the black fan with the eye-holes.

I looked among the collection of family friends and suddenly realized that Mark and Armorel were not in the room. I wondered who else had noticed their absence and if they were together somewhere. Then I caught my grandmother's black, penetrating gaze and I knew that she, too, had noticed.

"Greensleeves was all my joy,
Greensleeves was my delight—"

I leaned back in my chair and tried to listen. Immediately Harry's hand reached to adjust my cape. I glanced up and smiled at him.

How friendly and normal and a little dull he was! And yet how safe.

"Greensleeves was my heart of gold,
And who but Lady Greensleeves?"

The song was ended; the applause rose and fell. Around me people were rising, moving into little chattering groups. Wine was being served. I refused some and went to congratulate Mrs. Eyre. Then, carefully avoiding Harry, I slipped away.

I ran up the stairs to my own room, closed the door and leaned against it. The lamp burned; the fire flickered. I could no longer laugh and talk my way through the party. I was far too frightened.

Suppose this was a plan to kill me because someone in the house resented my being there? But what danger did I present to anyone, save someone who was mad—mad beneath the cloak of sanity? But surely such a person would give some sign! Madness was not so cunning that it could hide itself completely at will. Who, then?

I dropped to my knees on the rug in front of the fire and stared into the burning embers.

In my lovely green dress, in this handsome room, I again faced my own utter aloneness. There was no one to whom I could go and tell of this second attack on me because, like that first time on the stairs, there was no one who would believe me. I was loved; I was welcomed in this house, they would insist. It was beyond the realms of reason that anyone should wish to harm me.

I stirred the small fire and put my hands to the flames. There is no one so lonely, I thought, as one who has no childhood home, a place solid and permanent. The Dover cottage, my father and Rosie were gone. I must face it! This was my predicament!

Suddenly my spirit reasserted itself. I was young, I was strong, I believed I was good to look at. With those assets why stay here? More and more possibilities were opening for young women. I could perhaps, train for work in an office. That way, I could be certain of my life! I wanted it. I wanted a future . . . and if I stayed here, someone was determined to rob me of it.

I rose, smoothed down my dress and picked up the cape which had fallen to the floor. There was a light footstep outside my room and Aunt Geraldine's voice called to me softly, "Elizabeth, are you not well?"

I ran to the door and opened it. "I am quite well, thank you, Aunt Geraldine. I came upstairs to . . . just to tidy myself."

"People are asking for you. This evening is for you, my dear, you must not hide yourself away! Oh—" Her hand went to her face and her wide blue eyes saw the scratches on my shoulder. "My *dear* child, what *have* you done?"

I told her briefly about the kitten.

"I could not leave it out there in the cold," I explained. "You see, I heard it mew and I knew it must be lost."

"And you say it is in the kitchen with Mrs. Vine?"

"Yes. And it would be so lovely for Kenny if he could keep it."

"We must first see if someone claims it."

"I don't think anyone will. I think it was turned out to starve," I said angrily.

"Poor little thing." Her gentle blue eyes regarded me. "Then if Mrs. Vine does not mind looking after it, perhaps we could keep it. As you say, it would be company for Kenny. Now come along back to the drawing room. The evening is almost over." She laid her hand on my arm as we went along the passage together.

When we reached the drawing room, I drew back. I wanted, I said, to go down to the kitchen just to see how the little cat was.

"I have a feeling that it was almost in the last stages of starvation and I do not want it to die. I won't be long," I promised.

As I turned to go to the kitchen, I heard voices from immediately behind the Blue Room door.

"What are we going to do?" There was a clear ring of despair in Armorel's voice as though she was beyond caring if she could be heard from the other side of the door.

"What *can* we do? It is quite impossible."

"I won't let you say that! We can think of a way. We must! Oh, Mark—"

I stayed to hear no more. The green door swung behind me and I walked towards the bright lights of the kitchen.

I need not have worried about the little cat. It sat, purring gently, on Mrs. Vine's lap. She set it down on the rug as she saw me and covered it with her crochet shawl.

"Those scratches still look angry, Miss Elizabeth!"

"They *feel* angry!" I replied and felt the place tenderly. "Starvation hadn't affected the kitten's capacity for fighting!"

"You have a kind heart, Miss Elizabeth, to go out in the fog to rescue it."

"I am sure our Queen would give me a medal for that!" I teased her. But my gaiety was on the surface. I was grave as I went back through the hall.

Mark was there, standing alone at the bottom of the stairs. Above him, every crystal facet of the chandelier quivered and sparkled.

"I do not trust it!" I said.

Mark followed my gaze and then looked back at me.

"A young woman," he reproved, his eyes amused, "should go into life trusting everything and everyone. Nothing is more beautifying than trust!"

"You have," I observed, "what grandmother would call a facile tongue!"

"Surely you would not have me dumb!"

"I don't know." I mounted a stair and glanced over my shoulder. It gave me a pleasant sensation to be able to look at him levelly instead of always with my head a little raised, my eyes lifted as though to a superior being!

My shawl had slipped and he glanced at my shoulder.

"A cat clawed me," I explained, "a little cat Kenny heard mewing outside. I rescued him. He is in the kitchen."

"I don't like the look of those scratches."

"They are nothing."

"You must put some soothing ointment on them tonight. I have an excellent one. I will fetch it for you later."

"I, too, have an excellent one in my room, thank you, Doctor Bellenmore."

I saw the sudden angry flash in his eyes. His brows came together in a long dark line.

"That piece of mockery was not necessary, Elizabeth!" he said on a long breath. "I do not wish to have that prefix. You know why? Because I can write something of far more value after my name. Just three letters . . . but very important ones. Do you want to know them?"

"Not particularly," I said and avoided his gaze.

"But you shall. I am Mark Bellenmore. W.D.F."

I did not want to ask what the letters stood for, but I found myself doing just that!

"Well, and what do they mean?"

" 'When Doctors Fail,' " he said. "For that is when people in pain come to me."

"You have a colossal conceit!"

"I have faith," he replied very quietly.

"Mark, why do you not study to become a doctor?" I stopped taunting him. "You are clever. People would then accept you, respect you."

"How do you know that certain people do not already do that?"

"I am serious!"

"Why should you be? What can it possibly matter to you, whether I am called a charlatan or whether I am that most respected person, a London doctor?" The dark mood had passed and he was looking at me keenly.

I felt my heart quicken and I was afraid that at any moment I would do what I had boasted I never did . . . blush!

"People's opinion of you," I said, my voice as haughty as I could make it, "is of no personal interest to me! If you wish to waste the good brain God has obviously given you, then that is your affair!"

Turning to mount the stairs, I cast a glance at Armorel's door. Was it open just a crack, and was she listening and watching?

I began to walk up the stairs.

"You are an outrageous young woman!" Mark was by my side. "I believe you do battle for battle's sake!"

Let him think that way! I smiled. Yet, as we turned the sweeping arc of the staircase, I felt a longing tear at me. Not Mark! Oh, do not let it be Mark! And I did not know whether my plea was for him not to have been my attacker on the stairs and in the fog, or for it not to be he who made my heart race so wildly.

XV

IN THE END, it was James to whom I told the story of the attack on me.

He had returned, soon after noon the next day, from seeing patients and found me working in his study. We had scarcely had time for a word together since last night and he asked me how I had enjoyed the party.

I told him, a little cautiously, that it had been a glittering evening and that I had found the guests charming.

"And now," he came and stood before me, "let us dispose of formal phrases! Was it a happy evening for you?"

My first reaction was caution. I did not know even yet whom to trust. Then, looking into that broad and honest face, I was immediately ashamed. James would never harm me. To prove my trust in him, I told him the truth.

"I would have loved it had it not been for the terrifying incident when I found the kitten."

"What terrifying incident?" he asked sharply.

And then I told him.

He listened, leaning forward, his hands clasped between his knees, eyes staring down at the red and blue Turkey carpet. When I had finished he said nothing for a moment or two, but I saw his hands kneading each other as though his mind were in distress. Then he raised his head and looked at me.

"Why did you not tell me immediately it happened?" he demanded hoarsely.

"I could not burst into a roomful of guests quietly listening to music!"

"Indeed you could for something as serious as that!"

"But by the time I had run into the house and reached the drawing room, whoever had tried to harm me would have got away!" My voice was taut, my hands gripped tightly in my lap. I had told of my experience but I did not feel any relief from the telling.

I watched James start up from his chair and walk backwards and forwards across the room.

"I have been afraid for so long that some of the drunken roughs of the Quadrant might find their way here."

"You believe, then, that it was someone out to steal any valuables . . . jewels, perhaps?"

"What else is there to think?" He stopped and looked down at me.

Meeting his gaze, I wanted to be able to trust him, to trust someone.

"Surely no ruffian would attack a woman in a cloak unless he was certain that she had something worth stealing! It might have been a servant or a governess from one of these houses."

"But there *is* no other explanation, Elizabeth!"

I knew that I was being unfair to feel impatience with him. After all, from his point of view, what else was there to think. But in spite of myself, my voice was swift and ragged.

"For someone intent upon robbery," I cried, "it would not be necessary, or wise, to wait until a carriage came past! I am small. Someone wanting merely to snatch at any jewels I might have, had only to throw me to the ground and tear them off me!"

"He might have been so intent upon doing just that, that he did not hear the carriage!"

"You make the explanation too easy!" There was scorn in my voice.

"Then," he said helplessly and spread his hands, "what is *your* explanation?"

I rose and went to the window and looked out at the bare trees. The sun was as pale as candlelight.

"What," I countered, "was *your* explanation of my near-accident on the stairs the other night?"

"Dear God!" his ejaculation thundered out. "You do not for one moment imagine that there is a lunatic at large in this house? That someone tried twice deliberately to kill you?"

"I wish I did not have that thought, James," I said without turning round.

He was at my side in two strides, swinging me round to face

him and taking my hands. "Elizabeth, I cannot let you believe such a thing! No one in this house would harm you. We love you; you are one of us!"

I withdrew my hands. "Surely as a doctor you must know that the mad can love as well as the sane . . . and can kill that which they love."

I heard him draw a sharp breath. "What have you been reading to give you such an idea?"

"The medical books and pamphlets you receive interest me too, James," I said steadily. "Sometimes in odd moments I pick them up."

"Such reading matter is not for you," he reproached. "You are not a sick-nurse!"

"I wish I were," I said. "I wish I had been born a little earlier in the century and could have gone to Scutari with Miss Nightingale!"

"You do not know what you are saying!"

"I do." I nodded. "It is you who do not understand!" I turned from the window. "The point is—who followed me out of this house into the fog?"

James brushed his hand across his forehead. "I cannot believe anyone did. There is no violence here."

"You forget Helen," I whispered.

"She died as the result of an accident."

"Did she?" I forced him to meet my eyes.

"It is the only possible explanation," he said quietly.

"And a robbery attempt is the only explanation of what happened to me last night?"

He nodded. "It has to be, Elizabeth." He hurried on before I could protest. "Don't ever again go walking late at night in the streets of London! It is not safe. Every day one reads in the newspapers of acts of violence, of terrible things."

He was deliberately trying to frighten me! As though he had not spoken, I continued, "And then, there was Morag."

"It was a mere coincidence that she died in this Square," he said sharply. "You have got to believe that! We aren't so far away here from Regent's Quadrant and the dark alleys—"

I was scarcely listening. I was asking myself how I could trust him any more than anyone else in this house, after all? He had turned the conversation too neatly, making the danger come from the streets instead of from the house.

Yet could I believe that James, who had implied that he loved me, would allow a violence to go unprobed if he were certain that it came from this house?

I turned to the window. My fingers twisted the heavy tassel that looped back one of the curtains.

It was as I had feared! No one was going to believe my theory.

Looking out on to the desolate winter garden, I began to doubt my own certainty. These people were my family; they were proud and respected.

But suddenly I saw that in those very things lay my danger. Such was a family's faith in itself that it would be incapable of unbiased observation. Only when it saw with its own eyes would it believe what pride had mesmerized into invisibility.

I walked past James to the door.

"There is no possible doubt, Elizabeth," he said gently; "the man who attacked you was a thief. And you will promise me not to walk these streets alone again late at night, not even for a lost kitten."

I smiled at him and was silent.

As I crossed the hall, I told myself that a promise was futile, for if I wanted to keep my life, I must leave Manchester Square. Yet, as before when the thought had been so strongly with me, I knew that I would not. Foolish, falsely brave, I must stay until I knew what it was that tormented this beautiful house.

Don't let it be Mark! The words were like an agonized prayer in my mind. Frantically, I refused to ask myself why I prayed for Mark's innocence.

XVI

Mrs. Vine looked at Kenny over the tops of her steel-rimmed spectacles.

"If you pull that kitty's ear again I shall not let you play with him again!"

Kenny glared at her defiantly, his eyes made huge by the dark mauve smudges beneath them. The day was gray and without sunlight to lend its own glow to that pale, air-starved skin.

The kitten had forgotten that it had squealed with pain as it struggled down from the bed, caught by me before it flopped to the floor. I held the little thing against me and it began to purr.

"Give it to me. It's mine!" Kenny began to shout and a small rage began to fire his eyes.

Mrs. Vine looked at me and rightly interpreted my faint nod.

"I'm much too busy this morning to argue with you Master Kenny," she said, "and you leave that kitty alone!"

As the door closed firmly behind her, I sat down on the side of the bed, the kitten in my arms.

"When you were a baby," I said, "your Mama had to treat you very gently because your bones were easily broken and your skin tender. If she had harmed your head or pulled your ear, you might have suffered the effects of it for all your life. This kitten is like you were when you were a baby; it is very fragile. You could easily deafen or blind it. Would you want that to happen?"

"If you pulled my ear I'd squeal but I wouldn't go deaf!"

"You're bigger and your bones are stronger." I held up one tiny forepaw. "See, it is not as thick as my little finger! It was you who really saved it from starvation the other night, Kenny. That was kind! And now you must continue to be kind. The kitten has no home but this. Living things need to be loved; you do, don't you?"

He thought the matter over, frowning a little. Then he put out a finger and touched the kitten's paw.

"It *is* little, isn't it, Aunt Elizabeth."

I set the cat upon the sheet and it promptly sat down and began to wash itself. Kenny laughed and put out a hand and stroked the tiny head. I watched his fingers and saw that they were gentle.

When Miss Stanhope arrived for Kenny's lessons, I took the kitten back to the kitchen and sat it by the hearth. Then I went upstairs to my room to dust.

I had never quite liked the position of the escritoire. It was too much in the corner so that my own shadow fell over whatever I might be writing. I knew that Aunt Geraldine would not mind if I moved it and I set to work, first pushing a chair out of the way.

I am, however, not in the least muscular and as I bent to lift a corner of the desk, the carpet beneath it rucked. As I tried to smooth it with my foot, the desk slid from my hold and I felt a jolt. A pain stabbed my left hand. I let go of the desk, and stood for a moment holding my hand closely to me, trying by pressure to stop the pain. But it spread up my arm so that for a few minutes I thought I must have snapped a bone. There was no swelling, nor did there seem to be any break beneath the skin.

I sank into a chair and sat, trying to be patient, certain that the pain would go. But minutes went by and it did not ease. It was too acute for mere bruising and it seemed to me that the whole of my wrist was put out of joint.

James was still downstairs and his carriage waited outside. I could hear the occasional snort of the horses and the rattle of harness. I would ask James to bind up my wrist for me. I ran out of the room, anxious to catch him before he started his calls.

Half way down the main staircase I stopped. The pain was still shooting up my left arm to my shoulder. I heard James moving about in his room and from the other side of the hall, Kenny's young clear voice was repeating something after Miss Stanhope. I supposed Armorel was in their sitting room.

With a small surge of excitement at what I intended to do, I turned and went back to my room and put on my bonnet, tying the claret velvet ribbons with impatient hands. I wrapped my warm cloak round me, wincing as I inadvertently used my left hand to draw it round my shoulders. Then, picking up my reticule and muff, I went downstairs.

Half way down, I again paused, but this time it was because I could hear James in the hall. As much as I had hurried the first time to see him, I now held back, waiting for him to leave the house. For it was not James whom I intended to see, but Mark.

This was my chance to find out for myself something of Mark's form of treatment.

When I heard the front door close and the carriage drive away, I went down the remaining stairs and slipped quietly out of the front door. I tucked my head down before the blast of icy wind and walked quickly across the Square. As I opened his gate, I wondered at the reactions of the family to what I was doing. They would see my bound wrist and ask James what damage had been done. I would have to explain that I had been treated by Mark. I lifted my hand to pull the bell and at the moment when I heard it clang through the house, I knew that it was now too late to have second thoughts.

His housekeeper came to the door. Mr. Bellenmore was at home, she told me, and would I please come in while she enquired if he could see me. I was shown into a pleasant room where a coal fire burned.

I do not know how long I was kept waiting. But glancing through a copy of *The Englishwoman's Journal* I was quite unprepared for Mark's quiet entry. His amused eyes seemed to register everything about me in a single glance.

"So Miss Bellenmore has consented to pay me a social call."

"Miss Bellenmore," I retorted with asperity to hide my growing doubt as to the wisdom of my visit, "has done no such thing! She has come here because she wants advice. Medical advice."

He remained in the doorway.

"Then you should go to James, or to Dr. Rowlins, shouldn't you?"

"Not for what is troubling me," I said and held out my left hand. "This morning, trying to lift a piece of furniture, I jarred my wrist in some way."

"You did battle with a piece of furniture and hoped to win? Oh Elizabeth, have you not learned that you should always yield to that which is stronger than yourself?"

"I have learned no such thing. Such a generality would be weakness," I returned.

"And you are so strong."

As I sought a sharp retort, Mark reached out and took my undamaged hand and led me into his consulting room.

"Please sit down."

As I did so, he drew a chair forward for himself and sat opposite me. He took my left hand in his and his fingers probed lightly.

"Where is the pain?"

"In my wrist. But I do not think it is broken."

"It is not," he said and then he shook his head. "The damage is not where you think it is. It is here." He touched a place half way between my wrist and my forefinger. "You have a bone there and you have wrenched it out of its socket."

I exclaimed in dismay. "And it will take a long time to put right."

"Not necessarily."

I watched his fingers probe into the place which he believed to be the trouble spot and began to wish once more that I had not come. Why did he not get out bandages and bind the hand up instead of probing and feeling, separating my fingers as though he were merely playing with me?

Suddenly I felt him give my hand a sharp flick. It was so unexpected that I cried out.

"Come now," he said. "That didn't hurt you."

"No, but it will from now on, I have no doubt," I replied ruefully. "After such treatment—"

"Move your hand, Elizabeth. No, don't be too careful. *Move* it, bend it up and down."

With my eyes upon his face, I bent my hand, straightened it and bent it again. Five minutes ago I could not have done that without feeling violent pain. Now, there was no pain at all.

"What have you done?" I demanded.

"What I profess to do in such cases, returned the bone to its socket." He rose. "Now you can go home and do what you wish; but please don't lift furniture again."

"But the hand must be bound."

"The hand has no need of bandages," he laughed.

I felt the place where I had injured it, but there was no pain at all, not even with pressure. I rose slowly to my feet.

"Mark," I said softly, "I do not know what to call you. You are not a doctor and I know now that you are not a charlatan. So . . . what?"

He shrugged his shoulders.

"I suppose you could call me a rebel. I am at war with doctors who prescribe rest for all injuries. As I have said, I believe that I could cure Kenny."

"But you won't try, will you?" I besought him. "It's too wild a risk to take! If you should fail, then . . . then Kenny might be even more badly injured!"

"And suppose I did not fail?" he asked. "Suppose, in a few weeks from now Kenny could walk? Even James would have to admit then that I had succeeded where he failed!"

Was that what Mark wanted? To win where James had failed?

You, the physician, could not cure your son. But I, the charlatan, have given him back his strength.

"What is the matter, Elizabeth?"

I pulled myself together, aware that my gaze must have been long and unblinking as though Mark's faith in himself were mesmerizing me.

"Adults," I said, "might give you permission to experiment on them. But not a child. He wouldn't understand. Mark, don't do this thing! Your personal pride is not worth the terrible risk."

He reached out and his finger flicked my chin in a teasing way I remembered from my childhood.

"Suppose you leave me to decide!"

"And Armorel?" I said and waited.

His eyes narrowed and darkened. For one moment I thought his quick temper was going to lash at me. Then he controlled himself.

"You must learn not to concern yourself with outside problems, Elizabeth. Or keeping your hands in your muff will not prevent your pretty fingers from getting burned."

"Kenny is my nephew."

"No more closely than I am your cousin," he reminded me. "Now, I have half an hour before my next patient. Would you like to look over my house?"

Mark was smiling again, yet I could not check a small shiver as he laid his hand on my arm. I had no way of knowing how deeply significant had been his warning. It was possible to read much . . . or little into his words.

"Well," he demanded, "*would* you like to see my house?"

I was too inordinately curious to excuse myself on pleas of lack of time. "I would like to very much," I said.

I went with him up the staircase that was elegant enough but lacked the sweeping graciousness of our larger house.

Immediately I entered the drawing room I realized that Mark had collected beautiful pieces for his home.

Drawn up near the fire was a satinwood card table and beneath it a petit-point footstool. An infinitesimal glint of red caught my eye and I bent and picked it up with difficulty out of the rich pile of the carpet.

It lay glowing in my palm. A ruby, small but pure in color, and I guessed it had fallen from a ring or a brooch.

"One of your . . . your guests must have lost this," I said.

"Indeed she must!" he said without embarrassment and took it from me. "A fine ruby like that will have an anxious owner!"

"Perhaps," I suggested, "you have an idea to whom it belongs?"

"Perhaps," he replied lightly and his eyes went to the table on which stood a chess set.

It was only then that I realized the magnificence of the ivory and silver pieces, set on a mother-of-pearl board.

They were not the usual kings and queens and knights which I had been used to seeing, but were like Indian princes and dancing girls and the castles had domed eastern splendor about them.

I moved to the table and picked up a tiny figure wearing a minute silver crown.

"Mark, how lovely!"

He laughed. "That set was a gift . . . from a lady."

I put the piece down sharply on the mother-of-pearl board.

"I have shocked you."

"On the contrary, it is nothing to me who gives you presents," I said loftily and turned away. "But the very fact that you found need to inform me of the fact that a lady had given you the chess set seems to indicate how you enjoy your conquests."

"Oh Elizabeth!" He had flung back his head. "Look in the mirror," he said laughing and turned me round to face it. "See how flushed and indignant you look."

"You exaggerate your importance to me, Mark! I do not care—" I gripped my hands inside my muff and turned from the mirror.

"That set," he said, "was left me in the will of an old lady of nearly ninety. You see, Elizabeth, I had successfully treated her granddaughter after doctors had failed."

He had been teasing me and because I was chagrined, I was unreasonably annoyed.

"I cannot be too grateful for what you have done for me today," I said stiffly. "I . . . I came to you as a . . . a patient. Your fee, Mark?"

"Fifty pounds."

I gave a gasp.

Misty silver sunlight streaming in through the tall windows

caught his gray eyes and it was as though lamps shone behind them.

"There is an alternative," he began.

Before I could ask what it was, he had caught me and kissed me.

"This," he said and kissed me again lightly on the lips. "Thank you. Now I have my fee."

"I do not know," I breathed furiously, my cheeks crimson, "how you manage to keep such an elegant establishment as this if that is the usual fee you demand from your women patients!"

My skirts rustled round my ankles as I marched to the door. I held on to the banisters and descended the stairs.

But my flight was too swift, my eyes too blinded by anger. I tripped a little and as I righted myself, Mark caught me up. He steadied me with a hand.

"Careful! These stairs are not as shallow and manageable as those at home."

"And even easier to fall down and . . . break one's neck?"

Immediately the arm which steadied me dropped from my waist. He remained standing behind me, watching me. Heart racing, I went down the remainder of the stairs, opened the front door and half ran to the gate. I was only aware, when I found myself in the Square, that I had used my left hand without any sense of recurring pain.

I did not know whether Mark looked out of a downstairs window, watching me with hate in his eyes, or whether he was laughing at me. But, if he were really guilty of causing Helen's death, then I had placed myself in a dangerous position by that final challenging remark.

I was relieved to reach the house. My grandmother called me from the drawing room as I passed. I found her sitting in her usual chair, mending a rent in the black lace mantilla.

"You have been out, child." She paused in her stitching and looked me up and down. "Your face is flushed. Is the wind keen?"

I said that it was.

I watched her push the needle with uncertain fingers through the lace.

"I will mend that for you," I said quickly.

"And leave me nothing to do but stare into the fire?" she demanded. "I am not decrepit yet! You will remove your outdoor clothes and then come and talk to me."

Standing at my mirror, I tidied my hair, combing up the ruffled tendrils that had escaped from the neat coil and were curling at my neck.

I must never enter Mark's house again! And when he came here to dine, I would not let myself be alone with him. He was too free with women, too sure of his own charm. I burned at the thought of his kisses. I was quite certain that the ruby I had found had fallen from a piece of jewelry Mrs. Emsworth had worn last night when she had sat playing chess with Mark. Playing chess or— She had been proved an unfaithful wife. Perhaps she had lain in Mark's arms in that room.

And then I remembered that Armorel had a ruby ring. James had been called out to hospital last night and Armorel had, so we had supposed, spent the evening in her own sitting room. But had she?

It would be so easy, in the dark, to slip unnoticed from the house.

XVII

I NEVER AGAIN saw Kenny unkind to the little cat which had not been claimed and which he now looked upon as his. We called him Skippy because of his habit of bounding into the air for no apparent reason save that of sheer exuberance.

It had become a habit of mine to spend the hour after tea with Kenny. Sometimes he was listless and did not want to play or to read; sometimes he was quarrelsome. At other times he was so high-spirited and normal that it was difficult not to imagine him springing at me and saying "Boo!" as though lying in bed these past months had been a childish prank.

On this particular afternoon darkness had fallen early. Kenny and I had drifted from one pastime to another—reading, making shadow pictures—but he was already showing signs of becoming fractious when a cab stopped outside.

Immediately he leaned forward and pulled back the curtain.

"You must not do that," I said reprovingly. "It is not good manners."

"It is only Papa," he said without interest. "It's always ever only Mama or Papa or silly old Doctor Rowlins."

"You mustn't call him that. He's very kind."

"He just comes in and drags all the bedclothes off me and feels me with his cold hands. When I make a face and wriggle he tells me not to be a baby. He and Papa don't want me to get well."

"Kenny," I said severely, "you must not say such a dreadful thing!"

"Mama says Uncle Mark is going to make me walk again. She says—" He gave me a sidelong look and closed his lips tightly together.

I pretended to be absorbed in Skippy who was on my lap playing with a black bobble on the bodice of my red dress.

"You know," I pondered the question, "I think Skippy probably has a birthday soon. Let's suppose he is one year old and give him a party."

Kenny was not deceived by my quick change of subject. He looked at me suspiciously.

"I didn't tell you anything, did I, Aunt Elizabeth?"

"Tell me anything?" I feigned surprise. "No. Oh, except that nonsense about Papa not caring for you." I added as though as an afterthought. "Now, come along, shall we read again together?"

I set the kitten on the rug by the fire, where he promptly curled into a tabby ball.

I was still with Kenny when James came in. He had been to a meeting of the British Medical Association where, so he had told me beforehand, a paper was to be read on skin grafts.

I thought he looked tired as he crossed to the fire and warmed his hands. Kenny watched him doubtfully. I had a distressing feeling that he did not welcome James's intrusion into the room and I wondered whether Armorel was subtly turning him against his father.

"We've been playing with Skippy," I said, to break the silence. "He's so funny. He's been skating over the rug."

"Papa, when I'm better will you buy me some skates?" Kenny picked the word up with lightning speed.

I saw James's effort at a smile. "Of course I will." He came over to the bed.

"Because I *will* get better! Mama says—" Again that tight closing of the lips. It was almost more than he could do to keep his secret. I think he wanted one of us to force it out of him.

"Mama says you will get well and so do I," James said easily.

"But *you* don't promise. Mama does."

I picked up the kitten. "I'm going to take Skippy out to the kitchen now."

"Oh no." Kenny held out his arms, shouting, "I want him! Aunt Elizabeth, I want him!"

"He wants his supper, just as you do," I said firmly and smiled at James over the kitten's furry back.

At least I knew one thing. Mark had not yet begun to give Kenny treatment.

It was a long evening. Armorel and James were out; grandmother sat with her patience cards and Aunt Geraldine was hurrying to finish a beige shawl she was crocheting for an old servant, now in retirement. I found the music of some old Elizabethan songs and played them over once or twice. Conversation that evening was desultory and concerned people I scarcely knew. My own contribution to the talk was comparatively nothing. I was, in fact, being "seen and not heard!"

By half past nine I was alone in the drawing room. When Mrs. Vine came in for her customary round of the house before retiring, I told her that I would turn out the lamps and put the guard round the fire.

I had picked out a copy of Mr. Dickens' novel, *Our Mutual Friend* and found it too absorbing to put down.

Armorel and James returned home soon after half past nine. Their voices floated up the chimney with an angry rise and fall. Sharp single words stabbed the quiet, as though it were a duel of question and answer. Then a door slammed and there was silence.

I was soon absorbed in my book again. The fire had died down. Once or twice I heard a mouse scampering in the wainscot and an occasional late carriage passed by. Each time, silence settled again as though I were quite alone in the house.

When the clock down in the hall struck ten, I closed my book and yawned. Through the glass walls of the conservatory I saw that the moon had risen. It poured an almost shadowless light upon the garden so that I could see each bush as though it were day. I opened the conservatory door and went past the racks of green plants, palms and azaleas and geraniums, and stood at the far end looking down upon the lawn.

As I stood there, thinking how still the world was, I saw something move in the bare branches of the nearest tree. A bird, I thought, toppling from its nest. But what bird, staying with us through an English winter, would nest in a tree that had little shelter from the vicious north winds?

I looked again, narrowing my eyes in order to see more clearly.

A small living thing clung, scrambled and clung again to the tree. It was the kitten. With a sense of irritation at the little animal's insatiable appetite for adventure, I supposed that once again I would have to rescue it. The meager gas light in the hall lit my way down to the kitchen. There was a faint glow from beneath James's study door and I thought I heard the sound of movement from the Blue Room.

In the kitchen, I found matches and lit a lamp. I guessed what had happened. Susannah must have been sent to return a pail to the outhouse just before locking the back door and the kitten had slipped out unnoticed. I went into the moonlit garden, hoping that I could coax Skippy down without calling James to help me.

As I crossed the lawn, I called to the kitten. To my relief, it took hold of its courage and scrambled tail first down the tree, landing on its feet after a perfect somersault. I picked it up and held it in my arms, scolding, "You are not yet old enough for nocturnal habits," I admonished.

As I turned and walked back across the lawn, I glanced upwards at the house. The full moonlight lay upon it, silvering the walls. The light was out in the Blue Room, but at the top of the house, in the attic sewing room, someone passed across the window, holding a lamp.

For a moment I stood puzzled. The lamp and the arm moved out of my vision, but not before I had seen a gleam of Armorel's golden satin evening gown.

A memory flashed over me of myself sitting at the sewing machine and of Susannah standing before me, saying, "There be noises sometimes in the night—someone looking for somethin'."

So was Armorel Susannah's ghost? And what did she want up there in the attic? I knew that her boxes and trunks were stored in a cellar in the basement and that there was nothing of hers up here. Yet something drew her to the attic. Something to find.

I locked the back door and put Skippy into his basket. Then I turned out the lamp and went upstairs.

Before I entered my room, I glanced up the last curve of the staircase to the attic floor. It seemed from here to be in darkness. Armorel must have closed the door so that the lamp would not be seen by anyone.

I longed to go up there and confront her, but the whole thing could have such an innocent explanation. James might have asked her to look for something he had left there years ago. If I disturbed her I would look like some foolish, inquisitive young woman.

When I went into the servants' quarters the next morning to find Susannah and warn her to be careful that the kitten did not escape again, I found no one there. Mrs. Vine was in the pantry and from the large china cupboard leading out of it, I heard Susannah's voice: " . . . and she said to him, 'You hate me don't you? Ever since Elizabeth came to the house, or was it before, when Helen—' And then she cried out and I thought Dr. James had hit her."

"You and your gutter thoughts," Mrs. Vine interrupted angrily. "Doctor James is gentle; he would never hurt a woman!"

"Lot you know about them gents," Susannah squealed in derision. "Why, I bet—"

"Susannah," I called loudly.

She emerged, her over-large eyes bright and wary in her little pointed face. I told her about the kitten and left the kitchen.

What I had overheard was, after all, only backstairs gossip. James *was* gentle! He would not hurt a woman. And at that, the little worldly Susannah could have mocked at me, for what did I know of James? Of anyone in this house?

XVIII

When evening came and we gathered in the drawing room before dinner, James announced that Armorel had a headache and would not be dining with us.

Nothing gave me any suspicion that something was wrong until Mrs. Vine brought the trifle to the table. I thought she looked upset. She caught my eye, turned very red and hurried out of the room. I watched her in astonishment, wondering what the good soul had done to look so guilty.

When later she came to the drawing room with coffee, I saw that she was even more agitated. She dropped a little silver spoon, fumbled while picking it up, and finally, paused at the door and shot a look at me which I could not fail to interpret. She wanted to speak to me urgently.

I rose, murmured an excuse and slipped out of the room. She was waiting for me in the alcove on the landing.

"Miss Elizabeth, I don't know what to do . . . what to say." Her hands were twisting agitatedly.

"It is Mrs. Armorel. Her headache is worse?"

"Oh, Miss!"

"Well?" I asked impatiently.

"They've gone!"

I remember in that flash of moment, feeling a palm leaf brush my hair and the horsehair sofa which stood against the wall was smooth and cold to my touch as I leant against it.

"What do you mean? Who has . . . gone?"

"Master Kenny and his mother." The words fell over themselves. "She ordered me not to say anything. She said it would be the worse for me if I did! She . . . oh, Miss Elizabeth, what are we going to do?"

"Suppose you tell me exactly what happened." I tried to keep my voice calm, though my heart was hammering with apprehension.

"It was when I was coming up from the kitchen with the main dish. I saw Mrs. Armorel opening the front door. Miss Stanhope was there. I heard her say 'the carriage is here and I have asked the driver to help us!' And then Mrs. Armorel said 'Hush,' angrily and looked over her shoulder at me. I pretended, of course, that I had heard nothing. Then, when I came downstairs, leaving Susannah to serve the vegetables, Mrs. Armorel called me into Master Kenny's room. She had her outdoor clothes on and there were two packed bags at her feet. Master Kenny was lying, wrapped in rugs on the bed. He . . . he had a shawl round his head and he was looking frightened and whimpering a little. Mrs. Armorel told me she was going away for a while. It was for both their sakes, she said, and I was not to tell anyone until they had left."

"And so you waited?"

"What else could I do, Miss?" she demanded helplessly, her hands folding and unfolding.

"Did Mrs. Armorel say when she would be back?"

Mrs. Vine shook her head.

"Come with me," I said urgently and ran swiftly down the stairs and into Kenny's room.

The bedclothes were pulled back and I saw that blankets were missing. I dragged open the cupboards. A few of Kenny's playthings and his books were also gone. I flew across the hall and opened the door of the bedroom. All Armorel's personal things were gone from her frilled muslin dressing table.

"Mrs. Armorel took only two small bags with her," Mrs. Vine volunteered, watching me.

"She could have been planning this for some time and has taken things away gradually."

"She couldn't have taken her things without Doctor James noticing!"

I shot her a wry look.

"Some men are too busy to notice these things," I said.

"Oh, Miss, what will Madam say? She will be so angry!"

I decided privately that "anger" would not describe my grandmother's feelings!

"Will you go upstairs and ask Dr. James to come down here. Tell him I must speak to him urgently."

I went into the Blue Room to await him.

When I heard his footstep, I rose and stood with my back to him, holding my hands to the dying fire as though to give myself a semblance of outward calm.

"I'm afraid I have upsetting news for you, James. It's Armorel."

"What has happened now?" He sounded faintly impatient.

"While we were at dinner she sent for Miss Stanhope and they have taken Kenny!"

"Taken . . . Kenny?" He stared at me, then he was at the communicating door in a single stride. Flinging it open, he took one step over the threshold. Then drawing back he stood staring at the empty bed.

"Dear God! What has she done? She could kill him!" He swung round on me. "Where has she taken him? Did you know of this?"

His eyes, probing mine, had an odd, blind look.

"Of course I did not know until Mrs. Vine told me just now," I said. "And you must not blame her for not telling you right away. She is a servant; she has to take orders and Armorel gave her an order—not to tell anyone what she had seen and heard until she had gone."

"But where? And why?"

"She told Mrs. Vine that it was for both their sakes."

"Miss Stanhope!" he said in a violent undertone. "I must find her!"

"I doubt if she will tell you anything. From her actions, it seems that all her sympathies are with Armorel."

I saw the swift look of pain on James's face.

"Elizabeth . . . *you* don't condone this?"

"How can you even ask such a thing? But you must see that Miss Stanhope won't help you."

"It's Kenny," he cried, as though he had not heard a word I had said. "If there was any chance at all of curing him, rest and time would have done it. Now all the good will have been undone. Nothing I could do to Armorel is bad enough for this that she has done to my son!"

"What are you going to do?"

"First I must tell them upstairs. Then I shall see Miss Stanhope. I shall force her to tell me where Armorel has taken Kenny."

"And if she . . . refuses?"

He gave me a strange, hard look.

"Then, perhaps, Elizabeth, I shall not be responsible for my actions."

I hesitated for a second before following him. I am certain that he was so immersed in shock that he had no idea that I walked into the drawing room behind him.

I saw them, seated like some tableau, grandmother erect in her chair, her ringed hands deftly moving the patience cards before her. My aunt reading, using the large magnifying glass because her little touch of vanity refused her the comfort of spectacles.

I do not think anyone noticed me as I crossed behind James to the window. I heard him give them the news, heard the moment's utter silence before my grandmother spoke.

"Geraldine, ring for Mrs. Vine."

The tasselled bell-rope swung. I glanced at my grandmother. Her carved, sunken face had no expression.

I turned away, pulling aside the heavy curtain. In the fitful moonlight I saw how the keen wind bent the trees. Kenny, who had not stirred from the warmth of his room for months, had been carried into that bitter night.

I heard my grandmother question Mrs. Vine, heard her distressed replies.

Across my mind, blotting out everything that was happening around me, flashed one shocking thought. Had Armorel gone to Mark? In the rivalry between Mrs. Emsworth and herself, had she won? Mark was a rebel who was not concerned with the conventions and there had never been a real closeness between these two whom Aunt Geraldine had brought up as brothers.

I remembered the conversation I had overheard between Armorel and James when I had been caught in the conservatory. It was obvious that James believed his wife to be a dissatisfied, sensation-seeking woman. He had actually accused her of throwing herself at Mark whose interest lay in another direction.

I think he was past any real caring whether Armorel loved him or not. But how perceptive was he? And was the affair one-sided? What depth of morality had Mark? Did he believe that if a husband and wife no longer loved one another, either was fair game for an outsider?

I could not bear to believe that! My little-girl image of Mark was harder to die than my childhood belief in the truth of fairy tales.

And Armorel? Watching her, I had found her emotions all too obvious. I did not know whether she could be said to have any real experience of the quality of love. But she was sufficiently violently attracted to Mark to be reckless. Had she won him from Mrs. Emsworth by making some irresistible bargain with him? Had Mark's price been that Kenny should be placed in his care, so that he could be free to give him his unorthodox treatment?

A shudder ran through me so that for a moment I was deathly cold. Was a child to be the devil's bargaining point?

My thoughts jangled and tore at me with such force that it was a few moments before I realized that my grandmother had been speaking to me.

"Why do you still watch at the window? The carriage has been gone half an hour or more."

I dropped the curtain.

"If you cannot get in touch with Miss Stanhope, James," she went on, "you must try and trace the carriage that came for her. There cannot be many yellow broughams in London."

"Yellow!" I exclaimed.

"Did you not hear Mrs. Vine say that it was a yellow carriage which came for them?"

I had not heard. For a moment the room spun round me. I put out a shaking hand and caught sharply at the edge of an occasional table. A little Dresden figurine toppled. I saved it from falling and set it in its place with trembling fingers. A yellow carriage—

"You may go," I heard my grandmother say to a weeping Mrs. Vine. "But kindly bear in mind that it is your duty to inform me of anything unusual that occurs in this house. There are no final orders but mine! You understand?"

"Yes, Madam."

"And now." The black eyes swung round upon James. "You will find Kenny at once and bring him back."

"I intend to go to Miss Stanhope's lodgings."

"You have her address?"

"Yes."

"Then hurry! Hurry!" said my grandmother, beating the words out with her hands.

Aunt Geraldine was crying quietly, her eyes on her hands folding and unfolding the little cambric ball of her handkerchief. My grandmother had pushed aside her patience cards and was staring into the fire. I had wondered often how she could bear to look for so long into the furnace of dancing flames, but her eyes, even at her great age, were as strong as a hawk's. I had a feeling that she received some strange energy from the fire's heart.

"And where are you going, Elizabeth?"

I halted on the threshold of the room. "To Kenny's room, Grandmother. I believe I saw the kitten in there and it is probably shut in. I shall take it to the kitchen."

The kitten was chasing a feather that must have escaped from one of the pillows. I picked the little thing up and holding it against my cheek, took it to the kitchen. Mrs. Vine was seated in her rocking chair looking miserably into the fire. Her hair had straggled grayly from her cap and her face was blotchy.

I signalled to her not to get up as I entered the room and laid the kitten in her lap. She bent her head over it and burst into tears again.

"Oh Miss Elizabeth, I can never forgive myself! Had I spoken, I could have stopped this happening."

"You might have stopped it tonight," I said, "but it would have happened some other time. If Mrs. Armorel is determined on something, I doubt if anything would really stop her."

"It's Master Kenny I'm worried about."

"So are we all. But Mrs. Armorel is his mother. She would not let harm come to him."

"Wouldn't she? *Wouldn't* she, Miss Elizabeth? I don't know. I begin to wonder if she has taken him out of spite. It's a terrible thing to say, but I've lived in this house with her for years and—"

"And what, Mrs. Vine?"

She set her lips. "I'm sorry Miss, I shouldn't have spoken like that to you. But you see, I have no one I can talk to. No one in the whole world! And there's times when you're so full of all you want to say and daren't."

Like myself, no one in the whole world.

In that moment in the warm, cozy kitchen, smelling of baked cake, I felt very close to Mrs. Vine.

I sat down in the chair on the opposite side of the range and leaned forward.

"Couldn't you talk to *me*," I coaxed gently.

"You, Miss Elizabeth?" she asked, shocked. "But you're one of the family!"

"Not entirely," I said honestly. "Until I came here a few weeks ago, I was almost a stranger to them."

"I remember your father," she said dreamily. "He was such a wild little boy. But you know, I think your grandmama loved him best of all."

"Because in some ways he was like her," I said. "Wherever he was, he controlled. I believed he was a very good sea captain."

"I used to make peppermint creams for him."

"Mrs. Vine, you *did* see the carriage at the door, didn't you?"

"I told Madam so."

"And it was a yellow one."

"It was dark outside but I'm sure it was yellow. The front door was open, you see, as I came through the hall."

I was vaguely aware of someone coming down the area steps.

"That will be Susannah," Mrs. Vine said. "I sent her off immediately she had served the vegetables to see her sister whose new baby is ill. She promised she would not be gone more than an hour and she's kept to it. She can be a good girl when she likes."

"Did Susannah see anything?" I broke off as she came through the door.

Her pointed little face broke into a sly smile as she saw me.

"I trust your sister is better," I said as she took off her cape.

"Yes thank you, Miss." She disappeared into the pantry where there was a cupboard in which the servants could hang their outdoor things. I followed her.

"By the way, Susannah, did you see the brougham which took Mrs. Bellenmore and Master Kenny away?"

"I seed somethin', Miss." She gave me an oblique glance.

"I am asking you if you saw a yellow carriage," I insisted.

"Mebbe I did."

I held my breath. Then, as carefully as I could, I asked, "Did you by any chance recognize the driver?"

"Why should I?"

"No reason. I am merely asking." I pretended disinterest in my question. I was, however, watching her and I saw her mouth turn up knowingly at the corners. That decided me. I swung round, took two steps towards her and putting my hands on her shoulders shook her firmly.

She jerked back from me, wrenching herself from my grasp. "Let me go!"

"When you tell me what I want to know!"

She struggled at my renewed hold. "Whose carriage came for Mrs. Armorel?"

She gave me a wary look, then said sulkily, "That actress's!"

Until then, I had been unable to believe it. They were both in love with Mark. It was not possible between such women that the one would help the other!

Susannah could be lying. She was, after all, ignorant and untamed at heart. Yet, she was shrewd enough to realize that I could eventually prove or disprove her story and then woe betide her if she had lied! So, what she had told me must be the truth.

I went upstairs, slipping quietly past the drawing room where I heard a murmur of voices. I was certain that James had already gone out to search for his son. I was not concerned for the moment with what my grandmother and Aunt Geraldine had to say. I had something important of my own to do first.

I put on my cloak and stole out of the house, ducking my head against the first icy onslaught of wind.

I was going to see Mark.

XIX

I ALMOST ran across the Square so that I was breathless when I arrived at the house.

As I waited at the door, I did not dare rehearse what I was going to say to Mark in case I should find the words clumsy and lose my courage. I held the folds of my cloak tightly to me to keep out the vicious gusts of wind and, turning my back on the house, watched the black tossing tree branches above the sinister thickness of the bushes.

"Yes, Madam?"

I turned quickly and realized that the door had opened very silently and that the maid did not know me.

"I would like to speak to Mr. Bellenmore," I said. "And will you please tell him that it is very urgent?"

She shot me a doubtful look as I stepped purposefully into the hall. "What name shall I say, Madam?"

Her eyes were Irish blue and her cheeks pink. So Mark chose pretty maids, too!

"I am Miss Bellenmore," I said.

As I was being shown into a room to the left of the hall, there was a sudden burst of singing from upstairs. The piano accompaniment rippled and danced. I stood by the fire, listening and rubbing my frozen hands together. The singer was no drawing room amateur. I was certain that I was listening to Mrs. Emsworth.

> "I saw my lady weep,
> And Sorrow proud to be exalted so
> In those fair eyes."

Mrs. Emsworth was here! So how could she know anything about Armorel's disappearance? Susannah must have been lying after all, making up the story of the red-haired driver in order to gain some self-importance.

> "But such a woe, believe me, as wins more hearts
> Than Mirth can do with her enticing parts."

The song ended abruptly and then a moment or two later I turned and saw Mark.

"A visit from our little Elizabeth!" He held out his hands to me. "This is indeed unexpected. Won't you come along to the drawing room?"

I stepped back quickly. "This is not a social call, Mark. But perhaps you know why I am here."

He shook his head and, reaching up, drew the hood from my hair, his eyes laughing all the time. "I like you better without your *femme fatale* disguise."

I jerked my head from his audacious touch.

"I have serious news," I said and was gratified to see the laughter wiped from his face.

"What has happened?" he asked sharply.

"Armorel has left home and taken Kenny with her."

I do not know what I expected him to say or do. But, knowing his capacity for swift reaction I did not bargain for that cold, uncompromising silence.

"Mark, have you any idea where she has gone?"

"None."

His monosyllabic answer was as hard to bear as his suddenly expressionless face.

"Tell me the truth!" I said hoarsely.

"Why should I lie to you?" His gaze was grave and steady.

"Armorel talked to you a lot," I said impatiently. "She could have confided in you. If you know anything, please . . . *please* tell me! Or tell James. He is nearly demented."

"I had no idea he loved her so much!" Mark observed drily.

"It's Kenny! Mark, it's Kenny we're so afraid for. He hasn't been out of his room for months and Armorel has taken him into the night air, into a strange bed, moved him—"

"I don't imagine that will do him much harm."

It was the brief smile that made something snap inside me. I felt my face flame.

"How can you say such a thing? How can you be so calm? Have you no compassion? Are you not even a little human? Or are you ignorant of Kenny's danger? Is that it? That you know so little, after all, about illness and pain? Then I must tell you." I rushed on. "Such movement as Kenny has suffered, being lifted out of bed and into a carriage, jolted through the streets, has probably ruined his chances of walking forever." I stopped abruptly, and took a long breath.

Mark's gray eyes swam before me among a confusion of blurred images, of tables and chairs and pictures.

"Mark, *Kenny's* . . . gone." I whispered again as though I could not believe that he had heard me.

"And you have been quoting to me James's stock phrases of his possible danger."

"It will be Doctor Rowlins too, when he hears what has happened."

"*Old* Doctor Rowlins," Mark amended. "A nice man, but cosseted in archaic ideas."

"He is still very eminent in his profession . . ."

Mark gave a dry laugh. "It is interesting how a man can hold on to a reputation long after it has ceased to mean anything! Grandmothers, mothers and daughters, passing the word on from generation to generation, 'You must let Doctor Rowlins see you.

Wonderful old gentleman, Doctor Rowlins.' " He made an impatient gesture. "So eminent, indeed, that his words are treated as though handed down from God."

"That is blasphemy!"

"So is too much faith in old ideas!" Mark retorted. "Blasphemy against whatever gave us brains to use and progress to fight for."

"I do not understand you."

"No, you don't, do you Elizabeth? If it were not for the so-called quacks of the fourteenth century, there would be far less progress today. Did you know that?"

I rushed past him. "I did not come here to discuss medicine."

"I am trying to reassure you, Elizabeth," Mark said impatiently. "In my opinion, Kenny will suffer no ill-effects from being moved out of that infernal bed. And James will be a better doctor when he has ceased to treat Hilton's book as his Bible."

I had no idea who Hilton was or what his book was about. I had marched into the hall aware that I was wasting time here.

There was a sound and a flurry of color on the stairs. A woman was walking down, holding up her dress gracefully with both hands.

She was not in the least beautiful. Her mouth was too large, her cheekbones too prominent, her eyes elongated like those of an Eastern odalisque. But she had a glory of auburn hair and her shoulders, above her green gown, were like glowing marble.

"You will forgive me for interrupting, Mark," she said clearly and politely, "but I have to leave for the theater now."

"Of course. I'm sorry to have left you for so long. This is Miss Bellenmore and she would not stay. Elizabeth, this is Mrs. Emsworth."

She held out her hand to me and smiled.

"Mark has told me about your visits here as a little girl. I am delighted to meet you."

"Elizabeth has come to tell me that James's wife, Armorel, has disappeared with her small son."

"Oh, Mark!"

As an expression of dismay, it was entirely convincing. Yet, as I caught the look which flashed between them I was reminded that Mrs. Emsworth was an actress. I knew, in that moment, that it really had been her carriage which had come for Armorel. Susannah had told me the truth. But Mark had said, "Why should I lie to you?" And in asking, had implied his own lie.

I said shakenly, "You must forgive me! I am in a hurry."

My fingers fumbled for the catch of the door, slid and shook and failed to turn it. Mark's hand reached out and, brushing mine aside gently, opened the door for me.

I plunged into the black night, nearly pitching head first over the step. I was quite certain that, behind me, those two would exchange superior smiles at my lack of dignity. But I did not care. I felt as though the actress and the man of the world had quite coolly and deliberately humiliated me.

Aunt Geraldine had retired to bed when I returned. My grandmother sat alone. The patience cards were still scrambled on the inlaid card table in front of her. I tried to talk to her but she scarcely answered me. We sat in that unhappy, unsatisfactory silence for so long that I began to count the ticks of the clock.

"I don't understand," I burst out at last. "Grandmother, why aren't people happy in this house?"

She gave no hint that she had even heard me. Her restless ringed fingers gathered the tiny cards together.

"Grandmother, please tell me something of what you know!" I cried wildly. "Why did Helen die? It wasn't an accident, was it? And why has Armorel left James and—" My voice trailed into silence as I watched her.

She had dropped the cards and turning to the occasional table at her side, picked up the black fan with the eye holes.

"This," she said, spreading it out and holding it before her so that her face was concealed from me behind the dark lace, "is how one must view life. See it all. See it all, without seeming to observe that which is better hidden. It is the only way, Elizabeth, to preserve the dignity of one's family and one's self."

I could not tell whether her gaze was on me or not and it was an uncanny moment.

"I hate pretence!" I said violently. "I like everything open, spread about me so that I can see and understand."

"You are so young, Elizabeth," she said sadly and dropped the fan. "You will learn, and the process will be painful."

I saw her glance over my shoulder to the doorway. James had

entered quietly. His gaze was slightly stupefied; tired lines made deep cuts on his face.

"Miss Stanhope was not at home," he said. "Her landlady told me that she had left the house about an hour-and-a-half ago and appeared to be very distressed."

"As well she might be!" snapped my grandmother.

"I have kept the carriage," he said. "I shall go back and continue to go back until I can see her."

"You will be wasting your time," my grandmother told him scornfully. "Armorel has won the governess's loyalty."

"Nevertheless, I may be able to force her to tell me where they are. I must find her. . . . I *must* find Armorel!"

"Let her go, James. Let her go. She is of no use to you."

"She has Kenny!" There was a ragged edge to his voice.

My grandmother rose. She was very small and square-built, but as she stood there she seemed to dominate the room.

"Armorel has Kenny, but she cannot keep him. She cannot afford to," she said in a whisper that had uncanny authority. The green jeweled brooch securing the laces at her throat quivered. "She will be forced to return him to you."

"She has her own money," James said dully.

"Shock must have blunted your reason, James. You forget that upon her marriage to you she became no longer mistress of her own property." She paused, watching him. Then she said slowly, "It is for you to impoverish her, James. That way, she must give up Kenny."

"Her family are rich. She could go to them."

"Shall we not cross our bridges?"

"But I must consider the possibility. If she takes Kenny down to Somerset—"

"Country life bores her. You know that."

"But she might think it worth suffering the boredom for her son."

"You have far too high an opinion of Armorel's capacity for motherhood," retorted my grandmother. "She has taken Kenny with her to spite you and for no other reason. Make things difficult for her and she will return him, for she has no quality to withstand hardship." Her face was granite-hard. "There is so much agitation about the rights of women. But there is no law, yet, that can deny you the right to all she possesses. Do not be weak with her, James! Impoverish her!"

They had forgotten me so completely that I was able to watch them without embarrassment. But it was at my grandmother that I looked longest. The white-lidded eyes were wide open; the pale lips half smiled; the ancient head was poised high. My grandmother was like a woman who had thrown off a burden. And the burden must obviously be Armorel.

She rose slowly and taking her stick, crossed the room.

"I am tired," she said on a breath, "and it is late. Whatever you choose to do about this, James, I trust to your good sense and your consideration of the family."

She had paused in the doorway and although exhausted, there was an immense inner strength in her final glance as she bade James goodnight.

I was still no more than a shadow cast upon a wall. I had no place in this dilemma. I was merely the reprobate Nicholas Bellenmore's daughter, for whom a home had been found. And no one gave a thought to the fact that twice my life had been threatened, because no one believed it save myself . . . and my enemy.

"You will forgive me, Elizabeth, if I leave you?"

I started at James's voice. "You are going back to Miss Stanhope's lodgings?"

He nodded. "And this time, if she is not in, I shall wait in the carriage until she comes."

I sat alone and heard the brougham move off down the quiet Square. The fire was dying, but I drew up a chair and put my feet on the fender, pulling up my skirts a little to warm my toes.

There was nobody to see or disturb me. The day had closed upon still another link in the chain of questions. Why had Armorel left James?

My hair felt too heavy to bear. I took out the pins and let it fall around me, shaking my head at relief from its weight.

I leaned my head against the dark red brocade of the chair's high back and stared idly at the chubby gold cupids around the clock.

I do not know how long it was before I became aware that someone had entered the room and was standing silently behind me.

I gave a small, startled cry and shot a swift glance over my shoulder. Mark stood watching me.

"Did I startle you?"

"You know perfectly well that you did!" I told him crossly. "What are you doing here at this time of night, anyway?"

"I came to find you."

"Indeed." I withdrew my feet from the fender and tucked them under my skirt. I shook my hair from my shoulders and leaning my hands on the arms of the chair much as my grandmother did, felt that a little of my dignity was restored.

Mark moved near the fire, his eyes speculatively upon me.

"What do you want?" I demanded.

His eyes were amused. "The role of mistress of the house would suit you, Elizabeth. Even with your hair down."

"And now, suppose you come to the point?"

I refused to be moved by the obvious appraisal on his dark, handsome face. This was what charmed and was dangerous. But as he stood there watching me, I could feel the intense, stimulating power behind that light, outward show of amusement.

"Why does a young woman have to behave as though she were caught in a misdemeanor just because she has unpinned her hair?" he asked. "Remember, Elizabeth, when you were a little girl you used to ask me to pull it as much as I could, without hurting you, 'to stretch it', you said. Come, now. False modesty does not suit you."

"If your homily is over," I commented coolly, "perhaps you will now tell me why you want to see me. And how did you know that I would still be here and not in bed and asleep?"

"Because I heard voices when I first arrived."

"So you have been here some time?"

"I was not eavesdropping, if that is what you think. I merely intended to wait until I could speak to you on your own. You will understand, when I explain, why I could not interrupt."

"Indeed I doubt if I will. This is no game of hide-and-seek!" I said heatedly. "James is beside himself with worry. He has now gone round to Miss Stanhope's to try to force her to tell him where Kenny is."

"I can tell him."

"Then why didn't you?" I began angrily. "Why didn't you come straight here and put an end to his anxiety? Why, too, did you lie to me?"

I had risen and we faced one another like antagonists.

"Why do *you* not wait to hear what I have to say before you accuse?" he counter questioned.

It was a moment too serious for personal consideration. And yet I was conscious of my smallness before him and of my long hair flowing like a child's. To compensate for my sense of my own lack of dignity, I charged my voice with scorn as I said, "Well, Mark, suppose you now tell me the truth."

He did not take his eyes from my face. "Armorel has taken Kenny to Lucia Emsworth's house."

"And Mrs. Emsworth was with you when I called. I congratulate you both." I looked at him almost with hatred. "You played your roles of innocence admirably."

"Lucia had not told me then," Mark said patiently. "She was not finding it easy to broach the subject."

"So she decided that singing to you would put you in a good mood."

"It often does when I am tired," Mark said evenly.

"You are fortunate that you have so understanding and tactful a . . . a . . . companion."

"I am."

"And when Mrs. Emsworth saw me, and knew why I had come, she still did not say anything."

"It was not her secret to tell. Lucia is discreet."

"I'm sure she is." I heard the edge on my voice.

I had an uncomfortable feeling that, in spite of everything, Mark was still master of the situation. He bent and poked the glowing embers. I watched three little flames rise and plop.

"Lucia wants to help Kenny," Mark explained. "That is why she arranged an apparent chance meeting with Armorel at the house of a mutual friend. She suggested that if she brought Kenny to her house, she might manage to persuade me to treat him."

"Mrs. Emsworth goes to strange lengths for . . . for love of you." I choked over the preposterous words I had not meant to say.

"For *faith* in me," Mark corrected. "She wants to bring my methods to the notice of the medical profession."

"As though that will do you any good since you will not trouble yourself to qualify as a doctor."

He was not looking at me, yet I knew that he was as intensely aware of me as I was of him. The old childhood closeness and the new antagonism pulled and tightened between us.

"For myself," he said indifferently, "I am no longer interested in what people, professional or otherwise, think of me."

"You are fortunate in being so strong that you can stand alone."

He was not smiling and the eagle look which so characterized him when he was grave, was accentuated by the leap and dance of the flames playing on his face.

"You said . . . you came to talk to me tonight. Why?"

"Because I want you to go and see Armorel."

"I—" My voice faltered. I felt my heartbeats quicken at the outrageous suggestion of this conspiracy between us.

"Will you do this for me . . . for all of us, Elizabeth?"

For all of us. Clever, clever Mark to turn his desire into a plea of family duty.

"Why should I concern myself?"

He stood squarely in front of me, looking at me from under straight, dark brows.

"Because, if I treat Kenny, I want it to be *here*. It should not be hidden away from his father as though I were performing some secret magic rites I am ashamed of. So Armorel must be persuaded to return home."

"James would never allow you to touch Kenny."

"No. I don't believe he would," he admitted readily. "Then, let's forget I gave you that reason. Let's say that Armorel must come back for Aunt Geraldine's sake."

I reached up and began to trace the moulded leaf design of the carved mantelpiece.

"You think Aunt Geraldine minds, that she cares for Armorel?"

"I think she cares for the sanctity of marriage," he said. "By the way, the address is 749 Kensington Gore."

I wanted to say that I was not interested, that I had no intention of doing what he asked. But I could not. I turned away, aware of another perceptible change in the atmosphere between us. Quite quietly beside me, stood the shadow of the little girl who had found in Mark a friend to whom she could talk in this grand house. That little girl took charge of the adult Miss Bellenmore.

"Please tell me," I cried. "Do *you* think Armorel ran away for Kenny's sake? Or did something in this house frighten her?"

A trace of a smile touched his eyes.

"It's my belief that nothing could frighten Armorel. She has the fearlessness often found in beautiful, arrogant women."

"Mark." I could hold out no longer. I had to trust him! "There is something in this house that I don't understand, something secret. It is like . . . oh, like some beautiful apple which you don't want to bite into because you have seen a worm-hole on the skin."

"I always thought that even as a little girl, you had too much imagination." He spoke lightly, but the eyes he turned from me were shadowed and wary.

"So it's all in my imagination!" I said angrily. "Like everyone else here, you prefer that I should remain blind. Well then, let me enlighten you. How can I be blind to something that is a reality? To things I *know* happened. Things like—"

I caught my breath, holding back the wild words. I had been on the point of a revelation that might have been madness. From the very walls of the room I seemed to hear the echo of an unknown voice. *Ask Mark who killed Helen.* I did not dare tell him that I knew his wife's death was no accident.

He was waiting with infinite patience and when I did not reply, he prompted me softly, eyes narrowed. "Well? What are the things you think you know?"

"Mark, why do you not marry Mrs. Emsworth?" It was the last thing I had intended to say and I have no idea from what dark corner of my mind that little fiend of a question came.

I saw Mark's eyes darken; his brows drew together, then relaxed. He laughed, "My dear Elizabeth, you have a most surprising lack of reticence!"

"I am sorry! I should not have asked that!"

"But I'll answer you! The arrangement as it now stands between us suits us both admirably!" It was almost as though he welcomed the chance to shock me. Then he demanded, still amused, "Are my affairs of such importance to you, Elizabeth?"

"Not in the least," I said quickly. "I was thinking of James. Since Mrs. Emsworth cares so much about you, perhaps you could control her interference into the affairs of this household."

It was a swiftly thought-up reason, a despairing counterattack and I was not at all certain that it convinced Mark. He was looking at me thoughtfully. "You care very much whether James is hurt or not, don't you?"

"Naturally. He is a good man and a dedicated doctor."

"And I am a bad man and a charlatan."

"I have no idea," I said, desperately aware that I was becoming out of my depth.

He picked up a strand of my hair and let it ripple through his fingers.

"Go to bed, Elizabeth. It's too late at night to spar with me."

"And you?"

"I shall wait for James. And you don't have to worry on his behalf. I shall not quarrel with him. You are right. He has had enough trouble for one night."

I wanted to escape. Too many things were at war inside me. I wanted to stop believing in him and, against all the facts, I could not. As I moved past him to the door, he took my left hand and ran his fingers over the back of it.

"You have had no more pain?"

"None."

"So the charlatan has had his little moment of glory with you."

I avoided his faintly mocking eyes and withdrew my hand.

"Be kind to James," I pleaded and left him.

Up in my room, I lay and watched the softening wax round the candle flame. What had been said between those two women, Mrs. Emsworth and Armorel, that could induce them to share the same house even temporarily? It was like defying a jungle law, that a panther and a tiger should inhabit a common lair.

I slept lightly, with fits of startled waking. I heard James return and then men's voices in the drawing room below. They floated, too indistinct for recognition, up through the chimney. Mark and James. What were they saying to one another? What had they ever had to say to one another with their strong opposing views on most things?

I turned at last and picked up the little silver cone from the candlestick and snuffed out the light. The smell of smouldering wax hung for a moment upon the air.

Kenny! My thoughts filled with him. Lying somewhere in a

demi-monde's luxurious guest bedroom, was he in pain? Was he weeping and lonely for his own room and his father and his little cat?

I closed my eyes. I must not think of what Mark had asked me to do. For I could not, and would not, go to Kensington Gore and plead for her to return. It was for the three people concerned to argue out. I would not interfere.

XX

Since the two terrifying episodes in either of which I might have lost my life, I had walked warily, never quite trusting a deserted staircase, an empty hall.

I did not dare stop to consider too much the family's refusal to believe that I had twice been in danger from deliberate attack. I told myself that the episodes were so incredulous that no sane person could be expected to see them as anything but accidents. And yet, among themselves, did the family question the validity of their own easy explanations? I wished I knew.

In my own mind I was certain that it could only be Armorel who wished me harm. So, with her flight from the house, the tensions that were continually with me should have been eased. Instead, in the days after she had gone, I felt an imperceptible heightening and quickening of the pace of our lives.

James had not been able to see Miss Stanhope on the night Armorel left us. The governess's landlady had appeared like a dragon to guard her lodgers and when he returned the next day, Miss Stanhope had changed her address and no one admitted to knowing the new one.

I knew that a great deal of discussion went on behind doors closed against me. I knew that Aunt Geraldine's wide pale blue eyes were a little more swimmy than usual and that James was carrying on his practice under a great strain.

But it was as though I were a child, to have the ugliness of life kept from me, or a stranger to whom nothing of this was any concern. More than anything that had gone before, all this forced upon me the realization of my own utter aloneness.

The third morning after Armorel's departure was still and sharp. The birds hopped across the frosty lawn and I paused in the work I was doing in the study to watch their antics.

James came in just before luncheon.

"You look tired," I said. "Has it been a bad morning?"

"I've been to see Armorel."

"Have you? Have you really?" I began idly; then I stopped speaking suddenly and stared at him. "You *did* say that you . . . went to see . . . Armorel?"

He gave me a slightly apologetic look.

"I know I said I would wait for her to return to me and then take her back on my conditions. It was easy talk. I was too desperate to know how Kenny was to keep to my resolve."

"He's all right, isn't he?" I burst out. "I mean, he's not in pain, not further injured?"

"Why do you ask that?"

His question was so suspicious that I wondered if he knew, or guessed, that Mark was treating his son.

"Why do you think he might not be?" he insisted.

I avoided his direct gaze. "The drive that night to Kensington Gore," I said. "I thought it could have aggravated the injury."

He nodded as though accepting my explanation. "Armorel did not want me to see Kenny. But I heard him talking in the next room and I forced my way in. Mrs. Emsworth was with him. They were playing with her dog, a King Charles spaniel."

"Kenny was pleased to see you?"

He turned away and went to the window and I knew that he did not want me to notice how upset he was. "There was a little color in his cheeks and he seemed bright enough. But I do not know if moving him has harmed him because when I went near him, he broke into a storm of weeping as though he had been taught to fear me."

"But surely when you talked to him, he lost that fear?"

"I had no chance to say much. It seems," he added bitterly, "I am no match for two women guarding him."

Two women: rivals for a man's love, calling a truce over a little boy!

James opened the window and stood facing the cold wind that met him. I crept nearer the fire, shivering. I knew that, for the moment, he was beyond consideration for my comfort. I folded my arms tightly as though to keep within me such warmth as I could.

"James, why did Armorel leave you?"

For a moment I thought he hadn't heard me, that I had spoken too quietly, too tentatively. Then he closed the window and turned and looked at me. "I don't know. She refuses to discuss it with me, yet."

"But she can't just leave without an explanation. I mean, people don't. It's cruel . . . it's—" Words eluded me.

I stood helpless, feeling the hot blood pound in my throat at the whole seeming illogical situation. Something infinitely sinister lay underneath, something tied up, like a mystery bundle, with fear and the past. And Mark?

I was so caught up in my emotions that I started almost guiltily when James spoke again.

"It was always Armorel's form of torture that she withheld reasons for her seeming little cruelties. If she chooses, she will take one to the very edge of exasperation and suffering before she decides to explain!"

My arms still folded, I ran my hands up and down the smooth cloth sleeves of my dark green dress. The memory of Mark's visit fretted at me.

"Mark came here the night Armorel left," I said. "He intended to wait for you. He had something to tell you. I hope you saw him."

James nodded. "He told me, as you know, where Armorel had gone."

"No," I replied. "I didn't know. Someone forgot to tell me and I preferred not to ask."

My faintly acid tone was not lost on James. "I'm sorry," he said contritely. "We all felt it better that you should be as little exposed to such ugly things as possible."

"Mark had no such scruples," I retorted. "He told me that night where Armorel had gone. So you see," I added in silly childish triumph, "I knew where she was before anyone else in this house. Mark even asked me to call on her."

"The devil he did!" he scowled. "You should have told me."

"Why? I had no intention of doing what he asked. Besides," I added, "his motive for asking me was unselfish."

"I wonder." His lips curled in disbelief.

"Whether you credit him with consideration for you or not," I insisted, "it's true."

He made no comment. His eyes, under the still drawn brows, were turned from me.

So much had already been said that I decided I might as well know the rest.

"Did Mark say anything to you about giving Kenny treatment . . . his particular treatment?"

"He did. And I dared him to touch my son."

"But don't you see, that could be why Armorel left. She might have decided to take the risk of having Mark try manipulation treatment. And knowing that she did not dare have him attend Kenny here, under your roof, took him away."

"Armorel wouldn't jeopardize her position as my wife and the future mistress of this house for anything, even for the sake of her child!" he said savagely.

"But it's the only explanation." I frowned, waiting. "It is, isn't it James?" I asked at last.

"You really mustn't concern yourself so."

"Why? Because I am considered a child?" I demanded angrily. "Or because no one in this house will trust me with the truth?"

"Don't say such a thing. You know that is not so."

"I know nothing of the kind. Why must I not be concerned with what, after all, are family matters?"

"You are young."

"And the rose-tinted spectacles are not yet off my nose. Is that it?"

"Perhaps," he said indifferently. I saw the small pulse throbbing at his temple, saw his hands work with a tense, kneading gesture. "And perhaps you would like to know what Mark said to me when I came home that night?"

I stood quite still, making no movement.

"He accused me of jeopardizing the health of my own child by clinging to old-fashioned methods of treatment. He told me to tear up my medical books, and quoted Hood to me."

"Hood?"

". . . who wrote a paper deploring the treatment by rest for damage to joints," he said impatiently. "The danger with Mark is that he has a fanatical belief in his own theories. He brought home from America unorthodox ideas and he is defying all medical knowledge in pursuit of them."

"But he *does* do good."

"Luck is often with the charlatan."

"Mark is no charlatan," I cried swiftly. "I . . . oh James, I'm so sorry. Sorry for everyone here."

Unable to bear the pain in his eyes I crossed to the window and stood where he had stood. I could feel the draught cutting my folded hands as I stood there looking out.

"A house divided." I heard myself whisper.

"Strangely enough, we are not," James corrected me. "Mark is a rebel. The rest of us are very close. Grandmother and Aunt Geraldine and I . . . and you," he added with a smile.

I shook my head. "No," I said. "No, James, not I. But never mind that now. Tell me, how long does Armorel intend to stay away? Is it . . . for always?"

"It can't be," he said violently.

"You want her back so badly?"

"I want Kenny! That's why she'll be forced to come home. She can't live with Mrs. Emsworth indefinitely and there is nowhere else for her to go."

"She could return to her parents' home in Somerset."

"I think not." He leaned against the desk and studied his square, well-kept hands. "Armorel's parents are very conventional, religious people. They would never encourage a daughter to remain apart from her husband. I sometimes think it is their strictness that has made Armorel and her brother Gerald turn against conventions."

I watched the brown velvet curtains stir in the draught and, with a shudder, joined James by the fire.

Before we closed this conversation, I had to try to find out how deeply Mark was involved.

I looked into the overmantel mirror and said to James's reflection, "Suppose Armorel does go to Mark for help?"

"He won't involve himself in scandal a second time."

"A . . . second . . . time?" I held my breath and looked over my shoulder at him.

"It isn't exactly a secret that he has a friendship with a notorious divorcée."

But he was thinking of that as the first time? Or was he remembering Helen?

I watched his face. The savage bitterness was gone and in its place I saw such pain in his eyes that, on an impulse, I reached out and touched his sleeve.

"Don't be too unhappy, James. Everything will come right," I said with false, silly hope in my voice. "It *must!*"

"If by that you mean that in time Armorel will return to me, yes, she will. There will be no alternative for her. She could not afford to live away from me for long unless, of course, she finds some kind of employment. And she is trained for nothing."

"But she has her own money?"

He shook his head.

"Directly a young woman marries, her fortune becomes the property of her husband."

"That is wicked! It is unfair!" I cried.

He looked startled.

"I'm sorry," I said quickly, through the hammering of my heart, "I did not mean that as a judgment against you, but against the state that allows such an irresponsible law to remain. It means that love can . . . can make a woman a pauper." I felt color flame in my cheeks.

James did not smile.

"And," I rushed on, "just because the law gives you a right, do you have to demand it? Do you have to *starve* Armorel back to you?"

He stopped to stir the fire again as though he needed action. "Put it any way you like," he said coldly.

I sat down limply in a chair and stared into the fire. At the back of my mind I told myself that it was Armorel who must have been my enemy, whispering to me on the stairs, thrusting me almost under a horse's hooves. She, who had never, herself, gone in fear of her life. Yet she had fled from the house. And there seemed no rhyme or reason why.

"So you think that, in the end, Armorel will return to you?" I demanded.

"I cannot see that she has an alternative," he answered icily.

"And . . . and . . . Kenny?"

"He is my chief concern."

"Oh," I cried on a sudden impulse, "if only I could help!"

He took both my hands and the hardness, the muted savagery, went from his face. His brown eyes became dark with feeling.

"You help just by being here, Elizabeth."

I felt tears, releasing the pressure of so much emotion, well up in my eyes. James bent his head to me.

"My dearest Elizabeth," he said.

XXI

It was quite by accident that I found myself a few days later in Kensington Gore.

Aunt Geraldine had asked me to take a shawl she had crocheted, a carriage rug we never used, and a basket of food to Emma Marl. She had been parlormaid in the days when my grandfather was alive and now, an old woman of past eighty, she lived in retirement with relatives on the far side of Hyde Park.

A hired brougham called to take me to the street of tumbledown cottages in Fulham and waited for me. I stayed for twenty minutes talking to the half-blind Emma.

When I left, I breathed gratefully at the clear, sharp wind outside the stuffy cottage.

The horses started off at a brisk pace and we wound through the streets going north. When I saw that the driver intended to enter the Park, I called up to him that I would like to drive along Kensington Gore.

We had passed it on our way to Fulham and now I wanted a closer look at the tall, elegant houses.

I sat forward, peering at them, trying to read their numbers. At one point, however, the Albert Memorial attracted my attention and I turned back to the houses just in time to see a yellow brougham stop before a wide house with deep bow windows and a covered veranda stretching the length of the first floor.

A woman was hurrying up the steps. A bonnet of rose velvet hid her hair and sable, edging a mantle of dark green cloth, was swathed high about her chin. Yet, even with so little of the features visible, I knew that it was Mrs. Emsworth.

Mark had said, "I want you to go and see Armorel."

I had not done so. Yet the fact that I had turned back in time to observe not only the house, but Mrs. Emsworth herself, was like the hand of fate. I did not even try to resist it.

Leaning forward, I told the driver that I wished him to turn around and stop at Number 749. "It is that house where you see the yellow brougham," I said.

The man touched his hat, flicked his whip and the horses made a prancing sweep, pulling up outside the house. Mrs. Emsworth had gone inside and the heavy wooden door was closed.

I knew perfectly well that I was acting on an impulse which I would doubtless regret. Yet, as I walked across the pavement and pushed open the wrought iron gate, I felt a sense of excitement.

A trim maid in a brown uniform and a pretty frilled apron answered the door to me and announcing my name, I asked to speak to Mrs. Bellenmore.

I saw the immediate doubt flash over the girl's face, but she was well-trained in politeness and invited me in. I was admiring a table of ebony inlaid with mother-of-pearl when the maid returned.

"Mrs. Bellenmore will see you, Madam."

It was altogether too unexpected. Not at all certain what I would say to Armorel, I followed the maid past closed doors to the back of the large house.

I was shown into a room that was filled with light. Armorel stood in the path of a sunbeam, looking down at me as though she were mistress of the house. On a bed by great windows that looked out over a terraced garden lay Kenny. And he was crying in a small, quiet, hopeless way.

"Kenny!"

"I am not in the least surprised to see you, Elizabeth," Armorel said unpleasantly, blocking my instinctive movement to the little boy's bedside. "I guessed that sooner or later James would send someone round to plead for him."

"James did not send me."

"Then who did?"

Now that I was closer to her, I thought she looked strained and there were mauve shadows beneath her eyes as though she were not sleeping well.

"I was passing," I said, "and I called on an impulse. I was not at all certain that you would see me."

"In that," she retorted coldly, "you were quite right. I nearly didn't. Well, and who told you where I lived?"

"Mark."

She stared at me for a moment and I fully expected an outburst of anger. Instead, she began to laugh.

"Mark indeed. Oh, I suppose he spoke to you when I first arrived here. In the beginning, you see, he was full of loyalty to James and professional scruples. It is different now. James has himself to thank for that! His own bigoted arguments the other night when they talked, have reversed Mark's decision not to treat Kenny without his sanction."

"You can't be serious! You wouldn't dare let Mark experiment on Kenny without James's permission."

My voice was a thin defeated whisper of sound because I knew perfectly well that my protest was futile. I shot past Armorel to the bedside. There was the faintest bloom of color on Kenny's skin and his face was not quite so thin, but the tear stains on his cheeks were very real.

"Hello, Kenny," I said.

"Have you brought Skippy?" His over-large eyes looked up at mine with a small, lonely pleading.

"I'm afraid not," I said gently. "But you'll see him again when you come home."

"When can we go home, Mama?"

There was a flurry of silk, a sharp ejaculation.

"For heaven's sake, stop grizzling about going home," Armorel almost shouted. He cringed back in the bed.

"How is he?" I asked.

"You can see for yourself," she snapped. "Utterly ungrateful for all I am doing for him."

"But the treatment—" I moved so that I could confront her. "The treatment," I repeated. "Is it doing him any good?"

The cold dislike in her eyes sent chills creeping into my bones but I gripped my hands together in my muff and kept an unblinking gaze on her. It was she who averted her head first.

"You had better wait to find out. We had all better wait."

"But the treatment has started, you say? So you must know—"

"I know nothing yet," she said with a particular violence.

The chill continued, curling inside me, and I knew that it was fear. Something had gone wrong. At that point I forced myself to stop thinking. I did not dare consider what might happen if Kenny became worse as a result of Mark's forbidden interference.

Armorel had walked to a communicating door and was holding it open.

"Come in here," she said peremptorily.

I walked through the cream-and-gold panelled door into a smallish room furnished in ornate French style. The door closed.

"Mrs. Emsworth invited me here," she said with a touch of malicious amusement.

"I know."

"You are well-informed, then."

"Why should I not be? I am one of the family," I replied coolly.

"Kenny was not my reason for leaving Manchester Square," she said walking to the fire. "I had already planned that Mark would come to the house and treat Kenny in the afternoons there while I was . . . er . . . supposedly teaching him French and reading Shakespeare."

"Providing Mark would have agreed to that," I said drily.

She smiled. "Oh, but you don't know Mark. Nor men, my dear. You have no idea what ambition does to them. Nor what they will do for it."

I had no desire to pursue that subject with her.

"Why did you leave James?"

She turned and faced me. I saw the tip of her tongue moisten her lips.

"There is something I have to find out before I return . . . *if* I return! Something—" She broke off.

"Yes?" I prompted.

"Oh no!" She shook her head. "If I'm right, it will be *my* discovery. Sharing a dangerous secret is never wise."

"Whatever it was that made you want to escape from the house, surely it would be easier if you told someone. If there is danger in it, then sharing—"

"With you, I suppose." She threw back her head as though to laugh. But no sound came. "Let me point out, my dear, that your coming to the house has not made things easier. In fact—" Again she did not finish her sentence.

"I don't see how I can have complicated your life, Armorel," I said quietly.

She looked me up and down, a faint insolence in her expression. "Maybe you don't," she conceded. "Maybe you are completely artless, after all. I don't know you." She made a little sweeping movement with her hand. "But that is unimportant. What matters is that you do not come here again, spying upon me for the family."

"I have told you," I cried indignantly, "the family have no idea that I have come here. And I have no intention of telling them."

She sat down in a low chair, leaned her head back and closed her eyes. The bright half-sunlight fell upon her face and I saw to my surprise the shadow of depression upon the beautiful features. In that moment I felt a reluctant pity for her.

"Armorel," I said urgently, "please, if you are troubled, let me help in any small way I can."

She opened her eyes wide.

"I've already told you. *You* cannot help *me*. What I have to do, I do on my own. And when I have found out what I think is there to be discovered, then everyone in that house will sleep more easily in their beds."

I caught my breath sharply as the strange words registered. Inside my muff, my fingers gripped one another tightly.

"What—" I began and stopped, running my tongue over my dry lips. "What do you think . . . you can find out?"

She raised her dark blue eyes to my face.

"Who it is," she said in an almost inaudible voice, "who wishes to kill me."

I stared at her, wanting to cry. *You are quite, quite wrong! It is I who am in danger!* But I said nothing.

XXII

THE HORSES, chilled after their wait outside the house in Kensington Gore, fairly danced through the Park on their way home to the stables.

I sat huddled in my corner. I was obsessed with Armorel's last words. What had happened on the day just before she left the house to indicate that someone plotted to harm her?

I sought to recall the day and could remember nothing out of the ordinary.

The night before, I had gone into the garden to rescue the adventurous Skippy and had seen the light in the attic and recognized the glint of Armorel's golden satin dress. What had she been searching for? And had she found something? Was it that which had sent her fleeing from the house?

Something was wrong with Armorel's hint of danger to herself. For of all the people in the house only she could possibly have been guilty of those two attempts to harm me. Only Armorel.

Suddenly I saw her last words to me as a trick, her manner an act. To what false sense of security did she think she could lull me by what she had said? Armorel was in no danger. It was I! And she knew it.

I told no one that I had seen Armorel. It would do no good and probably only agitate Aunt Geraldine.

As the days drew slowly on toward Christmas, she did all she could do to plan a happy time for me. Harry Stanhope had persuaded his parents to ask me to a dance they were giving at their house in Fitzroy Square and the Winkworths invited me to a party.

There was no real rejoicing in our house. Kenny was not there and Mark came less and less.

We had a Christmas tree in the drawing room window because my grandmother insisted. I was allowed to decorate it. The great chandelier was lit from dusk to bedtime and presents and Christmas cards arrived for us.

Rosie remembered me. She sent me a petticoat which she had embroidered herself. I felt tears start in my eyes as I thought of all the hours she must have spent on work that was totally uncharacteristic of her. I had sent her a length of yellow silk.

But the house was too full of ghosts for gaiety.

On Christmas morning, Aunt Geraldine, James and I went to church. When we returned home, Mark was there. But he would not stay.

I guessed why. He could not sit down at a festive table with James while he visited Armorel in Mrs. Emsworth's house.

James knew where Armorel was staying, but his mind followed one track. Armorel had run away and taken Kenny in order to hurt him. He believed implicitly that time and his own control of her money would crush her defiant spirit and bring her back. All he had to do now was to wait.

Only I faced the dreadful probability that Mark had treated Kenny in his own unorthodox way and, since there was no news, had failed.

I should have taken Aunt Geraldine into my confidence, but I could not. I told myself that I would not be the bearer of tales. But something more deeply honest admitted that the less I said about things that did not actively concern me, the safer I would be. I could not un-know my knowledge. But I could keep it to myself.

It was soon after Twelfth Night, when the cards had been taken down and looked at for the last time, that I acquired a hobby. I was covering an old discarded screen with colored pictures and used Christmas cards.

I was working on it one late afternoon when I heard talking in the drawing room below. The sound rose through the chimney. As a rule it was impossible to distinguish particular voices save for Armorel's, which had a carrying quality. That voice was speaking now.

Armorel had come back.

I did not stop to think further than the fact that I had to know whether she had returned for good. Curiosity and dread went with me down the stairs. I heard Aunt Geraldine's voice, high and clear with bitterness, cut clear through the half-open door.

"You are evil! Like Helen, you have brought nothing but sorrow to us. Go away! Go back to that actress's house. You have destroyed all the peace and happiness here!"

"You know better than that, don't you, Aunt Geraldine?" Armorel interrupted her. "You know who—"

"Be quiet!"

"You and your two beloved sons! Look!"

There was a pause. Then a small, strangled cry and swift movement. I heard a thud and a series of tinkling crashes. A table had overturned.

Armorel was standing, seeming unreally tall, her face frozen into a mask. She was staring down at the crumpled and twisted figure of Aunt Geraldine lying at her feet.

I ran forward, falling on my knees.

"She seems to have fainted," Armorel said harshly.

"Get James!" I held a limp hand in mine. "And fetch Mrs. Vine. *Go on!*" I shouted at her. "Get help!"

I had never seen Armorel in a hurry before. Her limbs appeared to unfreeze in one single movement and she fled, as though with an almost hysterical relief, from the room.

But I had no time to consider Armorel's odd behavior. Aunt Geraldine was unconscious and her breathing was jerky. I put a cushion under her head and, waiting for Mrs. Vine to come and help me lift her, I was quite certain that this was not a mere faint. I watched the oddly flushed face anxiously.

"Oh! Oh, the poor Madam!" Mrs. Vine, smelling salts in her hand, swept across the room.

"Have you called Doctor James?" I demanded.

"He is out." She was loosening Aunt Geraldine's tight bodice.

"Then we must send for Doctor Rowlins at once."

"Don't you think your grandmama—"

"My grandmother will be resting. It will take her some time to dress. We'll call her, but the doctor must be sent for immediately." I got to my feet. "Susannah shall go for him; it will only take her a few minutes, if she hurries, to get to Harley Street." I went to the bell rope and pulled it hard.

Between us, we managed to lift Aunt Geraldine on to the sofa. She was small, but she was plump and quite heavy and she was still breathing strangely.

"I don't like her color, Miss Elizabeth," Mrs. Vine said.

"Will you stay here while I fetch my grandmother?"

Outside the landing, I found Armorel. She was standing with her back half towards me, staring at the stained glass window.

At the same time Susannah came running across the hall. I called my urgent instructions to her to fetch Doctor Rowlins. Then I turned to Armorel.

"What happened? What did you do to her?"

"Do to her?" The shock had left Armorel. She was herself once more, poised and hostile towards me. "Really, Elizabeth, do you imagine that I attacked her physically?"

"You were quarrelling."

"*She* was quarrelling with *me*."

"Aunt Geraldine is the gentlest person alive. What did you say to upset her so?"

"I came back," she answered.

"That doesn't account for what happened," I said impatiently. "You had been here some minutes before she collapsed. I know, because I heard you talking when I was in my room upstairs. So it was not the shock of seeing you that brought on this attack. And, come to that, why should it?"

"She was working herself up into a paddy," Armorel said composedly. "I could not help that."

"I overheard the last part of your argument," I told her. "The door was ajar and I could not help it. I think you showed her something."

"The worst of listening at keyholes," she remarked, her dark blue eyes wide like a cat's, upon my face, "is that one hears a little and imagination adds the rest. What in the world do you think I had to show her?"

"That is for you to tell me."

"There is absolutely nothing to tell."

Yet I watched her fingers closing and unclosing over the reticule at her wrist and I knew she was lying to me.

I did not dare remain arguing any longer. I pushed past her without another word and ran along the passage to my grandmother's room. She had finished her afternoon rest and was seated at her escritoire. A lamp shone on her gray and white hair and her dark skirt was splayed elegantly round her.

She looked at me absently over her shoulder.

"Well, child?"

"It's Aunt Geraldine," I said. "She fell and I don't know what is the matter with her, but she is unconscious. Armorel was there with her."

Grandmother reached for her stick and rose with difficulty. There was a small, hard smile on her face.

"So Armorel has at last been forced back, just as James intended."

"I don't think so. Kenny is not with her." I brushed that aside. "It's Aunt Geraldine, grandmother. I'm worried."

"A faint," said my grandmother placidly. "A useful escape when a situation gets out of hand."

I did not argue with her but followed her slow progress down the passage. As she went, she was murmuring to herself, "It would have been better if James had let her go. Much . . . much . . . better."

When she reached the drawing room, however, and saw Aunt Geraldine, my grandmother's serenity left her.

"This is no faint!" She turned and glared at us. "Geraldine has had a stroke. Fetch James at once!"

"We don't know where he is. But Doctor Rowlins is on his way," I ventured.

"Oh." Her authoritative tone wavered. "Then we will wait for him. He may even know where James can be found."

Before she finished speaking, she turned her head. Hate flashed in her eyes. "So, Miss, you have returned!"

Armorel stood in the doorway.

"I came, grandmama, to speak to Aunt Geraldine."

"To cajole her into interceding between yourself and James. To bargain?"

"My reason for coming was more personal than that."

"Indeed! Then what?"

Armorel paused. She looked at each of us in turn. I do not believe that she was conscious of her beauty nor of her dramatic pose. I think she was trying to make a decision.

"I wanted to see her about Ibbet," she said.

My grandmother did not move. Imperceptibly, something had crept into the room, silent as a ghost. It hovered, hesitant and invisible, the central figure of some forgotten incident—Ibbet, the little Welsh dwarf.

In the distance I could hear a lonely dog barking; I heard the tiny burst of muted thunder as the flames exploded from the coal; I heard my own heart thudding against my ribs.

Before coming to this house, Ibbet had been just a name to me. Then one day, I saw her as Morag's mother. Now, she was even more real. I shivered.

My grandmother was speaking. "Ibbet left here a great many years ago. She has gone to live with relatives. I do not know of what interest that is to you!"

My grandmother spoke with indifference. I could have been lulled and deluded by her manner had I not glanced at Mrs. Vine and seen fear spark in her eyes.

Doctor Rowlins' entrance broke the curious, malevolent spell. He shook the floor with his bear-like walk. His eyes were always mournful with drooping lids.

Armorel and I were sent from the room. On the landing, we parted without a word and I went up to my room.

I folded the screen, put away pictures, scissors, glue-pot and rags. Then I wandered from window to hearth, from hearth to dressing table with that shocked irresolution which often follows sudden illness or accident in a house.

Directly I heard James return, I hurried downstairs again. Aunt Geraldine had been carried to her great four-poster bed in her pretty room.

The first person I noticed as I entered the drawing room was Mark. Had someone sent for him, I wondered, or was this just one of his customary visits?

Doctor Rowlins had picked up his bag and was shaking hands with James.

"You will, of course, get a sick-nurse. Although there is very little to be done for her."

"I'll make enquiries for a good woman tomorrow."

"Oh no." I came quickly into the room, interrupting James. "Aunt Geraldine would hate a stranger fussing round her. I can look after her."

"You know nothing about sick-nursing. And you are too small. You could not move her."

From James's great height, I suppose I did seem small. But I was strong.

"We have a number of women in this house who would be happy to help me," I said. "There are Mrs. Vine and Mrs. Bell. And Susannah isn't exactly a weakling."

"You have no idea of the difficulties involved in what you are suggesting," James warned.

"Oh yes, she has," Mark interposed, smiling at me. "Let her try. If she finds it too much, she has a tongue in her head; she can tell us so."

"Elizabeth hasn't yet taken into account the unpleasant side of sick-nursing."

"I have not noticed," Mark said, still with that faint smile, "that Elizabeth is squeamish."

"I'm not. And so it's all settled." I turned to James. "You can give me all the necessary instructions."

I refused to look toward Doctor Rowlins, but I could sense his strong disapproval.

"Mrs. Bell stopped me on the stairs," Mark said, "and told me that she had experience as a sick-nurse. She said she would be very willing to come and live here temporarily and help."

"So there you are," I exclaimed with false brightness. "And now I am going to find grandmother and tell her what has been decided."

I escaped before there could be more argument. I expected strong opposition from my grandmother, but I was taking the difficulties one at a time. The important point was that I knew Aunt Geraldine would be unhappy with strangers touching her. I was determined that her life in bed should be as happy as I could make it.

As I reached the main staircase, my grandmother came out of the Blue Room. I stood aside watching her mount the stairs slowly.

The chandelier had been lit and the purple silk of her skirt gleamed through the arcs and curlicues of the iron balusters.

When she reached the alcove landing she paused, breathing heavily.

"I have just been talking to Doctor Rowlins and James," I said. "Aunt Geraldine will need a certain amount of nursing and since she would hate a stranger, I am to look after her."

"In my opinion that is a wrong decision."

To my relief, however, she spoke the words without any strong protest. It was as though her dominance had been momentarily spent.

"At least, I am to try. And Mark says that Mrs. Bell has offered to come and live here for a while and help."

She did not even retort, as she would normally have done, that it was not Mark's place to make arrangements in her house.

"She is helpless. She may be helpless for the rest of her life." The small, penetrating eyes stared at the tall window with its crimson and yellow panes. "My children. Thomas, your father, dead; Geraldine barely living."

I made to put an arm round her, but she avoided contact and began to mount the stairs to the drawing room.

"Grandmother, is Armorel coming back here?"

"If you mean, child, have I asked her to return, the answer is most definitely that I have not. I do not beg anything of one young enough to be my daughter."

"But surely she told you—"

"We did not discuss her return," she said sharply and left me.

I sped down the stairs to the hall, paused at the Blue Room and, on an impulse, called Armorel's name.

The door opened immediately as though she had been on the point of coming out. Her hand remained on the handle and she looked me up and down thinking little, I gathered, of my brown dress.

"Well?"

"I thought you would like to know that I am going to look after Aunt Geraldine. Mrs. Bell will be helping me."

"Why should I be interested?" The dark blue eyes studied me impersonally. "With your looks, I think you must be a little mad to shut yourself up with a dying woman."

"Aunt Geraldine is not going to die." I think I shouted the words for I saw her wince slightly.

"Or she may well be paralyzed for the rest of her life."

I had to agree with that and nodded my head miserably.

Armorel lifted a fold of her skirt and shook it as though she saw dust on the hem.

"Have you decided to come back?"

I think she found my direct question unexpected for she hesitated before answering me. "I have not yet made up my mind," she said.

"You have had four weeks in which to make a decision," I said tartly. "How long does it take you?"

"And since when do I have to suffer critical questioning from a young woman, living by Aunt Geraldine's charity, in a house that will one day be mine?" Her eyes blazed with icy anger.

"But it is not your house yet!" I felt my own quick temper rising. "And since I am not living on *your* charity, if I choose to pass an opinion on your behavior—" I broke off.

Something impelled me to glance swiftly up. The lighted chandelier was swinging gently. I moved instinctively to one side.

Armorel burst out laughing.

"You are a goose, Elizabeth! You stay here, wasting your life on two old people, for what else is there for you in this house? James is married and Mark—Mark, my dear, is everybody's charmer!"

"You don't like me being here, do you?"

"It is unimportant . . . for the moment," she said haughtily. "But you should be warned, you know, that you cannot look upon this house as your permanent home. When Aunt Geraldine dies—"

"She has scarcely taken to her bed!" I cried, furiously. "And you dare talk like that!"

"I face the obvious fact. Aunt Geraldine has had a stroke. She cannot live long. And grandmama is over eighty."

"You forget," I put in, "that Aunt Geraldine has not one but two adopted sons. There is Mark as well."

"I never forget Mark," she said softly.

"Perhaps it would be better if you did."

Armorel's hand lifted. I took a swift step backwards.

"Yes," she said, hissing her words. "You knew exactly what you deserved for that!"

"I'm sorry." I was honestly contrite. "Armorel, don't let's quarrel. Isn't there enough to contend with here? Aunt Geraldine may be dying and Kenny—How is Kenny?"

Her eyes glinted. "You would like to know, would you not, whether Mark is giving him treatment?"

"Yes."

"Then you must ask him," she mocked, and walked past me towards James's study.

When she was half-way across the hall, I called, "Why did you ask Aunt Geraldine about Ibbet?"

She whirled round, her hand reached out to touch the high, carved back of a chair.

"You must find that out from someone else, too!" she said, and shut the study door behind her.

Perhaps, I thought, I had not begun to understand where the source of the tension in this house lay.

I found the servants in the pantry. Mrs. Vine was crying quietly, her apple cheeks flushed. Mrs. Bell, who had taken upon herself the immediate duty in the sickroom, had slipped down to fetch a cup of tea for herself. Susannah's little pointed face was sharp with morbid curiosity.

I told Mrs. Bell to go home and fetch whatever she would need for her stay with us. When she returned, I would make a plan of our duties.

In the meantime, I asked for a bed to be made up for me in the boudoir off Aunt Geraldine's bedroom. I would sleep there at nights, I said, so that I would be near if she needed me.

"But your sleep will be so broken, Miss Elizabeth."

"Oh no," I reassured Mrs. Vine. "I do not need a great deal. And I doubt if Aunt Geraldine will rouse often during the night."

I imagined that Doctor Rowlins had left some time ago, but when I returned to the bedroom, I found that both he and James were there, standing by the bedside.

Aunt Geraldine's eyes were closed.

"She has not yet regained consciousness!" I cried. "She isn't going to die?"

"There is nothing much we can do in cases like this, Miss Elizabeth," Doctor Rowlins replied. "We must just hope and pray!"

"Neither of which," I replied swiftly, "are particularly practical ways of bringing her back to health."

Doctor Rowlins' drooping eyes looked sadder than ever. "I fear you have little faith."

"On the contrary," I returned, "I have great faith. I believe that we have been given brains to use in order to work out our own ways of living . . . and healing."

He shook his great head and I knew that he considered me both irreligious and far too outspoken.

"And now," I said briskly, "perhaps you will tell me what I have to do."

There was, I learned, pathetically little save to watch for signs of returning consciousness, keep her warm and clean and feed her.

When they left me, I stirred the fire and sat down in a chair half-facing her to wait for the slightest movement from that inert, remote little figure that was my Aunt Geraldine.

I do not know when Armorel left the house. But that night, there were just three of us seated at the long mahogany dining table.

I had thought that, since Mrs. Emsworth was sheltering Armorel, my grandmother would forbid Mark the house. But she did not. I think she saw the ranks of her family diminishing too rapidly. So, with the pathos of the old, she clung to the last remnants of it at whatever cost to her pride. Yet what tattered remnants, I thought. James, bereft of wife and child; Mark following a so-called quack profession and blatantly indulging his friendship with Mrs. Emsworth before our very eyes.

As the days passed, there was a decided change in Aunt Geraldine's condition. She recovered consciousness and could move her right arm and leg, although her left side seemed paralyzed. Gradually she managed to speak a few words and make a little grimace which I knew to be a smile.

It was fairly easy to nurse her, with Mrs. Vine and Mrs. Bell to help. What startled and distressed me, however, was that she was upset by my grandmother's daily visits. I did not understand this for there seemed to be a quietening of her aggressive personality, almost a new gentleness.

Why then, was Aunt Geraldine afraid of her? I could find no answer.

XXIII

I WAS SITTING by Aunt Geraldine's bed reading to her a chapter from a book she loved. Outside the wind howled like a pack of hungry wolves. There was a large fire burning in the grate.

As I sat near a lamp reading aloud, I did not hear the door open softly. Suddenly, however, I sensed a presence and turned, startled, to find James behind me.

"You can stop reading. She cannot hear you," he said quietly. "She is asleep."

I looked at the face on the pillow and saw the gentle features relaxed in sleep. James took the book from me.

"Your voice soothes her." He took my hand. "It is soft. Come over here." He led me to the rocking chair with the patchwork cushions and, himself, stood with his back to the fire.

"I am going to fetch Kenny home."

"And . . . Armorel?"

He shook his head. "I shall divorce her."

"James, you can't! You can't. There is no reason, no legal grounds."

"I shall find grounds!" He paused and looked at me closely. "Why do you seem so shocked? You are a modern young woman!"

"I am thinking of grandmother," I said soberly. "She is the one who will be shocked. And Kenny needs his mother far more than children who can run about and help themselves."

"I hope he will have a mother," James said.

I looked at him, frowning. In the firelight his eyes, meeting mine, were a burning brown.

"You mean you would marry again?" I rose, turning to look at the sleeping woman in the big bed. "But—"

"You do not need to ask whom, out of all the women I know, I would ask to be Kenny's second mother."

He left his sentence in the air, as though unfinished. In a few blind, swirling moments I realized what was in his mind. I reached out in a swift, involuntary gesture to ward him off, but James mistook my motive. He seized my hand and drew me towards him.

"My dearest Elizabeth!"

I was trembling and my heart was beating so hard that I was certain he must hear it.

"I am in love with you," he said.

His lips touched mine before I could protest. I wrenched myself out of his grasp. The head on the pillow did not move, the eyelids had not lifted. Our struggle had not disturbed Aunt Geraldine's sleep.

I felt James's arm round me. I used all my force to push him away.

"Before you can tell another woman that you love her, you must put your house in order!" I wished I could have stopped my voice shaking as I spoke. "And you are mad to think of divorce. You cannot!"

"I must. If I fail," his voice was ragged with bitterness, "I dread the consequences. I will get free, Elizabeth." His tone softened. "And when I do, will you be waiting for me?"

I turned from him, holding my hands out to the fire. "You are not in a position to propose to me."

"I am in a position, though, to ask if I may hope."

"A sick room is not the place—"

"In which to tell a woman she is loved? Oh, but sometimes emotions are the masters of ethics! And nothing would make Aunt Geraldine happier than that you and I might one day marry."

I gripped my hands together. "I think you had better leave."

To my surprise and secret relief, he walked away. I watched him stand by the bed and lift Aunt Geraldine's wrist. She did not stir and when he tucked her hand back under the bedclothes he said, "Her pulse is considerably stronger. I believe she will recover completely. Doctor Rowlins said that she would. He is an extremely clever man."

"But he could not help Kenny."

"No doctor can work miracles."

I was walking with him to the door in order to close it quietly behind him. Outside, the gaslight in the passage had been turned up too high and hearing its flare, I reached up and turned down the jet. Then I glanced toward the staircase.

For the first time since illness had struck my aunt, the chandelier had been lit. Grandmother must have ordered this. It was like a sign that, in spite of all adversity, the house must return to its splendor.

I crept to the head of the stairs and looked down. The great crystal cluster of festoons and diamond drops winked and danced and sparkled as though the house were preparing for festivity. And very, very gently, the mass of lights moved; the candles dipped and rose in the draught.

"What is it?"

I started, not realizing that James was behind me. I turned to him to speak and, before I could avoid him, he bent his head, swift as a hawk, and kissed me.

My protest was muffled, my body held closely so that I could feel a heart beating without knowing whether it was James's or my own. Through my half-closed lids, the lights were prisms of purple and emerald and ruby upon my lashes. I heard James say my name again, felt my hands press against his chest in a puny effort at release.

"Perhaps," said a slow, frozen voice above us, "I have arrived back at the wrong moment!"

We broke away and turned together.

Armorel stood on the drawing room landing and lights turned her hair to a golden halo. But the hand which reached out to touch the baluster was like a long white talon that could willingly have clawed my throat.

My one thought was that she seemed everlastingly to be there catching me out in a moment's forbidden impulse. There was something of the witch about her that knew when to appear.

XXIV

I SHALL NEVER know what Armorel and James said to one another. I fled, lifting my skirts in a flurry of speed, down the stairs and into the kitchen.

"Mrs. Vine. Mrs. Bell." I called, my voice high with agitation, "Will one of you please go at once and sit with my aunt?" I saw their alarm and added lamely, "I need a rest."

Mrs. Bell's thin, angular body moved past me. "Don't worry at all, Miss," she said soothingly. "I'll stay with Madam."

I remained for a while, warming my hands at the great range, shaken and dismayed by what had happened. Then, when I felt more calm, I went up to the drawing room. There was no one on the stairs now, but I slipped almost guiltily past the place where I had stood when James kissed me.

A conversation ceased abruptly as I entered the room. I avoided James's gaze and greeted Mark. "It is some time since you have visited us," I said with false brightness. "But then, when you are not working, I suppose you are caught up in the social whirl."

"Balls and theaters and the opera." He shot me a lively glance. "Indeed, I burn the candle at both ends. Can you not see the signs of dissipation on my face?"

"The lamplight is too kind," I murmured.

James was staring into the fire, his expression blank. My grandmother, too, was not amused by our banter. Only Mark and I, I thought, had any conversation that would lighten the heaviness that hung over this house.

Suddenly I was aware that both grandmother and James had lifted their heads, listening. I heard sounds, too. Horses stopping with a clatter of hooves, voices calling to one another.

I went quickly to the window, saying over my shoulder to James, "Are you expecting a patient out of consulting hours?"

I did not hear him reply. I had pulled the curtain aside.

Someone was alighting from a carriage and behind her I could just discern another figure. As the driver climbed down, the carriage lamp fell upon his face. It was Thomas, Mrs. Emsworth's coachman, and in the circle of light I saw a patch of color, polished, shining buttercup yellow. Then, from below, I heard a little boy's clear voice.

I dropped the curtain and looked at James. He had risen and was standing quite still staring at nothing. He knew—we all knew—that Armorel had come back.

My grandmother broke the silence in the room. Her fingers had begun a restless beating on the chair arms.

"What is the meaning of the noises downstairs?" she demanded. Then, after a pause, "James, why do you not answer me?"

"I think Armorel has returned."

My grandmother sat up straight in her chair. "Did you know this was going to happen?"

"She called on me this afternoon and told me that she intended to come back," he said evasively. "You were resting at the time so I said nothing. I did not even know if she meant it."

"You should know your own wife by now!" When my grandmother was angry, she scarcely seemed to breathe. "Bring her here!" she commanded.

We were still standing in an attitude of listening when Armorel walked into the room. She wore purple cloth and sables round her throat. Beneath her bonnet, her eyes were very bright and defiant.

"I have brought Kenny home," she said. "Will you please, all of you, come down and see him? Grandmother?"

There was a long, poignant pause. No one in this house ever asked my grandmother to do anything. But Armorel did not wait for either protest or refusal. She turned and swept out of the room.

Without a word, my grandmother reached for her stick and rose. We followed her down the stairs and the movement of five people set the chandelier swinging gently.

Half way down, I found Mark by my side. I glanced up at him and suddenly, meeting that dark, steady look, I knew why we had all been summoned to the Blue Room.

The gaslight shone on to the sofa drawn up near the fire. I saw a dark, tousled head, and large, bright eyes darted from face to face as we entered.

"Kenny!" We spoke together, three of us. For, with two small hands gripping the arched back of the horsehair sofa, Kenny stood before us. *Kenny stood!*

I had a swift, irrelevant thought that he was such a little boy for his age. And then I heard James say, "Dear God! What are you thinking of, forcing him to strain his legs like that? Sit down, Kenny! Sit down at once!"

As James strode towards his son, Armorel's fingers closed on his arm.

"You can leave him alone. He doesn't need your help. He doesn't have to lean against anything. Kenny . . . walk!"

"I—" He took one hand off the couch and I saw that the whole of him, from arms to his thin little legs, were shaking.

"Walk, Kenny!"

"I . . . I can't. Mama, I . . . can't!"

"This is criminal!" James thrust Armorel aside and took a few steps towards his son.

"Let him be!" Mark's voice commanded. "Armorel is right. Kenny is quite capable of walking. It is merely nerves that prevent him."

"I am not interested in your opinion!"

Mark ignored James. "Now Kenny. Walk to me." He held out his arms.

Kenny took an awkward, stumbling step forward, still clutching the couch.

"Let go!" Mark commanded.

First one hand and then the other dropped to his side. Kenny swayed and gave a small, scared sob.

"Come on!" Mark's arms were held wide and steady.

Kenny took one halting step and stopped. "No!" He groped for the sofa. "I can't. Uncle Mark, I can't!"

"Either you take five steps . . . just five, or you remain in your bed, helpless, for the rest of your life. Now, which is it to be?"

I turned to Mark, shocked at the lack of tenderness in his voice.

"For God's sake!" James, beside himself, moved forward.

"I said stay where you are!" Mark rapped out.

I turned and looked at grandmother. She was leaning against the wall, her face paper-white. I went to her and put an arm round her shoulders. For the first time since I had ever known her, she did not reject the comfort of my touch.

"Kenny—" All this time Mark's eyes had not left the little boy's white face.

My own eyes burned because I was scarcely daring to blink.

"You are going to walk . . . to me."

Slowly Kenny's little legs, beneath his short night shirt, moved. He wobbled, put out his hand and finding himself too far away from the support of the sofa, began to whimper again.

"When you are near enough to me to touch my fingers," Mark said, "I will let you off any more tonight." His arms remained miraculously steady.

I saw the glint of desperate determination in Kenny's eyes, the under-lip caught tightly between his teeth. He put out a leg and set his foot on the ground, then he moved his weight and took a step with the other foot. Slowly, with terrified indecision, Kenny walked. He took not five steps but seven and then flung himself into Mark's arms.

I felt rather than heard the sigh of released tension in the room.

"Kenny can walk! He really can walk!"

It was some seconds after I heard the words that I realized I had said them. I had broken the rock-like silence.

Mark picked Kenny up in his arms, kicked open the communicating door and carried him to his bed.

"I walked! Uncle Mark, I did what you told me! And now I'll be all right, won't I?"

The words trailed off; the door was swinging to. Armorel looked at James. "So much," she exalted, "for Dr. Hutton's fine teaching that pain needed rest! You were so sure, weren't you, that old theories could not be improved upon. My clever, my very clever husband!"

"That will do!" Grandmother moved between them. "James, did you give Mark permission to treat your son?"

"Of course he didn't," Armorel retorted. "If it had been left to James, Kenny would still be lying helpless in his bed."

James shot her a long, dazed look. Then slowly, as though shock had slowed up his reflexes, he walked into Kenny's room and closed the door. I could hear the murmur of voices.

"I do not know what to say to you." My grandmother was leaning heavily against the sofa which Kenny had clutched so wildly. "I . . . do . . . not . . . know."

Controlled elation made Armorel's eyes shine like blue stars. "You see now, Grandmama. Today's charlatan can be tomorrow's master."

My grandmother turned her gray, expressionless face away. "Will you tell Mark I would like to see him in my room?"

When she was out of hearing, Armorel laughed. "You see, they are all lost for words!"

"I'm so glad," I said quietly, "that you had the courage to make this decision."

"What do you think my life would be, having a helpless child like a millstone around my neck all my life?" she demanded. "Kill or cure, I had to take the chance."

For *her* sake, not Kenny's! I watched her loosen her furs. With a soft, light step, she crossed to the communicating door and closed it behind her. Standing there alone, I hated her.

I longed to be in the other room to hear what Mark and James had to say to one another. Instead, I turned and went into the hall.

Mrs. Vine was half way up the staircase, leaning over to light the candles in the chandelier with a long taper. I watched the little flames spring to life. When she had finished she saw me and her face creased into smiles.

"It is wonderful news about Master Kenny. The Lord has been good!"

The Lord? Or Mark's magic hands?

Later, when I knew that Kenny was alone, I took Skippy to see him. We were playing with the kitten when James entered.

"Supper soon," he said, "and then we tuck you in for the night."

I left the kitten with Kenny and moved over to the fireplace where James stood.

"Was Mark's treatment just a wild experiment that succeeded?" I asked him. "Or is it something revolutionary in medicine?"

He stared into the fire. I had a feeling that he did not want to meet my gaze. He was either ashamed of his earlier behavior or angry at my resistance.

"We tend to call that which we don't understand, a miracle," he said in his most formal voice. "We doctors are cautious; we have to be, since the sick trust us. I decried Mark's theories and he has proved me wrong."

"It is generous of you to admit that."

"My son is cured," he said simply.

I knew then that the relationship between Mark and James had changed in the miracle-moment when Kenny had walked into Mark's arms. The idea which Aunt Geraldine had dreamed of, that they would become close as brothers, had only now become a possibility. Too late, perhaps, for her to know.

James was saying that he had sent a message to Doctor Rowlins asking him to call.

"And Mark's treatment will become universal for such injuries as Kenny's?"

"It is not that easy. Mark is an unqualified practitioner. There could be failures too. One success does not make a method infallible."

An exciting idea struck me. "Have you thought that, with your professional skill and Mark's gift of healing you could, together, achieve something great?"

His smile was indulgent. "You reduce everything to such simplicity, don't you, Elizabeth? In this matter, my dear, you have ethics to consider."

"You are pompous," I retorted.

"What's pompous?" Kenny asked from the bed.

"You tell him," I said over my shoulder and walked out of the room.

If only Mark would study medicine and take his degree. I brushed my hand over the leaf of an ugly spike plant standing on the hall table. It seemed to matter so very much more to me than it did to Mark himself that men called him a charlatan.

XXV

At four o'clock every afternoon, I took tea with my grandmother. Sometimes James was there. But it was always a formal occasion with the ornate silver tea service set upon the Buhl table before my grandmother.

Contrary to the common saying, March had not roared in. It had come with soft blue skies and little snow-white puffs of cloud. And one afternoon I could no longer resist the radiance outside.

I put on my gray velvet bonnet and my broadcloth cape. Then, knowing that Aunt Geraldine was being watched over by Mrs. Bell, I let myself out of the house.

The air was soft as I lifted my face and there was a faint yellow light in the west as though the sky were mirroring a distant field of daffodils. I walked, feeling a sense of release as though all the ponderings and the questionings could be solved by fresh air and a view of green grass.

The questionings! There were so many that my brain reeled at the thought. I still did not know why Armorel had come back. To humiliate James? *You could not cure your son, but see what Mark has done for him!* Or because Aunt Geraldine might be dying? I was still no nearer knowing who had twice tried to harm me and why the attacks had ceased. And then to the last, the final and most dreadful question: Had Helen's death been murder?

I began to walk more quickly, forcing myself to notice things: the children in the distance flying bright paper kites, the tiny yapping pomeranians.

I walked as far as the Serpentine and then turned back. I had reached the path that ran parallel to Park Lane when a man rose from a seat and came toward me.

"Taking the air, Miss Bellenmore?" asked Mark, lifting his hat.

"It is a beautiful afternoon," I said formally, pretending not to be surprised to see him. He fell into step by my side without even bothering to ask my permission.

"Why are you wearing gray like a matron?"

"I happen to like the color," I retorted.

"But you should wear jewel colors, always. Do you not know the rhyme?

'Amethyst, silver and gray for the dove,
But crimson and purple and green for my love.'

You are no dove, Elizabeth."

"It is a stupid piece of doggerel." I was angry with myself for flushing at his amused, sideways glance.

"Doggerel, perhaps. But artistically correct. You have a flame in you. Shall we sit down?"

I nodded. I had not had an opportunity of talking to Mark alone since Kenny had returned.

"If we sit here," Mark indicated a seat, "you will be a little sheltered. But we must not sit for long because your coat does not look to me to be particularly warm."

"It is a mild day." I sat down, tucking my feet out of sight and folding my hands inside my muff. I could have wept with annoyance that Mark had caught me at my least attractive.

I said abruptly to break the silence, "Suppose you had failed!"

"In what? Meeting you in the Park?"

I knew he was watching me and fixed my eyes on a child bowling a hoop. "To cure Kenny," I said coldly.

"Save yourself the wasted effort of supposition," he counseled. "I knew I would not fail."

Omnibuses trundled towards Marble Arch, the sun reflected in the black polished blinkers which the horses wore. I lifted my face to the March sunshine.

"You are fortunate," I said, "in having Mrs. Emsworth's faith in you."

"I am," he agreed.

"Armorel tells me it was your . . . your actress friend's idea that you should treat Kenny."

"I was called to her house in Kensington Gore and found him

there. For the first time, I was able to examine him properly and that was when I knew without a doubt that I could cure him."

"How did you do it?"

"Technicalities would mean nothing to you," he laughed, "but in principle, I refused to let those back muscles of his become wasted with disuse any longer. Resting was only fixing Kenny's dislocated vertebrae. If he had remained immobile for much longer, nothing could have cured him. As it was, it took weeks."

I wanted to ask him how Mrs. Emsworth and Armorel had managed to live in any sort of harmony in the same house. But I could not find the words that would not, perhaps, sound sour to him.

"Mrs. Emsworth must love children very much. Has she . . . has she . . . any of her own?"

"No. She is a dedicated actress."

I said nothing.

"When she marries again," Mark went on, "she will give up the stage for good and then devote herself to her family."

"She had better hurry up then."

Mark's laughter was anything but restrained. It startled a blackbird.

"It's a pity you don't like Lucia Emsworth. She's a woman of great charm and generosity. One day, perhaps, you will find out for yourself."

"Really Mark, I do not think our paths are ever likely to cross. She is never likely to set foot in our house."

"I shouldn't be too sure on that point."

I turned my head quickly and met his eyes. They were not smiling. At that moment some trick of memory flashed the image of Helen at me. The lovely profile of the destroyed silhouette was there with a jumbled, swirling impression of the staircase at Manchester Square and the chandelier. The pear-shaped candle flames streamed and danced across the three images. Suddenly I was aware that I had started to my feet.

"What's the matter?"

"Ghosts!" I whispered. "Oh . . . ghosts!" and fled.

Mark made no attempt to follow my seemingly inexplicable flight. He must have thought me a little mad.

I went quickly along the lane between the trees and faced the fact that one day Lucia Emsworth might walk through our house as her right. Her right as Mark's wife.

A light wind danced round me. A March wind. March! Just fourteen months ago Helen had been killed. The time of mourning was well over.

XXVI

THAT EVENING Armorel joined us for dinner for the first time. Beneath the surface normality there was, between my grandmother and James's wife, an unhappy truce. Armorel had, of course, to be accepted in the house. She should have returned, an erring wife, shamed and contrite and humbled. Instead she had brought Kenny back cured and so had silenced even my grandmother's condemnation.

Across the long table with the silver candelabra I watched James. He was polite and attentive to Armorel. But I wondered whether, behind the facade, he hated her. I gave a little shiver.

"You are cold?"

From the top of the table, my grandmother's eyes were focussed on me. "You were out a long time this afternoon, child. Perhaps you were not warmly enough clad."

"I went for a walk in the Park. It was lovely."

"You did not sit down anywhere and get chilled?"

"I did sit down." Secretly I wondered at her persistence. "But not for long."

"In the Park? On your own?" Her eyes narrowed at me. "My dear child, you must remember you are in London. You should not sit alone on a public bench inviting—"

"I met Mark," I said quickly. "We sat for a few minutes, talking."

I glanced at Armorel without meaning to. She held my gaze with a cold, expressionless stare.

"If you have finished your soup, Elizabeth," said my grandmother, "will you please ring the bell?"

I felt I had displeased her.

After dinner, I went to sit with Aunt Geraldine to relieve Mrs. Bell.

Since the evening when he had told me he loved me, I had been wary of James's sickroom visits. But, now, each time he came, he behaved with almost exaggerated good manners.

I had gone into the little room next to my aunt's, which was my temporary bedroom, to fetch a shawl when I heard James enter. I had known which drawer to open to find the shawl so did not light the gas. As I slid it round my shoulders, I heard Armorel's voice and realized that she must have entered with James.

"How is she tonight?" I heard her ask.

"Very drowsy, but her pulse is steadier."

"There is nothing you can do for her, is there?"

"Unfortunately, no."

"Yet you find enough excuse to be constantly here when Elizabeth is in attendance."

"I should be doing less than my duty towards someone whom I cared for if I did not keep a constant watch."

"A constant watch upon whom?"

"If you wish to argue, we will do so outside," he said with low anger. "You appear to forget that Aunt Geraldine is no longer unconscious. She does not wish to lie here and listen to our quarrels."

I moved forward, coming through the door into the lamplight. James had gone. Armorel had remained. She knew perfectly well that I was there, but she did not remove her gaze from the bed. I think she was beyond caring, in that moment, who saw the stare of hate on her face. My heart beat in my throat with fear that Aunt Geraldine might have seen.

I went swiftly to the bed and pushing her roughly aside, leant over and took my aunt's limp hand in mine.

The fingers made no movement to curl round mine. She lay inert as though the little life that had stolen back to her these last few days, had been peremptorily extinguished. I laid the limp hand down and walked to the door.

"Will you come outside?" I said to Armorel.

In the passage I faced her. "Don't ever do that again or I will not be responsible for my actions!"

"Do what?" Her eyes were insolent.

"Look at Aunt Geraldine as though you hated her."

"She neither noticed nor cared. She was asleep."

"She was not asleep!" I said heatedly. "And if your anger was against James, I will not have you carrying it to the sickbed!"

"*You* will not! My little Elizabeth, you are the last person to give orders in this house. Though you would like to have the right, would you not?" she added softly.

"Yes, I would love to be mistress of this house."

My honesty startled her.

"But if I had no love for the occupants," I added, "I would be ashamed to admit it."

"You are impertinent!"

"You forget," I parried, "that you have made your dislike of most of us very obvious."

"You need only concern yourself with my feelings for you," she said rigidly. "You see, I have not the slightest intention of losing James to a poor relation who is looking for a husband."

I gripped my hands so hard that they hurt. Had I not done so, I would have slapped that beautiful, cruel Medusa face. While I still had control of myself, I swung back into the bedroom and closed the door firmly behind me.

Aunt Geraldine had not moved. I went to the bell and rang for Susannah to bring up warm water. It was time to sponge Aunt Geraldine's face and hands.

Hitherto, she had enjoyed this half hour before I settled her for the night. Tonight, she lay like a stone, her eyes mostly closed, making no attempt to speak.

When Mrs. Bell came up to sit with her for a while, I went to find James.

He was in the drawing room. Armorel was playing the piano and singing. Her hair was living gold. Her voice rose, well-trained, soft and clear.

> 'In Scarlet, where I was born
> There was a faur maid dwellin'. . . .'

She turned her head as I entered and, still singing, watched me go to James.

As I passed her chair, my grandmother looked up from her patience cards. Black five on red six, Knave on Queen.

"I am anxious about Aunt Geraldine," I said to James. "She seems so listless, as though she has had a relapse."

"You worry because you do not understand the nature of her illness," he said. "In fact, her condition is improved."

"But this evening she does not respond to anything I do or say."

"That is the sad part for which no one can help her," he said gravely. "Physically, she is making a wonderful recovery. But her will has gone. She seems to—"

"To what?"

"To fight against her body's desire to recover its strength."

"But why, James?" I stopped because I could not make myself heard above the sudden crescendo of Armorel's singing.

> 'All in the merry month of May,
> When the green buds they were swellin'. . . .'

I wanted to shout to the soaring voice to be silent.

Then, clearly above the singing, my grandmother said, "You must call Doctor Rowlins in the morning, James. We will tell him we wish for another opinion on Geraldine's condition."

The music ceased. Armorel rose from the piano. Her dress, in the soft lights of the room, had all the lights and shades of a pink rose. She faced us, looking gentle and fresh as though she had put on the mask of an angel's face for some role she was about to play.

"Do you not think, grandmama," she asked, "that now I am home again, I might perhaps do my share of looking after Aunt Geraldine?"

"*No!*" My voice was so loud that I startled myself.

"You do not need to shout, child," said my grandmother.

"Our little Elizabeth guards her duties jealously." Armorel leaned against the piano, smiling and watching me. "But she is young. She should be going out and enjoying herself more than she does."

I was frightened. I saw the gleam of speculation in my grandmother's eyes, the grudging agreement in James's. She would win them over easily. Whatever happened, I decided, even if I had to lie like a guard-dog on the mat outside Aunt Geraldine's room, Armorel must never be left alone with her.

"I am perfectly capable of carrying on with Mrs. Bell's help." I made a last desperate stand. "There is really so little to do."

"But that 'little' could be less, could it not, if I did my share?" Her voice was dove-soft.

My grandmother laid down her patience cards and leaned back in her chair. "You have been here for some months now, Elizabeth, and you have had very little opportunity for enjoyment. At first we were still in mourning for . . . for Mark's wife. Then there was your aunt's illness. Armorel is right. You will divide your duties with her."

Fears eddied and capered in my mind. What would they say if I shouted at them that Armorel wanted Aunt Geraldine to die? I bit my lip. Out of the quiet, I heard my grandmother speaking to Armorel.

"You will make arrangements with Elizabeth to take over some of the sickroom duties. She will tell you—"

Blackness danced before my eyes. I heard my own voice, pitched high, over-loud. "The arrangement is perfect as it stands. I do not want anyone's help!"

"Your love for your aunt does you credit, child. But you must do as you are told."

Sick terror gripped me. I put out my hand and my fingers caught a little Dresden figurine. I swept it to the floor and heard it crack twice.

"If anyone dares to interfere with my nursing Aunt Geraldine, then . . . I shall go to the police and ask them to reopen the investigation as to how Helen died!"

I do not know whether anyone in that room moved or spoke. I spun round, trampling the broken skirt of the shepherdess under my heel and ran out of the room.

As I fled along the passage, I faced the fact that if they defied me, I would be forced to carry out my threat. And if I did, then perhaps Mark would be indicted for murder. Mark, who had been kind to the wild, shy child from a Dover cottage.

XXVII

TO MY SURPRISE, nobody followed me. The matter was never referred to, nor did Armorel make any attempt to share my duties with me. It was as though the family looked upon my outburst as that of an over-imaginative, hysterical young woman. For the sake of peace in the house, she should have her own way. Or was it that they were afraid?

I was a very light sleeper and sometimes in the middle of the night I would wake with a start and lie listening. But there would be only stillness around me and Aunt Geraldine's little bell, placed at her right hand, did not ring. I was certain that it was my own nervous tension that woke me and I would go to sleep again wondering how many mice there were in the wainscot or why old furniture talked to itself in the night.

One night, however, waking this way, I sat up and listened. Through the curtain which had not been fully drawn, I could see a slit of moon-washed Square. Perhaps the sound had come from outside—a late carriage, a barking dog. I began to relax, slid down again in bed and closed my eyes.

Then I heard the small, protesting creak of a floor board. I swung myself out of bed, reached for my dressing gown and lighting the candle, crept into Aunt Geraldine's room.

She lay on her side, her breathing steady. The ribbon that bound her pretty gray hair had slipped a little. I put the candle down and gently slid the ribbon into place. She did not move.

There was the faintest light at the door and I saw that it was ajar. I knew then what had disturbed my sleep. Someone had been in the room.

I went quickly to the door and glanced into the passage. An empty blackness stretched into the far domed ceiling. Down in the hall, the tiny glimmer of gaslight burned, as it always did, all night.

Yet someone had been moving along that passage.

I stood in doubt, wondering whether to call James. To tell him what? That someone had walked past my door, someone who had been in Aunt Geraldine's room? It could have been my grandmother, since old people sometimes walked at night. Or James or Armorel might have been moving about in the room below: restless, sleepless, quarrelling. I, myself, could have been responsible for the unclosed door. I . . . or the wind.

I went back to bed, snuffed out the candle and lay listening. There was no more sound. But it was a long time before I returned to sleep.

The following morning I found Aunt Geraldine very much brighter again. She smiled and managed to chat while I washed her. "How was Kenny?" she asked.

"Mark worked a miracle," I said softly.

"For others . . . but not for himself." The sadness returned, clouding her eyes.

"He loves his work, Aunt Geraldine. Perhaps that is how the miracle works for him."

She moved her head restlessly on the pillow. "Mark is in . . . d-dan . . . danger again!" "Danger" was a difficult word for her twisted lips. "Elizabeth, dear, don't let him . . . marry that actress!"

My heart gave a lurch. "But if he loves her," I began tentatively.

"It is . . . enchantment. And all enchantments die. . . ." She closed her eyes and sighed.

I bent closer. "Mark has known Lucia Emsworth a long time now," I said, "and the enchantment has not died. So perhaps it is real."

"The unattainable," she murmured. "An everlasting mirage. That which touches the surface . . . of the senses . . . is not love."

Her head fell to one side. Quickly I lifted her wrist. The beating of her pulse had not changed. She was just tired with talking.

I left her and crossed to the hearth. Staring into the fire, I saw burning crimson stars because tears blurred my vision. I was so lost in my distress that I did not hear the knock on the door. As it opened, I turned expecting Mrs. Vine.

It was Mark.

He went across to the bed and leant over.

"You are wearing a very pretty shawl," he said kindly. "When I was a small boy you used to have one just like that with little bobbles on the fringe."

I saw her eyes lift, shining with silent love, to his face. "You should be with . . . your patients."

"It is good for them to have to wait for me."

"Mark, you did . . . a wonderful thing for Kenny! Or," her brow furrowed, "have I already told you? I forget so easily."

"I wish I could do something for you, too."

"Nobody can."

"Except yourself, Aunt Geraldine." He sat down by her side. "And if only you would help yourself, you would be doing it for us, too."

"How little you understand," she said sadly. "I do not want to be ill."

"But sometimes it is easier to give in to incapacity. It releases us from our responsibilities. We lay down our burdens." He still spoke gently, but there was point and deliberation in his words.

Tears sprang into Aunt Geraldine's eyes and coursed down her cheeks.

"Mark, don't!" I cried and wiped her face with a handkerchief.

"I am trying to make her see that lying here is a renunciation of responsibility. And that to be loved carries a responsibility."

"Did you use those tactics with Kenny?"

He smiled at me. "More or less. I had to after I had first made it possible for him to walk again because he still did not believe that he could. In brief, I bullied him."

"And now . . . you are . . . bullying me." Her swimming eyes smiled at him.

"Yes. You see, I want to take you and Elizabeth to the theater again. Do you remember *Trial by Jury?*" It was at me that he glanced.

I felt the blood rise to my face. I even believed I could feel a ghostly kiss upon my face.

"Yes," I said shortly. "I remember very well."

He stayed with her a little longer and when he left, I saw her eyes follow him to the door. I bent and put more coal on the fire, and for a moment the room was quiet. Then, into the stillness, came Aunt Geraldine's voice, crying out in the wilderness of her private abyss.

"Where did I go wrong? How did I . . . mistrain them? They grew up . . . to think that . . . beauty was all good!"

She was not talking to me, and the bright, honey-gold evening beyond the lace curtains, the distant sound of a barrel organ playing in a side street, were not there for her.

That night I felt unusually tired and I went to bed early. Lady Dyron had called to talk to my grandmother and Armorel and James were dining out.

Just before I got into bed I heard the quiet opening of the gate. Curious as to who could possibly be calling at this late hour, I pulled aside the curtain and saw Mark.

It did not unduly puzzle me. I supposed Mark had called to talk to my grandmother. I climbed into bed and was immediately asleep.

I had awakened on the previous night to the merest stir of sound. Tonight I woke with a start to a single, wild scream, followed almost instantly by a sharp crash.

I sprang out of bed and in my nightdress, ran across the room. My hand, held before me to feel my way in the dark, stopped against unyielding wood.

Someone had closed the communicating door.

"Aunt Geraldine!" My fingers sought the handle in panic and twisting it, flung the door open.

I rushed to the bed. It was empty. But the door leading to the passage was wide open. A gas jet, turned low, illuminated the length of it.

Aunt Geraldine was leaning up against the wall, her body so off-balance and rigid that the slightest touch would have sent her keeling over.

There were sounds below me in the hall. I wanted to rush forward and see what had happened, but first I had to get Aunt Geraldine back to bed.

"Oh Miss! Oh Miss! Let me help you." Mrs. Bell was behind me and her strong arms went round the plump, rigid shoulders. Together we got Aunt Geraldine back to bed. I lit two candles.

"You can walk!" I said as we tucked her up. "You heard that scream, too, and it forced you to move, to find out what had happened." I bent and kissed her. "I will be back." I looked at Mrs. Bell. "Who screamed?" I asked.

"I don't know. I . . . I didn't dare leave Madam to find out."

"Stay here," I cried and ran to my room. I dragged on my dressing gown and sped down the passage to the staircase. No journey had ever seemed so long.

I paused instinctively when I reached the landing and leaned over the wrought iron baluster. One hand flew to my mouth to stifle a cry, the other gripped the cold iron scroll-work.

In the hall below, her crimson cloak spread round her, lay Armorel. She was beautifully bedecked, diamonds dazzling her cloak, her hair, even her face, tiny, sparkling prisms split into multicolors by the chandelier. The chandelier!

I looked up. It was not there!

Moving my head as stiffly as though I were crippled from the neck down, I stared down into the hall. Someone had lit the gas. By its light I saw what remained of the chandelier.

It lay, a thing of twisted metal, its crystal festoons torn apart. The "diamonds" scattered over Armorel were splinters of glass.

Mrs. Vine and Susannah, her plaited hair standing out like two little sticks from her head, were stamping out the tiny, licking candle flames. The smell of burning wax was acrid and sickening. James was kneeling by Armorel.

Then I saw that among the diamond sparkles on her hair, there was also blood.

"*It is quite safe*," they had said to me as a little girl. "*It has swung that way for fifty years.*"

XXVIII

I KNEW before they told me, that Armorel was dead.

The next hour was a bewildering and muddled nightmare. No one took charge, gave orders. And yet, on the other hand, no one lost control. We all moved with a numbed mechanicalness.

Doctor Rowlins was sent for and James shut himself in the bedroom with Armorel. My grandmother went in to him, but no one else.

Kenny had been disturbed by the noise. I went to him and found him out of bed, clinging to the edge of a table. I told him that the chandelier had fallen and when he wanted to see, I explained that it had all been cleared away. I persuaded him to get back into bed, tucked him in and kissed him goodnight. To my relief, he did not ask for his mother.

There was no one in the hall and I sat on the stairs and waited for Doctor Rowlins. When he came out of the room where they had laid Armorel, I told him about Aunt Geraldine.

"It could happen," he said nodding. "It could well happen. Shock could force her limbs to work." He spoke as though he had known all along that it might and I was quite sure he hadn't.

I asked him if he would give her a sleeping draught. He said absently, "Of course, of course," and followed me up the stairs to her room.

Mrs. Bell rose and, as Doctor Rowlins went to the bed, I held back. Looking at her, lifting my eyebrows, I tried to convey an unspoken question. She interpreted my glance and shook her head very slightly. Aunt Geraldine did not yet know that Armorel was dead.

Suddenly I heard her ask, "Doctor, something terrible happened! What was it?"

I looked at the aged face on the pillow and waited.

"Don't you worry your head about anything Miss Bellenmore," he said with false ease. "The chandelier fell. I am afraid it is quite beyond repair." He gave her a sleeping draught and then turned and gave me his brooding smile. "She will sleep very soon now," he said.

I went downstairs with Doctor Rowlins and showed him out.

Mrs. Vine was clearing the hall of the splinters of glass. She had found a thick stick lying by the mahogany table and she showed it to me.

"It wasn't there earlier in the evening, Miss Elizabeth," she said.

I took it from her. It had been heavily coated at some time or other with white paint and this was now peeling off. If looked to me like a curtain pole and I told her so.

She shook her head. "I can't think how it got there unless your grandmama told Susannah to throw it away and she forgot. She's like that sometimes; she goes off into dreams."

I straightened the fine old Isfanan rug by the hall table and, guessing that I would see none of the family that night, I climbed the stairs to bed.

Mrs. Bell was standing at the door to Aunt Geraldine's bedroom. She was twisting a handkerchief and crying quietly.

"Go to bed," I urged gently. "There is nothing more for us to do."

"She was so very beautiful and so young. I always said that chandelier was dangerous and now it has killed her!"

Yes, I thought when I was at last alone, the chandelier had killed her. But why had it fallen? What freak of coincidence caused it to crash just when Armorel was passing underneath it? Lying in bed, staring up at the black vacuum of the ceiling above me, I knew that Armorel's death at that particular spot had been no coincidence.

I wanted desperately to sleep, to stop thought, for my thought must be mad. Yet, stark, brilliant, malevolent as a cat's eye, the thought stared back at me.

It was I, not Armorel, who should have lain beneath the crushed crystal chandelier.

I tossed and turned and at last rose, and buttoning my dressing gown, went down to the kitchen for some milk. I looked all ways before I descended the staircase although I was certain that the killer would not try twice in one evening.

The house was very still and the staircase lit only by the dim globe of gas. The kitchen was warm and the juicy smell of the roast beef we had had for dinner, lingered. I found milk and heated it. Then, turning to take it upstairs with me, I saw someone standing in the doorway watching me.

"James!" I wheeled round and some of the milk spilled. "You startled me." I went for a cloth to wipe up the milk.

"Let me." He took it from me, wiped the spot clean and returned the cloth to the sink.

As I watched him, a strong urge told me to escape, to hurry upstairs while I was yet safe. For now I knew that I had been entirely wrong in thinking it was Armorel who wished to harm me. And, but for the servants, who else was there but James?

I was alone with him and nobody would come into the kitchen until morning. The green baize door shut us off entirely from the rest of the house.

"The milk will help you to sleep," he was saying. "But it might be as well if I gave you a draught."

I refused to meet his eyes; my voice was over-clear.

"I must not sleep heavily in case Aunt Geraldine should need me." As I spoke I edged out of the kitchen and when my elbow came in contact with the green baize door, I felt more brave. It was only then that I realized that James was still fully dressed.

"You had been out to dinner," I said. "Armorel was all right? I mean, she didn't complain of being ill . . . or dizzy?"

"No. As a matter of fact she had seemed over-excitable all the evening. I merely supposed she was enjoying herself."

"And when . . . this happened?"

He shook his head. "We had only been indoors a few minutes before the Merriman's parlormaid came round to tell us that her mistress had had another heart attack. I went round and remained there for about a quarter of an hour. When I returned here, the house was quiet. I went into my study and then it was that I heard Armorel scream and the crash."

He was talking to me, I thought, as though he were rehearsing for police evidence, stating the facts as they were. Or as he would have them appear.

"Armorel still wore her evening cloak," I said. "Yet she had been indoors some time."

"That is what puzzles me, too."

I remembered, then, that moment by the window when I had seen Mark enter the house. Had I been a moment earlier, would I have seen Armorel precede him through the gate? If so, it meant that directly James had left to visit his patient, she had crossed the Square to see Mark. Or had sent a signal from a window for him to come to her. And, up in my quiet room looking over the Square, I had not heard him leave.

"What is the matter?" James asked abruptly.

Immediately I sought and found a reason for the stare I must be giving him. "That stick—"

"What stick?"

"A thick white-painted one. Mrs. Vine found it near the hall table."

He shook his head. "I don't see—" he began.

"It could have been lying on the stairs," I said, "and Armorel fell over it."

"It was much more likely to have been left where Mrs. Vine

found it," he replied. "I don't imagine the stick had anything whatever to do with the accident."

"Accident!"

"Of course." His eyes widened, the pupils seeming unnaturally large in the half-light. "It was a million-to-one chance that the chandelier should fall on someone. And it happened. Though I can't understand it, for the bronze rods that secure it are inspected regularly."

I made a move to push the door open.

"That's strange," he said slowly as though he were still dazed. "You said something about a stick. You did, didn't you? Or did I dream it?"

"I spoke about it only a second ago," I said cautiously yet gently, aware that he must be suffering terribly from shock.

"And Armorel said—"

"Yes?" It was a breath rather than a word.

He shook his head like a man shaking away sleep. "I remember now. Armorel murmured something about a stick just before . . . she died. But her voice was so remote that I thought I had not heard correctly."

"What exactly did she say?"

For a moment he did not answer. It was eerie standing there in the half-light, our voices whispering backwards and forwards. "Say? Just that it was a stick that had caused her fall."

I felt the touch of an icy hand steal over me. *How* the thing had happened and *why*, I did not know. But *what* it was I was no longer in any doubt. It had been murder.

"You will have to call in the police," I said.

I was sure that it was anger that flared for a moment upon his shadowed face, although his voice was quiet, answering me.

"There is no need. In an accident such as this—"

"Like the accident that killed Helen . . . that nearly sent me crashing down the staircase!" My voice rose. "What is everyone in this house afraid of? Why are eyes shut, ears closed? Is there someone here who wants to eliminate the whole household? Is there such hate here? And are we behaving like suicides, walking through this house to our deaths, one by one?"

"You are talking nonsense!" His voice was harsh. "Helen's death was an accident and so far as you are concerned, there was no attack. You stumbled over your long dressing gown. As for Armorel, do you think someone waited on the landing over the hall in order to smash the pins that held the chandelier at the precise moment when Armorel walked underneath? If you do, then you have an alarming imagination!"

"I did not fall over my dressing gown!"

"In real life, tragedy lies more often in circumstance than in intent. The Bellenmores do not admit to much imagination, so you must have inherited yours from your mother's family. Now go to bed."

The changed, peremptory voice convinced me that whatever James might think, or suspect, he had no intention of confiding in me. I was to be placated with easy explanations while, behind closed doors, the truth would be faced, thrashed out and hushed up.

"But James—" He took two steps toward me. His eyes burned; I saw his whole body tense, coiled as though preparing to spring. And suddenly I was afraid again. I pushed open the baize door with my elbow and, with the milk I carried swinging in the glass, escaped.

I knew that James watched me go upstairs. But he watched from below. The evil which had followed first Helen and then Armorel, had watched from above. I kept saying to myself, I mustn't ask questions! That way lies danger, for me. As I passed the shadowy alcove with the black outline of palm and sofa and the tall, frowning stained-glass window, I quickened my pace.

Aunt Geraldine had turned on her side. Her eyes were open and she was staring into space. The milk I had carried upstairs was still warm and I offered it to her. She shook her head.

"Armorel is dead. Armorel is dead." She kept saying it over and over again in a voice like a sleepwalker's.

"Yes."

"How did . . . she die?"

"The chandelier fell," I explained softly, "and caught her."

She closed her eyes and small, strange keening sounds came from her twisted mouth.

"Dear," I urged. "Don't! Oh, don't! You should be asleep. And tomorrow—"

"Tomorrow!" She gave a long sigh. Then she looked at me and

tried to smile. The lids closed over her eyes. The laudanum was taking effect at last.

I sat there, with her hand in mine, until she was really asleep. The question that had been at the back of my mind all that terrible evening rose to the surface. Where had Mark been when Armorel was killed?

XXIX

Mark visited us early the next morning. I knew he had already seen my grandmother and James and so had heard, before I told him, that Aunt Geraldine had recovered the use of her limbs. He came to her bedroom.

"It is wonderful, isn't it?" I said.

"Wonderful."

I looked at him sharply, for he had spoken the word as though it were a lie.

We were standing by the fire and Mark's face was half-turned from me. With the blaze of firelight behind it, his eagle profile had a harshness that was almost sinister. He crossed to the bed and bending down, said, "We must watch over you with care."

To my utter surprise, she turned her head sharply away from him and withdrew her hand from his with a movement more swift than I had believed her capable of.

I heard him say, "Good-bye," and promise to come back that evening. Then, when he went to the door, I followed him.

In the passage, with the door pulled to, I faced him. "You were here last night."

"Yes. But how did you know?"

"I saw you from my window. But never mind that. Mark, did you see . . . what . . . happened?"

"If I had, would I have kept it to myself?"

"You might, if you thought it . . . expedient." I tried to outstare him as I spoke the daring, dangerous words.

"To whom would it be expedient?"

The dark, bent head was in shadow. I could not tell whether

or not he was angry with me. Nor could I answer his question. Instead, I asked him another.

"Mark, *did* you see Armorel last night, speak to her?"

"I did."

"Does James know?"

"No."

"But surely—"

"Go on. Surely what?" His voice was not quite real, as though he were on guard, watching me, watching himself.

"If you told James that you had been with Armorel just before she . . . she died, it might help him to piece together what exactly happened."

"How can you explain the circumstances of a split-second accident?"

"As I see it—"

"You know nothing, Elizabeth. Don't try to be too clever."

"It is not always wisdom that supplies an answer," I retorted.

My grandmother was coming slowly down the passage. I left Mark abruptly and went back into the bedroom, closing the door.

Aunt Geraldine's fingers were plucking the snowy embroidered sheet. She seemed far more animated than she had been since the evening of her attack, and yet in some strange way, infinitely more ill.

I had already washed her, brushed her hair and put her pink shawl round her shoulders. I picked up her right hand. "Now I'm going to make your nails look pretty," I said, and went to fetch scissors and buff for light polishing.

With her plump, soft hand in mine, I splayed her fingers and studied her nails. Under two of them was a dull white substance.

"Oh, Aunt Geraldine!" I chided with mock gravity. "What *have* you been doing?"

I thought I spoke lightly, as though to a child. To my amazement the hand in mine went rigid. A tiny chip of the white stuff edged, with the pressure of my fingers, from under her nail into my palm.

The chip was of old, hard paint scraped off something. Involuntarily my fingers tightened round hers. There had been a curtain pole with chipped paint lying near the dead Armorel. But it couldn't . . . it couldn't be! I pushed a monstrous thought out of my mind and said quietly, "How did this get under your nails?"

I had no idea what I expected her to say. I only knew that as her eyes met mine, I wanted desperately to see innocence. Instead, I saw the look of a sudden knowledge shared, a terrible resignation that the truth was inevitable.

The monstrous thought was there again. *Don't let it be like this! Dear God, don't let—*

Prayer was useless. I bent over her, my voice a whisper. "Aunt Geraldine, dear, what happened?"

She had closed her eyes. I sat, scarcely daring to breathe.

"They were evil!" Again her voice had a dream-quality. "They made my sons . . . bad wives. I failed—"

"You failed no one."

The twisted lips fought to protest. I wanted to leave her, to call James so that he would hear what she had to say. But I did not dare move from the bed. Watching her face, I think she was fast forgetting that I was there.

"It was my fault," she murmured. "I should have taught them . . . not to trust a look of innocence."

I measured the distance to the bell rope at the side of the bed.

"You wanted them to be happy," I said softly.

"Why did you wear red?" She turned her head toward me, pleading, speaking with difficulty. "My eyes are bad—I could not tell. I thought it was Armorel. You nearly died, my dearest Elizabeth. The red dressing gown . . . the red cloak you wore in the fog—" The old red cloak hanging on the peg in the cupboard under the stairs!

"Last night." I bent over her, knowing almost all now. "Last night . . . how did Armorel die?" I held her hand in mine, gently.

"I've watched and waited . . . for so long! For the right moment. It came last night. She had been seeing Mark again. I took the curtain pole . . . to help me walk. I hid behind the palm in the alcove. But I had not the strength to do to her . . . what I had done . . . to Helen. So I threw the pole at her. She fell sideways over the baluster. She flung out her hand and caught the chandelier. It . . . crashed with her . . . weight. I . . . I could not get back . . . to bed before you found me."

I lifted my head, listening. Someone had entered the room

and stood behind me. I saw Aunt Geraldine's eyes lift and look over my shoulder. I turned round.

My grandmother was there with Mark.

"Fetch James," I said.

Mark took no notice of me. He came round to the other side of the bed and sat down upon it, stroking her hair.

"You have been able to walk for some time, haven't you?"

"You know that?" She nodded. "At night . . . I practised walking. I had to! I had to finish what I had set out . . . to do."

"What did you have to do?" Mark's voice was infinitely gentle.

"Give my sons . . . my sons . . . a chance of happiness."

The room had become deathly quiet. I felt a hand on my arm, strong as a claw.

"Go," my grandmother said, "and wait for me in the drawing room."

I hesitated and looked at Mark. He gave me an almost imperceptible nod. It was like a reprieve. I was not to hear more of that torn and twisted confession. Before I left, I bent and kissed Aunt Geraldine.

"I love you so much!" I whispered. At the door I turned. "Goodbye," I said. And I did not know what made me take so solemn a farewell of her.

I reached the drawing room as though I had walked there in a dream.

I sat waiting. I did not know for whom or what.

The gilt clock under the glass dome pointed to ten minutes past eleven. Outside, the sunlight lay opalescent across the misty sky. It could just as well have been evening. For there was no moving time, only a great and terrible sensation of an accumulated past lying, immovable as rock, around me.

The story of a sin that was not seen as sin, of violence committed in the name of love.

And as I sat there, hands folded, feet crossed at ankles, Mark came to me. He stood before me, facing the window so that I saw the unusual gravity that aged him. It was, however, I who spoke first.

"Aunt Geraldine killed Helen. She did it to rid you of someone she believed evil. She did the same thing last night."

A piece of coal fell into the grate. We watched its glow.

"If only I could put the clock back and not do what I did!" I cried. "Mark, it was I who made her confess. She thought I knew when I pretended to scold her about her nails. She thought it was all over for her. That's why, in despair, she explained to me the reason why she did it. If only I had taken no notice."

"It would have made no difference." He opened his hand and I saw that he held a piece of printed paper.

"You told me you saw me come to the house last night. I did. Armorel came to see me and I walked back with her to the house. I did not come in."

"She came running to you when James was out." My voice held scorn.

"Yes. She had found this." He held the piece of newsprint out to me. It must have been from a very old newspaper for the print was fading and the paper yellow.

It was a brief account of an attack with a knife made by a nine-year-old girl upon a little boy. It had happened at a children's party in Fitzroy Square. The little girl had slashed a boy mocking the midget woman who had brought her to the party. I felt no surprise as I read the names of the chief actors in this strange, ancient drama. Geraldine Bellenmore and Ibbet.

"She loved Ibbet," I said, and the piece of paper fluttered from my fingers.

I remembered the party dress packed in the attic chest. The torn muslin.

"Just before Helen died," Mark broke my thoughts, "she managed to speak a few words to Armorel. Someone unseen behind her had whispered to her to look at the chandelier. As she did so, she was pushed. She spoke a name, Aunt Geraldine's. But Armorel thought she was merely asking for her. Then she whispered something about a newspaper cutting. They were her last words."

"And Armorel was curious and searched for the cutting."

He nodded. "Yesterday she found it, in the pocket of a dress at the bottom of the chest."

"Helen," I said, "must have found it there and put it back. Perhaps someone disturbed her and she had no other place to hide it."

"And meant to come back for it. But that night she died."

Perhaps, I thought, Aunt Geraldine herself had found her in the attic and Helen's discovery had sped her death.

"Why did Armorel bring the newspaper cutting to you?" I asked. "Surely she should have gone to James?"

Mark shook his head. "Perhaps because Helen was my wife. I don't know."

Or as an excuse to go and see him? I wondered. We would never know now and it did not matter, it was too small a point!

"When I had that . . . that accident on the stairs I thought you were here, in the house."

"I had been. I left a note for Mrs. Vine with the name of a man who would mend her rocking chair."

I heard what he said, but my thoughts had already moved on to another track. "Sometimes," I said, "I woke in the night because of some sound. It must have been Aunt Geraldine stealthily exercising the limbs I had thought so helpless." I looked up and caught Mark's eyes on me. "Do you think grandmother guessed? And was that why she treated Aunt Geraldine like a child, dominated her and watched her? Do you think she hoped to keep that streak of violence under control?"

"I think she did," Mark said gravely.

We looked at one another. Then, out of the silence another voice spoke. "Would either of you betray to a relentless law a child of yours who had killed, not out of viciousness or greed, but because she loved too much?"

Mark and I turned simultaneously. My grandmother had entered the room so quietly that we had not heard her. She looked from one of us to the other, her voice vibrant with her own self-defence, "Would you hand her over to the law, to a prison, or an asylum?"

Mark had risen and I saw that she was waiting for him to speak. It was I, however, who broke the pitiful silence.

"Aunt Geraldine did not kill Armorel," I said quietly. "The chandelier—"

"It is hopeless to divert the blame! You know now, Elizabeth, that she had planned this long before she suffered the stroke. Will power made her carry it out against the obstacle of her feebleness."

"The day Armorel came to see her and showed her the newspaper cutting—she knew, then, that she had little time in which to do what she wanted! She must have been terribly afraid that Armorel would make public what she had found out."

"And the emotional upset brought on a stroke," Mark said.

"I still can't think why Armorel didn't tell James," I said.

"Perhaps she would have, had Aunt Geraldine not had that stroke. I think she believed that she would die. In which case, Armorel intended to say nothing. When I died, she would be mistress of the house and the less scandal that surrounded her, in that case, the better. But when she realized that your Aunt Geraldine's health was improving, she knew she must tell someone. She told Mark."

My grandmother glanced at him. "Perhaps you know, for I don't, why she did not choose to confide in her husband."

Mark said, "This past few weeks they had nothing to say to one another. Socially, they went around together. Behind their doors, they were virtual enemies."

We had been talking in shocked voices.

"Come and sit by the fire," Mark said gently to my grandmother.

She shook her head. "I must go back to her," she said.

When her slow, light tread had died away, I crossed to the window.

"Ibbet had a daughter," I began.

"Yes, she did. Why?"

I told him, then, of the strange meeting in Marylebone.

"Why have you kept it to yourself all this time?"

"I . . . I told James."

He gave me that small half-smile of his. "I suppose you didn't trust me enough."

I made no attempt to explain.

"I thought at the time Morag had some personal grudge. Now I know that *she* knew about Aunt Geraldine. I suppose Ibbet told her. That Aunt Geraldine had fought out of love for Morag's mother obviously meant nothing to her. She was after money."

"Yes," Mark said. "She tried to blackmail the family. Then grandmother threatened her with the police."

"So she thought she could take revenge on them through me," I said. "She wanted to make me suspicious . . . to probe . . . to bring to light again the whole tragic story."

"We can only surmise that part," Mark said. "That is something Aunt Geraldine has not spoken about."

"But Mark," I cried with a last rebellious stand against the truth, "Aunt Geraldine was so gentle. I can't believe she killed three people! She was the least violent—"

"Some people have dark, secret sides," he said. "They are good and kind and are loved. But when the dark side gets uppermost, they become mad." He turned away from me and in a changed voice, said, "Our marriages broke her heart."

And it will break her heart, too, if you marry Mrs. Emsworth!

Suddenly I could not bear to face him with that thought. I turned and went swiftly across the room. Mark followed me. He opened the door and looked down at me. Then, before I could escape, his fingers touched my face, lifted my chin forcing me to meet his eyes.

"Bad things pass, Elizabeth," he said.

Bad and good, I thought, as though the future mattered. There was only one important moment in any life and that was the everlasting present.

That night Mrs. Vine slept in the room adjoining Aunt Geraldine's and I went to my own bedroom on the floor above. Sleep, when it came, was a restless thing fraught with fragments of nightmares from which I awoke at intervals with a racing heart.

Next morning I heard that Aunt Geraldine had got up again in the night and gone to the head of the stairs. Why, we would never know because they found her there unconscious. The strain of everything had been too much for her and that afternoon she suffered another stroke.

I was sent to fetch Mark.

The yellow carriage was outside his house and when I had given him the message I could not wait to escape. But he held my arm as though he had no intention of letting me go.

"I would like you to come with me."

I strained away from his grip, but it only tightened. I said, my face set and angry, "This is no time for a social call. I do not wish to meet Mrs. Emsworth. I gather she is with you."

I glanced towards the stairs and then I saw her. She came with that graceful, unhurried walk of hers down towards us. "Miss Bellenmore—"

"My aunt will not live long," I said in a high, tense voice. "I have come . . . to fetch Mark."

I saw their eyes meet in deep understanding.

"Please, Miss Bellenmore, spare me just five minutes," said Lucia Emsworth.

"In here." She had thrown open the door of the downstairs room in which I had waited once before. The fire was bright and the light danced on her face as she crossed to it. I had been drawn into that room against my will and I heard the door close softly behind me. Mark had gone. I was certain that my dislike of her emanated so powerfully that she must feel it.

"Please sit down." She patted the back of a chair.

She wore a dark gold cloth dress and a topaz and diamond brooch held the frills at her throat. I could feel her magic and steeled myself to withstand it. If this was an attempt to try and make friends, to insinuate herself, through me, into the household, then she was going to be disappointed. I did not hate her; I did not disapprove of her. For the first time I faced my feelings for her. I was deeply and furiously jealous.

"You know, of course, that Mark and I have been friends for a long time."

I stared at her stonily without answering. I resented her copper-gold hair, her smooth, lovely forehead, tawny eyes.

"But you did not know, did you, Miss Bellenmore, that I owe Mark a very great debt of gratitude. I owe the continuance of my career to him."

"To . . . to Mark?"

She sat there, a little smile on her lips. "A year ago I had a bad fall and injured my foot. I was appearing at the time in *Gay Lord Valentine*. The understudy had been taken ill and I *had* to go on. It was Mark who made it possible, by manipulation. Then, a few months ago, I stumbled on an icy patch of road outside my house and hurt my back. The pain was very bad. Four evenings a week, before I was due at the theater, I would come here for treatment. Now, I am much better, but I still need treatment. I come here for it in the late afternoon and rather than go all the way back home, I rest here. Mark and I play chess together, as you see." She indicated the board on the table before her with the little ivory and silver pieces.

"Armorel . . . knew this?"

"When I suggested she should bring Kenny to my house for treatment by Mark, I had to explain to her why I was so certain he would succeed. I had kept the fact of my injury a secret from those in my profession. There are too many waiting for a chance to take over a star's role and I am not so young that I can afford to be over-generous to my rivals." She smiled. "The way up has been hard enough for me as it is."

"Why are you telling me all this, Mrs. Emsworth?"

The small smile deepened, "I think you will know soon enough!"

I felt at an extraordinary disadvantage. I had entered the room prepared to be distant, uncommunicative, antagonistic, even. Yet I found myself warming to Mrs. Emsworth so much that I put out my hand.

"I am glad," I heard myself say, "that Mark could help you. And do not worry, I shall not tell anyone."

She shook her head. "I am so much better that it does not matter any longer."

I rose, glancing out of the window at our house seen through the still-bare trees.

"You will forgive me if I go now?" I asked. "My aunt is very seriously ill and she may ask for me."

"Of course."

"I hope," I said a little shyly, "that we will meet again."

"We shall." She nodded and the mysterious little smile broke out again. "We shall meet often, I think!"

Four days later, Mark asked me to marry him.

We were alone in the drawing room in the hour before sunset. The Square was stained with the glow of it. We had stood very silently by the window for a long time before Mark spoke. When he did, he said four words, "I love you, Elizabeth."

My heart did not leap; I did not even feel a wild joy. It was strange. All I felt was the inevitability of it, that from the very beginning my life in this house had been coursing towards this end. It had been my private hell that, loving him, I faced the possibility that he had killed Helen. And a greater hell that, had he been branded a murderer, I could not have stopped loving.

I turned to him. He was watching my eyes in that way he had. I knew that he had his answer without my speaking a word. He drew me towards him.

"My dearest Elizabeth!"

For a moment I withstood his arms. So short a time ago James had told me he loved me. I spared him a thought. James! But he had Kenny. And I was not for him.

I moved towards Mark and closed my eyes as he kissed me.

Moments or hours or aeons later, grandmother found us together.

Mark turned to her. "We are in love," he said.

She neither smiled nor congratulated us. Instead, she made a swift, dismissing gesture with her hand.

"Go quickly, both of you, and tell your Aunt Geraldine before it is too late."

Mark took my hand and we went together into the big, shadowed room.

Aunt Geraldine's eyes were closed and her face had the curious remoteness of the very ill. She would not hear us, I thought in despair, if we told her. It was already too late.

Mark bent down. He took my hand and laid it firmly with his own over Aunt Geraldine's.

"Elizabeth and I are in love," he told her in slow, clear tones.

All my life I shall remember that, although she did not open her eyes, her face changed in some subtle way, settling into a mask of peace.

James and Doctor Rowlins said afterwards that she had been in a coma for two days, that she could not have heard what we said. But I know she did. And Mark knew it, too.

I think it was because he wanted to do a last act for her sake that he immediately began to study medicine. We had been married two years when he took his final degree and became a qualified doctor. We were living in his house in Manchester Square and even my grandmother came across for the celebration. James was there, too, and Lucia Emsworth came.

She was now one of my closest friends and for a moment, we found ourselves alone together at the party. Wine glass in hand, I stood by the mantelshelf and told her, laughingly, how resentful

I had been whenever I had seen her yellow carriage outside Mark's house.

She smiled; she was looking lovely with topaz and diamonds round her smooth, bare throat. "If I could not have Mark for myself, there is no one I would rather have seen him marry!"

"I shall never understand why he chose me, when you—" I broke off, shaking my head.

She turned me round to face the mirror. In it, I could see all the people in the room reflected. But I sought and found Mark. His mirrored eyes smiled at me.

Falcon's Shadow

I

THE TWO SUITCASES on the rack opposite me still looked new. I had used them so seldom since they had been given me three years ago on my twenty-first birthday. I was a nurse in a great London hospital, and I had very little time for traveling.

The cases were dark blue, aircraft weight, and the initials stamped crosswise in the corners looked rather like two rows of grinning golden teeth. "L.B." Loran Brant. A name given me by strangers at my christening; a name by which my own mother and father, if they heard it, wouldn't know me.

That was the reason for this journey I was taking. I was on my way to try to find my parents, my real roots. Only I faced the forlorn fact that I scarcely knew where to begin. I had only one fact to go on. I had been born in Dorset, near the seaport town of Arlesthorne, and if I could trace my parents from that slender clue, it would be a miracle—and miracles didn't happen.

The deep hush of the country outside the halted train seeped into the compartment where I sat alone. I leaned forward, looking over the green fields towards the gray, distant hairline of the sea.

Saxon Magna could not now be far away. The train began to crawl forward, rattling over points into Lark Abbas. I glanced up at the abbey ruin dominating the town.

It was an unimportant little station and our stop was brief. I sat there, impatient for the train to start again. Then, as the whistle blew, a small figure dashed through the ticket barrier.

My compartment was directly opposite. Flying feet raced towards me; short arms reached up and wrenched at the door.

The train was already moving and the old stationmaster

shouted. Frantic fingers clung to the handle of the compartment door and turned it. An orange from the child's basket rolled onto the platform. For a flash it seemed that the train would drag her along with it. Then, swiftly, I bent down and with both hands hauled the child into the carriage.

"That was a very silly thing to do," I began, catching the swinging door and slamming it shut. "You might . . ." And then I stopped.

It was no child who sat opposite me, breathing hard and laughing. It was a miniature woman of about thirty. Every limb was tiny but perfectly formed; her skin was tough and suntanned. She was a doll of a woman with eyes that seemed to fill her face and long, tossed hair, raven black in the sunlight. She wore an old tweed jacket, much too large for her, and a wide, bright blue skirt. Her sandals were kicked and dirty and in her ears she wore enormous and beautiful gold earrings.

"I don't ever know the time," she said with a hint of dialect.

"You might have been dragged along the platform and badly injured," I said reprovingly. "You could even have been killed."

The woman laughed. "Not me. I won't be dying for a long time yet." She spoke like a little gypsy foretelling her own future.

I watched her scrabble in her basket among the oranges, windfall apples and a limp and browning cauliflower. But the poverty of the contents made me self-conscious about my curiosity and I looked away.

The train gathered speed, and the silence between us lasted for a few minutes. Then the woman said:

"You don't live in these parts, miss?"

"No."

"You going all the way to Exeter?"

She was being curious, but it didn't matter. If she wanted to talk, I wanted to talk too, in order to stop my own thoughts.

"I'm going to Saxon Magna," I explained. "To stay with . . . friends." I found the inaccurate word hard to say.

"You'll be staying with Mrs. Cranmer up there at Saxon Manor."

I said in surprise, "Why, yes, as a matter of fact I am. But how did you know?"

The woman smiled. Her little pointed teeth were very white.

"These be tiny villages around this part, and lonely. Folks know everyone's business."

"I suppose they do," I admitted.

"And *I* know Mrs. Cranmer." There was a wily look in her eyes. "You a great friend of hers?" She asked the question as a child would, with frank inquisitiveness.

"No. In fact, I've never met her. She was a friend of my . . . father's." Again, I stumbled over the last word. It was one I was no longer able to say with ease.

The woman's bright black eyes regarded me. "You haven't never been to Saxon Magna before?" she asked.

"This is my very first visit."

"It's wild around them parts." She sat nodding her head like a mandarin toy. "I know. I've lived there all my life. Maybe you won't like it. Maybe you'll wish you'd never come."

"Why do you say that?" I demanded, startled.

"I only said 'maybe.'" She sat swinging her little legs which could not reach the carriage floor. "I meant no offense, miss. Only, I know people around here. I know all they know and lots they don't. I know . . ." Her eyes, staring into the distance, seemed to be looking at secrets.

I waited a moment and then urged, "You know what?"

The woman shook her head. "Never you mind. Secrets is best kept."

Her voice was so brisk and final that I decided our conversation, with its intriguing hints on her part, would get us nowhere. I turned back to the book I had been reading.

I had borrowed it from the Marylebone Public Library because I felt I should know something in advance about the corner of Dorset where I would be staying. I had already read that Saxon Magna had shrunk with the centuries and was now merely a village, that Black Ash Heath on its borders was wild and uncultivated.

I found my place in the book and looked first at a photograph of tall cliffs, outstretched like wings. The caption read "Falcon Point." Beneath it was one of those strange stories that scatter the coast of Britain.

In the winter of 1910, during a hurricane, the sea stormed into submerged caves causing a landslide. A church, an inn and a row of cottages crashed into the raging water. At certain times, when the wind was soft and from the south, legend had it that the sound of bells ringing could be heard from the belfry of the sunken church.

I looked up from my reading, aware that the train was slowing down again. The sea was nearer now, and I saw a high, jagged outline similar, from this angle, to the cliffs in the photograph.

"Is that Falcon Point?" I asked the doll-woman.

She followed my gaze, then swung her head around and stared at me, her eyes sharp and suspicious.

"What d'you want to know about that place for?" she flung at me.

Nonplussed, I tapped the book lying on my lap. "I was merely interested: I've just been reading about it."

"Funny." She surveyed me. "You askin' about that place and going to stay with Mrs. Cranmer!"

Her manner put me again on the defensive. "What's funny about it?"

"Could be you'll find out, could be you won't," she said disinterestedly and craned her neck as the train slid into a station. "Trenthide. This is where I get out. Your station's next." She collected her basket and slid to the floor.

Her little grubby fingers were on the door handle. As the train stopped she turned and the strong sunlight made her squint so that her eyes became glittering slits.

"You been kind to me, miss. I'll tell you something." She leaned towards me. "Be careful. Don't you get too nosy about Falcon Point if you know what's good for you."

My hand shot out to detain her, but she wriggled free and jumped down on the platform.

"Wait, please!" I called.

But she took no notice. I leaned back in my corner and watched her without much interest. I decided, matter-of-factly, that it was more than likely the woman had warned me to keep clear of that patch of coast because she thought I was here on holiday. She could have supposed that I was prepared to brave the cool autumn seas and go bathing. There were probably dangerous currents around Falcon Point.

The train plunged through dark woods. In five or ten minutes

I would arrive. I glanced at myself in my compact mirror and decided that I had better not appear before strangers looking shiny and travel-stained. First impressions were important. I had never met the woman who was to be my hostess and I badly wanted her to like me because I needed help from her.

I collected my handbag and went along the corridor to wash. My hair was always difficult to comb and I tugged at it. It was dark and heavy and I wore it sweeping back from a side parting. It needed quite a bit of discipline to keep it neat under the cap I wore at the hospital where I was a third year nurse. My eyes were gray and I had high cheekbones that gave me, when I was tired, mauve shadows under my eyes. I drew lipstick across my mouth. It took up quite an area of my face and I remembered my father's old cook-housekeeper saying once, when I was a little girl watching her pare apples for a pie, "If you open that mouth of yours much wider I'll pop this green apple in. Then see if you don't get a pain in your tummy."

I turned on the tap and ran cold water over my hands, wondering if in a week's time I would be returning on this very train with nothing accomplished.

And if that was so, what would it matter? *I am me*, I reasoned, *answerable to myself, not to any parents, for what I make of my life*. But the words mocked me, and still, like a flame inside me (other people, I supposed, would call it an obsession), was the urge to find out who I was: my name . . . my parents . . . the world into which I had been born.

I dried my hands and brushed dust from my suit. Pinned to the lapel on my coat I wore a large topaz. The stone hung from a triangle of gold scrollwork by a small gold ring. On the deep yellow surface of the stone was carved a strange bird. It wore a high crown, its wings were upstretched, and it rode a spear. I had been told that it was a replica of the legendary phoenix—the bird that rises from its ashes. It was the one thing I had possessed since I was a child, and although I would have hated to lose it, I hadn't yet got around to taking it to the jewelers to have the join in the ring soldered in order to secure the stone.

It was given me when I was seven years old and I was told that it had been a gift at my birth. At seven, it made no impression on me—it neither sparkled nor jingled. So it was no hardship to put it away. I had forgotten it for years. Then, when I came upon it only a month ago, I decided I would wear it as a lapel ornament.

When I returned to my compartment I no longer wanted to read. The train was passing through a copse of spruce. Gazing into the blackish-green depths, I saw them as a backcloth against which lay spread the shocking, immediate past.

One picture, the crux of my whole predicament, was spotlighted in my mind. Even the newspapers had used black and prominent type for their headline.

FAMOUS SURGEON DIES IN CAR CRASH

and in smaller type,

DAUGHTER ESCAPES WITH SLIGHT INJURIES

In the solitude of the train a helpless compulsion took me back to that evening nearly six weeks ago I had been trying so desperately to forget.

I was in the car, sitting by the side of the man I believed to be my father as he swung the Rover around a serpentine bend in the road. I could see, as I had seen a hundred times since then, his hands suddenly wrenching the wheel; I could hear again the hissing of the tires, the moment's terror, the sound of my own scream. Because of a misjudgment of inches, Richard Brant, senior surgeon of the Marazon Hospital in London, lay dead beside me in a wrecked car.

Save for a wrenching pain in my back, I was uninjured. Trapped but conscious, I had been aware of everything that had happened —of cars stopping to offer help, of the police, the ambulance. "What happened?" they asked. What happened? Just that on an unrestricted area, Richard Brant had taken a double bend with his usual impatience, had skidded and met a giant elm head on.

If I had been knocked unconscious at the time, the whole thing would not have been imprinted so dreadfully on my mind.

My own comparatively slight injury, a strained back, had meant that I was on sick leave for some weeks from St. Osyth's Hospital where I was a third year nurse. I remained at home in the Wimpole Street house with Adéle, my stepmother. She was blonde and pretty and without a mean thought in her charming head.

She was stunned and in no state to cope with all those poignant duties that follow a death—the letters from sympathizers, the sorting of papers, the dispatch of clothes to a charity. She had left all those things to me.

My hardest task had been the clearing of the great Queen Anne desk in the study. Old letters, old bills had all to be glanced at before being torn up. It took me two full mornings and then, on the second day, I found at the back of a drawer a sealed envelope. Inside was an ancient photograph cut from some newspaper. My father, as a young man, stood at the door of a house and by his side was my mother, holding a baby.

The caption read: "Mr. Richard Brant, the surgeon, and his wife with the baby girl they have adopted. They are calling her by the unusual name of Loran."

I stared at the blurred faces of the two people and for a few moments I couldn't think. Then the truth hit me, leaving me raw and shaken. I was not living in this house because I belonged here. Richard and Irene Brant, the people whom I had believed to be my mother and father, had picked me out of an anonymous cot and taken me home with them. I, Loran Brant, was as alien in that tall, dignified Wimpole Street house as a changeling.

The cutting was yellow with age and at the top I saw part of the newspaper's name: . . . *thorne Gazette*. It was not a London paper. Where, then, had I been found? A hospital? An orphanage? Was I the product of a wild and hopeless love? Of some gay hour after a party, with empty champagne glasses, a crumpled dance dress and a fallen rose on the hearth? But the wild romantic imaginings of that last picture didn't soften the shock. Perhaps if I had not still been suffering from the aftereffects of the car accident, this second shock might not have struck so deeply.

As it was, I sat there holding a yellow cutting in such tight, tense fingers that my nails tore the paper in the center.

Why had I been allowed to grow up with a false sense of my own belonging? Why hadn't I been told years ago that I was adopted? They could have explained to me, while I was young, that they had chosen me out of all the babies they had seen because I was the one they loved most. As a child, I would have accepted that and been secure in being loved. As I grew older I would be so used to the fact that I would not even question. Now, coming upon the truth by accident, I felt certain that there must be some shameful reason why I had not been told. I tried to push my suspicions away, but they nagged and twisted in my mind. Could there be something sinister behind my adoption? Not just the pathos of an unthinkable physical act, but something more catastrophic, something that it would be better for me not to know?

Was that why it had been kept so secret? In case I should ask awkward questions? And suddenly, filled with a sense of loneliness, of ache and bewilderment, I knew that I was going to do just what my adopted parents had obviously hoped I would not do. I was going to find out why I had been given away at my birth.

One thing, however, was now clear. My "mother" had loved me. Until my seventh birthday, when she had died, I had been happy. But Richard Brant—it was now terribly easy to think of him by his own cold name—had probably never wanted me. I supposed he had merely indulged his childless wife's longing in adopting me. Certainly he had shown me neither love nor interest. It was common knowledge that he was a dedicated surgeon. The hospital was his beloved place; his hands were his most treasured possession.

I was twenty when he surprised everyone by marrying again. I never quite understood why Adèle adored him, save that for all her prettiness she was not particularly intelligent and she had a childlike awe and wonder towards learning. Perhaps, for all his coldness, his preoccupation, Richard was capable of a passion which only Adèle knew. So far as I was concerned, Adèle was like a charming acquaintance from whom I could never ask much or expect much. She had her own friends and her own life—Richard had forced that on her. I knew that she was planning to sell the Wimpole Street house and take an apartment for herself. I would then have to make my home in the nurses' wing at the hospital. I would find myself at odd times wondering what, among my possessions, I would take there and what to get rid of or store. There was something rather sad in having to be ruthless about things with which I'd grown up—the rosewood desk, the pink and green Chinese carpet, even the bed I'd slept in and dreamed in.

That morning I went to find Adèle and asked her if she knew I'd been adopted. She said yes she had, but added that Richard hadn't discussed it with her.

That I could well believe. Richard discussed nothing with anyone; that was perhaps why he had no friends—nor, for that matter, seemed to want them. It was also why the few relatives he had had drifted out of his life years ago.

Of one thing I was certain. I had not been kept in ignorance about my adoption because of Richard's genuine affection for me. I couldn't remember a time when I had gone to him for comfort, for a loving hug when I was little. I was always shy of him so that sometimes I had stammered when he spoke, looking down at me with that cold, withdrawn expression. I wondered, now, how he would have behaved had I really been his daughter.

I glanced at my watch. As I did so, an express train tore by, its whistle screaming, its speed rattling the compartment. I started so violently that I knew that shock was still with me.

I closed my eyes. During the week following my discovery, I had sought everywhere for someone who might know about me.

My letters poured to Richard's few relatives in Scotland, to his bank, his solicitor, in fact to everyone who was in touch with his affairs. People were kind and polite, but nobody told me anything. Richard's fatherly solicitor advised me firmly to leave matters alone. "Once a child learns the name of his real parents, he can't rest till he finds them. It nearly always makes for unhappiness. Leave it; leave it, Loran."

He was right, I supposed, but it made no difference.

I knew that Irene, who had come to England from South Africa as a young girl and trained for the stage, had no known relatives still alive, so I drew a blank on both sides of the family. It seemed, as the days went by, that I might very easily have been found under the proverbial gooseberry bush for all the knowledge anyone had of me.

The letter that changed everything came a week after Richard's death. It was signed "Charlotte Cranmer," and as I read it I remembered one with the same signature which I had found in Richard's desk. It had been written to him a year ago after my success in winning the St. Osyth Hospital's Annual Nurse's Award. The letter had expressed pleasure "that Loran is doing so well in a branch of your own profession." It finished with an invitation to the three of us, Adèle, Richard and myself, to stay with Mrs. Cranmer in Dorset.

I had known nothing of the letter or the invitation. I had never even heard of Charlotte Cranmer. It was both typical of Richard not to have passed on the congratulations to me and, with his hoarder's instinct, to have kept the letter.

Now, in this note of sympathy to Adèle, Mrs. Cranmer repeated her invitation:

"I had known Richard for thirty years, although I hadn't seen him for a long time. He was a friend of my husband's when they were both at Oxford."

I read the letter with its condolences over twice. And, as I did so, something crept out of the past and became linked with the present.

Once, when I was a little girl, Irene had been showing me colored photographs on a calendar. One was of Corfe Castle. She had said:

"You were born between that castle and Arlesthorne, which is a big seaport on the Dorset coast."

I wished desperately now that I had been more interested.

I remembered, too, part of the name of the newspaper where my baby photograph had appeared—". . . *thorne Gazette*." And now Mrs. Cranmer's letterheading read: "Saxon Manor, Saxon Magna, near Arlesthorne, Dorset."

Arlesthorne. . . .

These were the three strong reasons for writing to her. I wrote on an impulse and therefore without restraint. After all, I had nothing to lose. I told her of my discovery and begged her to tell me if she knew anything about my adoption. My pen raced over the pages.

"I just feel," I wrote, "that I've got to know why I was given away. I want to know about my real parents. Please don't think I'm being hysterical about this. I suppose everyone wants to belong somewhere, to know he has real roots, not borrowed ones. I keep asking myself, 'Who am I?' Is there anything you can tell me to help me to find out? I'd be so grateful for the smallest lead."

I didn't pause to read the letter over in case second thoughts and shyness might induce me to tear it up. I sealed it, stamped it and went out at half past eleven that night to post it at the box on the corner of Harley Street.

Mrs. Cranmer's reply came three days later.

"I can tell you little, I'm afraid, about yourself. When Richard came down here to lecture at the Arlesthorne General Hospital he brought Irene to see me. I met her, in all, just three times. Then a year later my husband met Richard in Wigmore Street and he told him they had adopted a baby girl. We went abroad soon after that for three years and lost touch. It was six years later that I read of Irene's death. My husband wrote to Richard but he had no reply. That is all I can remember at the moment. If you would care to come down here for a visit, I should be delighted to see you and perhaps I can rake my memory for something that might help you."

I accepted her invitation by return of post. If I did not go immediately, then I might not be able to go at all, for in another few weeks I would be back nursing and there would be no time for journeys to Dorset.

The few days before I left London were filled with a restless impatience. Nothing was more important than my meeting with Charlotte Cranmer.

Temporarily I lost my longing to get back to St. Osyth's and nursing. I was going to find my real parents, and in searching for them I would be searching for my own identity.

II

SAXON MAGNA could not now be more than a few minutes away.

I was all things at once: excited, doubting, apprehensive. Then common sense steadied me. The question was not what would I find out about myself, but, would I find anything at all?

When the train stopped I lowered the window, reached down and opened the door.

A solitary, skinny, gray-haired man in breeches stood peering at the train. As I stepped onto the platform he came forward.

"Miss Brant?"

"Yes."

"I be Josh, Mrs. Cranmer's man." He didn't smile, but his glance was friendly. He picked up my two cases and walked with me to the ticket barrier.

"You'd a slow journey, I reckon, miss. These branch line trains bain't like your main line expresses." His *a*'s were broad, his speech slow as though, for him, tomorrow was as good as today for finishing what he had to say.

"It was quite good, really," I said. "We came almost non-stop to Salisbury."

Outside the station the moor and sea air were clean and sharp. A young man leaned against an emerald green sports car watching me. He was slightly built and his hair was so light that it was almost silver. He had unusually regular, deeply molded features and his eyes were very light and sparkling with amused curiosity.

He tossed his cigarette away and came towards us. "Good evening, Josh."

"Evenin'." Josh spoke curtly, looking ahead of him.

"Let me have one of those." The man reached to take a suitcase. "You get the trunk open."

"Do 'ee think I bain't able t' manage?" Josh scowled and shrugged free.

"All right, my old ox! Keep your burdens." The young man laughed and reached for my cream coat. "I like being useful," he said and his eyes were merry.

The coat slid from my arm before I could retort that I didn't need an amateur porter either. He matched his step with mine and Josh marched on ahead, every line of his back stiff with offense.

"Since you'll have to know everyone in the village," said the man by my side, "I'll introduce myself. I'm Martin Cavall, and as you see, I'm not popular. That's because I'm new here. They don't like 'furriners.' You're Miss Brant, aren't you?"

"I haven't a clue what my claim to fame must be," I said laughing, "but you're the second person who seems to know me."

"The second?" He looked about him as though expecting the first to materialize out of the empty space around us.

"Someone in the train who got out at the last station," I explained.

"Oh, well, that's life for you in a remote village. Nothing is secret. Well, almost nothing!" he added thoughtfully.

Josh had stowed away my suitcases. He was still scowling as he held open the back door of the big, ancient car.

"I'd rather sit with you," I said.

The scowl disappeared. When he smiled the brown, grizzled face lit up. He settled me in the passenger seat and Martin Cavall laid my coat in the back of the car.

"We'll be meeting again, Miss Brant." He waved an airy hand and walked away.

I waited for Josh to say something about him, but he climbed into the driving seat, started the car and clutched the wheel with his brown, knotted hands without saying a word.

We had driven about three hundred yards down the road when the emerald car roared past us.

"Proper daft, 'e be, drivin' like old Horney hisself."

"Old Horney?"

"The divil."

"If he came to meet someone on the train, he was disappointed," I said.

"He be come to look at 'ee, miss."

"Then he must be very badly in need of something to do," I retorted in amusement.

"'E be a strange one. Doan't ever know why 'e come to our village, thaat I doan't."

The car's speedometer never registered more than twenty-five miles on that journey. We drove between thick hedges and past dark woods. Presently we came to vast open land studded with clumps of salt-burned trees and gorse and bracken.

"Black Ash," Josh said succinctly.

I looked with interest at the heath I had read about in the library book I still clutched.

"It's huge," I said.

"It goes right up to they hills."

We drove through a narrow street of cottages built of Purbeck stone.

"Saxon Magna," said Josh. "Manor's over yonder." He jabbed a crooked finger towards the horizon.

A dappled horse dozed in the shafts of an empty cart.

"It's all very peaceful," I said, "after London."

"Oh, aye," he answered noncommittally.

Yet the peace was only in the quiet. We had passed the village and were on the open heath. I looked at the wind-racked trees, and the torn gorse stretched below a sky raked with angry vermilion.

The car slowed down before two stone pillars that had once supported gates.

"Went in t'war," said Josh, and he drove between them.

There was a bend in the lime avenue. We rounded it and then I saw the house.

It stood in a semicircle of great chestnuts which threw conical shadows over the ill-kept lawn, the few flower beds and the heavy mass of rhododendron and laurel. The house itself was of gray stone, three storied with one wing thrusting into a cluster of bushes. The windows were tall and blank and closed. The huge door could have belonged to a fortress. I was staring up at the uncompromising house when Josh said, "Go 'ee up an' ring t'bell, miss."

I walked up the five steps to the front door and lifted my hand. Before I could press the bell, there came a piercing shriek from behind me. I swung around. Another shriek followed. Josh came towards me, chuckling.

"Doan' 'ee let 'em scare you. 'Tis only they peacocks."

And then I saw them, two beautiful strutting birds gliding out of the laurel bushes into a last pool of sunlight on the lawn. The cock spread its tail. It was beginning to suffer from autumn molting, but patches of color still burned, emerald and sapphire and gold. They had both turned their small, imperious heads to look at me.

"Loran. Loran Brant."

I hadn't heard the door open. I turned. A short woman with white curly hair and dark brown eyes held out both hands to me. She was, I guessed, in her sturdy, country-bred sixties.

"Mrs. Cranmer?"

She nodded. "I hope the peacocks didn't alarm you," she laughed. "I've been looking forward so much to your visit that I'd hate you to turn and run away." She had a voice so clear and light that it could have been a young woman's. Her warm hands drew me into a large hall made gloomy by three stained glass windows through which the outside light came, brooding as in a cathedral.

I was aware of a tall woman hovering in the shadows. Mrs. Cranmer caught sight of her too and called her forward.

"This is my housekeeper and friend, Miss Ferrier—Ferry to us all. She'll tell you how impatiently I've been waiting for you. We have so few visitors here."

The woman Ferry came forward. She was as thin as a beanpole with gaunt bones that stuck out at her neck and wrists and elbows. Her face was very flat except for a sharp nose and her eyes were quite emotionless. She said in a voice entirely without expression, "How do you do, Miss Brant."

"Isn't it lovely to have someone young around again?" said Mrs. Cranmer.

"Yes, madam. It's very pleasant."

I decided that her flat answer was purely mechanical and that she wasn't in the least delighted to have me there.

"I'll let you know when we want tea. Come, Loran."

The room to the left into which Mrs. Cranmer led me was large and lofty. The last of the sun's rays glinted between the tree branches shafting onto shabby walls and fine old furniture. In a large grate, logs burned redly and a man stood very still beside it, watching me.

"Let me introduce you to Sarne. Sarne Algar," Mrs. Cranmer said. "He owns the farm which was once part of the estate. This is Loran."

I looked up at him. He was tallish, tanned and strongly built. His hair was a rich chestnut and looked as though he had got it wet and had just rubbed it dry. It curled a little. Blue-gray eyes met mine.

As I shook hands, I had an impression which I had only felt once before, when I had met a Rhodesian tobacco planter, of tremendous stored vitality and at the same time of a curious, almost arrogant, aloneness. I could explain it no other way about the Rhodesian. I could explain it no other way about Sarne Algar.

"You must be a lucky traveler." His eyes were disconcertingly direct. "We've had three days' incessant rain. And now you've come and it's a fine evening and a good forecast for tomorrow."

"If that's the way you want it, I'm glad," I said. "I never know when farmers want rain and when they want the sun."

"We're all King Canutes," he replied. "We all want to rule the elements."

"That's an argument for later," said Mrs. Cranmer lightly.

"Loran is probably longing to get to her room and freshen up. Then we'll have tea." She laid a hand on my arm, calling over her shoulder. "Oh, Sarne, let the dogs in for me, will you?"

We were crossing the hall when the doorbell rang.

"I'll answer it," Mrs. Cranmer called to Ferry in the kitchen.

She left my side with quick, light steps. I waited by the curved staircase and thought what a curious smell the hall had, like an old church impregnated with the odor of ancient wood and dusty hassocks. Not that this hall would have any dust, I thought, remembering Ferry.

A girl had entered the house.

Mrs. Cranmer greeted her with an affectionate hand on her arm.

"I'm so glad you could manage to get off in time to have tea with us." She turned to me. "This is Gillian Tasker. Her parents were close friends of mine. And, of course, you've guessed, Gillian. This is Loran."

As I watched the girl cross the shadowy hall, my impression of her was so curiously unreal that I blinked to clear my eyes of any mistiness. Only when she stood in front of me and gave me her slightly limp handshake was I able to understand that blurred, colorless impression.

Her hair was of an odd cinnamon tint, sweeping back from a low, very white forehead. Her light eyes had mauve shadows beneath them and she wore a very pale lipstick. Her skirt and sweater were both well-shaped, but beige was most certainly not her color. She looked as though she were dressed and made up to merge with a landscape like a fawn.

"I slipped away early," she said to me, and her voice was, surprisingly, a little hard, "because I wanted to meet you."

"I'm just taking Loran to her room," Mrs. Cranmer said. "Sarne is in the sitting room. Go along in, I'll be down in a minute." She began to climb the stairs and I followed.

Everything about that big, lofty house had the same air of old luxury and encroaching dilapidation. Even the stairs dipped and sloped as though too many generations had trod them.

When we reached the landing, Mrs. Cranmer paused a moment for breath.

"Gillian works at the Arlesthorne Public Library." She was panting and I wondered if she had a bad heart. "I particularly wanted you to meet her because it'll be nice for you to have someone young around. I'm hoping, you see,"—she cast a smiling, sideways look at me—"that you'll stay some time. It's a tonic to me to have someone young about the place."

"Don't make me too happy," I warned, "or I won't want to go. And the hospital isn't giving me unlimited sick leave."

Mrs. Cranmer gave a small chuckle and opened a door leading from the gallery that ran around two sides of the house. The room into which I walked was large with long windows. The shabbiness was well-hidden by its homeliness. There were flowers in a blue and white ginger jar; paperback books stood on a shelf, and a tin that obviously contained biscuits and a little transistor radio were on the bedside table.

"Everything," I said looking around, "for my comfort. You're being so very kind."

"It's bribery." There was a touch of wistfulness in her light tone. "As I've told you, I want you to stay as long as you can. Though there's nothing much for you to do here. Of course, if you had come in the summer there would have been bathing."

"At Falcon Point?" I don't know what made me ask that.

She was at the window. She jerked her head over her shoulder and gave me a strange, long look. She began to fidget with her hands.

"You know something about this coast?"

"Only what I read coming down in the train."

At once I saw her relax.

"It's good bathing in the bay immediately below here. Sarne's children almost live on the beach in the summer. If you lean out, you can see the sea from this window. It's just across the edge of the heath. And over there, through the trees, is Sarne's farmhouse." She was talking hard and I couldn't stop a suspicion that she wanted to cover up my mention of Falcon Point with as many words as she could.

My suitcases stood on a carved oak chest. I wondered why she didn't leave me but continued to wander around the room touching the green and white padded counterpane, the asters in the blue vase. I felt she wanted to say something she felt was important and did not know how to begin.

"It's kind of you to ask me to stay," I began, as though I didn't think her loitering strange. "I feel that perhaps, down here, I can sort myself out."

"And meet new people. That's part of a cure after any shock," she said. Then she stopped fidgeting around the room and I knew I had given her the lead she wanted.

"About meeting people for the first time," she began, conversationally, "I always feel it makes everything easier and saves embarrassing moments if one knows something about them beforehand. I'm thinking of Sarne mostly. You see, he's like my own son." Her voice became soft. "His parents died in a cholera epidemic in Persia and I brought him up from the age of twelve. He has a native's obsessive love of Dorset, even greater than mine." She straightened a bedside rug with her foot and moved across the room to the door. I thought she was going, but with her hand on the painted door handle she again hesitated. She was looking at me curiously, almost shyly, as though there was still something she wanted to tell me that was proving difficult to say.

I stood politely, expectantly, hugging my coat.

"Sarne has three small children, Marnie, Simon and Nina. His wife isn't with him." She stopped and flashed me an uncertain look. "You're bound to hear about it from someone in the village so it's better if I tell you. Sarne's wife disappeared one night nearly a year ago and nothing has been heard of her since."

"Oh," I said inadequately. "You mean she walked out and left them? Just like that?"

"It's the only explanation, though we all thought she adored her children. The whole thing is like a cloud over the village. It's so long ago, yet the whispers, the gossip, the horrible insinuations go on."

"They'll die down." I smiled at her. "Just give them time."

"They might, perhaps, if only the police would leave us alone."

"The police?" I asked, startled.

She nodded. "As the months go by, you get to thinking it's all over. You think: she's gone and Sarne can remake his life. And then back he comes—that policeman, Inspector Gray, I mean—to ask another little seemingly inconsequential question, to open the wound again for us all."

"But why keep questioning? Hasn't anyone any idea where Mrs. Algar is?"

"None. That's what's so terrible. Sarne's children think their mother has gone away because she is ill. I think I should also tell you . . ." She stopped abruptly, flashed me a look and seemed to fold herself in. With a smile that was obviously forced, she went on. "But I won't bother you with any more talk. The rest is—unimportant, anyway. I'll leave you now to tidy up, my dear. The bathroom is two doors along. Come down when you're ready and we'll have tea. There's no hurry."

I don't know why, as she closed the door, I felt that what she had checked herself saying had been very important indeed—too important, in fact, on second thoughts, to tell to a stranger.

III

THE DEEP SILENCE that spread over the room when Mrs. Cranmer left had a sound of its own, a kind of rhythmic beat. Only once, when I had washed and made up my face, was the hush broken. Somewhere, not so far away, came the lonely half-bark, half-braying, of a dog.

I unpacked only a few essentials, kicked off my shoes and put on dark red leather pumps. I was excited, wondering whether Mrs. Cranmer had managed to recall any point, however small, about my adoption. I'd know tonight. Perhaps by this time tomorrow I'd stand in this very place, facing the antique triple mirror, and know who I was. Perhaps I'd be very happy . . . or very sad.

When I returned to the sitting room three faces were turned towards me. Mrs. Cranmer and Gillian sat together on the great, shabby settee; Sarne, standing by the mantelshelf, moved forward to draw up a chair for me.

Two boxer dogs at Mrs. Cranmer's feet thrusting sentimental heads on her lap. They had to be introduced formally and gravely.

"This is Juliet and this one is Viola. They're silly names to give dogs, aren't they, but my husband was a Shakespeare fan. You've already heard the peacocks. Ever since I was married there have been peacocks at the manor. I hope they won't disturb you, but they don't screech much."

"I won't mind, anyway," I assured her.

Lamps had been lit. Everywhere about me was the friendly untidiness of scattered newspapers, books, an open and tumbled needlework box and a big pile of something wrapped in a polythene bag. The cold, formal façade of the house was softened inside by its mistress's warm, slightly haphazard personality.

Ferry brought in tea, set the tray on the inlaid table in front of Mrs. Cranmer, and went out again without once raising her eyes. The dogs drooled at the old-fashioned cakestand.

While we had tea I discovered that Mrs. Cranmer was "Aunt Charlotte" to Gillian, as well as Sarne. Although there was no relationship between them, it seemed to draw them into a close little circle. Once Mrs. Cranmer must have been extremely attractive. She was still pretty to look at; the lines of her face were gentle and uptilted as though she were a naturally happy person. But there was something about her that was not quite in keeping with this impression, a kind of shadow, a darting restlessness in her brown eyes.

Gillian put questions to me about London. What cinemas and theaters had I been to? Did I live right in town? I felt that she was being polite rather than particularly interested.

Sarne asked if I knew Dorset well.

"I've never been here before."

"They've spoiled parts of it," he said frowning. "They've brought down their factories and their radar stations. But this part is still untouched, thank God."

"Sarne is medieval," Mrs. Cranmer laughed. "He'd have feudal ways if he could."

"Maybe they weren't so bad, at that! A good landlord looked after his people, was employer and lawyer, doctor and confessor to them. Nowadays we have to spend our time filling in forms and leave welfare to the State."

Gillian leaned forward. Her pale oval face looked unreal in the lamplight.

"But the landlords could be bad ones. Now, at least the workers have free medical advice and a wonderfully efficient police force which solves most crimes. There aren't many . . ." Her voice jerked to a sudden stop.

The silence was immediately charged with hidden tremors. Something significant had been flung, pulling and tightening, between the three people sitting there.

I looked first of all at Sarne. He leaned back in his chair, a cigarette between his fingers, his eyes hidden by tanned lids, his dark brows drawn—in anger or in thought, I couldn't tell which. Mrs. Cranmer was fidgeting with the teapot, pouring in unneeded hot water. Her lips were a tight line. And Gillian sat frozen in her unnatural position, leaning forward, chin jutting out, awkward, hand raised to make her point.

The curious stagey moment held. I found myself searching frantically for a topic of conversation. Before I could do so, something moved outside the French windows. A huge dog rose from the darkening terrace and turned its great head and looked in at the windows.

Instantly, noticing my startled gaze, Sarne glanced over his shoulder.

"Don't go by appearances," he said. "It really *is* a dog you see there and not something escaped from a circus. He's a Great Dane—and a bit outsize at that!"

I felt they were all relieved by the diversion.

"Let him come in," Mrs. Cranmer urged.

Sarne went to the window and opened it.

The dog entered slowly, muscles rippling under his bronze coat. Sarne slid a finger through the heavy brass-studded collar and led him over to me.

"Meet him, Loran. He'll be your friend for life if I say so."

"He's a very unusual color," I began, pushing the jealous boxers out of the way and fondling the great head.

"He's come from a rare species of the breed. They're much larger than the usual Great Danes and their coats are a deeper color. His name is Remus."

"The children love him," Mrs. Cranmer said with affection. "Loran must meet them, Sarne."

"Of course. Why waste time? Come and have lunch tomorrow, both of you. And Gillian too, if you can."

"I won't be able to get away. It's my Saturday for working full day." She glanced at her watch as she spoke. "I'll have to go now, Aunt Charlotte. I'm awfully sorry to break up the party—"

"My dear girl, you've only been here half an hour!"

"I have to catch the shop open. We only have two shops in our village," she explained to me, "and I want to give Monty a good supper tonight; he hasn't eaten much all day."

"It sounds," said Mrs. Cranmer briskly, "as though Gillian is going home to feed a cat or a budgerigar, doesn't it? Really," she turned with affectionate impatience to the girl by her side, "why can't Monty shop for you sometimes? He has nothing to do all day. You spoil him."

"He *is* my lodger," Gillian reminded her, "and if it weren't for him I wouldn't be able to keep the house on."

"Why do you bother when you could get a nice little apartment in Arlesthorne?"

"I don't want to leave here." The pale face became suddenly animated. "It's my home! Everything I . . . I love is here. Besides, I like looking after Monty. He's lonely and heaven knows, that son of his in Australia never bothers to write to him."

"It's your life, my dear," said Mrs. Cranmer evenly and rose. "I've got a jar of blackberry jam for you. Ferry made a lot last week. Come, and we'll fetch it."

Sarne hadn't spoken during the gentle brush between them. As they left the room, he came over to me and offered his cigarette case.

I refused, and as he lit his own I wandered to the fireplace. The shelf above it held an old-fashioned marble clock, two fine cloisonné vases and a small, lovely little porcelain dove. I leaned forward to look at it.

"It came from Copenhagen," Sarne said. "Do you know who gave it to Aunt Charlotte?"

I turned and looked at him questioningly.

"Your mother," he said.

My heart gave a sudden jerk.

"You knew my *mother*?" I began. Then I stopped. Deeply disappointed, I realized that he meant Irene.

Sarne missed the poignancy of the stressed word.

"Your parents went to Denmark one Easter and brought the dove back as a present for Aunt Charlotte. I remember your mother so very well although I only saw her twice. She was lovely, wasn't she?"

"Yes . . . yes she was. She died when I was seven." I turned from Sarne's steady gaze. Then glancing sideways, I looked at Sarne's reflected face.

How strange, I thought, that a mirrored face can look subtly different from the original. Shadows fell on his mirrored face making it a little more hawklike, not cruel exactly, but too strong, too savage.

I wondered whether my reflection in the mirror seemed different to him, too.

At that moment he raised his eyes to me. I tried to smile at him and couldn't.

There was a faint stir behind us. A voice said:

"I was told to come straight in."

We both swung around. I had a clear impression of a woman with black hair sweeping from a wide forehead, of a beautiful nose, straight and delicate, and greenish gold eyes focused on me. She wore an enormous coat of cornelian-colored wool so soft in texture, so fluffy, that I wondered what material could look so fragile and yet stand up to hard country wearing.

"Hello, Deborah," said Sarne.

She walked lightly across the room, her eyes on me all the time. Sarne introduced her—"Mrs. Millbrook," he said.

She was assessing me, my hair, my face, the suit I wore. I felt young and awkward and small before her.

"We heard you were coming. I wonder how you're going to like it here; it's the back of beyond, you know." Without waiting for my reply, she turned to Sarne: "I've stalled my car down by Withy Lane. It's usually quite easy to cross that runnel of water, but the rain these past few days has swollen it and I suppose I've got water in the carburetor or whatever bit of the engine doesn't like being flooded."

I noticed that when she spoke, she had a way of half closing her eyes. It gave her the look of a lovely sleepy cat. She turned back to me. "I know nothing about the insides of cars. I merely drive them."

I nodded vaguely, wondering who she was. Sarne's sister? Cousin?

"Women and cars have such a superficial relationship," Sarne remarked to me. Then he asked Deborah if she had left the lights on.

"Of course. And I'd better hurry back home or the children will be playing up to Chauncey. You know she can't discipline them! Chauncey," she explained to me, "is our Girl Friday—she does all the chores that I hate doing. But she can't manage people. She spoils them if she likes them. It's a work of art, anyway, to discipline three strong-willed children—four if you count their father. First you have to love them . . . then feed them . . ." Her eyes flicked, dancing and challenging, to Sarne's face.

He said slightly, "That could be a point for argument, but there's no time. Come along, I'd better do something about that car of yours before it gets towed away."

Deborah protested that no one was likely to use the lane that night, but Sarne moved to the door as Mrs. Cranmer re-entered the room. There was a kind of battle gleam in her brown eyes as she looked at Deborah, but her tone when she spoke was perfectly pleasant.

"What a nuisance about the car," she remarked coolly. "We shall have to do something sooner or later about that stream, you know, Sarne. I think the lake up at Coveyhyde is enlarging itself and if we're not careful we shall have a permanent hazard down at Withy Lane."

"I'll get on to the local authorities tomorrow about it," Sarne promised.

Deborah was moving out of our small circle through the door, wrapping her coat around her.

"You must come up and see the farm sometime," she said to me.

"Oh, they're coming to lunch tomorrow," Sarne said.

"Why, that's lovely. I hope the weather keeps fine so that you'll be able to see around the farm." She turned from me to Mrs. Cranmer. "You come to see us so seldom!"

"I do, don't I?" she agreed pleasantly. But the coolness remained in her eyes.

Sarne reached out his hand and Remus came and stood beside him as good-byes were said. He was a very still dog and his great head was almost on a level with Sarne's thigh. They stood quietly, and I had a feeling that the beautiful bronze animal understood his master better than many people did.

Mrs. Cranmer went into the hall with them. Left alone, I wandered across to the fire and held out my hands to the blaze.

The front door must have closed, for suddenly I was aware of silence outside. Then there were voices again and I gathered that Mrs. Cranmer was talking to Ferry just outside the sitting room door.

"Yes. Yes, one has to be careful. But it's cruel that it happened like this. She has come too late. *Much . . . too . . . late!*"

Although I had no idea of the meaning of her words, I knew they were talking about me.

"Well, my dear, and I hope you found all you wanted in your room." Mrs. Cranmer smiled at me from the doorway.

"You've thought of everything," I said gratefully.

"This is an absurd house, isn't it, for one old woman?" she observed, crossing to a corner cupboard. "In fact, it's a millstone around my neck."

"Oh, no," I cried. "It couldn't be, not if you have deep roots here. Nothing you love could ever be a burden."

"Oh, but it can." She took out two little sherry glasses, closed the cupboard and walked to the uncurtained window. "I'm too old to leave now. But I wish to heaven I'd uprooted myself years ago and taken Sarne with me, before he grew to love the place. We might have escaped so much."

I let the silence hold for a few moments, wondering what to say. I saw Mrs. Cranmer give a deep shudder and move from my window back to the table. "But it's no use getting introspective. Nothing can undo what's done. Now let's have a drink. I hope you like sherry."

I said I liked it very much.

"Is Mrs. Millbrook a relation of Sarne's?" I asked.

She set my drink down on the low coffee table and gave a dry, surprised laugh.

"My dear child, no. She runs his house and cooks superbly and looks after his children. Didn't he explain? Or no, I suppose there wasn't time. And it wouldn't amuse Deborah, anyway, to be introduced to a stranger as a housekeeper," she added dryly, and sat down in the big chair with the carved arms in which she had sat at tea. It seemed to be her special chair.

"I tried to sell this house after my husband died six years ago." She had deliberately changed the conversation. "Prospective buyers came to see it and their expressions said: 'What, buy a house in this dead-and-alive hole?' and they smiled at an apparently insane woman trying to sell them a white elephant, and went away."

"From what I've seen of it, it's very beautiful."

I'd pleased her and she smiled, shaking her head. "Visiting a place and living in it are very different matters, Loran. I'm lucky to have Ferry and old Josh. He's a native and Ferry has been with me for a great many years."

"It's strange, isn't it," I said irrelevantly, "that no one knows where Mrs. Algar has gone?"

As soon as I had spoken I regretted it. I would not have been surprised if Mrs. Cranmer had ignored my burst of curiosity, but she gave me a long, troubled look.

"When I invited you down here, Loran, I had no intention of drawing you into all this. But you can't live in a village even for a short time without someone making it his business to tell you the gossip." She paused and brushed her hand across her brow. "If you hear about us from someone else, the story could sound ugly and suspicious and you might not want to stay here. I couldn't bear that."

Her brown eyes pleaded so hard with me that I said impulsively, "I'll stay. Whatever you have to tell me, I'll stay."

She nodded. "After all, you have your own strong reason for being here. And our affairs can't be anything to you."

I sat holding the little crystal glass in my hand, staring at the tawny dregs of sherry. I wanted to hear what she had to tell me, but I was even more anxious to know whether she had remembered anything that could help me to find my parents.

"Sarne's wife has taken this terrible step out of revenge."

The word startled me. I looked up sharply and met the clouded, bitter eyes.

"I told you she'd walked out and completely disappeared, didn't I? I believe the whole thing was premeditated, that she packed clothes and jewels some days before and awaited an opportunity when suspicion would be most likely to fall on him."

"Suspicion?" I echoed.

"Of course. The affair began very oddly. Sarne and his wife had been to a little dinner party I gave that night and Claire had sulked the whole evening. In fact she created such an atmosphere that it was obvious there would be a scene when they were alone—Sarne has a wild temper, I'm afraid. That's why I think that evening was deliberately planned by Claire so that everyone would foresee a quarrel when they were alone. She *wanted* to make him suffer, Loran. She wanted people to whisper and rumors to begin: 'What happened that night? Is Claire Algar still alive or—?' " She broke off.

Or dead? I thought.

So heavy was the tension in the room that I felt drawn into the mystery and the tragedy of these people. It was curious, for my life at the hospital had taught me that the only way to keep sane in the face of tragedy was to steer a course between sympathy and impartiality. Yet here I was, sitting with a woman I had never met before today, caught in the grip of her pain.

"But in these days," I said, trying to be matter-of-fact, "how could anyone just disappear?"

"The strange thing is that they can—and do. You read of such cases in the newspapers almost every day. Claire has done it because she was frustrated in her insane possessiveness. She couldn't bear to let Sarne out of her sight in case he should look at another woman. Even Gillian didn't escape suspicion, though it was absurd to suspect her. Gillian has no time for men—for, er, romantic attachments, that is."

I held back a smile at the dated phrase.

"Then she's a phenomenon," I said wryly.

"But you don't know Gillian. She has a perfectly mediocre mentality. She was devoted to her parents and looked after them till they died. Then she took in Monty—he's old and selfish, but she seems to enjoy having him around."

The dogs suddenly raised their heads. I looked over my shoulder. Ferry stood in the doorway and asked Mrs. Cranmer if she wanted wine with dinner.

"Of course. It's an occasion," she said and smiled at me. "I'll come and choose it myself."

Ferry held the door for her. I saw her eyes, small and deep-set, rest on her mistress as though in inquiry. I wondered whether she had been listening outside the door and was silently questioning Mrs. Cranmer's wisdom in confiding in me. I tucked my legs under me and stared into the fire and tried to visualize Sarne with a possessive wife, Sarne in a temper. There were circumstances when even the best of men could be driven to such distraction. Had Sarne been violent with her?

"I hope," said Mrs. Cranmer from the doorway, "that you like roast veal. I quite forgot to ask if you were a vegetarian."

"I'm not," I said firmly.

Over dinner in the somber dining room I told Mrs. Cranmer about my meeting with Martin Cavall.

"He intrigues the village," she said with amusement. "They can't understand why he lives here, and there are all kinds of rumors, none of which I agree with. Some think he's just a newspaper reporter. Others that he's a—a policeman." The amusement died out of her face. "You see, they have to link even a stranger with Claire's disappearance."

"I met someone else, too," I said. "An odd little woman—she could have been a gypsy. She was tiny, like a child."

"That must have been Babette. She comes from a mumper family."

"Mumper?"

"They're a breed of idlers despised by the true gypsy. Babette lives with her family in what's little more than a shack on the heath. There are eight children in the family, and no one knows who were their fathers."

"Are they all under-sized?"

"Oh, no. Only Babette. Be careful of her, Loran. She talks, and her talk is malicious. No one here takes any notice of what she says—she's a terrible little liar. But you're a stranger. You might believe some of her wild, silly stories. Now you've been warned, though, you'll be on your guard, won't you?"

"I doubt if I'll see her again," I said.

"You will. She's often on the beach searching for anything she can find there. There's a particular kind of seaweed these people collect for eating. They fry it. Personally, I can't bear it. And Babette's a gregarious little creature. *She'll* talk to *you* if she catches sight of you. Don't listen. Don't ever listen to her nonsense."

She was so very anxious that I wondered if she really believed it all to be rubbish.

When we were drinking coffee I glanced up at a sea picture over the mantelshelf. As I looked, enjoying the lovely liquid silvery grays and greens, a thought came to me out of the blue. Only the sea and quicksands could hold their dead forever. I heard myself blurt out:

"Sarne's wife could be—dead? Have met with an accident."

I sensed a tensing of Mrs. Cranmer's sturdy body. The fingers of her left hand plucked at the worn fringe on the chair arm.

"What makes you say that?"

"It crossed my mind that she might perhaps have been drowned. The sea is near here . . ."

"I believe that's what Claire wants people to think. That Sarne . . . that Sarne . . ." She choked over the words and put her hand to her throat, catching at the single strand pearl necklace. The thread broke and a few pearls dropped into her lap. She dragged the broken string from her neck and cradled it with the loose pearls in her lap. It was as though she scarcely knew what she had done.

"The heath is a large place," she continued. "I think when they searched it Claire was somewhere far away, perhaps reading about it in the newspapers and laughing."

"She could have been drowned," I insisted. "Perhaps she went for a swim. There are people who like night bathing."

"Not Claire. She hated the sea. Everyone knew that."

Once again, almost as though she were listening, Ferry broke into our conversation. She looked around the door and said, "If you don't want me any more, I'll be off as soon as I've finished washing up."

Mrs. Cranmer gave her a half glance. "Yes, of course. It's Friday, isn't it? Your night for visiting your sister."

"Yes, madam. Good night." She forgot me, and, without even looking my way, closed the door.

Like the pearls, the thread of our conversation was broken too.

Mrs. Cranmer gathered the necklace and put it in a little Sèvres dish. Then she picked up the big polythene bag from the chair in the corner of the room and brought it to the fireside. She sat down and opened it. Ivory silk damask flowed over her lap; gold thread glinted.

"How beautiful." I leaned forward and touched a design of fleur-de-lis.

She nodded. "It's a bed cover from Jessily Court, one of our great Dorset show houses. Some of the hangings there are badly worn and a few of us have undertaken to repair them. It's lovely work, isn't it?" She spread it out for me to see.

Her workbox, a coil of gold thread, and some crimson and green silks were on a table by her side. I watched her thread a needle, wondering if I could ask more questions about Claire.

"I've talked so much, Loran, about our problems here. You must forgive me. But it would have been futile to have hoped that you could stay here and not know. Now, let's try to forget them and discuss yours. I wish there was something I could remember that would help you, but there's nothing. I don't even know where you came from."

"It was somewhere around this part," I said and told her about the Corfe Castle photograph on the calendar. "And I think the cutting about me was taken from a local newspaper. Is there an *Arlesthorne Gazette*?"

"Yes, it's our weekly," she said. "The young man you met, Martin Cavall, works on it. You know, of course, that Irene and Richard were married in Arlesthorne."

"No," I said excitedly. "But that's somethnig that could give me a lead."

"I doubt it. Irene wasn't a native of the town. She was an actress and she had joined the local repertory company. Her home, you see, was in South Africa."

I nodded. "She used to tell me bits about it."

"My husband and I were away at the time of their marriage. It was a very quiet affair, I believe, and afterwards they went straight back to London. I doubt if anyone in Arlesthorne remembers it now—it's such a long time ago."

"But they came back here and found me," I said. "It's just possible that the vicar of the church where they were married might know something. But which church?"

Her curly head was bent over the meticulous golden stitches. "It was probably St. Jude's. That's the parish church."

Then I would go there tomorrow, I said. It might not help at all, but at least it was action, and I had to start somewhere.

I thought Mrs. Cranmer looked tired. People kept early hours in the country, and although it was only nine o'clock I suggested that I go to bed. I could read a book and write a few letters in my room, I decided.

"It's such a lovely night," Mrs. Cranmer protested. "Why don't you take the dogs and go for a walk? The fresh air will do you good. The moon is so bright that you can't lose your way, and if you do, the dogs will bring you home."

It was what I wanted—to walk, to breathe the keen night air and to sort out my thoughts.

When I had fetched my coat, she came with me onto the terrace outside the sitting room window.

"Go across the lawn and through a small gate you'll see by the rhododendron bushes. It'll take you onto the heath. Then, if you want to go down to the sea, you can't miss it, it's there in front of you, not seven minutes' walk away. When you come back you'll see the lights of the house all the way."

A little wind sang in my ears. I lifted my face to it and called the dogs. They eyed me doubtfully until Mrs. Cranmer hustled them.

I was across the lawn and was nearly at the little gate that led onto the heath when something made me turn and look up at the house.

There was a light in a top window and someone stood there watching me. It could only be Ferry. I supposed that she had now finished washing up and had gone to her room to fetch her coat. Why shouldn't she be looking out of the window? She probably wanted to see if it was a fine night. But as I continued walking, I felt uncomfortable at the thought of that cold, still woman staring down at me.

The capering shadows of the dogs went before me, brushing through the bracken so that it whispered. I passed quite close to the boundary of Sarne's farm garden and heard music. I paused to listen. Someone was playing a piano or phonograph. It was a little nostalgic thing of Beethoven's called "For Elissa." I had the record at home.

Were Sarne and Deborah in that long, low house I could see

through the trees, listening together? A strong, very vital man and a beautiful woman . . . master and housekeeper.

I pushed back my intrigued thoughts. It was nothing to do with me, anyway. I had my own problem.

I was glad I had put on low shoes, for the going was rough with puddles from the recent rains and tricky little rises of earth and coarse grass. At the cliff's edge there were bushes and stunted trees. There was no rail or fence to guard whoever walked there, and the drop was heady.

I stood well back and looked down. Far below me the waves creamed over the black rocks. The moon dazzled the water. The dogs watched me.

To my right I saw what looked like a double hut standing almost at the cliff's edge. Whoever lived there, I thought giddily, had better keep sober, because a crooked way home would mean a quick and horrible death over that great plunging cliff.

The thought and the fact that I was staring down at the sea made me feel a little dizzy, and I turned and made my way back.

It was very quiet. The sea was a mere sigh and the wind had dropped. There was no movement except my own.

Then where were the dogs? I stood and looked about me and called them by their silly names. "Juliet! Viola!" My voice was high and urgent.

Nothing moved. So much, I thought, for their training in obedience. I tried again, and as I did so a cloud crept over the face of the moon and I was in complete darkness.

I walked on, trying to recognize my way by clumps of trees and massed black clusters of gorse. But I was taking so long to get back that I knew I had lost not only the dogs but my way.

It was ridiculous to feel a small, rising panic. Nobody was going to jump out of the bushes at me; no living things were around, anyway, except rabbits and hares. I was scared because I was used to city lights and pavements.

All the same I walked more quickly, and then, quite unexpectedly, the house loomed up in front of me.

Mrs. Cranmer had said, "You will see the lights of the house all the way."

Only there were no lights. . . .

I called to the dogs again, no longer in panic but because I knew Mrs. Cranmer would expect them to return with me.

I had reached a thick rhododendron hedge, but I couldn't find the little white gate. I was, I guessed, on the wrong side of the house, but there was no point in going all the way around. I parted the rhododendron bushes and pushed my way blindly through.

As I did so I heard one of the dogs bark. It continued on a sharp, excited note. I felt my way towards the sound, my voice, calling their names, drowned in those powerful yelps.

Heavy leaves brushed my face like fingers as I plunged through the bushes. Their depth seemed endless. I must be in the part of the grounds where the peacocks were.

At last I felt the end of the thicket. I stepped forward onto rough ground, still blindly because of the hidden moon.

"Juliet!" I shouted.

She, or Viola, went on barking. I went towards the sound.

I will never know what would have happened had I been walking less cautiously. I was putting one foot carefully in front of the other, not knowing the hazards in my way. My right foot lifted, moved downwards, and felt nothing beneath it. There was no time to think, to try to see where I was going; no time to do anything but what I did. At the very moment I touched emptiness, I flung myself backwards.

It was the swiftest reflex of my life. For a flash, just before I stumbled onto the firm ground behind me, I saw the blackness of a great hole.

I crouched, shaken, and stared at the snaring thing just ahead of my chin.

The dog had stopped barking and the silence was heavy.

I edged myself forward and peered down. At the same moment, the cloud partially cleared the moon face and by its light I saw a horrible, seemingly bottomless pit. I saw, too, stretched over the far half of it, two large, solid-looking planks.

Slowly I got to my feet and stood for a dazed moment, wiping my wet palms down the rough surface of my coat.

"Juliet. Viola."

My voice did not carry further than my lips.

But suddenly the dogs were there, as if nothing had happened, sniffing around me and wagging short stubs of tails.

I skirted the horrible pit and began to walk quickly toward the house. I didn't care if the dogs followed me or not. I was safe now. Safe from what? On the face of it, all I had done was to come across some dug-up place which had been inadequately covered.

I trod on cobbles, crossed them and found myself at the back door. It was locked. I skirted the house and went up the steps to the front door, grateful for the reassuring lights in the hall and the sitting room.

My hand shook as I rang the bell. Mrs. Cranmer let me in.

"Did you enjoy your walk?" she started to say. Then she looked sharply at me. Her eyes fell from my face to a long muddy streak down the front of my coat. "Loran, what happened?"

"I fell." It was so grotesquely inadequate that I could have laughed if I hadn't still been shaken.

"My dear, did you hurt yourself?"

I shook my head and followed her blankly into the sitting room.

"Where was this—on the cliff?"

"No, here, near the house. There—there was a deep pit and I nearly went into it."

"A pit? But there isn't—" she began. Then, sharply, "You mean the well. But how did you find that? It's right at the back of the house and nowhere near the gate."

"Clouds came up," I said, "while I was halfway back and I lost both the dogs and my way. Then I heard one of them barking—"

"But they don't bark," she said in surprise. "I've always said they're no earthly use as house dogs."

"One of them did—very loudly. I followed the sound and that's how I . . . I found the pit."

"But this is dreadful!" she cried. "Josh is filling in the old dried-up well in his spare time. He has always been very careful to cover it with planks when he's not working on it."

"One side was covered," I said, "the other was gaping."

She stared at me for an unbelieving moment. Then she said firmly, "I'm going to see for myself. If there'd been a dreadful accident, Josh would be responsible."

I followed her through the neat, almost clinically clean kitchen; the smell of meat roasting still lingered. We went down the passage that led to the back door and across the cobbled way and onto the grass.

The moon lit up the old well. Thick planks covered the entire hole.

Mrs. Cranmer looked at me.

"It's perfectly safe, you can see for yourself."

Her voice was relieved and her tone gentle as though reassuring a child who had had a bad dream.

"But those two far planks weren't there just now," I said.

"It was dark, wasn't it?"

"A bit of moon came out, but not much," I admitted.

"Then you probably stubbed your toe against the plank and felt that tiny gap between it and the wall of the well—you can see it quite clearly. Your toe must have slipped through the space and that's what frightened you. But the gap isn't wide enough even for your foot to go through, so you'd have come to no harm."

I hadn't stubbed my toe. I had put my foot forward and found emptiness. I knew perfectly well that those two planks on the far side nearest the rhododendron bushes hadn't been there five minutes ago. I wasn't mad and I hadn't the kind of imagination that can turn a fancy into a reality.

But there was nothing I could do or say. I was a guest and a comparative stranger. It was ludicrous, anyway, to suspect that it had been deliberate, and so far as the dogs were concerned one of them had probably barked its head off at a fox-hole.

Walking by Mrs. Cranmer's side back to the house I listened to her telling me that in the morning she would speak to Josh about covering the well more completely. "Even a tiny gap can be alarming at night," she said.

I agreed and went on thinking my own thoughts. I guessed that the obvious explanation must be that Josh had been called away while putting the planks across the old well and had forgotten to return and finish the job. Then, tonight, hearing the dog bark, he had probably come out of his cottage to see what was wrong and found me there. Realizing what he had done, he could have remained hidden until I went into the house and then, scared of what Mrs. Cranmer might say if she found the well inadequately covered, he must have placed the rest of the planks across the hole while I was in the house. It was all so clear now that I was calm and could think again.

IV

Mrs. Cranmer had told me the previous night that she preferred her guests to have breakfast in bed.

I lay in the morning light and heard the grandfather clock down in the hall strike eight. I watched the tops of the gold-leafed trees waving across the misty sky and thought about my first task today. I had to find the church where Irene and Richard were married and hope that the vicar or the verger had been there long enough to recall it. It was faintly possible that when they had decided to adopt a child, they had sought the vicar's help. Then, too, I would have to visit any adoption society there was in Arlesthorne.

When the tap came on my door, it was Mrs. Cranmer herself and not Ferry who brought in my breakfast.

I sat up in bed, my dressing gown around my shoulders, and she set the tray down on the bed table.

"I won't ask you if you slept well. First nights in strange beds shouldn't be inquired into." She stood smiling down at me. "I've been thinking. Instead of searching for the church where Irene and Richard were married, you could ask Adèle if she knows where the marriage certificate was kept."

"She'll be in France," I said. "Friends in Avignon invited her to stay with them. I could contact Somerset House for a copy of the marriage certificate, but I'd rather take a chance on St. Jude's. It'll be quicker."

Mrs. Cranmer gave me a searching look. "Does it occur to you that it might be better if you fail in all this?"

"Because knowing the truth would make me unhappy?"

She nodded. "Not all family reunions are pleasant."

"I know. But I've got to do it. I won't rest if I don't try."

"I think if there were any of Irene's or Richard's relatives around, people you had grown fond of, you wouldn't feel this way. It's finding yourself quite alone without even borrowed roots. I only hope the end will make you happy, Loran. Now drink your coffee while it's hot. I'm sorry there's no newspaper for you, but we don't get ours until about ten o'clock. By the way, can you drive?"

"Yes."

"Then take my car this morning. I won't be needing it."

"Oh, no," I said quickly. "Thank you all the same, but I don't want to drive just yet. It . . . it's too soon after the accident."

She understood and didn't press me.

"There's a bus service every hour," she said. "One passes the end of the lane at ten o'clock. If you catch that and get the twelve o'clock one back, you'll have plenty of time to go to the church.

"I spoke to Josh this morning," she said. "He says he distinctly remembers covering the well completely. But his eyes aren't as good as they were and he probably missed that few inches on the far side. I told him to be very careful in the future."

I saw that she believed him—after all, she had seen the planks in place with her own eyes. Only I knew that they hadn't been there. I liked old Josh and I wasn't going to get him into trouble for lying about it.

I settled down to too leisurely a breakfast so that I didn't have time to clean the mud stain off my coat before I had to run for the bus.

The long road to Arlesthorne skirted Black Ash Heath and then dipped into a wooded valley before reaching the ugly outskirts of the town.

I found St. Jude's Church easily and a woman doing the flowers went to find the verger, who was checking stores in the vestry.

My hopes rose when I saw that he was very old. But when I mentioned the Brant wedding, he shook his head.

"I've only been here ten years and the vicar, Mr. Vernon, is comparatively new. The old vicar died some years ago. But I'll help all I can."

He found the registration of the marriage, but that didn't help me at all.

I thanked him, put some money in the offertory box, and went out into the sunshine.

On the opposite side of the road was the library. They could probably tell me there the names of adoption societies in the town.

The building was large and modern and the reference library was on the ground floor. Someone was talking to the assistant and as I stood at the long counter waiting, I saw a pile of telephone directories. I picked one up. I wasn't looking for anything in particular, but I flicked through the B's. "Ba" . . . "Bl" . . . "Br". . . .

There were two people with the name Brant listed there.

A sudden excitement seized me. I whipped out a pen and an old bill from my handbag and wrote down the telephone numbers and addresses. Then I snapped the book shut and left without speaking to the assistant. That could wait. There were more possibilities here, on the back of a Selfridges bill. My heart lifted with excitement and I almost ran out of the room.

The library floor had been well polished. As I pushed my way through the swing door I ran full tilt into someone.

"I'm sorry . . ." I began, and then I recognized her. "Gillian!" I stared at her a little stupidly.

"It's no coincidence," she said. "I work here."

I laughed at my own surprise. Of course, I remembered now. "But what are you doing here? Do you want a temporary reader's ticket?"

I said I didn't, that Mrs. Cranmer had supplied me with enough paperbacks to last me my whole stay. "I've made a note of two people with my name, Brant," I said, "and I'm just going to telephone them. Oh—" I broke off and said apologetically, "You probably don't know what on earth I'm talking about!"

"Yes, I do. Mrs. Cranmer told me why you came here. You don't mind?"

I didn't, of course. The more who knew, the easier would be the search.

"You're not wasting much time about it, are you?" She studied me with her pale, curious eyes.

"I haven't got much time to waste. I have to be back at the hospital by the end of the month."

"If it were I . . ."

I never knew what she was about to say, for she was loudly and peremptorily interrupted.

"Young women these days seem to spend their time gossiping in corners," bellowed a voice at our elbows.

We turned together. An old man in a wheelchair with chaotic white hair that seemed to grow all ways swung himself out of the reading room next door.

Gillian looked at him without surprise. "I hope you enjoyed your morning papers."

"On the contrary," he shouted for the whole library to hear, "they were exceedingly dull. Nobody does anything these days to make hotblooded news. Nobody lives dramatically any more."

"In other words, there's no Van Gogh to cut off his ear and send it to a friend," she said, teasingly.

He scowled at her. "I'd rather receive someone's ear through the post than advertisements for washing machines."

She eyed him calmly. "The trouble with you is you're bloodthirsty," she said. "If you want excitement, why not go out yourself and create it?"

"If you mean something like murder, you've got it already, right on your own doorstep."

Gillian's face went quite still.

"There's no murder that I know of, Mr. MacQueen," she said icily. "Or perhaps you have some premonition of one about to be committed. Anyway, I hate joking about death."

"I'm not joking and you know it," he snapped and turned his vivid gaze on me. "Can I be introduced?"

Gillian pulled herself together. She said with visible effort, "Loran, this is Mr. MacQueen. Miss Brant. She's staying with Mrs. Cranmer."

"The woman who owns the near-ruin on that godforsaken heath? I've met her and her scraggy housekeeper. Fine study for an abstract painting that one would make. I'd title it 'Woman without Virtues.' And I'd mean physical virtues. No bosom, no behind. And I like a behind on a woman!" He shook with laughter and propelled himself towards the door. A woman held it open for him and he shot through. "Enjoy your stay, if you can," he roared back at me.

"That," said Gillian frozenly, "is Deborah's father. He's an artist—or rather, he was one. He doesn't paint much now, but his pictures fetch big prices if ever they get on the market. You may have heard of him in London. Tom MacQueen."

I hadn't and said so. "He seems to enjoy shocking people," I added.

"He's always like that," she said. "Even before the accident when he fell and injured his spine, he was violent in every way. He doesn't mean half of it, though."

"That's something to know," I laughed. "He must liven the

town." I glanced over Gillian's shoulder at the clock over the door. "And now I suppose I'd better go and telephone these Brants," I said.

She murmured something about my coming to have tea and meeting Monty. I said I'd like to and we parted, smiling brightly and rather meaninglessly at each other. She was one of those people to whom I would never find very much to say because there was no real point of contact.

I had an uncomfortable feeling, however, as I went out into the street, that for all Gillian's reassurances, Tom MacQueen had meant what he had said about murder.

There was a confectioners next door and I bought a slab of chocolate and collected a heap of coins. I found a telephone booth and rang the first of the two numbers. Maggy Brant was a dressmaker and she had never heard of Richard Brant, the surgeon. Brant, she explained with a little giggle, was really a trade name. I thanked her and called the next number.

An old and slightly tetchy voice answered me. Who was I? I explained.

"Richard was my great-nephew," she said. "I read that he'd been killed, but I haven't heard of him for years. You're his adopted daughter? Well, what do you want?" She sounded as though she were afraid I was coming begging.

"I would like to come and see you."

"What for?"

She deflated me. But my excitement at having found her spurred me on.

"It's not very important, Miss Brant," I said. "Please, if I may come I won't keep you long."

"Then it'ud better be now. I shall be going out later. Do you know the way?"

She gave me directions and I found the small Victorian house easily. It was ringed around with dusty laurel bushes. Miss Brant herself opened the door to me. She would have been very tall if she hadn't been so bent, and her hands were like claws with rheumatism. She led me into an over-heated sitting room, sat me down in an uncomfortable chair, and asked me what I wanted.

I told her. She listened, shading her face from the fierce fire with one heavily ringed hand.

"Richard never bothered with me once he became successful," she said, matter-of-factly. "He was always too busy cutting people up. But I remember Irene. He was staying with me, making use of me while he was visiting Arlesthorne Hospital. He met Irene here and brought her to see me. A charming girl. I did hear they had adopted a child, but I've no idea where they found you."

"I believe I was born between here and Corfe Castle, which could mean in one of the little villages like Saxon Magna itself."

"How old are you?"

"Twenty-four."

She looked directly at me for the first time.

"Then my advice to you is, be satisfied with your adoption and forget you ever had any other parents. You can't have mattered much to them."

I stood my ground. "It needn't have been quite like that. There could be some good reason why they parted with me."

"Illegitimacy?"

"Perhaps," I said steadily. I'd met her type before. She'd have no time for anyone she could intimidate.

"No." She screwed up her face into a hundred tiny wrinkles. "No, not illegitimacy; that wasn't it. I heard . . ."

"You heard what, Miss Brant?"

She let me wait while she pondered, perhaps on whether to tell me or not. Then, when I could scarcely bear her silence any longer, she said:

"That there was already one child in the family, a boy."

"I have a brother?" I felt that I almost shouted the words.

She nodded. "I can even remember his name. It was Anthony. Odd, my remembering that, but that's age. You remember long-past things."

I leaned forward, tense and suddenly excited.

"Where can he be?"

She raised her eyebrows at me. "How on earth should I know? And I don't see that my bit of information can help you at all."

"You don't by any chance know his surname?"

"No, I don't." The tetchy note was in her voice again. She moved as though to rise.

I got to my feet. "Thank you for seeing me, Miss Brant." I held out my hand.

She looked me up and down. Then, leaning forward, her claw-like fingers touched the topaz and gold fob on my coat lapel.

"That's very unusual."

"I've had it all my life," I said and added on a wild hope, "you haven't seen it before, have you?"

"I'm not sure." She had for a moment forgotten that she was bored with me. She was staring at the topaz.

"The thing looks vaguely familiar."

I stood and let her turn and twist it, puzzling to remember.

"It's a queer-looking bird. Now where was it?"

I held my breath.

"It's no use." She dropped her hand and rose with such difficulty from her chair that I made a little move to help her but sensed just in time that she would resent it.

She straightened herself, her hand resting across her back.

"Perhaps later on you might remember where you've seen this before. If you do . . ."

"I shan't," she snapped with a child's sudden petulance. "Why should I? Bits of nonsense like that are probably sold in their hundreds in trinket shops."

They weren't, and I knew it. Not pure, brilliant topaz in gold scroll settings. But Miss Brant made it plain that she had nothing more to tell me and wanted me to go. I felt that she didn't much like people, particularly young people.

I heard her brown front door close behind me before I had even reached the gate. I blinked in the sunlight.

My footsteps down the street were like the background beat to a song, and the song was mine. I have a brother and his name is Anthony . . . I have a brother . . .

The line for the bus to the outlying villages was quite long. I joined it, hoping that it would take the twenty-four would-be passengers. I was the twenty-fourth.

I began counting again to pass the time when a car stopped. Deborah Millbrook was ducking her head towards me.

"I'm on my way home if you'd like a lift."

I climbed in gratefully beside her.

"That was clever of you, to spot me."

"Most people passing here cast a glance at the bus line for familiar faces," she said. "If you didn't you'd have it chalked up against you that you were inhospitable, and it doesn't do to get on the wrong side of villagers. No shopping?" She glanced at my empty lap.

"I've been trying to trace the Brant family," I said, "but I've drawn almost a blank. I did meet a great-aunt of Richard's, but she wasn't very interested and knew nothing about me except that somewhere I've got a brother. But as I only know his Christian name, Anthony, that doesn't help much."

She accelerated and shot past some slow moving traffic. She was handling the big car with splendid assurance, sitting almost nonchalantly in the driving seat. "If my parents had given me away, I'd think myself well rid of them."

I didn't answer that one.

"I met your father in the library," I said. "Gillian introduced me."

"So that's where he got to!" she exclaimed impatiently. "I called on him and he was out. He's getting too venturesome on his own. He uses that awful wheelchair of his like a weapon. One day he'll knock someone down with it and be had up for assault." She gave a dry laugh but I felt that she was more angry than amused.

"I hear he's a great artist."

"He was. He doesn't paint now. He has enough money for his needs, so he says, and if he wants more he only has to sell one of his mass of paintings. He hoards them like a miser, while collectors clamor for them."

The car slid effortlessly up the hill and, passing a huge factory, reached the decontrolled zone. The speedometer leaped up and steadied at sixty-five.

"I suppose you know Dorset very well," I said.

"Fairly. I'm a native, though I was abroad during my marriage. It broke up, and I came back."

I watched the road ahead of us. "Did you know Claire Algar?"

She answered with perfect ease.

"Oh, yes. I was hostess for a while at the Arlesthorne Yacht Club and Claire and Sarne were members. Sarne was too busy to own and sail a boat but he was always welcome at the club."

Was?

As though I had asked the question aloud, Deborah said, "He resigned after Claire went away."

"She did go away, then?"

"Of course." I felt her swift glance. "Didn't Mrs. Cranmer tell you? There was a quarrel after a party at the manor and Claire just packed her bags and left. Sarne has a hot temper. I can deal with him, but Claire never could. I've learned the way his mind works. He's arrogant and self-willed, but I think those are the very things that make him such a fine farmer. He fights the land —and usually wins."

"And Claire never contacted him after she went away? Never let him know whether she was alive—or dead?"

"That's one form of revenge, isn't it? To vanish without a word so that Sarne will have to wait seven years to get free of her."

"And suppose," I said, "that after seven years are up, she came back!"

"It would be too late. Men like Sarne don't cling to memories. They're virile. A woman to own and a piece of land to fight."

I watched her hands. They had tightened on the wheel.

"It's terrible for him," I said. "If he loved her . . ."

"Loved her?" She broke into sudden loud, unamused laughter.

I turned my head expecting her to explain. She didn't. Her right foot moved gently on the accelerator and we were doing seventy, flying with a silken purr of engine past Black Ash Heath.

I was aware of her next to me; her lovely coat felt soft to my hand as I bent to retrieve a dropped glove; the single aquamarine on her finger glittered like blue sunny water. I began assessing her. She was almost beautiful, well-dressed and a fine cook—according to Mrs. Cranmer. With all those qualifications there must be many houses in the cities which would welcome her. Why, then, live at a lonely farm where she had to mother three children and know that the fashion shops weren't just up the road?

The answer was surely Sarne Algar.

I was obviously looking at the woman who would be the second Mrs. Algar.

V

WE HAD REACHED the cross lanes, one turning towards the manor and the other to the farm.

Deborah stopped the car. "I'm rather late. Do you mind if I drop you here? It isn't far for you to walk."

"I'd like a walk anyway," I said, "and thank you for the lift."

"We'll see you at one o'clock," she called.

As the car drove on, I checked my watch and found that it was only ten minutes past twelve. As we were not due at the farm until one o'clock there was plenty of time for me to go down to the sea. All my life I had loved being by it, in it and on it. I couldn't resist the steel blue line I could just see beyond the high cliffs.

As I walked I heard the screech of peacocks. I looked back and stood for a moment watching them on the far lawn. Bronze-green, silver-blue, tinged with vermilion and old gold . . . lovely birds with voices like old saws, strutting proud as crowned kings through the emerald grass. The picture fascinated me. I stood counting the colors like a child. Then, when they disappeared behind the rhododendron bushes, I walked on.

I came out on the cliff top, just by the hut I had seen last night. Daylight showed it to be a neat, solid little building of reddish-brown pine logs, built picturesquely with a double roof as though it had been designed for two families.

"Good morning."

I recognized the voice at once, but that didn't stop my giving an absurdly guilty start as though I were caught trespassing.

"Don't be scared," said Martin Cavall. "I'm quite harmless." He emerged from the path that ran at an angle to the one I had taken. He wore a thick dark green sweater and he was carrying two morning newspapers.

"They don't deliver," he explained, noting my glance. "In fact, it's been said that I live too far out for letters and not quite far enough for cables." His dancing, restless eyes missed nothing of me from my hair to my shoes.

"I can't think how you exist here in winter," I said, turning from that frankly appraising stare.

"I haven't done so yet, and I doubt if I will. I'm one of those birds of passage."

"At least you're living a healthy life. I should think you're a good mile's walk from the village, and if you have to do that every morning . . ."

"Who said anything about walking?" He turned his head and I saw the bright green car drawn up under some trees in the lane. "Will you have coffee with me? I don't work on Saturday mornings and I haven't had breakfast yet. I promise I make excellent coffee and the hut's quite comfortable inside. You won't have to sit on a soap box."

"Thanks, but I must be getting back. I'm lunching at the farm."

"*Are* you?" His eyes suddenly lost their merry look; they were bright and conjecturing. "Well, I hope you enjoy it. They keep a good table there, so I'm told. I don't get asked."

Still with his eyes on me, he reached out and flung open the door of the hut. I had an impression of a many-colored Afghan rug tossed over a divan, of a table and a big armchair.

"I make good coffee," he said again.

"I'm sure you do. But some other time . . ."

In another moment I would have gone my way and the door would have closed. But there was a movement in the bushes and the great Remus stood sniffing the air and watching us.

Then I saw Sarne.

"Hello," I said easily.

He scarcely acknowledged me. His glance was on Martin. "I'd like a word with you."

"Fine. Come on in."

"No. Outside. Here and now."

I turned away, but Sarne's hand came out and gripped my wrist. I looked up at him in astonishment and saw that he was rigid with anger. His peremptory hold annoyed me and I gave a quick twist to my wrist. His grasp only tightened.

"Please," I said in a mocking voice, "can I have my wrist back?"

"Since my tenant ignores my warnings when I give them, perhaps he'll take more notice if I have a witness," Sarne said with barely controlled fury.

"I don't like being held captive," I murmured and dragged at his fingers.

His grip held. I might have been nothing more than a dog on a lead, I thought angrily.

"Sarne, will you please—" I began, and then I gave up. He was speaking, his voice for all its deadly quiet, drowning mine; his reddish-brown head bent to Martin, who was half a head shorter.

"I've already warned you about racing your damned car down my lane. You know that cattle cross it."

Martin's shrug was faintly insolent. "There wasn't a cow in sight when I came along this morning."

"I'm talking about last night. One of my heifers panicked and stumbled against some barbed wire and cut itself. I don't breed cattle for your pseudo-sporting amusement."

"I'm sorry." Martin's head was thrown back in order to try to meet Sarne's gaze levelly. "My 'damned car,' as you call it, wasn't speeding. Unless, of course, in this one-eyed hole you consider forty miles an hour only suitable for the race track."

"I consider forty miles an hour too fast on a twisting lane which cattle use. And I won't warn you again. Next time it happens, you pack up and leave, or if you prefer violence I'll come and throw you out."

In the moment's silence while the two men measured each other, I wrenched my wrist free from Sarne's grasp. I was furious with him for having forced me to stay, and yet now that I was free to leave, curiosity as to the outcome of this verbal battle held me there.

Martin tossed his newspapers through the open door of his hut and they landed with a plop on the rush matting. It was a gesture of irritation and frustration.

"You know, Algar"—his tone still held controlled insolence—"it's time you stopped behaving as though the whole country belongs to you."

I was trying to push Remus out of the way, but he stood across the path I had come up, unyielding as a five-barred gate. If I stepped around him I would plunge either into the gorse bushes or over the cliff. So I pushed past Sarne and decided to go down the hill and chance my way through the thick copse back to the manor.

"This bit of country belongs to me," I heard Sarne say. "One more exhibition such as last night and I'll have the police—"

"Police?"

I paused, my head half turned.

"By all means call them," Martin went on. "I think they're already quite interested in *your* bit of country. You must be careful, Algar. With a wife who has disappeared and a very attractive housekeeper . . ."

There was a sharp crack and a thud. I swung around and saw Martin slumped against the wall of the hut.

My training made me react as I did. I ran back to his side. As I bent over him, I flashed a look at Sarne.

"Do you have to resort to violence to make your point?"

Sarne's eyes, brilliant in the sunlight, looked at us from under straight-drawn brows.

"If you'd given yourself time to think," he said coldly to me, "you'd know that if I had hit him I'd have caught his jaw, not the back of his head."

It was true. Martin was getting up slowly, cautiously feeling the back of his head as he did so.

Sarne knee'd his dog gently out of the way.

"He'll live," he said briefly.

I ignored him and reached up to Martin. "Let me see if you've cut yourself," I began. "You're too tall for me. Bend down."

But he ignored me and walked into the hut and slammed the door after him.

Sarne stood a few steps away, watching me.

"I'd have enjoyed hitting him," he said. "That's really why I wanted you around—as a check to my impulses."

"Your impulses seem to have done quite well, checked or not. He must have thought you were going to hit him and tripped and fell."

"That's right. That's just what happened. Perhaps the fact that you witnessed his moment's humiliation will teach him more than all my warnings."

"Threats, I think you mean."

"Very well, threats, then." His face lit up with sudden amusement.

I glanced sideways at him as he walked with me across the cliff top. His profile was strong with its craggy nose and brooding forehead. His anger was over, but his temper was something to be careful of. Temper born, in this instance, of righteous anger at a man's veiled hints? Or fear because behind the words lay a truth, and, in that truth, danger for Sarne?

Suddenly I didn't want to walk back to the manor with him. He disturbed and distressed me. We had come to the steps cut in the cliff face and leading to the beach.

I said, pausing, "I'm going down to the sea."

"You'll spoil those town shoes. Why in the world wear such a smart pair for walking in rough country?"

"I've been in Arlesthorne," I retorted, "and even if I hadn't, I don't see—"

"What business it is of mine?" he asked easily. "No, except that I don't like wanton destruction, even to a nice pair of obviously expensive shoes."

"You seem to care more for the feelings of shoes than of people." I met his gaze challengingly, and was sorry I'd said that, for he had been justified just now in his anger with Martin.

"Whoever your parents were," he said slowly, his eyes riveted on my face, "they gave you the gift of always having an answer."

"Oh, I forgot," I flashed at him, "you like feudal ways, don't you? 'I'm king of the castle and no answering back!' Well—" And then I stopped. I saw the light of real laughter in his eyes. He had been taunting me and I had risen to the bait. "Really, Sarne—" My mouth quirked. I felt idiotically happy that we were still friends. I made to turn away, the little exchange over. But he was stronger than I and he held my gaze. The moment was hypnotic. It was as though he had stripped off all the façade and looked into my mind.

My heart began to thud uncomfortably; I felt the color rise to my throat and cheeks. People didn't embarrass me—and this man wasn't going to. I wasn't naïve enough to fall for a steady, penetrating glance. I fought his will and turned sharply away towards the beach steps. I went down two of them.

"We'll meet at lunch," Sarne called after me. "I hope the thought of a man's sore head won't put you off pheasant."

I didn't answer. When I reached the place where the steps curved, I paused and looked upwards. I saw the sun shining on the dog's bronze rippling body and on Sarne's russet head.

The cliff steps were rough-hewn and I walked cautiously, watching where my feet went. That was why I didn't notice, until I'd reached the beach and my shoes slid into the soft silver sand, the doll-woman, Babette.

I watched her scrambling over the rocks, her hair blowing back, her little brown feet bare. She had some seaweed in her hand.

I hoped she wouldn't see me, but her eyes, swift and darting as a bird's, looked my way. She lifted her hand and beckoned me as though we were friends. I decided to pretend I hadn't seen, but she came running towards me. She had lifted her skirt and put the seaweed in it, holding it to her like a bundle. She stood right in front of me and I couldn't ignore her.

"I've learned your name," I said. "It's Babette, isn't it?"

She nodded, watching me with bright, suspicious eyes.

"You come down here to hide?"

"Good heavens, no. Hide from whom?"

"Him." She nodded towards the cliff top. "Him. Sarne Algar."

"I've no reason in the world to hide from him," I said with over-emphasis. "I had ten minutes to spare and I thought I'd come and look at the sea."

Babette hoisted the bundle of seaweed higher in her damp skirt and said in her rough little voice:

"His kids have only just gone. They're always down here playing. They talk to me," she added, nodding her head and smiling.

"I shall be meeting them presently," I said, and peered at the great winged rock jutting into the sea ahead of me. "Is that Falcon Point?"

She gave me a long, sideways look. "Yes."

"There's a cove beyond it, isn't there, where a village is buried."

She looked from me to the cliff and nodded.

"They say when the waves are light and the wind's from the south you c'n hear the church bells ringing. Only I know . . . I know they ain't bells. They're Mrs. Algar crying from her grave."

I jerked back involuntarily as though the terrible little sentence had hit me in the face.

"That's a silly and dangerous thing to say," I told her, my voice sharp. "Mrs. Algar has left her husband. I know because I was told last night. Lots of married couples part."

"I only know what I know." Babette eyed me sulkily. "And I don't tell no one. I don't tell the police, neither. They've bin lookin' everywhere, even 'mong them rocks. But they didn't find nothing. They couldn't. Not under them rocks and that thing that makes the sea sing."

"What thing that makes the sea sing."

"Don't know. That organ, maybe, that got buried with the church."

"It's all too fanciful to listen to," I said impatiently. "What you hear are the waves crashing against the fallen stones."

"Oh, no. They come together, the sea singing and her crying."

"Then you'd better tell the police that," I retorted.

She gave me a look which had all the cunning of her hybrid race.

"They don't listen to me. And I ain't told you nothing, either, so don't you go saying I have."

"And if I do?" I parried.

She put out a foot and stepped down into a little rock pool.

I watched her wiggle her toes in the clear water and knew that I had no intention of going to the police with her story. I was a stranger here and I had no intention of becoming involved.

Babette was tearing at a clump of brown seaweed. I turned to go, my shoes heavy with fine sand.

"Miss—"

I said, "Yes?" and waited.

"You like Mrs. Cranmer, don't you?"

"Very much."

"So you won't say nothing."

"I don't see that I've got anything to say. What you've told me is obviously not new to the police since they've searched Falcon Point. And, come to that, what has liking Mrs. Cranmer got to do with . . . with the terrible thing you . . . suggested about Mrs. Algar?"

She was swinging a piece of wet seaweed and smiling. "You don't know now, but you will. You will. . . ."

Suddenly I had to get away. I hated the hints and the sly looks. Babette, I decided, was just a malicious child who had fastened onto me with her tales because I was a stranger here. On her own admission, no one here would listen to her.

I looked pointedly at my watch and said I must go.

"And if you hear someone crying among those rocks," I said over my shoulder, "then it's a ghost. And, personally, I don't believe in ghosts."

The hall clock was striking a quarter to one as I came up the steps of the house. The front door was open and the dogs sat on the steps, alert and with ears twitching, like shorn lions.

Mrs. Cranmer met me with a protest. "You went out this morning without getting that mud mark cleaned off your coat."

"I'll go and tidy up and then I'll do it before we go to the farm."

"Ferry will do it for you. She has cleaning fluid in the kitchen. Here, give it to me."

She took my coat from me firmly, and thanking her I ran up the stairs to my room. It didn't take me long to do my face and wash my hands. When I was ready, I picked up a green chiffon scarf and tied it over my hair because the wind was whipping up from over the sea.

I found Ferry in the hall with my coat.

"It was an oil stain," she said, holding the hem of the coat for me to see. "You must have got it from the train."

I wondered whether she always avoided looking at people. I was beginning to dislike the sight of those white lids always closing her gaze from me. I pretended to look for the place where the stain had been.

"It's cleaned so beautifully," I said, "that I can't even see the place. Thank you, Ferry."

As I walked by Mrs. Cranmer's side along the private lane between outhouses and trees and a duck pond, I told her about my meeting with Martin Cavall and the scene with Sarne. I kept my main piece of news until last. After describing Miss Brant, I told her that I had a brother and that his name was Anthony.

"A brother." Her eyes shone. "Oh, Loran, if you could find him!"

"He could even be living near here," I said. "There might be people here who know him, even some who saw me before I was adopted."

"It's a long time ago."

"Twenty-four years?" I said unbelievingly. "Why, people of fifty would easily remember that time back. If I went from village to village between here and Corfe, asking if there was a family there who had given a baby away for adoption . . . Mrs. Cranmer," I was suddenly so excited that I stopped quite still, "there can't be so many villages! I'm going to do just that. I'll take a few places each day."

I felt suddenly glowing and very happy. I had hit on a plan that was certain of success. I would comb the villages. I would ask and ask and not be put off by headshakes and bad memories. Someone was going to remember something of a couple who had a son called Anthony and a baby girl they had given away. Someone . . . somewhere. . . .

I heard the chattering before I saw the little cavalcade of children storm towards us with such speed that I automatically braced myself for an impact. Mrs. Cranmer was laughing.

"Here they come," she said. "Marnie and Simon are the two eldest on bicycles; Nina is the little dark one on the scooter."

With cycle bells ringing and Nina hooting like an express train, they bore down on us. They stopped within two feet, and three pairs of eyes looked me over keenly.

Mrs. Cranmer introduced them and they said, "How do you do," with a small, grown-up graciousness.

"We're the outriders," said Simon, screwing up his eyes. "We've been sent to escort you."

With bicycles and scooters weaving between us, we walked to the farm.

Sarne's children were slender with long straight legs and they all wore red shorts and white shirts.

The two elder ones had thick, light brown hair and charming, short little noses; but Nina's hair was black and she wore it in a top-knot tied with red ribbons. She had Sarne's blue-gray eyes and some of his imperiousness. Looking at the two older children, I felt I knew a little what Claire was like.

The manor farm was long and low and built of Purbeck stone. It was very old, but much had obviously been done to modernize it. There was one magnificent picture window which commanded a view right over the heath to the sea. There was also a patio, and the gardens, although not large, stretched down to the orchard and were full of ragged autumn color.

The children led us along the gravel path skirting the house and through wide French windows into a huge, oak-beamed sitting room.

Sarne watched us enter in laughing surprise. Greeting us, he said to me, "My children seem to have forgotten that every house has a front door."

"But, Daddy, we couldn't bring them in that way," Marnie said reproachfully. "You know Mrs. Maggs is having babies in the hall cupboard and we didn't want to disturb her."

"I hope you realize," said Sarne to me, "that Mrs. Maggs is a cat."

"She's not just a cat!" Nina's eyes flashed to her father. "You *know* that! She's an Aby . . . Aby . . ."

"Abyssinian," Marnie told her in her soft, hesitant voice.

"You should have all seen that she had her confinement elsewhere," Sarne told them. "Or would you have liked the best bedroom for the purpose?"

They giggled, and Deborah, entering, asked what the joke was.

"Your cat is having kittens in the hall cupboard," said Mrs. Cranmer.

"For positively the last time," she protested to the children. "If it happens again, out she goes, to the stables or the vet."

"Oh, Deborah-h-h!" they wailed.

She took no notice. She greeted us with smiling apology.

"I didn't hear you come. I was in the kitchen with Chauncey."

"I think we told you," said Sarne, "that Chauncey is our valuable help. She and her husband, Ned, live in and we couldn't imagine life without them."

"Come and take off your coats," Deborah said, "while Sarne gets the drinks."

Mrs. Cranmer was untying the scarf over her head.

"We could leave them down here, only I'd like Loran to see the view from your landing window."

"By all means." Deborah shot me a bright, brittle smile. "Let's go up."

The view from the half-landing between the floors was far finer than any I had seen from the manor. Here one had a clear view over Black Ash Heath to the Purbeck Hills, covered in amethyst mist, and in the hollow were the crenellated towers of Corfe Castle.

We left our coats in a bedroom decorated in yellow and white.

"The room has been redecorated," Mrs. Cranmer exclaimed looking around.

"I always hated the dull red hangings in here. They were far too somber against the oak beams. Sarne agreed with me."

"You've changed the picture, too. There used to be one of your father's here—a rather curious picture of black and white and brown."

I followed her gaze and looked at the little harbor etching that hung on the far wall.

Deborah said, "It seemed a pity that it should hang in a room that was seldom used. I moved it into my bedroom. I rather like it."

"Sarne liked it, too," Mrs. Cranmer said quietly. "I remember very well when he bought it. He and Claire had gone to an exhibition of your father's works in London."

Standing by the window looking out over the farm, I felt that she had deliberately brought Claire into the conversation. I would have to steel myself against becoming emotionally involved. It was no concern of mine that Claire had vanished and Deborah was changing things about the house.

Downstairs again, with Sarne, the atmosphere eased. Lunch was a gay meal—the children saw to that. I was a stranger whom they had decided to like. Therefore there was so much that I must know about them. Simon and Nina were alike, vital and uninhibited. Marnie was the one who interested me most. She had a grave little face with a mouth far too sensitive for a child. Deborah's manner towards her was very different from the indulgence she showed to the two younger children.

Marnie, screwing up her eyes, peered over the table for the salt. Deborah pounced.

"Why are you squinting like that? Can't you see properly?"

"Yes—I was th-thinking."

"You weren't, dear, you were looking for something. Sarne, I really believe she needs glasses."

Simon pointed at her in delight. "She's going to wear goggles."

"Stop that," Sarne ordered.

"I won't wear g-glasses." Marnie's face flushed. "I *can* see. You'd hate me to—to look p-pretty, wouldn't you, Deborah?"

"Marnie, stop that," Sarne said again, but more gently.

"It isn't f-fair." She was sitting next to me and her distress touched a memory in me. I too, as a little child, used to stammer miserably when Richard dropped his cold questioning gaze on me, feeling my childishness, my inadequacy. I reached out under cover of the table and found Marnie's small stiff little fingers and squeezed them. Immediately I felt her relax.

The pheasant was perfect, and the trifle, which I'd never before liked, was rich with sherry and apricot preserve and cream. When we went into the sitting room for coffee the children were banished.

"When I first took over this farm," Sarne said to me explaining the long, lovely room, "this floor was a succession of small rooms leading out of one another and with such low ceilings that I was always hitting my head. I'm too large for cramped spaces so I had walls knocked down and the ceiling lifted. I can just manage to walk about now without feeling like a giant in a birdcage."

Deborah, sitting cool and at ease behind the coffee pot, said:

"And one of these days, Sarne, we'll really have to think about building on a sun room. It would be lovely for the summer."

There was a sudden clatter. Mrs. Cranmer had knocked the spoon out of her saucer. Sarne bent to pick it up for her.

"One thing one has to guard against in old age," she said apologetically, "is growing clumsy!"

But I had seen the deliberation in the movement that had sent the spoon flying. It was the only way she could think of to change the flow of the conversation.

I said, over-brightly, "Where's Remus?"

"Out with the children, I expect," Sarne said. "I hope he didn't disturb you last night. Two things happen on this farm at full moon. The coots on the lake fly up and cry to it, and Remus does a kind of bewitched baying."

"I didn't hear him," I began, and then said, "Oh, but I did hear a dog barking when I came back from the cliff. About nine o'clock. I thought it was one of the boxers."

"It must have been. Remus was indoors with me until after eleven," Sarne said.

"Loran had a scare last night," Mrs. Cranmer said, and told them about it.

Their eyes were on me. Sarne said, "Josh should cover the well face with a double set of planks, going crisscross. It's the safest way until the well is filled in. If you haven't enough boards for it, I can let you have some. Now," he turned to me, "would you like to see the farm?"

I said I'd love to, and Deborah, glancing out of the window, said we would need our coats and she would fetch them.

Wrapped up against the wind, we inspected the farm, the coots and grebe on the small lake, the fine herd of Friesians in the fields. In the stables I saw Marnie's skewbald Perchance, the pony Simon and Nina took turns to ride, and Sarne's big gray with the snow-white mane. I was shown the fine Dutch barn and the children's small pets—a tortoise, some angora rabbits and a budgerigar called Jenny.

VI

It was three o'clock when we left. Sarne offered to run us back, but Mrs. Cranmer chose to walk. She wanted to return by way of the swollen stream at the foot of the lane, she said. Something would have to be done about it before the winter since it seemed to be rising higher each year.

It wasn't until much later that I missed my topaz. I had written a letter to Adèle after tea and put on my coat to go to the village to post it. It was then that I saw that the little ring in the center of the gold scrollwork that had held the topaz was swinging emptily. I had had it when I went into Arlesthorne this morning because Miss Brant had remarked on it. I didn't remember seeing it later because Ferry had held my coat for me when I put it on to go to the farm and my big chiffon headscarf had covered it.

I searched the floor of my room, the stairs and the sitting room.

Mrs. Cranmer had gone into the village to visit a retired servant who was ill. I went onto the heath and across the cliff top. The topaz could have fallen off anywhere—down on the beach, even, when I had talked to Babette. In either place it would be almost impossible to find.

Back at the manor I asked Ferry if she remembered seeing the topaz on the fob when she cleaned my coat.

"I was in too much of a hurry to get the stain off before you went out to lunch to be quite certain," she told me. "I do remember something on your lapel. Something gold."

In her usual somber silence she helped me search the rooms again, but I knew I wouldn't find it.

The loss depressed me—not for the intrinsic value of the topaz, but because it had *belonged*, as nothing else I possessed had done.

To lose it was like a bad omen. I was angry with myself for not having had the join in the ring securely soldered.

When Mrs. Cranmer heard about it she was upset for my sake. She made me telephone the farm. Deborah answered me. No, she was afraid she hadn't really noticed the topaz, she said. She'd carried my coat and Mrs. Cranmer's over her arm when she brought them to us. The topaz could have fallen on the stairs; she'd have a look and ring me back if she found it.

But she didn't ring me back and I gave up the search. I knew I would never see it again.

That night I wrote to a friend at the hospital telling her all that I'd been doing.

"It's a queer feeling," I wrote, "to know that I have a brother and that I wouldn't know him if we met. But it makes the search even more exciting, and funnily enough, not quite as hopeless, because I've got a name to go on."

Mrs. Cranmer was watching television. I said I was going to post a letter and might I take the dogs with me. She said "of course," and prodded a sprawling Viola with her foot. This time, she said, I must take a flashlight with me.

There was a postbox at the cross lanes near the farm. As I slid the letter into the box, someone was again playing music. I wandered nearer the house and listened. The gates were open and the dogs, supposing that I was going to visit the farm, bounded up the short drive and onto the terrace sniffing at the French windows.

I called them and they ignored me. I went up the drive, wondering exasperatedly why people didn't teach their dogs to obey.

Viola began whining to be let in. I darted onto the terrace and seized her collar. At the same time, the glass doors opened and Sarne looked down at me.

"You're fighting a losing battle, Loran," he told me. "When these dogs set their minds to a thing, nothing stops them. Viola, you're a spoiled bitch." He gave her a slap on her strong rump and she shot into the room. "I was stealing half an hour from bookkeeping. Chauncey's just going to bring me in some coffee. Stay and have some with me."

I took a step over the threshold and looked around the huge room and into the shadowy far corners.

"Deborah is out," he said, and I felt he had been reading my thoughts.

He pulled around a chair and I sank into it. "What were you playing just now?"

"A Chopin Nocturne."

"It was lovely. Please go on."

"First I'll tell Chauncey that there are two of us for coffee. Cigarette?"

"No thanks."

I sat alone in the room and watched the flicker of firelight on waxed wood, the luxuriant vases of autumn flowers, the great jar of golden beech leaves. My fingers stroked the brocade of the chair. This is where Deborah sits to hear Sarne play, I thought. I'm leaning my head against her cushion; Remus usually lies as he is now, filling the hearth with his great body.

Deborah, so sure of her position, her golden claim firmly staked. The second Mrs. Algar. Because Claire was gone forever.

Sarne pushed open the door with his foot. He came in carrying the coffee tray and set it down on the low table in front of me. "I always like my women to pour," he said.

The coffeepot was of fine green-and-gold china. I began to pour. Sarne was lighting a cigarette. As I handed him his cup I looked at him. In the red firelight his face was gaunt and stern. Then he raised his eyes and looked at me and smiled. A small thrill ran through me. This was it, the thing that had caused Claire so many jealous hours, the thing that had attracted women. That sudden smile that transformed the remote, arrogant face. I understood. It conceded the power to you, of all women, to make a difficult man happy. Whether it was deliberate or not I had no way of knowing, but my excitement was like a little electric shock. To cover any give-away on my part, I said the first thing that came into my head.

"This must be one of the few peaceful spots left in England!"

"So long as the heath separates us from Arlesthorne," he said, "it will remain that way. My one dread is that some local council will decide to develop it."

"I suppose if people want houses—"

"They want food, too. And that's what I won't be supplying if the paved streets come to my door."

"If it's in your blood to be a farmer," I said, "you'll stay."

"There's always Canada and Australia," he said.

"I can't see Deborah settling in the Dominions."

The thoughtless words were out before I could stop them.

Sarne picked up his coffee cup and drained it. I couldn't bear to look at him as he stood near the fire, one foot touching Remus's silky flank. I waited, dreading that his quick temper would flare up and he would say, "That's our affair!"

Instead, he moved, sat down in a chair opposite me and said, "Aunt Charlotte told me why you were down here. I hope you don't mind."

"Of course not."

I wondered whether, behind his deliberate change of conversation, he was angry. If he were, he held it well in check.

"She explained about your search for your parents because she decided that the more people who knew, the better. Someone might remember something that could be a lead for you."

"I've got a busy week ahead of me," I told him, and I explained my plans.

He sat back, looking at me through a soft coil of cigarette smoke. "It matters a lot to you, doesn't it, Loran?"

I nodded.

"In one way," Sarne said, "our childhoods ran parallel. Both of us were brought up by people who were not our parents."

I couldn't say, "And there the parallel ends. You were happy. I was lonely and the only person who wanted me died when I was seven." It savored too much of self-pity, and Sarne would have no time for that.

"It's an odd feeling," I said, "knowing that you've been living on a borrowed identity all your life."

"Hasn't it occurred to you that you're an identity in yourself? You aren't your parents, nor are your future children."

"That's easy enough to say," I told him defensively. "But I belong to the *reason* they had for getting rid of me. Would you just give up if you were faced with a mystery? I mean . . ." The two words faltered lamely. The silence of the room vibrated, and near the window Juliet and Viola sighed, one after the other.

"I *am* faced with a mystery," Sarne said.

"I'm sorry. I didn't think when I said that!"

"It's all right. It's public knowledge, why should you be sensitive about it? My wife walked out and promptly vanished. She may be anywhere in the world and she'll probably never come back."

"Whatever she felt for you," I said uncomfortably, "how could she have left her children?"

"Yes," he agreed. "How could she?"

"It must be terrible for you, not knowing."

"If you can live with a thing for a year, you can live with it forever," he said, and rose and flung away his cigarette.

I wasn't cold, but I shivered. Sarne missed nothing. He laid the back of his hand against my cheek.

"Get closer to the fire. You don't feel cold, but the wind's in the west and there could be a draught from under those windows."

"I must go," I said.

"At nine o'clock?" he said in amusement. "If you're wondering if Mrs. Cranmer will think you're lost, I'll ring her and tell her where you are."

"No, it isn't that."

"Then don't you like my house?" His tone was still amused.

"It's beautiful," I said. "And I'm very comfortable." I looked around at the darkly gleaming walnut, at Sarne's grand piano, at the rich, deep-blue damask of the upholstery.

"We chose that damask in Italy on our honeymoon," he said. "We loved it so much; we said, 'It's wonderful quality. It'll last us forever.' Forever! . . ." His voice held bitter derision.

I felt that for a moment he had forgotten me. Ghosts had crept into the room and they were the realities, I the shadow. I sat very still wondering whether, if the ghosts remained, I might learn something more about them all, about Sarne and Claire and Deborah.

"If we could only realize how we fool ourselves." His voice cut harshly through the silence and the specters. "'Forever' never means longer than the period of wanting something."

I watched his profile as he stared into the fire. Was he talking of himself or of Claire? I wanted very much to know, to understand. The silence beat about us and I had to break it.

"I should be going home, but would you play to me first?"

"What would you like to hear?"

I said I didn't mind, and settled myself on the settee and

watched him go to the piano. He sat for a moment, head bent, hands lightly touching the keys. Then the music began.

I had no idea what he was playing, but the lovely flow of notes seeped into the room.

I watched Sarne's fingers—strong farmer's hands that could touch the keys with such delicacy that for some of the passages I held my breath, afraid that the sound of my breathing would drown the tenderness of the music.

Sarne was not with me any longer. He was absorbed, identified as though every note had come from inside himself, every cadence belonging to him. The light fell on his copper hair. I remembered him as I had seen him standing in front of Martin, tanned face set with fury. And then I remembered that first strange encounter. His face and mine in the mirror. . . .

Whatever happened in my life, I had always tried to be honest. I faced the fact now that Sarne was a force too strong for me. I could love this man. I could defy all that I knew him to be, swift-tempered, arrogant and more.

The music came to an end. He paused and without looking at me, began again. This time it was the music I had heard on my first night, when I'd crossed the heath to the sea.

When it came to an end, I said, softly:

"That was lovely. It's called 'For Elissa' isn't it? I've got a record of it at home."

He sat staring at his hands. "I've often wondered who Elissa was."

"One of his loves," I said. "I suppose, like most artists, he had many."

"If it gave him inspiration for such lovely music, why not? A man's morals are his own affair. It's what he gives to the world that should matter."

Like farmers, for instance, giving food to the people. . . . Sarne's morality, too, was his own affair.

I stayed to listen to one more piece of music, a special request of my own—the Moonlight Sonata.

I was too happy, sitting there listening, too shut off from reality. Time was an enemy. I leaned my head back against the cushion and dreamed of such evenings being my right—of a long and lovely room and firelight and a man playing to me, dogs sleeping and children dreaming upstairs.

Suddenly the dogs by the window lifted their heads and growled. Remus sprang to his feet.

Sarne stopped playing and went to the window.

"What in the name of heaven is the matter with you? There's no one there, you idiots. Look!" He flung the window wide. "Go out and see for yourselves."

In one bound the three dogs dived into the black night. I heard Remus barking.

"Someone *was* there," I said, joining him at the window.

"They probably heard a footstep in the lane."

But the lane was on the estate and no one would use it unless he were coming to the house. Besides, it was quite a distance. There was the drive and the lawn and the hornbeam hedge between us. Yet the dogs had scented danger.

I had an uncanny feeling as I stood with Sarne looking out into the dark garden, that someone had been very close to us, watching us through the window. No stranger from Arlesthorne would be walking through this remote country at night. Then it must be someone we knew—and someone the dogs disliked and mistrusted.

The magic of the evening was gone. I looked at my watch and said that I must really be getting back or Mrs. Cranmer would be worried about me. Sarne made no attempt to keep me any longer, but he came with me.

The autumn smell of leaves, damp earth and wood smoke was in the air. We walked quietly in a comfortable silence, with the three dogs leading us.

When we reached the manor steps, Sarne stopped.

"I won't come in," he said. "It's late and Chauncey is alone in the house except for the children. Her husband, Ned, is playing darts at the village pub."

"You think there was a prowler?"

"There could be. We haven't had a burglary in the village for as long as I can remember, but I still don't want to leave Chauncey on her own. She's town-bred and there are times when the quiet scares her."

I stood on the first step and put out my hand.

"Thank you for an unexpected and lovely evening."

"Thank the dogs for bringing you."

Our fingers touched. I felt his eyes on me in the darkness and I wondered how much he could see of my face by the faint light from the manor hall, seeping through the stained-glass windows.

"Good night, Sarne."

"You'll come again." He was stating a fact, not asking me.

"I'd like to very much."

Swiftly he bent his head and kissed me. Then he turned and walked away and almost immediately was lost in the shadows of the trees.

The dogs were sniffing impatiently at the front door. I stood and stared at it. Sarne had kissed me. A man kissed a girl good night. It was friendly, harmless, and meant nothing more than "It's been nice knowing you!" I put out my hand to the bell and dropped it again. I didn't want to break the link with Sarne just yet. I leaned against the door frame and put my forehead against the cool wood. All in a moment you met a man and loved him. There is no sequence, just something lovely and immediate like the birth of a flame. But this wasn't it. I steadied my capering emotions. This was just a strong attraction. Sarne merely made me very aware that I was a woman.

Viola leaned her heavy body against me. I felt it warm against me leg. I felt Sarne's kiss warm, too, on my lips.

I rang three times but no one came to let me in. Switching on the flashlight I went around the house. The back door was open and I entered.

The kitchen was in darkness and there was no one in the sitting room. Only the hall light gave a wan glow that was not strong enough to penetrate the shadows.

Mrs. Cranmer must be in her bedroom and I would go up and call to her that I was in. Ferry had also gone to bed; then I must lock up. I was a little surprised, though, that the back door wasn't bolted.

I shut the dogs in the small room off the kitchen where flower vases and garden chairs were kept. Then I turned to go upstairs.

There was no sound from above me, but suddenly as I looked upwards I saw someone run across the dark landing. It was a woman. She wasn't tall enough for Ferry nor broad enough for Mrs. Cranmer. My glimpse of her was so brief, shadowy and foreshortened by my view at the foot of the stairs that I couldn't possibly identify her.

Immediately I recalled how the dogs had been alerted in Sarne's sitting room. Had she been around and had their barking scared her off the farm? Had she come instead to the manor? There was probably plenty of old silver to steal in a house like this.

I tore up the stairs and paused on the landing. She had run from the lived-in side of the house to the unused west wing. I went over and turned the handle of the door leading to it. It was locked.

I couldn't have dreamed I saw someone. But looking about me in the uneasy silence, surrounded by darkness, I was quite alone. My heart was pounding although I wasn't aware of being afraid.

Suddenly there was a loud crash and a thud from Mrs. Cranmer's room, which was up a few stairs on the left. I swung right around and took the stairs two at a time.

"Mrs. Cranmer!" I flung open the door of the room without knocking.

The light was on, a chair was overturned, and she was crouched on the floor, her hands clawing at her chest.

I knew at once what was wrong.

"Your pills—"

She managed to point to the table by her bed. I found the bottle and shook out a pill and gave it to her. She gasped for a moment or two and gradually the livid look left her face; her hands dropped to her sides. I righted the chair and, helping her to her feet, got her to the old rocker by the fire.

"That's better," she breathed, leaning back. "Thank you."

"How long have you had a bad heart?" I asked.

"Some years. . . . But it doesn't bother me much. . . . Not unless . . ." Silently I finished her sentence for her. *Not unless something upsets me.* And I was quite certain that something had. I drew up a chair and sat down by her side and waited. The green marble clock on the mantelpiece ticked away the minutes. Apart from that there was no sound except her breathing, which became gradually easier.

Presently she laid her hand on mine.

"I'm sorry about that, Loran. It was silly of me not to have taken a pill earlier. I—I felt the attack coming on. You know what the pills are, don't you?"

"Yes," I said.

"I'll be all right now. I don't often have attacks and they aren't bad."

"Did something happen to upset you tonight?"

"No. Of course not," she said decisively.

"Is Ferry out?"

"I don't think so. She's probably up in her room."

I looked at her wondering if she were recovered sufficiently for me to question her about the woman on the landing. I had little doubt that something alarming had happened and that the woman I had seen had been the cause. I realized now that she had come from Mrs. Cranmer's room. But how she could have disappeared so completely I had no idea.

The rocking chair swung gently. "I shall go to bed," Mrs. Cranmer said.

"I'll help you undress."

"Thank you, dear, but I'm really quite all right now. Just a little exhausted, that's all."

"I've undressed a great many people in my career," I said steadily, "and you've no idea what a lot of effort I can save you. Please let me."

"If you'd just undo the zip of this dress . . ." she conceded.

In the end she let me help her get to bed. I sponged her face for her, settled her pillows, and was relieved to see that her color was normal again.

She had her usual thermos of hot milk on her bedside table, but she didn't want anything to drink, she said.

I saw as I smoothed the sheet and straightened the eiderdown that although she was better she was still agitated. There was a quick, nervous look in her eyes and her fingers plucked at the sheet.

Something was very wrong. I took her hand in mine and said gently, "Mrs. Cranmer, please tell me what's the matter."

"Nothing is the matter. I've told you."

"You had a visitor, didn't you, just before you were taken ill, and she upset you?"

"A visitor?" She stared at me in such astonishment that I was almost convinced I was wrong. "Loran dear, what on earth are you talking about? I was just about to get ready for bed when the attack came on."

"Then the woman I saw on the landing must have been someone visiting Ferry."

"You *saw* someone?" She tried to out-stare me. "But you can't have. Ferry never has visitors. She's a lonely person, but she likes it that way."

"There was someone," I insisted.

She silenced me with her steady, measured gaze.

"You are mistaken, my dear. There is no one in the house but you and me and Ferry."

"Mrs. Cranmer," I began patiently, "perhaps—" The calm stare gave way to agitation deepening in her eyes, and, afraid of upsetting her, I shook my head. "Then, as you say, I must have imagined I saw a woman crossing the landing."

"That tree outside the landing window sometimes throws a shadow," she said. "Especially if the moon is bright." She turned her face away. "I'm so tired," she said with a touch of childlike petulance.

She wanted me to go. Her head lay to one side on the pillow. Her eyes were closed and I saw the gray sheen of weariness on her skin. Whatever had happened before I came in tonight, she had no intention of telling me.

I bent down and kissed her cheek.

"Good night," I said. "I'm a very light sleeper, if you should want me."

A ghost of a smile touched her features.

"You're also a very dear girl," she said. "Good night, and bless you."

I turned on the bedside lamp and switched off the main light by the door. As I left, she called out to me.

"Ferry is probably in her room. Perhaps you'd lock up, and on your way to bed call up to Ferry and tell her that you've done so. She won't need to come downstairs again then. Are the dogs in the flower room?"

I said they were and that I'd do what she said. Lying in the big bed she looked small and so fragile that I had a queer protective feeling towards her. I closed the door quietly and didn't turn on the landing light. I knew that as the house made its own power, it was not wise to keep turning lights on and off. And anyway, though the hall light was faint it was adequate.

I had no idea which was Ferry's room. As I paused halfway up the second flight of stairs, hers could be any one of the doors facing me.

I called out, "Ferry? I'll lock up downstairs and put the lights out."

No one answered me. I supposed she must have gone downstairs while I had been in Mrs. Cranmer's room. I turned back, stepping down cautiously because the stairs were very dark and rather steep.

That was why I was back on the half-landing before I realized that I was not alone. Someone watched me.

With my hand on the banister, I stopped dead.

The door leading to the west wing was open and from what I could see, a passage stretched beyond it into blackness. My view of it, however, was limited, for someone stood on the threshold, her hands folded over her long, dark dressing gown. My heart turned over, then settled itself when I realized that it was Ferry.

"You startled me," I began.

"I'm locking up."

Her flat, cold voice annoyed me.

"Do you check the doors in the empty wing, too?"

"I check every part of the house each night before I go to bed."

"Then perhaps you know—" I began, and then stopped.

"Know what, Miss Brant?"

"Never mind." I had a feeling that if she knew who the strange woman was whom I had seen dart across the landing, she wouldn't tell me. And if she didn't know, it was Mrs. Cranmer's affair and not for me to talk about.

"I've just been in to see Mrs. Cranmer," I said. "She has had a slight heart attack."

Ferry became alert at once. "I must go to her."

"No. Don't do that." I stood in her way. "I've settled her for the night. She'll be quite all right now. She'll sleep."

"*You've* settled her, Miss Brant?"

I chose to ignore the insolence of her tone. "I heard her fall as

I came up the stairs and went in to her," I explained. "I *am* a nurse, you know."

"If Mrs. Cranmer is ill, it is I who should be called."

"But there was no time. I gave her her pill. It was a very slight attack, anyway."

She didn't answer me. She turned and closed the door to the west wing carefully.

"Don't you lock it?" I asked.

"It is self-locking," she said.

So now I knew. The woman on the stairs had slipped through the open door and it had locked after her. Were there back stairs leading from that wing and had she escaped down them? Or was she still somewhere in the house, hiding until Ferry and I went to bed?

I heard the soft rustle of Ferry's gown as she moved down the passage. That she disliked me was one thing. That she should have stood there, unmoving, and let me call out that I would lock up without bothering to reply was quite another. She had been caught there in the doorway and hadn't wanted me to see her. I wondered why.

Twice, as I went to my room far down the dark passage, I looked over my shoulder. I suppose I was expecting to see that little figure again—the one so small that it could have been a child—or Babette.

VII

I WENT IN to see Mrs. Cranmer first thing the next morning and found her preparing to get up.

"You should stay in bed," I scolded.

"What nonsense! I always get up early."

"But after last night . . ."

"Last night I wasn't myself for a while, that's all. Today I feel fine."

She didn't look it. Her brightness was like a film over her tired face. She was putting on a brave front, but whatever it was that was tormenting her, she didn't want me to know, and I must humor her and pretend not to notice.

The morning was lovely, soft as spring, windless and golden. I was going into Arlesthorne to visit the adoption societies. I was much too early for the bus, so I decided to walk to the next stop. The lane went past the farm; the only sounds came from the machines in the cow stalls and the distant sound of a motor tractor in a field. Wherever the children were, they were keeping extremely quiet.

Farther down the lane the thorn hedges began. They were fairly high and were broken here and there by field gates. I thought how I would love to take some of the hedge color back to the hospital with me to decorate the wards. The fruit of the elderberries was purple-black and the lovely, evil bryony was heavy with its waxy yellow-red grapes.

I paused at a gate to look at the fine herd of brown and white dishorned Ayrshires.

Two people were somewhere near me, talking. Their voices were low but I recognized them. There couldn't be much private about a conversation out here on a field path and I opened the gate to go in and just say good morning to Deborah and Sarne. They were, however, farther off than I had imagined; in the quiet, their voices had carried.

Deborah wore russet slacks and a green sweater; Sarne was in corduroys. I heard him say something to Deborah; I saw her turn, laugh and bend her head slightly to his shoulder. It was the smallest of gestures and yet it was as intimate as a kiss. I turned quickly, angry with myself for having stood and watched them, angrier for being so irrational as to mind.

A few yards farther on there was a gate in a hazel hedge which led into the next field. As I came level with it I heard the thud of hoofs over earth. I paused and saw Marnie riding across the field on her little horse Perchance. I watched them for a moment, small horse and small rider, and even from a distance I sensed the little girl's happiness. She was free and alone, with no one to watch and nag her.

Suddenly someone darted out of the hedge. I had a swift impression of bright yellow material against the soft green of the hedge. The color came and was gone. But that momentary flash had been enough to startle Perchance. He reared, shied, and kicked up his heels. I thought Marnie cried out just before she fell, but everything happened too quickly to be sure.

The horse was prancing across the field; Marnie lay on the ground. I stumbled over the rough grass to her. There was no one else in sight. Whoever had darted out of the bushes had vanished.

"Marnie!" I dropped down by her side. She stirred, moaned a little, and then sat up.

"My foot!" she cried. "Oh, my foot!"

I ignored the long bleeding wound on her arm and gently straightened her leg.

"Where does it hurt most?"

She touched her instep and winced, wriggling painfully away from me. Her eyes looked away over my shoulder. "Here's Daddy. He'll be so c-cross."

"Of course he won't," I comforted her. "You couldn't help it if someone frightened the horse."

"But he told me I m-mustn't ride unless there's a grown-up with me." Her dark, prettily-tilted eyes were focused on Sarne's striding approach.

"I told you not to ride alone," Sarne said.

"I know, Daddy, but I was going to stay in the f-field. Nothing much could happen here, c-could it?" She watched him anxiously. "And m-my foot—Daddy, m-my foot hurts so." She was stammering badly. Surely she wasn't afraid of him too. . . . But her eyes held trust.

"Your arm's bleeding," Sarne said, and he knelt down by her side. "You must have caught it on the jagged edge of the tree stump. And did you have to fall in the muddiest part of the field?" His hand touched her face gently and she rubbed her cheek against his palm.

"People don't w-want to fall," she wailed.

"It wasn't her fault," I said. "Someone darted out of the hedge and frightened the horse."

"Who?" He looked at me for the first time.

"I don't know. I was watching Marnie. She was managing very well until then. Perchance reared and by the time I looked to see what had scared the horse, whoever was there was gone. All I saw was something yellow like a scarf. Be careful," I cautioned as he bent down and touched her foot. "I think she might have broken a little bone."

"Poor Perchance," Marnie said sadly.

"It's you who're hurt, not your horse. Come on, this is where I carry you." He picked her up in his brown arms and, holding her close to him, carried her like a doll across the field.

"Can I come too?" I called. "I might be able to help."

"Of course," he threw back at me.

Deborah met us near the house.

"What's happened?" She was frowning into the sunlight.

"Perchance reared and threw Marnie. Get the doctor."

I followed Sarne through the French windows and into the sitting room. He laid his little daughter gently on the couch.

"Her arm will have to be cleaned," I said. "And the doctor may want to give her an anti-tetanus injection. I'll boil a kettle of water."

"There's no need," Deborah, standing at the hall table with the telephone receiver in her hand, called back into the room. "I can see to everything. Thank you, Loran." Her tone dismissed me.

"If you really can cope—" I began.

"Don't go." Marnie clung to my hand. "Please, oh please, stay with me, Loran."

I hesitated and looked at Sarne.

"Would you?" he asked.

"Of course." All thought of my journey into Arlesthorne went from my mind. "I'll bathe her arm for her."

Deborah, waiting at the telephone, heard us. "I've already said—" she began.

"Thank you, Loran, if you would stay." Sarne's voice cut across her clear protest. "Deborah has her hands rather full this morning."

I heard her speaking to the doctor, say charmingly, "Thank you. We don't think she's done herself serious injury but if you would come right away . . ." Then she replaced the receiver and came back into the room. "Doctor Baines will be here in ten minutes." She looked from me to Sarne. She was holding her annoyance in check. "Chauncey usually has a kettle almost on the boil. I'll go and see."

"Have you got a rug?" I asked Sarne. "I think she's cold. It's shock."

He went immediately to fetch one and I drew up a chair and sat by Marnie's side. I put an arm around her and cradled her against me. She lay quietly but I could see that her foot gave her a lot of pain. I laid my cheek against her soft brown hair and stared into the garden.

Who had darted out of the hedge? And why? Had it been deliberate? But no one, surely, would endanger a child's life. . . .

From that hedge, dividing the two fields, someone could have been watching Deborah and Sarne, could have suddenly been afraid she was seen and so had shot into the next field. But who? Who wore a bright yellow scarf?

I had cleaned the wound on Marnie's arm by the time the doctor had arrived. He gave her an anti-tetanus injection and then told us that she must go immediately to the Arlesthorne General Hospital for an X-ray on her foot.

I would willingly have gone with her, and I know she wanted me. But this was obviously Deborah's place, and all I could do was settle her on the seat of their big car, tuck a rug around her and give her a final hug.

Sarne stood with me as the car drove off.

"If there's a fracture at all," I said, "I'm sure it's only a small bone."

"She hasn't been riding long enough to go out alone," he said. "But at least she didn't induce the others to go with her, which is one blessing. I wonder where they are."

"Would you like me to go and find them?"

"No. I hate children who have to be watched. They'll come home soon enough when it's time for food."

"And Perchance?"

"Oh, he's all right." He looked down at me. "Would you like a drink? Some coffee?"

I shook my head and on an impulse reached out and laid my hand on Sarne's arm. "Don't worry about Marnie," I said. "She fell lightly. Children do."

He smiled at me. "And they have to experience a few cuts and bruises," he said. "I'm not worried. Do you wear a blue uniform at the hospital?"

"Ours is rather special," I said in reply to that unexpected question. "We wear green, and as I'm a third year nurse my belt is a darker green."

"You must look very pretty in it," he said.

It was the most casual flattery, but I stood silently savoring the words as though he'd paid me some great tribute. I didn't look at Sarne but I felt his deep awareness of me. It was a moment when I longed to say something clever or startling, something to hold his admiration. Instead I looked at my watch and said flatly, "I'd better be going."

"I hope this hasn't upset your morning."

"Oh, no."

"Of course there was no real need for me to ask you to stay," he admitted. "I yield to impulses, you know."

"Do you?"

He laughed down at me. "When they suit me! And Marnie wanted you to stay."

"She'll be all right at the hospital with Deborah, won't she?" It was an idiotic question, but then, I was ill-at-ease.

"Oh, yes. Deborah will look after her—for my sake."

There was no reason on earth why I should mind the gentleness of his voice as he said that, but I did. It flung a spear right through my awkward happiness. My wide mouth smiled brightly at him. I'd ring up later, I said, to find out how Marnie was. Then I left him.

I had missed the ten o'clock bus and there wasn't another until eleven. If I caught that, I would have too little time in Arlesthorne.

I would go this afternoon. In the meantime a car hooted at me. Martin pulled up.

"Going my way?" he sang at me.

"I shouldn't think so. You can't take the car onto the beach," I said flippantly.

"You could change your mind about beachcombing and come into Arlesthorne with me."

I hesitated. "I'd planned to go there. But I got held up. Marnie had an accident. Her horse took fright and she had a nasty fall."

"She's Sarne Algar's brat all right," he said gruffly. "She'll ride to her death one of these days."

"That's a most horrible remark," I flashed at him. "And quite wrong if you mean to imply that she's as unlikeable as *you* think Sarne is."

"I merely mean that there's a devil streak in that family."

"Not in Marnie. She's gentle and shy and her riding was perfectly all right," I said indignantly. "I told you, something scared the horse."

He grinned at me. "All right, all right, you don't have to wave the flag for the Algars quite so frantically. Come on, jump in and I'll take you to Arlesthorne. Then you can have a drink with me and I'll get you back well in time for your lunch."

He had leaned forward while he talked, and opened the door on the passenger side of the car. I got in, and almost before I was settled he was away with a roar which I guessed was infuriating Sarne.

"There are some sugared almonds in the glove compartment," he said. "I always keep some; I like them. Have one."

"Not now, thanks."

We turned into the main road. I cast a cautious sideways glance at Martin. The silvery fair hair gleamed in the sunlight; in profile the sculptured lines of his face were handsome but did not exactly denote strength. As he grew older, if he were not careful, he would become fleshy like the portraits of Roman Emperors.

Quite suddenly he turned and looked at me.

"Do I pass?"

"I'm sorry," I said and glanced away.

Immediately my heart leaped in alarm. The car was steering straight for a green bank.

"Be careful!" I cried, remembering the great elm where Richard had crashed. I closed my eyes. When I opened them again we were on a steady course again.

"You *could* keep your eyes on the road," I said, letting out a breath.

"Don't worry. I'm an expert driver. I was curious to know why you were staring at me. Were you looking for the bump I received yesterday morning when Algar threatened me?"

"No. I wasn't that interested. It was entirely your own fault anyway. Sarne was right in wanting to knock you down."

"You've got medieval ideas," he said. "You'd probably have enjoyed seeing us fight it out. All I did, you know, was tell him the truth."

I sat staring ahead of me, saying nothing.

"How long are you staying here?" he asked.

"Until next Saturday."

"Good. That's not long enough for you to get involved."

"Involved in what?"

"Something," he said in an instant's seriousness, "that isn't exactly pretty."

"But *what*?" I demanded exasperatedly.

"Don't ask me! I can't solve the riddle."

"Just who *are* you?"

"Martin Cavall. Aged thirty-one—"

"What's your job?"

"Oh, this and that."

"You work on the *Arlesthorne Gazette*, don't you?"

He threw back his head and laughed as though I'd said something funny.

"You should have gone in for law," he said. "You'd look charming in a counsel's wig! And you're dogged about questions, aren't you?"

I decided not to ask any more. He would answer only those he chose and as he chose. I lifted my head a little and the wind blew my hair back. In spite of my warm coat and the mild day, I felt cold. For some reason which I couldn't discover, I wasn't enjoying my ride into Arlesthorne with a merry young man. It was that very merriness which troubled me. I had never before felt a sinister element in laughter.

He was a truly magnificent driver. We roared into the town, powerful engine zooming. I told Martin I had one or two jobs to do and he dropped me at the market square. I promised to meet him at the White Hart for a drink in an hour. That would give me time to look up the names of adoption societies here and visit them.

As it happened, I had too much time. The one adoption society in the town couldn't help me. It had been formed only fifteen years ago, and before that the two charitable establishments run by various society women with headquarters in London had closed down. I was up against the law, which erected its own barrier between me and my parents. I was also up against the impenetrable fact that I did not know the name of the people I was searching for.

With time to spare, I telephoned Miss Brant, apologized for troubling her, explained that I had lost the topaz from the fob I wore and asked if by any chance she had found it.

"If I had," she said in that tetchy voice, "I'd have sent it to you. It was very careless of you, wasn't it?"

"Very," I said humbly and thanked her and heard her replace the receiver.

I wandered around the shops, bought a silver belt for my sapphire dress, and a tiny little blue-and-gilt St. Christopher keyring for Adèle, who loved gewgaws. Then I found my way back to the White Hart.

For all that he was a stranger in the village, Martin seemed to be on casual greeting terms with almost everyone in the White Hart. I had never been introduced to so many people at one time before. Though Christian names were used for them all, I had a strong feeling that in the case of most of them he had no more idea of what their surnames were than they had of who he was. And the more I saw of him the more I wondered, too, what he was doing living in a shack that was like a sinister little woodman's hut in a fairy tale, on the edge of Black Ash Heath.

Martin kept his word about getting me home around twelve. He dropped me at the manor gates. As I turned to wave, I caught sight of a tiny figure disappearing down the lane. She wore a blue skirt and a yellow scarf on her head. I had seen that patch of color before. It had frightened Marnie's horse. And as Babette scuttled up the road the ends of the scarf bobbed and blew in the wind like sunflowers.

Mrs. Cranmer met me in the hall. Sarne had telephoned and told her of Marnie's accident.

I slid out of my coat and hung it in the cloakroom in the hall.

"I know now who frightened Perchance," I said. "It was Babette."

Mrs. Cranmer had her back to me. She was running her finger along the top of a picture frame.

"Are you quite sure?" she asked carefully.

"Yes. I recognized her yellow scarf."

"I suppose she was blackberrying on Sarne's private property, saw someone coming—perhaps Sarne himself—and started to run away. Then, when Marnie fell she was frightened and darted back into the hedge to hide."

"Will you speak to her about it?"

"Nothing can be gained by doing so now, can it?" she said evenly. "And the less we have to do with Babette, the better. By the way, Marnie had had her X-ray when Sarne phoned. A small bone in her foot is broken and the gash on her arm is rather nasty. But thank God it was nothing more serious."

"Are they keeping her in the hospital?"

"No. She's home, though Sarne will have to get a nurse to come in and dress her arm every day. It's a deep gash and needs careful watching. The trouble is," she added, "nurses are in short supply and it's difficult to get someone to come right out here."

"I could do it for her," I startled myself by saying.

Her face lit up. "Would you? Would you really, Loran?"

"Of course. I'm here on the spot and it wouldn't take long each morning to dress her arm."

"I must tell Sarne at once." She reached immediately for the telephone, as though frightened that I might change my mind.

I perched on the Italian cassone in the hall while she got through to Sarne.

"I've found a nurse for you," she said. "Someone on the spot. Loran, of course."

As I waited, watching Mrs. Cranmer's face, I didn't ask myself why it was so imperative to me that Sarne should let me come.

"But she *offered*," Mrs. Cranmer was protesting. "She really did. . . . No, of course I didn't suggest it to her. I wouldn't do such a thing . . . I *know* it sounds as though you're imposing on her, but Loran wouldn't offer unless she really meant it. Look, she's here with me. Let her speak to you."

She held the receiver out to me and I took it. Leaning against the table, I said, "Hello, Sarne. Mrs. Cranmer is quite right. I offered to come in each morning to dress Marnie's arm because I would really like to."

"Even so, I don't know that I can let you." I could picture his face, stern and final. "I'll get the district nurse to come in."

"She's probably got quite enough to do," I protested. "Really,

Sarne, there isn't any argument. That is," I added hastily, "unless you don't want me around."

"That's the damnedest silly thing I've heard."

I held the receiver away from my ear as the explosion hit it.

"Very well, then don't say the kind of thing that makes me think it. The matter's settled. I'll be along tomorrow at ten. And this," I added firmly, "is to be a labor of love. That's understood. I like Marnie." I felt a certain satisfaction in putting the receiver down, finally and firmly. For once Sarne was at the receiving end of a decision. I glanced at Mrs. Cranmer. Her face was alight with pleasure.

"This means you'll be staying here a little longer, doesn't it? I'm so glad. I'm so very glad, Loran."

I smiled faintly, murmured that I wanted to tidy myself up before lunch, and escaped to my room.

I hadn't stopped to think, when I offered to nurse Marnie, that it would mean I must stay here longer than my week. I hadn't stopped to think at all. I stood at the window, drying my hands on the pink towel, and stared out at the black lightning-struck top of a distant tree. A week would have given me plenty of time to complete what I had to do here. I felt a small rising panic at the thought of staying longer. But I was committed now. Torn in two, I wanted to escape and I wanted to stay.

VIII

MARNIE'S PREOCCUPATION in the days following her accident was not with herself, but with her little horse. "I love him more than anyone in the world. He's the bravest, most beautiful—"

"He's a silly," I said. "He shies at a yellow scarf."

"People shouldn't frighten horses."

"And horses shouldn't throw little girls."

Every time we talked about Perchance, we reached an impasse. To Marnie he had wings on his feet and his mane was silver fire. I secretly thought him dangerous. I'd seen for myself. He hadn't merely shied; he had reared and kicked and danced in temper at being startled.

I soon discovered that Marnie liked me to tell her stories about hospital life. I talked to her about some of the odd patients I had had; I talked about the babies I had to deliver.

"I wish Mummy would have more babies when she comes back," she said. "I'd like lots. Daddy once said he wanted eight children."

"And you'd be the eldest and boss them all," I laughed.

"You know Mummy's gone away? She's ill," she said solemnly.

"Yes." I noticed that she seldom stammered when she talked to me.

"I wanted to write to her, but Daddy said we mustn't. It's funny, because she always wanted us to love her a lot and now she doesn't want to *know* that we love her."

I said gently, "She knows without your having to write letters."

"Grown-ups cry a lot, don't they, Loran?"

"It all depends on the grown-up." I secured the bandage and patted her hand. "There you are. Now you're all set for the day."

"Mummy did. Cry a lot, I mean." Marnie was staring out of the window towards the apple orchard. "She was awfully pretty and she kept wanting us to tell her how pretty she was and how we loved her." She turned her heartshaped face towards me, her low brow furrowed, her eyes far too sad for a little girl. "She will come back, won't she?"

"Of course." I pushed a table laden with books, paints and drawing paper nearer to her. "What are you going to paint this morning?"

"I don't know," she said. "I want to go back to school."

"You'll go when you can walk again," I comforted her. "It won't be very long. You like school?"

"Not much. But I don't like home, either. Not without Mummy. I . . ."

A voice cut in from the doorway. "If you draw your mouth down like that you'll grow up into a very ugly girl. Heaven knows you're no beauty as it is."

We both turned. Deborah watched us. There was no kindness in the look she gave Marnie. "It's you who're the baby of the family, not Nina," she said.

"I . . . d-don't . . . care." Her little stammer defeated the defiance of her words. "I d-don't care about anything a-any more."

"That's enough of being sorry for yourself," Deborah said

authoritatively and turned to me. "It's so good of you to do this for Marnie. But we really can't continue to take advantage of your kindness."

As she spoke the formal, uncompromising words, a man's long stride sounded on the paved terrace and Sarne joined us. Deborah smiled up at him. "I was just telling Loran that I'm sure I can look after Marnie now. There's no need for her . . ."

"No, Daddy, no! I want Loran. Please let Loran come. Daddy, I want Loran." Her voice became a little sing-song plea. Sarne took no notice of her. He came and stood in front of me. Someone had to speak.

I said calmly, "I always like to carry a job through to the end. I suppose that's part of my training."

"But Deborah's right."

"That gash on her arm is a brute," I said. "It still wants watching." I was aware of Marnie's little raised face, full of hope. "I'd hate to leave my job half done," I added.

"You win," he conceded with a laugh, "and thank you."

I dragged my eyes from his face and glanced at Deborah. She was looking at Marnie and her face was like a stone mask. Behind it she was hating her, and just *how* she was hating her for being the cause of my visits to the farm!

The beautiful Indian summer continued over Dorset. There was rain in eastern England, there were gales in the north. We basked in sunshine.

Every day I took Mrs. Cranmer's car and visited the various villages between Saxon Magna and Corfe. I knew the names of all the inns, for it was there that I began my search. Sitting at bars, talking to landlords, sipping a sherry or a lager, I found out who were the oldest inhabitants. I met them, asked them questions, and each time I drew a blank.

One afternoon when I could not believe the lovely weather would last much longer, I decided that I would have what would probably be my last sunbath of the year. It was a Wednesday and the day Mrs. Cranmer went into Arlesthorne for a W.V.S. meeting.

I had visited three villages that morning and had arranged to go to the farm immediately after lunch to dress Marnie's arm.

I told Mrs. Cranmer of my plan to go to the cove at Falcon Point. "I'm interested in that lost village."

"There's really nothing to see there except a few stones and bricks. The hamlet is buried under the sea and that great cliff makes the place rather depressing. But if you've set your heart on going then I suggest you take your tea with you. I'll ask Ferry to fill a thermos and you can tell her what you want to eat."

I went upstairs to change into low shoes and an off-the-shoulder jersey that I could pull down when I sunbathed.

I didn't hear the doorbell ring, but when I went downstairs again Gillian was standing in the hall. She was looking at her reflection in the Regency mirror over the table and doing something to her hair.

"Going picnicking?" she asked pleasantly, indicating the thermos and the little packet of biscuits.

I nodded.

"Monty hasn't been well," she said, "and I slipped home at lunch time to bring him some pills the doctor has prescribed. Now I'm off back to work. Though I've got a feeling I'm going to be late. My car's giving me trouble. I just looked in here to pick up a magazine Aunt Charlotte promised me."

Ferry came out of the back room with two magazines in her hand. "I don't know which one, Miss Gillian. You'd better take both."

"Thank you." She turned and smiled at me. "Can I drop you anywhere?"

"No thanks," I said. "I'm going to walk across the heath to Falcon Point."

Immediately I sensed a heightening of attention. Their eyes sharpened, watching me. Gillian said, "I really must be going or I'll get sacked."

I walked with her to the small Hillman. Just before she got in, she paused and listened. A car was coming up the lane towards the farm.

"So now Deborah's got a new car out of Sarne!"

"She could have bought it herself."

"If she managed to steal one of her father's pictures to pay for it I suppose she could!" She gave me a pale, sour smile. "And I wouldn't put it past her. He gave her one some years ago, but he hangs onto the others. It'd be really funny, wouldn't it, if when he dies he wills them to some art gallery?"

"Would it?"

She looked in the direction of the lane, one foot resting on the car floor. Her angular body was still rigid with resentment.

"You wouldn't say she's a patient person, would you?"

"Who? Deborah?"

She nodded. "Seven years is a long time. She won't stay the course. And then . . ."

"Then what?" I watched her.

She gave a short, sharp laugh. "He laughs best who laughs last," she said.

I stood by as she got into her car. I knew quite well that that last remark wasn't as irrelevant as it sounded.

I watched the car out of sight and then hoisted my shoulder bag and turned towards the farm. It was all so beautiful and so serene with the lush green of the fields and the misty emerald of the distant Purbecks. Only the people who lived in this wild corner of England had no serenity. Perhaps to have had perfection in everything would be too much. . . . I reached the farm and dumped my things in the hall, then I went to find Marnie. I saw Sarne out in the distant fields and Deborah was in the patio filling two red luster jars and a bronze urn with flowers. I watched her for a moment or two putting long stemmed russet chrysanthemums in the urn. She felt someone near and turned and greeted me in the cool, unenthusiastic manner I had come to expect from her.

"I'll find Marnie," I said.

"She's around on the sheltered side of the house in the sun. Sarne carried her there after lunch. We've had a few tantrums from her today."

"She must miss Simon and Nina when they're at school."

"I suppose so," she said boredly, without sympathy.

"It's a pity Marnie has hurt her foot, because otherwise I'd have taken her with me."

"Where are you going?"

She snapped a stem and fitted a late white rose well down in the vase.

"To Falcon Point to do some mild sunbathing. It's too cold for a sundress, but at least I can let my face and hands bask in it," I laughed.

She turned and looked at me half over her shoulder.

"It's quite a walk."

"Oh, I'm taking my tea with me."

She said nothing, and, dismissed, I went to find Marnie. It was becoming routine that while I dressed her arm I told her stories about hospital life. She said once that she'd like to be a nurse when she grew up. This afternoon she was very reluctant to let me go. Every time I was with her she brought her mother into the conversation. I had a feeling that she sensed something had happened to Claire, something that would never bring her back. Not that she had ever said so. Marnie kept things inside herself: the fears of this small bewildered child showed merely in her stammering, her shadowed eyes and her small, sensitive gestures.

I stayed with her longer than I'd meant to, and as always when I left she put her arms around my neck and kissed my cheek lightly, shyly.

"Bring me some shells back," she said softly. "You can find lovely ones there."

I promised and left her.

Falcon Point was quite deserted. I stood for quite a while at the water's edge, looking out at the huddle of rocks and stone. Some of it must belong to the submerged hamlet. I wondered if people had been drowned or if they had all escaped. It was all so far in the past—long before I was born—yet I had been told this wasn't a happy spot and I felt it very strongly for myself.

I went back and sat down in a patch of sunlight and drank some tea. Then I lay back and stared up at the sky. I closed my eyes.

I don't know how long I lay there in the warm sun, but presently I heard a sound and it was not like the sea at all. Half in dream, I thought: It's the sound of bells, just as the book said. Bells from the submerged church tower. . . . But Babette had said, "It isn't bells that you hear. It's Sarne Algar's wife crying. . . ."

But they *were* bells, growing louder and louder. Their sound was lovely, liquid as water. Water. . . . I tried to open my eyes. I was suddenly aware that all my limbs were stiff with cold and that no sun shone onto them. I dragged one eye open and felt something at me feet. I needed all my force to rouse myself. I pulled myself with dull, heavy limbs against the cliff and stared. Bells, I'd dreamed.

Not bells but water—all around me. Waves, no longer gentle and limpid but strong and white-foamed crashing around me. I struggled up and looked about me. I was entirely cut off. What was more, the foot of the cliff path which I had come down was submerged. Behind me the great wall of granite rose in a concave sweep.

I found that I was clinging to the rock. My feet were wet but the water had not quite reached the rest of me. I stood in a patch of beach no larger than a small traffic island and getting smaller every minute.

I leaned against the cliff face, my hands splayed behind me, and stared at the sea. My eyes had difficulty in focusing and my limbs felt as though I had no muscles. This must be the kind of feeling one had when forced to wake from a drugged sleep, but I'd no idea why I should feel like that.

I took off my shoes and climbed a foot of rock to a tiny platform. It was narrow and sloping, but for the moment it was above sea level. Perhaps the sea was already at full tide and I would be safe. My full wits rallied a little and I looked around for the thermos flask. I saw it, some way out, being tossed with my shoulder bag up and over the strong waves.

The sky was now heavily overcast and I was cold. I measured the distance between myself and the cliff steps and knew that for some odd reason my limbs felt too heavy to swim the distance—not that I was much of a swimmer anyway. I shouted, but the waves drowned my voice. Besides, I doubted if anyone would be walking across the cliff top in that isolated place. I glanced at my watch. It was nearly five o'clock. I had slept for over two hours.

Who knew I was here? Mrs. Cranmer—but then she would not be home yet to discover that I hadn't returned. Ferry? I doubted if after I'd gone she would give me another thought. Deborah? But she wouldn't know that I wasn't yet back at the manor—if *she* gave me a thought. Gillian? No, I thought again. Gillian was working. And Marnie would merely think I had gone straight home and forgotten her seashells.

There was no one, then, who would think for hours yet of searching for me. For hours . . . and the tide was still coming in.

I still felt a little lightheaded. I closed my eyes and again I thought I heard the sound of bells. But shutting my eyes, even for a few moments, was dangerous. I opened them and looked at the sky. The clouds were being blown from the south. I couldn't understand how I had slept so heavily and for so long. I was never a deep sleeper, nor did I wake with this sense of heaviness. I was certain that this feeling was exactly what people experienced when they had been drugged. But how could I be? What could have drugged me? All I'd had since one o'clock was half a cup of tea. The tea. . . .

I stared in growing horror at the bobbing thermos crashing against the rocks. I tried to laugh at the idiocy of my thoughts. No one had drugged me. Why should they? Why should they, any more than anyone had lured me by a dog's bark to the old well and removed a plank? Yet suddenly I was very afraid.

The sound of the waves crawling higher towards me forced me to try to think again of the immediate problem of saving myself. I looked up at the cliff face curving inward and thought a little hysterically, even if I were a mountain goat I couldn't climb that.

Slowly, as my brain cleared, panic took its place. Suppose I had been drugged? Suppose someone, knowing where I was going, had planned for this very thing to happen because he—or she—knew that at high tide the cove would be flooded?

There wasn't even a dinghy in sight. But if there were, it wouldn't see a girl in a gray skirt and a blue sweater clinging to a cliff. I was too small, too merged with the color behind me, too much in the shadow of the vast black wing of Falcon Point.

"Don't you get too nosy about Falcon Point if you know what's good for you. . . ." Babette's harsh little voice came to me like an echo out of the waves.

But I hadn't been nosy. I had come here to lie in the sun. Just as, on my first evening, I had gone innocently for a walk to look at the sea—and had almost lost my life down an old well.

Haphazard happenings? Near accidents without design? I wanted to believe it.

I tried to think more clearly and couldn't. The sound of bells seemed to grow louder, to mingle with the crashing of waves, no longer musical but dully rhythmic. I pushed my hair out of my eyes with a wet ice-cold hand.

And then I saw the motorboat. It was well out from the great rock and it was turning to cut inwards towards the cove. As it sped nearer, I saw that someone was raking the cliffs with binoculars. A second man was at the wheel.

They were looking for me. Pressed against the rock face, I watched the boat draw close. It tacked this way and that as though whoever steered was negotiating the tumbled mass of the piled hamlet lying there.

Then the little boat made a last dash, riding a wave, towards the place where I was crouched. The man lowered his binoculars.

"Sarne!" I think I cried his name aloud. There was a sudden welling up inside me of a tremendous emotion. I closed my eyes against a sudden dizziness. When I opened them again, Sarne was wading through the water towards me.

I suppose I must have swayed a little, for he called:

"It's all right, Loran. Hang on."

He climbed to my side and put his arms around me. Against the warmth of his body I felt my own shuddering coldness. I clung for a moment. Then he put me a little away from him and picked up my shoes.

"It's all right," he said again and half carried me down through the water to the boat.

I have never fainted in my life, and it wasn't exactly faintness I felt now. My head swam and I felt as though my body had melted away. I lay in the boat with Sarne's right arm around me and heard him giving instructions to the man at the wheel. I guessed that it was a tricky business getting free of the rocks, which might at any moment scrape the bottom of the boat and perhaps hole it.

It seemed that I was the only one of the three of us who didn't care. Against Sarne's lean, hard shoulder I could even have faced drowning. It was a wild, hysterical thought because I wanted to live, but it dominated me. To die with Sarne rather than live without him. . . . I was raving. I was delirious with the aftermath of panic.

I was all those things. But behind them, something real in me faced a moment of truth. I loved Sarne Algar.

I moved swiftly out of his arms.

"Careful!" he said.

"I . . ."

"What is it?"

I shook my head. My wet skirt clung clammily to my legs.

"My feet are so cold," I said faintly and began to rub them hard. It was my wild effort at an escape from Sarne's touch.

The little boat was clear of the rocks. It made a wide, cautious arc around the point and then turned into the stretch that bordered Saxon Magna.

Sarne moved to the floor of the boat and took one of my feet between his hands and began to massage it.

I sat there wanting desperately to cry, watching the dark bent head, the strong brown hands gentling the blood back in my numbed legs.

The man at the wheel took no notice of us. I gripped the seat on either side of me, not daring to let my fingers relax, afraid that if I let go I would reach out to Sarne. More than anything in the world, I wanted him to kiss me. This was what happened, I supposed, when fear weakened one's will. Emotions took charge. I gripped the seat harder.

The sun came out for a second or two and threw the great shadow of Falcon Point across us. I shivered. Sarne raised his head and our eyes met and held. His were strangely shining. And mine? Afraid my eyes would give me away, I turned my head quickly.

The waves creamed over the rocky pile in the cove, almost submerging them. Did Sarne know what people were whispering? What Babette was saying of that place where the sea sang? "It's Sarne Algar's wife crying . . ."

I shut my eyes and felt my feet tingling under his strong massaging hands. I was loving it and it was unbearable. He moved back, squatting before me like a Red Indian.

"Is that better?"

"Much . . . much . . . better," I said and burst into tears.

He moved to my side on the seat and took me in his arms as though I were a child.

"I'm sorry," I sobbed. "It's idiotic of me."

"No, it isn't. It's quite natural. It's reaction."

I felt his cheek rest on my hair; I felt his hard body through his shirt and the steady beating of his heart. Or was it mine, so close to his?

"Loran," he said. "Loran."

Sometimes a man says your name and it's as though he's saying, "I love you."

Soaked and cold as I was, I would have liked that moment to have lasted forever. I clung to him while the boat made for the shore. The sun had gone again, but so had the shadow of the Falcon's wing. The wide silvery sands on this side of the point were not covered at high tide. The little boat beached swiftly and without trouble and I was helped out.

I put on my sandals to climb the cliff, Sarne steadying me. I turned and thanked the boatman. His smile showed two rows of splendid teeth, milk-white in a brown face.

"'Ee be safe, miss. Do 'ee now go an' get waarm."

Sarne said something to him that I couldn't hear. He said, "Thank 'ee sir," and turned back to his boat.

Sarne put an arm around me. "Can you walk or shall I carry you?"

"You'd be sorry. I may be a small package but I weigh heavy," I laughed. It was a funny, jerky sound that came out like a hiccough. I walked without his help up the cliff steps. Mrs. Cranmer was waiting for me at the top. She was almost tearful with relief.

"My dear Loran, thank God you're safe!" she cried. "What happened?"

"I fell asleep," I said.

"Without knowing that the tide came right up? How *could* we have let you go without warning you? I blame myself."

"Don't, please," I said, distressed. "Everything's all right."

"She's shivering," Sarne said practically. "Put that rug around her and take her straight back to the house."

"Of course. Come, Loran, the car's down in the lane. You can walk?"

"I'm fine," I said, trying to stop my teeth chattering.

Mrs. Cranmer unfolded the rug she carried and slipped it around my shoulders. I almost ran to the car.

"I'll come around later on to see how you are," Sarne said, tucking the rug around my feet.

"I've given everyone enough trouble," I said, shivering. "I'll be all right."

"All the same"—he straightened and looked at me—"I'm coming around."

He watched Mrs. Cranmer back the car, turn on a grassy place and then drive off. I didn't turn around to look but I knew he was watching us until we were out of sight over the brow of Black Ash Heath.

IX

FERRY WAS COMING down the stairs as we entered the house.

"I've put hot bottles in Miss Brant's bed," she said. "Shall I run a bath?"

"Thank you, Ferry," Mrs. Cranmer said before I could protest that I could do it for myself, "and I think a brandy would be best for her when she's tucked up."

"Oh, no," I said quickly. "No, thank you. I'll just have a bath and then I'll come downstairs. I'm all right, really I am."

"You can get pneumonia in London if you really want it, my dear," Mrs. Cranmer spoke briefly. "But while you're here you're going to be looked after. Now go along and have that bath."

"But not brandy," I said. "I—I'd rather have tea."

"Very well. But I thought young people today liked strong drink."

I said lightly, "As a matter of fact, they prefer coffee bars." But my thoughts weren't gay as I dragged off my clothes and huddled into my dressing gown. My hair hung damply around my head, and my face, devoid of make-up, looked pinched and white and not in the least pretty. But Sarne hadn't cared. Sarne had knelt and held my frozen feet in his hands.

I lay in the hot bath and wondered how I could explain to Mrs. Cranmer. "I fell asleep because someone drugged my tea. Someone who wants to frighten me away from here—or to destroy me." I used the word "destroy" even to myself, because I couldn't face the word "kill." The whole idea sounded as implausible as a nightmare. I tried to face it, to think it out step by step. Why? Who?

And then, what would have happened if I had drunk all the tea? But slowly, as I grew warmer and more relaxed, the idea became more outrageous. In the end I stopped thinking about it.

I was dressing when Mrs. Cranmer entered with tea on a green painted tray.

"Loran dear, do get into bed!"

"I'm not tired and I feel quite warm now. I'd much rather stay up."

"Then come and sit by the fire." She pulled an armchair forward for me and sat down opposite in a straight-backed chair.

"Thank God Deborah rang up."

"Deborah?" I stared at her.

She nodded. "She called me because you'd apparently told Marnie you'd look in on your way back and bring her any pretty shells you found. When you didn't come, Marnie thought you'd forgotten her. Sarne and Deborah were with her and Deborah rang through immediately and asked if you were back. When I said no, Sarne went to Falcon Point to find you. I followed in the car. We were all terribly worried, though we never dreamed you'd fallen asleep. You must have slept very deeply."

"I did. It . . . it was almost as though I were drugged."

"With sunshine. I shouldn't have thought there was enough power in the sun for that."

I didn't know what to say. I drank some tea, almost welcoming the scalding sensation in my throat. "I went to sleep so quickly," I said. "So easily. I've never taken any sleeping pills in my life, but I've nursed enough people who have, to know what it must feel like. I felt like that."

"How extraordinary!"

I set my cup down and because my hand wasn't steady it rattled slightly against the spoon. "I suppose," I said, staring into the electric fire, "there couldn't have been . . . dregs of anything in the thermos."

"My dear child, what *are* you asking?"

"Just that perhaps, by accident, something might have been dropped in. Something . . ."

"That thermos is used to keep hot milk in. It stands every night on my bedside table. And every morning Ferry washes it out with boiling water." She wasn't exactly annoyed, but she watched me closely, almost as though she were discovering something she didn't like about me, some irritating complex. But I couldn't drop the subject.

"I'm sorry. It was a stupid suggestion. Of course Ferry left nothing in the thermos, but I'm not imagining how I felt."

"I'm sure you aren't—not consciously, that is," she said soothingly. "You were probably tired after your walk and the sun was more powerful than we thought. After all, it's not so many weeks since that car accident and you're probably not fully recovered yet." She sat forward, watching me, puzzled and unhappy.

"I'm sorry about your thermos," I said. "It got washed out to sea. I'll get another tomorrow."

She waved the offer aside. "There's another somewhere in the house. Don't bother about that. It's this feeling you had of being drugged that worries me. Sometimes at night I take a pill," she admitted. "I don't sleep very well these days. But I couldn't have accidentally dropped one into the thermos, and anyway it would have been sterilized before your tea was put into it. There couldn't have been anything . . . Loran, there *couldn't.*"

Her distress was so sharp, so poignant, that I felt the onus to pacify was on me. She had enough to cope with without my mysterious sleep.

I said gently, "I expect it was the sun and the sound of the sea that made me doze off. But I'm fine now."

Relief crept over her face. "I blame myself for not warning you about the tides around the point. I'm afraid I didn't think."

"But everything is all right now," I reassured her.

She gave me a long, affectionate look. "Dear Loran. . . ." The door closed behind her.

After supper Mrs. Cranmer explained that she had to go into Arlesthorne to fetch an altar cloth, from Jessily Court's private chapel, which needed repair. She glanced across the room at the polythene-covered heap on a corner chair. "Though I'm afraid I haven't finished mending that quilt yet." She drew her hand in that characteristic way she had across her forehead. "Ferry is going out after she has washed up. But you'll be all right, won't you? There may be something good on television. And you'll have the dogs. I won't be very long."

She didn't wait for coffee, and I heard her hurry through the hall and out of the house. Ten minutes later I thought I heard Ferry leave. I was alone with the dogs, the fire, and a television program about Ireland. I watched for awhile, and then, unable to concentrate, switched off.

The curtains weren't drawn over the window and I stood looking out. The dogs watched me, willing me to take them for a walk. I said, "Not tonight," and as though they understood, their broad noses settled down again on their paws and they sighed.

It was strange how the black, wild heath drew me. Perhaps it was merely because my life had been spent in a house in a narrow West End Street and I looked out onto cars parked outside doctors' houses and women airing their poodles. And at the hospital my room gave onto a well, and the noises I heard were the thud and roll of oxygen cylinders being trundled from the trucks. This was strange to me, this black gorse-and-fern isolation.

At the very moment of thinking how silent it was, I heard footsteps along the terrace. Instinctively I drew back and my fingers went out to check the lock on the window. I was perfectly safe. I reached out to draw one of the heavy velvet curtains, and as I did so a man came out of the shadows.

It was Sarne.

My fingers shook as I unlatched the window and let him in.

"You're looking remarkably well," he said, "after nearly drowning."

"Oh, I'm fine." I heard my voice high and excited. "It would take more than that to get me down! I'm enormously strong!"

"Your strength must lie in your spirit, then," he said in amusement, "because to me you're just a scrap of a girl!"

"No nurse is a scrap of a girl. We have to be strong."

His amusement became out-and-out laughter.

"Then I'll call you a pint-sized Amazon. You're so little . . . so very little!" He tilted my chin and looked deeply at my face.

I knew that he misinterpreted the sharp way in which I jerked my head away. He had no idea that as soon as he touched me I had begun to tremble. I moved to the fire and held out my hands to the glow, my back to him.

"Mrs. Cranmer is out."

"Is she? Well, never mind. I didn't come to see Aunt Charlotte. I came to see you."

I turned and faced him. "I haven't thanked you for what you did. I might easily have been drowned."

"Yes," he said reasonably, "you might."

We were standing looking at each other. Every line of his face was clear and sharp as the light fell on it. His eyes were no longer silver-gray; they were storm-dark and they held my own gaze as though they were the eyes of an enchanter.

Nerves made me break the silence.

"I'm so grateful."

When he frowned, his brows almost met.

"Do you imagine that's what I've come for?"

"No. No, of course not. But I suppose gratitude is always nice to have."

"I can do without it. I can do without every damned, noble emotion," he said with a low violence.

"Have it your own way." I closed my eyes against his strange powerful gaze.

"Do you really think that it's gratitude I want from you?" he burst out. "Just a pale, patient emotion like that? Dear God . . ."

My eyes were still closed but I sensed his movement towards me. I knew he was going to touch me even before his arms went around me, drawing me hard and hurting against him. I felt his lips speak against my cheek. "This is what I want."

His mouth hurt mine, his chin bruised my face with its roughness. He had drawn me so close that I could feel the violent beating of his heart and his body. Odd, that you never realize how soft you are until a man holds you close to him. The little thought came and was immediately crushed out of my mind by the power of Sarne's kiss. I could have no thought at all, no mind, only sensation and a glorious and terrible all-over need for him. There was no passing time, only the everlasting present vibrating with our desire for each other.

"Loran. Loran." He said my name twice, just as he had done in the boat, his lips opening my mouth. I had never before found my name so beautiful.

I think I made a little sound, a cry—a laugh, a moan perhaps, because joy and pain are sometimes one.

Sarne moved, bent his head and kissed my neck, where a pulse throbbed.

"Oh, Sarne . . . darling. . . ." My eyes were closed. I opened them. Far away, in another world, at the door of the quiet room, Ferry stood and watched us.

I stiffened. Before Sarne noticed my sudden resistance, the door had closed and we were alone again.

"Ferry," I said breaking away from him. "She saw us. She was at the door."

"I'm glad."

I leaned against the big chair, drained of energy, plunged into life again.

"I'm glad," he said again, "because it brought us to our senses."

Unable to speak, I watched him take out a packet of cigarettes and offer them to me. I saw that his hand was unsteady. I shook my head and he lit a cigarette for himself. He walked away from me and stood near the fire, blowing out a small coil of smoke.

"Do you think I ought to find out what Ferry wanted?" I asked faintly.

"No. Leave her." He was looking at his cigarette with absorbing interest.

His coolness was a cruelty. I crossed to the fire and stood near him, leaning to the low flames.

"I'm cold, too," I said. "Suddenly cold."

He didn't answer me. I was standing so near him that our arms almost brushed. Why did he have to delight me so? I could hate him for my love for him.

"I think the fire needs another log," I said.

He reached for one and threw it on without a word. I watched him. He seemed a world away from me.

"It's all over, isn't it?" I said frozenly. "Ferry, as you say, brought you to your senses. So hadn't you better go?"

He turned and tossed his barely smoked cigarette into the fire.

"Sometimes we think we can perform miracles," he said, "wipe away the past, ignore the present. We get to thinking we're the exception to every human limitation and can catch and hold a dream."

I looked at him in amazement. He was powerful and earthy. Miracles and dreams were not his kind of speech. His meaning was, however. It was that of a realist. He could never entirely forget that two women stood between us. Claire, his wife, and Deborah. Deborah, his mistress?

I shuddered. "I'm very cold," I said.

"Aunt Charlotte has some brandy. I think one would do you good. I'll get it for you." He pushed forward a chair. "Sit down."

"That log isn't burning very well."

He prodded it with his foot. "It's too damp. But it'll burn up. In the meantime I'll fetch the brandy. Or would you rather have Scotch?"

My hands flew to my face. The awful anticlimax of our remarks made me shake with uncontrollable laughter.

"What's amusing you?"

"Your solicitude," I shouted at him. "Your damned solicitude."

I walked past him and out of the room because I couldn't have borne another moment. When I reached the hall I began to run. I tore up the stairs to my bedroom, slammed the door and flung myself on the bed. There I turned my face into the soft blue quilt and for the second time in one day I, who never cried, burst into tears.

For a while it was very quiet. Then I heard my name.

"Loran."

I lifted my head. Sarne was outside my door, hammering on it.

"What is it?"

"I'm coming in."

"No!"

I was shouting not at a closed door but at one open with Sarne on the threshold, looking at me from under black brows. "I don't want you," I said stubbornly.

"Then," he said, "you'd make a thundering good actress. That was a fine performance you put on downstairs."

I sprang off the bed, swift as a cat.

"Sarne, please go away." I turned my head so that I wouldn't have to look at him.

"We're both rather overdoing the enmity, aren't we?" His hands were on my shoulders drawing me to him. I kept my face turned away.

"Loran, look at me." He took my face none too gently in his strong fingers and forced me around to face him. "That's better. I don't like talking to the back of a girl's head."

"I didn't invite you in."

"But you're going to listen to me."

I waited, looking at his mouth, harsh and tender. I tried to stop the trembling of my lips by pressing them tightly together. Sarne said softly, "Why the devil did you come here?"

I knew that a word, a gesture from me, and it would start all over again. I wanted it to, but some momentary sense of self-preservation made me break from him. I put my hands to my burning face.

He was looking at me with such intensity that he didn't seem to blink. Passion and anger gave him the same dark expression. I thought: If he were ruthless he could have me now and I wouldn't try to stop him. I wanted to give myself as much as I knew he wanted me. I'd never felt this way before and I knew it was mad. I waited. Our eyes never left each other's faces. The tick of the little clock seemed so loud, and outside the window the wind fretted around the house.

Then Sarne moved. He crossed the room. He's going to turn out the light. I thought, and stood quite still, trembling. Then I saw him pass the light switch and put his hand on the half-closed door and swing it open.

"I'm no good for you, Loran," he said.

"Sarne—" I think I spoke his name aloud. But he was gone. The door was wide open and no one was there. He fled from me as though I were a witch.

X

I REALIZED as I walked across the lawn towards the orchard where Nina and Simon were playing that it was none of my business. But Deborah was out; Sarne was somewhere on the farm and someone had to see that Marnie was not left alone. She brooded too much anyway, and when I had finished dressing her arm and had said good-bye her little face had a sadness that it hurt me to see. Nina and Simon were going to be taught to be considerate of her. They were coming to play with Marnie in the patio if I had to drag them by their hair.

For some time I'd heard a dog's excited barking. I knew it wasn't Remus. The sound was so similar to the almost hysterical yelps I'd heard one of the boxers make on that first night by the well that I stopped being purposeful and moved cautiously towards the sound. I didn't want to do anything to stop that bark—and if Viola, or Juliet, saw me she might well stop. I wanted to know what excited her.

I went through the little gate into the orchard. The apples were golden on the trees. Beneath them I saw Simon on his hands and knees, small dark head thrust forward, staring at Viola. And, front legs braced, she was gazing at him as though hypnotized. Simon's lips were parted and he was hissing softly at the dog.

"Simon, what *are* you doing?"

He looked up at me, his face impish. "Viola's silly. She never barks at strangers like she should. But if you hiss at her, she barks her head off."

A cold wave shivered through me. I looked at the dog, quieter now, but still making small punctuated yelps. So, had someone deliberately hissed at her that night, to draw me to the well? I tried to shake off the cold clutch of fear by being angry with myself. Dear heaven, don't let me start on that tack again. . . .

"You and Nina," I said firmly to Simon, hoisting him to his feet, "can go and keep Marnie company."

"I don't want to."

"Marnie didn't want her horse to throw her," I said.

"All right, *I'll* go," said a matter-of-fact little voice behind me. Nina had been making a bouquet out of grass and leaves. She clutched it in a small hand and said, "I'm a queen's bridesmaid," she marched, slow-stepping across the lawn. "Come on, Simon."

He picked off the tiny seed pods on a blade of grass. His hair was untidy and he scuffed as he walked. But Nina dominated him. She didn't even bother to look back; she knew he'd follow her.

As I left the farm and walked up the lane back to the manor, I knew I mustn't let my mind dwell on Viola, who only barked when someone hissed at her.

After lunch I helped Mrs. Cranmer in the garden, tidying up the mass of leaves, snipping off dead flowers. When we'd had tea I walked to the village to buy stamps and post some letters. I came out of the little general shop and ran slap into Gillian. A tall, thin, elderly man was with her. I knew even before she introduced me that it was Monty. He had pale blue eyes and a pointed, well-trimmed beard. He was the kind of old man of whom people say, "What a charming old man! How sad that he's all alone in the world"—and then proceed to spoil him. He traded on his gentleness as a beggar traded on pity. I knew his type. But his gentle charm touched me, too.

"Come and see my house," Gillian said after introduction.

I told her I'd like to very much, and we dawdled at Monty's pace down the main road and turned into a lane with tall hedges.

Gillian's house was stone-built, bright, and not in the least pretty. But she took me in, showing me around the rooms with pride. When the telephone bell rang, Monty took me into the garden to see the roses. He knew the names of them all. "This is an Ophelia; this is a Christopher Stone. . . ."

Up against the wall of the house was one particularly beautiful rose, yellow as butter. "Smell it," he urged. "It's all right, you can step on those bits of rock over to it, that's what they're there for."

I stepped cautiously onto the stones and leaned forward to smell the rose. But the ground was soft and the stones sank a little. To keep my balance I put out my hand quickly to touch the wall. A nylon curtain from an open casement window on eye level was fluttering out and my hand caught it, pinning it against the wall so that the window was clear. As I stumbled, I caught sight of the room with a table set at right angles. On it were some books and a blotter and a photograph in a silver frame. The photograph was of Sarne.

"Careful." I felt Monty's hand at my elbow. "Here, turn and jump."

I turned and jumped and landed unsteadily on the path. He was grinning at me like a schoolboy.

"That's Gillian's secret room in there. She calls it her study. No one goes in but her. I tease her and ask her if she's got a lover hidden away. But she doesn't think it very funny. She's an odd girl. She has no sense of humor, you know."

He stopped speaking abruptly as Gillian came out.

"Isn't it wonderful to have roses in October?" she said. "Claire gave me that yellow one." She pointed to the one against the wall.

"Claire Algar?"

"Why, yes. I knew her very well." She gave Monty a quick glance and then looked away. "Claire loved gardening."

"She played at it, you mean." Monty corrected her in his gentle, tremulous voice. "It was Ralph Cranmer who planted the roses at the farm that time when Claire was being so restless and jumpy. He thought he'd try to give her an interest. Ralph," he explained to me, "was Mrs. Cranmer's husband."

I touched a full white rose and petals fluttered about me. "I haven't seen the roses at the farm," I said.

"How could you?" Gillian cried. "There's no one to look after them now that Claire has gone. Sarne is too busy with the farm to do gardening, and Deborah—well, can you see her grubbing about with earth?"

"She housekeeps and that can be quite a grubby job," I said.

"Chauncey and Ned do all the work."

"In a place that size, Deborah must do some," I said.

Monty chuckled. "And if she doesn't, what does it matter? That girl's an ornament in a house and a very lovely one. Sarne's lucky."

Gillian turned on him like a pale fury. "You don't know what you're saying. How do *you* know what Sarne considers lucky? You don't really understand him, any of you. Only I—" She checked herself and color flooded her neck and face. For a moment she was almost pretty. "I've known him since we were children," she added in embarrassed explanation. "We were friends—real friends. We even used to go to dances together. But I—I hate dancing now."

Monty looked up at the sky. "It's getting cold," he said, and shivered. "Gillian, don't you think I ought to start wearing my woollen vests?"

The change of conversation was so marked that a moment's awkward silence fell. Then I said I must go or Mrs. Cranmer would wonder where I was.

Gillian made no attempt to detain me. Her mood had changed and I felt she wanted me to leave. Monty insisted on coming to the end of the road with me. I had a feeling that he liked a new face around occasionally. We had almost reached the corner when he said:

"Gillian doesn't hate dancing, you know. In fact she's got a passion for it. Sometimes when I'm in the garden and I'm near that private room of hers, I see her dancing with the radio on and a cushion in her arms."

"I've done that!" I said, laughing.

"Oh, but you're different. You go out a lot, don't you?"

"Being a nurse doesn't give one that much chance. But I make the most of my time off."

"Gillian never goes out, except to her job and for shopping. Nobody ever asks her."

"But why doesn't she join some social club?"

"She wouldn't enjoy it. She's one of those people who nurse their grievances and hate God for forcing them on them."

I knew what he meant. Neurological wings were full of patients in advanced stages of this.

Monty would have continued talking for ages, but I didn't want to hear any more. I said good-bye to him and made my way through the village. And all the way I carried the memory of Sarne's photograph in Gillian's private room. It was a tragedy, I thought, in a tiny village, for one man to be so dominating and so damned attractive to women.

XI

Marnie was soon allowed to walk a little. Waving a book she hobbled down the path to meet me. Her little heart-shaped face was pretty when she was happy. "Look what Uncle Tom has sent me."

I guided her back into the house, settled her by the fire, and then took the book from her. It was a volume of animal stories. In the wide margins on almost every page and in the spaces at the ends of chapters were the most enchanting little paintings of animals.

"They're hand-done," I exclaimed.

She nodded. "Uncle Tom's awfully clever. He chooses books for us and paints pictures in them."

"That's the sort of uncle to have!" I said jauntily. "Someone who takes time and trouble over what he gives you!"

"Oh, he does these awfully quickly. He painted little pictures in a book of fairy tales once for Nina's birthday and I watched him. He just wiggles a brush over the paper. That's all."

Tom MacQueen with his leonine head and his roaring voice was difficult to associate with the Tom MacQueen who could execute such minute, exquisite things for children's delight.

"Deborah says my book will be worth lots and lots of money one day so I mustn't ever give it away for the jumble sale."

It would, of course, be worth lots and lots of money, but I wished Deborah had not told Marnie so.

"Let's see how your arm is getting on," I said briskly.

Soon now there would be no solemn promise to a little girl to keep me in Saxon Magna. Her arm was almost healed. Yet I argued that I would keep an eye on her for a few more days just to see that she didn't use her foot too much. It was an unnecessary chore, since Deborah was perfectly capable of watching over Marnie. It was also like keeping my own wound open. But some perversity drove me to hold onto my visits here for as long as I could.

I had been adjusting the bandage on Marnie's foot. "There you are," I said and glanced up at her. She was gazing at me forlornly.

"I don't want to get better," she said.

"Why ever not?"

"When I'm well you won't come and see me any more," she said.

"Then you'll have to come and see me in London. We'll go to the Zoo and the Planetarium, where they show you the stars—"

To my dismay her eyes filled with tears.

"Mummy took us there before she went away. I wish she'd come back."

"You'll be back at school next week," I said, "and then you won't be lonely when Simon and Nina aren't here."

"They don't care," she said. "They don't think everything's horrible." Then she added defiantly, "It was me Mummy loved best."

The sad little favorite, I thought, and looked up and saw Deborah in the patio. She beckoned me.

"We were talking about a painting of father's the other day," she said. "I've got one in my room if you'd like to see it."

I didn't want to see Deborah's room; I didn't want to be aware of anything that established her too firmly in this house. But I had no excuse for a refusal.

Deborah took me up the stairs and opened a door. I walked into a room full of light, of soft nylon curtains billowing in the rush of breeze. I had an impression of subtle color, of oyster and dusty pink, of rosy lampshades and a bed-head of wood so black that it resembled ebony and carved so finely that it was like lace stretched across the wall.

"What a lovely room!" I said, helpless to check my admiration.

"It is, isn't it?" she said with satisfaction. "I told Sarne when I first came here that I had no intention of living in a bedroom that was essentially someone else's choice. After all, we spend a good deal of our lives in bedrooms, so I was going to enjoy mine. Sarne agreed." She gave a slow, thoughtful smile. "I brought most of these things with me. I'm afraid Sarne thought it all rather theatrical, which of course it is, and too glamorous for the country. But he's got used to it now and he even likes it."

Staking her claim in every room, in every corner, I thought, my fingers tracing the shadow pattern on the silk bedcover.

"This is what I think you wanted to see."

I looked up and found Deborah standing underneath a painting on the far wall.

"My father's idea of moon clouds over Black Ash Heath."

There was a quality of excitement about the painting. He had caught something of the eeriness that I, too, felt for that heath. The silver was all in the sky, ringing the clouds, paling the stars. On the ground the colors were sober and yet violent, laid on thickly—indigo and purple and sable mingling in a kind of torment as though the place held no peace, no placidity, for him. One tiny splash of silver in the bottom right-hand corner of the painting, where a tiny pool of water reflected the moon, broke the dark, angry colors.

"It's lovely," I said.

"It doesn't go with this room, but I don't mind." She stood back, staring up at the painting with a queer little half-smile playing about her lips. "Whenever I look at it, I remember all those paintings he has stacked in his house. He refuses to sell them and gloats over them like a miser. He may think himself immortal, but he's not. He'll die of high blood pressure and then those pictures will be mine." She looked at me. "You see, Loran, where other women have diamonds, I have paintings."

A fortune, I thought, in canvases. And Sarne as well. And beauty and youth and health. I looked around the room as she went to the window to close it. Sarne had walked over this thick carpet . . . had admired the ormolu desk that served as a dressing table, probably touching her scent bottles, her big crimson swansdown puff, the necklace of garnets tossed carelessly onto the glass top. Sarne here, in this room. . . .

I swung around and walked to the door. I wanted to go and pack my two suitcases and never see or hear of Saxon Magna again.

The hospital—the hospital is where I belong. I have a vocation. I am a nurse. One day I may even be a matron. Nothing could be more satisfying than this life I had chosen for myself—to have in my charge sickness that would one day, by my care, become health. My vocation . . . my vocation . . . I said it like a refrain, as I went down the stairs.

And there, in the hall, stood Sarne. Vocation? Of course. To love and be married, bear children, have a home. Whom was I fooling?

"Hello, Loran," said Sarne as unemotionally as though I had been his sister.

"I've just been looking at Deborah's father's painting."

"It's a very fine piece of work. Deborah, why don't you take Loran to see your father and get him to show you his canvases? Why not go this afternoon?"

"I'm afraid," said her voice from behind me, "I'm going to be rather busy all today. The Baineses are coming in tonight for drinks and—"

"I've never known you not to take entertainment in your stride," he laughed. "Go on, Deborah, take Loran this afternoon. You never know, your father might be able to help her about her parents. After all, he's lived here for years."

"Tomorrow . . ." she began.

"Tomorrow," Sarne said, "you're taking Nina to the dentist's."

"Oh, I forgot!" She was standing next to me now at the foot of the stairs. "Very well, this afternoon, if you'd like that, Loran. I'll call for you about three o'clock if that would suit you."

"Perfectly," I said, "and thank you."

When I told Mrs. Cranmer where I was going, she said:

"Sarne's right, Tom MacQueen has lived here for years; but I doubt if he would be able to help you to find your parents or your brother. Arlesthorne was a large town even twenty-four years ago. But you never know. It's faintly possible that he might have met your brother somewhere. *Just* possible."

My brother called Anthony.

It was ridiculous to feel a sense of excitement at my meeting Tom MacQueen. After all, that same sensation had been mine on every occasion I had gone into Arlesthorne to check on some point that might lead me to the secret of my identity—and in every case I had failed.

Deborah was punctual. Her car drove up outside the manor precisely at three o'clock. She said as I got in:

"We won't be able to stay for tea, I'm afraid. I want to get back. Chauncey can do the simple cooking, but puddings and fancy things are always left to me."

"You like cooking?"

"Strangely enough, I do. Though I shall prefer it when things are more settled and I can get a really good cook whom I can train to do things my way. Chauncey's rough; she's best at housework."

Tom MacQueen lived in a small house in a cul-de-sac. It was a rackety road with a few houses and sheds and a lot of tall dark trees.

"It was once a coach-house," Deborah explained as we stopped outside. "But it has been very cleverly converted."

We got out, walked through the black gate and between the untidy flower borders to the front door. There was a queer Henry Moore-ish stone animal on one side—at least I supposed it was an animal—and the knocker was like a green bronze claw.

No one answered the first knock. Deborah hammered more loudly. Again there was silence.

She stood back and looked up at the little house. All the windows were closed. She said, "I'll go around the back."

I stood where I was, peering after her until she disappeared. When she came back, she said irritatedly:

"I rang him after you'd gone this morning and told him we were coming. I said we'd be here by half past three. This is just like him. He has no thought for a living thing except Tom MacQueen. I'm sorry, Loran, I'm afraid it's no use, he may not come home for hours."

"Never mind," I said. "Another day, perhaps. I'm only sorry you had this journey when you're busy."

Deborah did a little shopping in Arlesthorne and dropped me at the fork lanes when we reached Saxon Magna.

The afternoon was cloudy but calm and I didn't want to go indoors. I walked towards the beech woods, and once inside sat down with my back to one of the great trees. It was breathlessly still, without a bird's song, and the light and the interlaced branches above me made a bronze cave. Out of the corner of my eye I saw something move between the trees. It was a woman wearing a yellow scarf, and the woman was Babette.

I scrambled up and called her name loudly.

She turned and saw me, hesitated for a moment and then began to run.

"Babette!" I shouted. "Wait!"

I began to run fast after her, but she was fleeter of foot than I. I was surprised, therefore, when suddenly she stopped, turned, and waited for me to catch up to her.

"What d'you want?" She was scowling at me.

"Just a word," I said. "I haven't had a chance to speak to you since Marnie Algar's accident. I've seen you two or three times hanging around the manor."

"What's that to do with you?"

"Nothing," I said coolly, "so long as Mrs. Cranmer knows and doesn't mind your trespassing."

The woman looked at me, mockery in her sharp little face and something almost like venom in her brilliant eyes.

"That's funny, that is! 'So long as Mrs. Cranmer don't mind,' " she mimicked me. "You ask her. Go on, when you get back, you ask her."

"I certainly shan't. I'll wait for her to find you near the house." I was angry at her mockery. "What I'm interested in, is why you rushed out of that hedge and frightened Marnie's horse."

"I didn't."

"Oh, don't lie to me."

She swung away from me and began to run again. The last shred of my patience snapped. My movements were purely instinctive. I flew across the coarse grass and gripped her arm.

"Let me go!" She writhed against me.

"Not till you admit that it was you who darted out of the hedge that morning."

"Well, suppose I did?" she demanded sulkily. "What do you care?"

"You might have caused Marnie to be killed."

"Oh, no." She gave a little smirk. "Oh, no, miss. Kids don't fall heavy like grown-ups. She fell soft. And it won't do her no harm."

"It did," I said. "It broke a bone in her foot and gashed her arm badly."

"Well, then, p'raps Sarne Algar'll care about *that!*" she said viciously. "He don't seem to care about the other."

"What—other?"

"Why, Mrs. Algar being dead."

"Every time I see you, you seem to take a delight in telling me that. Is it because you think that if I tell the police what you say they might take some notice, whereas they don't listen to you?"

"I don't care whether you tell them. They'll find out in time."

"And meanwhile, you watch and listen and dog the footsteps of the people at the farm. You do, don't you? You were in the hedge watching Mr. Algar and Mrs. Millbrook on the day Marnie had her accident. They probably turned and you thought they saw you and that's why you ran out into the field on the other side of the hedge. Then when Perchance reared, you got scared and ran back and hid."

"Ain't you clever?"

"No, just trying to use my common sense," I snapped back.

Quite suddenly the defiance went out of her. Her fingers started plucking at her grubby blue skirt.

"Those two, miss, they're no good; really they ain't. They done all this. You watch out. Could be they think you're just sayin' you come here to find your ma and pa."

"What else might I be here for?"

"Could be they don't believe you. Could be they think you're sent here by the police to snoop on them."

"Of all the absurd ideas!"

"So's lots of things, but they happen."

I had dropped my hand from her arm but now she made no move to run away. Above us the silence was broken by a thrush's sudden singing. The leaves of the trees moved lightly and the sun made a pattern of little golden coins on Babette's dark face.

"You was down at Falcon Point, wasn't you?" she said. "And you nearly got drowned."

"I went to sleep," I said.

"Oh—huh?" She narrowed her eyes disbelievingly at me.

"If you think you know so much, then go to the police again!" I cried. "Keep going until they listen to you. It's the only way. . . ." I stopped abruptly. The dreadful thought struck me that what I was urging her to do could mean Sarne's arrest. I knew suddenly that she mustn't go to the police again. I was wondering how to stop her when she said:

"You never been to prison, have you?"

"No."

"Well, I have and Sarne Algar put me there. That's why they won't listen to me. They know I want him to go to prison like he sent me; they think I'm making it all up."

"Why did you go to prison?"

"He said I stole something."

This, I decided, was not for me to argue about. Otherwise, with her limited type of mind, we'd just go around in circles.

"Nobody here suspects me of being some kind of policewoman," I said. "Mrs. Cranmer knows why I've come. She knew my . . . my adopted parents."

"That don't stop making you a snooper, do it? You get clear of the lot of 'em, miss, like I told you before."

"While you go about hinting and hating?"

"You don't understand." She thrust her small face up at me. "Even if I didn't hate Sarne Algar, I'd still know what I know, wouldn't I?"

It was child's logic, and as such it had a shattering simplicity. I made one final effort to stop her avid little tongue.

"You'd better be very careful what you say. There's a world of difference between suspecting a thing and knowing it for certain."

She began kicking at the mossy bole of a tree. It was all I could do to stop scolding her and saying, "That's why your shoes look so scuffed at the toes!" as though she were a child. But she was a woman and she was standing there in the quiet wood and a terrible accusation hovered like a ghost at our sides.

Suddenly I felt I couldn't bear this place any longer. "There's nothing more to be said," I told her. "But you'd be wise to take a piece of advice from me. From now on be careful what you say or it'll be you, not . . . not someone you hate, who will be harmed."

She laughed at me. "I ain't scared. But Mrs. Cranmer is. She's scared to death 'cos *she* knows. That's why she lets me do as I like, come an' go, because she knows I know."

She turned her back on me as she spoke, and ran off, skipping over the rough, leafy earth. Her hair bobbed, her little skirt flounced around her.

Somewhere a dog barked. I heard it as though it were part of a dream. I watched Babette until the bright blue skirt became merged with the mist and the breaking sunlight in the distance. Then I turned and walked slowly back to the manor.

When I came to the lane that ran parallel to the farm drive, I saw two cars there. One was Deborah's blue Zodiac and the other a large old-fashioned chauffeur-driven Daimler obviously used for taking invalid carriages. A wheelchair came around the side of the house, furiously propelled by Tom MacQueen, and Deborah walked by his side.

The old artist was shouting something at his daughter, and as he reached the big car the chauffeur got out and placed a wooden ramp to the door of the back seat.

I crossed the grass verge and made my way towards them. Deborah looked around and saw me as Tom MacQueen was being pushed by the chauffeur up the ramp and into the car.

For a moment she hesitated and I had a feeling she was going to pretend not to see me. But Tom MacQueen, settled in the huge hearse-like back of the car, hailed me.

"That the young woman? Oh, I remember. We met at the library."

I said we had.

Deborah ignored me and leaned between us and tucked the rug around his feet.

"Are you all right, Father?"

"No, I damned well am not. You've pushed me too far in. I can't move."

"Of course you can. Don't fuss so!"

"If I say I'm uncomfortable, then I am. And I've got to drive twelve miles in this blasted mini-car."

"It's the car you always have. And for heaven's sake, don't keep the chauffeur hanging about. He's probably got another job after taking you home."

"And who forced me out here, anyway? You told me to come because you had someone you wanted me to meet and when I arrive you tell me airily that you said *you* would be calling on *me*."

"That's just what I did say. But we've had all that out. You don't listen half the time."

"I wanted so much to see your paintings, Mr. MacQueen," I said.

He glared at his daughter. "You said nothing to me about anyone seeing my pictures."

"That's something else you didn't listen to," she retorted. "Now do get going."

"Bring her along now."

"I can't," she said exasperatedly. "I've got people coming in for drinks."

She reached in front of me and slammed the car door. Behind the glass window old Tom MacQueen scowled at us.

"I pity any chauffeur who has to drive Father around," she said wryly. "But they must be used to him by now. He has this special car that will take his wheelchair."

"He's very crippled?"

"He lost the use of his legs after a spinal injury when in a temper he fell down the stairs from a hayloft," she said.

"But he had all this journey for nothing," I said. "What a shame!"

"It's his fault. He never listens." She looked towards the house. "That's the telephone ringing. Excuse me."

It wasn't, but it was as good an excuse as any for getting rid of me. I said goodbye and cut through the farm's private lane to the manor.

XII

Ferry was building up the fire in the sitting room when I arrived. She turned and saw me watching her from the hall.

"Madam has had to go into the village," she said. "She told me to tell you she won't be long."

"Thank you." I slid out of my coat. On the fob the little gold ring swung emptily.

"No one ever found my topaz," I said sadly.

"If you lost it on the heath, it would be almost impossible to find." She had replaced the fire tongs and was coming towards me, brushing her long thin hands.

"Funny, isn't it," I said, "how we seem to lose only those things we really value."

"It was of considerable value?" She stood near me, her light eyes as usual not quite looking at me.

"The value was in the fact that the stone was given me at my christening. I was superstitious about it."

"A good luck charm."

"If you like." I laughed to try to break her icy manner. "Do you think it means seven years' bad luck, like breaking a mirror?"

"I couldn't say, Miss Brant. It could mean, of course . . ."

"What?" I asked as she hesitated.

"That this is an unlucky place for you," she said.

I had no answer for her. I went to hang up my coat in the little cloakroom off the hall, and when I turned back she was no longer there. How silently she moved. Like a black ghost, watching me from a high window; from the open door of the unused wing; listening at a door—and throwing it open once to find me in Sarne's arms. . . . Had she told anyone of that? Somehow I doubted it. She was too secretive. But I guessed that if the opportunity came she would use it as a weapon against me.

I went into the sitting room and closing the door, crossed to the fire. The dogs, who had returned to the hearth after Ferry had disturbed them, rose again and sniffed.

"Hello," I said friendlily.

Viola gave a little snort. I bent down and hissed softly at her. Immediately she backed, her forepaws braced, and broke into loud, staccato barks.

"Be quiet!"

She was too hysterical to stop.

"Come here," I said, "and don't be an idiot."

The door behind me opened. I looked around and Ferry said, "What is the matter with the dogs?"

"I'm sorry. It was my fault. Simon told me that Viola only barks if anyone hisses at her, so I tried it."

"She has that ridiculous habit, but Mrs. Cranmer doesn't encourage it."

It was a reprimand. I ignored it.

"She barked like that on my first night here, when I went for a walk with them and lost them both. I wonder who hissed at her then."

"Oh, she probably saw a rabbit," she said coolly. "Is there anything you want, Miss Brant?"

I thanked her and said there was nothing. The door closed very softly behind her.

Mrs. Cranmer was back in time for tea. She was nervous and jumpy. Her hand shook so that a little of her first cup of tea spilled in the saucer, and I noticed that she was careful not to fill her second cup too full. She ate nothing and her effort to appear normal was almost pathetic, so that I longed to ask her what was wrong. I let her chat about the little affairs of the village, and watched her.

Her eyes flew with a haunted restlessness from fire to window, from door and back to window. It was as though she were afraid of an unnamed guest.

When we had finished tea, she pushed the trolley away and, sitting back in her chair, looked directly at me. I surprised such naked misery in her face that I could hold out no longer.

"Mrs. Cranmer, please don't mind my asking, but something is very wrong, isn't it? If I can help . . ."

Immediately her expression became cautious. "My dear child, nothing is more wrong than it has been since Claire vanished. Perhaps I'm a little tired. I walked to the village and it's quite a way for an old woman. I should have taken the car."

She didn't speak again until Ferry came in for the tea cart. She wheeled it halfway across the room; then she stopped.

"I think I should tell you, madam, Josh has just come in. He tells me that a police car is standing outside in the farm drive."

Mrs. Cranmer sat so still that I thought for a moment the news was unimportant. Then I realized that what I thought was stillness was frozen shock. She said, her lips scarcely moving:

"Ferry, why . . . have the . . . police come?"

"I don't know, madam. But Josh says that the man who got out was the one who called last year—you know, when Mrs. Algar disappeared."

"Inspector Gray."

"I suppose so, madam."

"I must ring Sarne." Charlotte Cranmer pushed herself up from her chair and almost ran to the telephone in the hall.

Ferry remained standing in the middle of the room, hands folded, quiet and listening.

In that moment, with only the clock ticking and the murmur of Mrs. Cranmer's voice from the other side of the closed door, I felt a rush of real terror. Not for myself but for Sarne. It welled up in me, choking in my throat so that I had to speak, to say something, as an outlet.

"Why have they come?" My voice jerked. "Do you think they have news of . . . of Mrs. Algar?"

Her small black eyes swiveled around at me.

"I don't know. How should I?" Her voice was flat and dead-sounding. "But if the police are re-opening their inquiries, it won't be very pleasant here."

I swallowed. "No."

"There will be so much coming and going, so much questioning. We shall have no private life."

I rose and went to the window. I understood her meaning perfectly.

"If Mrs. Cranmer wishes me to leave here, of course I shall go at once," I said quietly. I had my back to her but a moment later I knew she had gone. She had made her point.

I was still at the window when Mrs. Cranmer returned.

"The police have gone and Sarne is on his way over here." She leaned heavily against the high-backed chair. Her face was paper-white, old and drawn.

"I'll go to my room," I said. "I have letters to write."

She nodded vaguely. "If you wouldn't mind, dear."

I moved over to her and laid my hand on her arm. It was rigid. "If you want me to go back to London I'll understand. I'll go at once."

"No." She turned to me so fiercely that she stumbled a little. "Loran, don't go. Please, I need you. I need someone around at the moment to keep me sane."

"Then I'll stay," I said gently, "and if there is anything I can do . . ."

"There's nothing anyone can do. Claire chose to have her revenge and nobody could have thought out a more perfect and complete form. For the rest of his life Sarne will never know whether she is alive or dead; the police will never stop suspecting him and the whisperings and the gossip will go on and on."

"You believe Claire is alive."

"She must be." She turned on me fiercely. "Loran, *she . . . must . . . be . . . alive.* If she's dead . . . if they find her body, then God help us all!"

I heard Sarne's footstep outside the French windows and left the room just as he entered. I didn't turn to look at him. I couldn't. If Mrs. Cranmer was beside herself with anxiety, I was beyond that point. His torment had become mine. He couldn't help that; he hadn't laid his burden on me. But because I loved him it was as much part of me as if we were married and had shared the most intimate moments so that we were one. It's a curious feeling to love so deeply without any certainty of being loved in return. I climbed the stairs slowly, hand on the banisters.

In my room, I crossed to the dressing table and looked at myself. Loving hadn't given me a new radiance—how could it? Nor had fear for Sarne aged me. I was the same, except that my eyes were darker and so dry that they hurt. I leaned towards the looking glass. "I love you so much," I said to the man downstairs. And then I turned my face away.

I tried very hard to write my letters. I turned on the lamp on the little bureau and pulled a pad of writing paper towards me. But with the pen in my hand, all I could do was scribble on the page before me. Through blurred eyes I saw that I had drawn the shape of the topaz I had lost and a very bad outline of the engraved phoenix. I saw letters forming words, looped and spidery and unlike my usual writing. "*My darling Sarne.* Whatever happens to me in the future this you must know. . . ." I had written as though I were about to die and this was my last shaken message.

I tore the sheet of paper into tiny pieces and threw them into the wastepaper basket. I wished there was someone to whom I could talk. My friends would be intrigued and curious and sympathetic. But they couldn't help. No one could.

I drew a clean sheet of paper towards me, pressed the spring of my pen and began to write:

"Dear Adèle . . ."

The tap on my window was feather-light. I thought it was a hard brown leaf tossed against the pane by the wind. But when it came again, more loudly, I got up and went to see if a sudden storm had come up.

There was no rain spattering on the window.

Below me I could just see a man standing in the darkness looking up.

I opened the window and leaned out and recognized Martin. "What do you want?"

"To talk to you," he called softly. "Come along down. But don't make a noise or I shall be thrown off the estate!"

"I'm writing letters."

"Then postpone them."

I said ungraciously, "Very well," closed the window, and went down the stairs. I could hear voices in the sitting room as I got my coat out of the hall closet and flung it around me like a cape. Then I opened the door and went into the chilly night.

The wind immediately caught my hair and whirled it about my face so that, blinded for a moment, I gave a gasp as Martin's hand touched my arm.

"Come and sit in the car," he whispered.

I felt curiously like an accomplice in some lawlessness as I crept away with him towards his car which was parked in the lane, close under some trees.

"Now," I said cautiously as we sat together. "What do you want?"

"You know the police are around again?"

"Why?" I evaded a direct answer. "Didn't they complete their inquiries a year ago?"

"Yes, but something has come to light."

"What . . . ?" My heart began to hammer.

"A suitcase with some clothes in it. Claire's clothes."

"Oh, *no!*"

He was watching me. "A police dog dug it up on the heath."

I felt as though I were being stifled. I pushed my hair back free of my forehead.

"What . . . what do they think . . . that . . . proves?"

"That Claire didn't pack her things of course. Someone packed them for her and hid them. Now I ask you—why?"

I remained silent, refusing to turn my head and look at that face which I guessed was as smiling as ever.

"It's obvious, isn't it," he said, "that Claire didn't go voluntarily. But someone wanted it to seem that she did."

His handsome face, thrust at me, held muted triumph. I found suddenly that I was beating with my fist at his arm, which lay across the wheel. "Stop gloating. You *want* something dreadful to be discovered, don't you? You *want* to sit back and see a man ruined."

"A life . . . for a life!" said Martin and took my clenched fist in his hands and held it tight. "This is the first step, the first clue to what has happened to Claire."

"She *is* alive." I almost choked over the words. "Martin, she's got to be alive." And my voice became small and shaken. By the light of the dashboard I saw a change come over his face.

"You fool! You bloody little fool!" he breathed at me. "Pack up and get the hell out of here while you're safe."

"Safe?"

"You've got a short memory!" he said. "We had this out once before and I warned you. Your apparent reason for being here is all very fine, but guilty people are suspicious people. A stranger from London—a girl detective? You don't have to watch television, or read, to know that there are such people. Scotland Yard employs a strange assortment for their purpose. Well, do you get me this time? Or do I have to explain in words of one syllable that you are in danger here because someone doesn't quite believe the story of your search for your parents."

I managed to open the car door. I felt as though I had been frozen into an inhuman serenity. I was cold, too, yet I didn't shiver.

"I think," I said in as normal a voice as I could manage, "that you meant kindly in warning me, Martin. And thank you. But I must stay here—just a few days more."

"Why?"

"Because I have promised Mrs. Cranmer."

"Why bother about a promise to *her*? She's only using you. She's terrified because in her heart she believes that Sarne killed Claire, and Sarne is her world. Your being here gives her a kind of moral support—God knows, Ferry gives her none! Get out and leave the lot of them to solve their own problems. It's not yours."

The wind blew at me through the open door of the car. I stared ahead into the blackness.

From the village, the church clock struck six. Then I heard the sound of the bells: single ones tolling, double ones, a scale. The bellringers were at practice. The sound came lonely and achingly beautiful on the thin black air.

"I like you, Loran. You've got spirit and a sense of humor. I'd hate to see anything happen to you. Go home."

"No," I said. "I can't."

"You mean you won't."

"I won't," I said and got out of the car.

"Oh, by the way," he called after me. "There were initials on the suitcase that contained Claire's clothes. Just two letters. C.C."

I heard the car rev up and roar away. "C.C." Charlotte Cranmer. I ran the rest of the way to the house.

At half past eight that night Mrs. Cranmer made a brief telephone call. She came back into the room and told me that she was going to see Dr. Baines. "I'm not ill," she assured me quickly, "I want to consult him on a . . . a private matter. You'll be all right, won't you? I won't be long."

When she had gone I switched on the television, watched a program about Ireland, and when it was over, called the dogs. "Come on. Out!" I said.

As though each had been sleeping with one eye open, they bounded up and leaped to the door.

I fetched my coat and then went to the kitchen to tell Ferry I was going for a walk. The place was in darkness. She was probably up in her room. I wouldn't disturb her.

I kept to the lanes, walking quickly in the keen, cold air, and although the dogs tried to lure me that way, I didn't go near the heath.

It was so dark and moonless that I was glad I had brought a flashlight. A few drops of rain began to fall as I turned back. I looked up at the sky and then at the house. There was a light in the hall and one in Ferry's bedroom. There was also a third light. I saw it shining out to sea from a room in the unused west wing. Someone had been there and forgotten to switch it off. I knew that the house had its own electricity plant and that one had to be careful with lights.

I let myself into the house, shut the dogs into the sitting room, dropped my coat on the mahogany chest in the hall, and went up to the first floor. The landing was dark and I felt for the switch and turned the light on.

The door to the west wing was not quite closed. I pulled it open and saw a dim light at the end of a long, twisting corridor. I had no feeling of trespassing. Mrs. Cranmer had promised me on my first night here that she would show me the rooms in this wing; she had urged me to treat the house as my home.

At the end of the passage I found the lighted room. The door was half open.

"Is anyone here?" I called.

There was no answer. I pushed the door wider and went in.

The room was partially furnished. There was a roughly made divan bed with a red rug I had seen in the hall cupboard lying across it. An old armchair was pulled up by a fire that had gone out and on some shelves stood a jumble of pots and pans. There were also two tables. On one was a portable cooker. The other was covered with a white sheet, and on it lay a brocade cloth similar to the one Mrs. Cranmer was mending. On the table, too, were silks and a spool of gold thread.

Who was camping out, roughly and secretly, in the unused west wing?

And then I saw, on a rush-bottomed chair in a corner, what looked like two lumps of Plasticine. I moved over and picked one up. It was a clay model of a woman—roughly made and yet discernible. I recognized the smooth head, the splodge of clay on one finger to represent a ring. Someone had tried to model a likeness of Deborah. With it in my hand, I looked down at the other and knew that it was Sarne. Ugly, badly made, they had a sudden horrible meaning. For pins were stuck brutally into the heart and head of each model. I dropped the grotesque thing and it missed the chair and fell on the floor. I stood staring at the primitive display of hatred, of ill-wishing. . . .

And suddenly the light went out.

I caught my breath sharply and put my hand up to my throat. "Who . . . who's that?"

There was no answer. But someone was standing behind me. I moved and knocked against one of the tables. I felt the stir of air as though someone breathed heavily at my back. The blackness and the silence could only have lasted a few seconds. To me it was like an eternity.

Then the lights came on again.

I swung around; Mrs. Cranmer stood watching me from the doorway. She gave a gasp of surprise.

"Oh, it's you. Why are you here, Loran?" Her voice was so quiet that it frightened me.

"I was out with the dogs. I saw a light and I thought someone had left it on by mistake. I . . . I just came to turn it out for you. I thought you probably had to be careful with electricity. It . . . failed," I finished unnecessarily.

"Ferry had probably gone out to see to the pump," she said, "and accidentally switched the mains off for a moment. They failed just as I reached the door. I didn't see who was here."

I scarcely heard her. I had turned my head and was staring at the clay figure lying on the chair.

"Who . . . who hates him so much?" I whispered.

She pushed past me, picked up the model, and dragged out the pins with shaking hands.

"Come downstairs."

I looked back. She had left the other clay figure, the one of Deborah, lying on the floor where I had dropped it. The pins stuck out like little silver spears of rain.

She switched off the light and in silence I followed her out of the room. We walked in procession down the stairs and into the sitting room. The fire flames, the dogs' friendly faces, the soft lamplight, brought me back to a sense of sanity. I wasn't living in the Dark Ages after all.

"Sit down, Loran."

She went to the wastepaper basket by the desk, dragged out a discarded newspaper, and wrapped up the hideous clay model. Then she went out of the room with it. I supposed she put it in the dustbin.

I was still sitting by the fire, my hands in my lap, when she came back.

She took the chair opposite me and sat very upright, her eyes on my face. "I'm a foolish old woman. I thought I could get away with having someone in the house without anyone knowing. I thought: Big houses are turned into flats and often the tenants never see their neighbors, so it would be safe."

"Who?" I asked, unable to believe my hunch.

"Babette."

I was right in that hunch.

"Loran, I *had* to," she was urging. "It was coercion."

"You can't mean she's threatening you and you're letting her get away with it."

"That's just what I am doing."

"I don't understand."

"How could you? How could anyone understand someone else's fear?" She was leaning forward, her hands clasped over her knees.

"It concerns Sarne, doesn't it?" I asked.

She nodded and began speaking softly as though telling the story to herself.

"Before Babette went away with her family, first to the hop fields and then apple-picking, she made herself a nuisance with the police, telling them that she knew Claire was buried among the hamlet ruins beyond Falcon Point."

(*It isn't the sea, it's Mrs. Algar crying. . . .*)

I waited.

"About eighteen months ago Babette went to prison for the theft of some money from the farm. It was Claire who had her charged, but Babette insists that it was Sarne and has developed a blind hatred of him."

She got up from her chair and began wandering around the room, picking up a reel of silk from her needlework box and winding the loose green thread, tossing yesterday's newspaper into the little painted bin. I watched every racked, restless movement and tried to be patient.

"Some days ago, the night you found me ill in my room, Babette came to me and told me that she had quarreled with her family and that they had turned her out. She had nowhere to go. She said she wanted to live here, 'in a big house,' as she put it. I ordered her out. But she stood where she was and gave that little inhuman chuckle of hers and told me that she had overheard Deborah and Sarne talking. She said they knew Claire was dead. She said that she would go to the police and tell them a lot that she'd heard them saying if I didn't let her come and live here."

"But Mrs. Cranmer," I said bewilderedly, "the police wouldn't listen to her stories. And she's afraid of them, anyway; you said so yourself."

She put her hand hard against her chest and I watched her face for any change of color. Emotional upset was the very last thing she should have with her heart condition.

"Please sit down," I urged. "Can I get you a brandy?"

She shook her head but sat down again and leaned her head back against the red damask cushion.

"I believe Babette would go to the police," she said, "and if what she has to tell them is damning enough, they'll listen."

"But it can't be! What *does* she know?"

"She wouldn't tell me. She said it was her secret. That's why I had to let her come here. I told her she could live temporarily in a room in the west wing and that I'd provide a few pieces of furniture. But I stipulated that she must look after herself, always use the back stairs, and keep out of my way. In the meantime, I intend to find out what it is she knows about Sarne and Deborah."

"Does it occur to you that it could be merely something she has made up? Mrs. Cranmer, how could you possibly believe her?"

"Of course it can be lies, but I daren't chance it. Loran, I just daren't!"

"Why not?"

Suffering had turned her face gray. "Sometimes," she said, "you're three-quarters certain that something is a lie. But you have to believe it to be the truth because if you don't you could place someone very near you in terrible danger."

"Sarne?"

She put her hands to her face. For a moment she couldn't speak and I stayed quiet. I looked down. She had little green slippers on and her feet were very pretty. I kept my eyes from her face as her voice came muffled in despair.

"Sarne has a wild temper," she whispered. "If he and Claire had quarreled that night and he had hit her, she could have fallen, knocked her head against something and been killed. Sarne could have . . . panicked."

"I don't believe it."

"How can you say that? You don't know him. No one knows how anyone else would behave in any given circumstances. We don't even know how we'd behave ourselves."

"You think Sarne might have killed Claire, and . . . hidden her body? Oh, no. No, you couldn't believe that."

"I don't. But I dare not risk the faintest possibility. I love Sarne so much."

"But this is madness!" I cried. "You're only piling up trouble for yourself by letting Babette come here. It's a case of blackmail. Mrs. Cranmer, you can't realize what you're doing."

"Oh, but I do. Only too well."

"What about Sarne? Have you told him that Babette is here?"

She turned to me with a sudden spurt of energy. "Of course not. He must never know."

"Do you really think Babette will keep quiet about it? She may have promised you that she will, but I'm quite sure a promise means nothing to her. Soon the whole village will know, if they don't already."

I watched her beat the palms of her hands on her knees. "Loran, don't you see, I'm trying to convince myself I did what was best for Sarne. It was done in a moment of being terrified for him. It was mad, do you think I don't know it? But it's done now and there's no way I can turn her out until she chooses to go. I daren't, God help me—I daren't."

She was caught in the trap of her love for Sarne. Fear must have distorted her mind, muddled her thinking. And then I asked myself what I would have done in her place. I wasn't so certain. I sat huddled in my chair, staring at the gently-sleeping dogs. By telling me what she had, she had given me a kind of oblique responsibility for her.

I felt suddenly that she was the child and I the adult.

"Tell Sarne," I said.

"No, I'll never do that."

"But you know he'll find out."

"All right," she said, nodding her head wearily, "he'll find out. But it won't be from me."

"I suppose Ferry knows."

"She had to because of moving the furniture."

"And what does she say?"

"She's devoted to me. She'll never talk."

"But surely she didn't approve?"

"For the first time in my life, I've shocked her by what I've done. But she dreads the police as much as I. She hates upheaval. We're just two aging people wanting quiet in our lives. It's so little to ask and yet it seems so much to expect."

"This, of course, accounts for my seeing Babette near the house a few times. I even warned her once about trespassing and she laughed at me."

"The staircase in the west wing leads straight down to the back door, so we won't be troubled by her."

"The needlework I saw on the table in her room—" I began.

She nodded. "She is helping me mend some of the embroidered bedspreads from Jessily Court. When she was a child, she was put into a convent school. I think her father, whoever he was, could have been a Catholic. But when she left the convent she reverted to her old ways—she had no chance, with that dreadful family of hers. At the convent, however, she learned to embroider beautifully. One of the conditions I made for her staying here was her silence. The other was that she must help me with the repair of the embroideries."

"Her clothes could do with a few repairs, too," I said dryly.

"She'll always be slovenly in herself," Mrs. Cranmer said. "It's in her blood. Please, Loran, just try to forget that Babette is here. I don't think she'll bother you—or indeed any of us—now I've given her a roof over her head. She won't dare to go too far with me."

I sat quite still, and above the despair of my own heart I had the incongruous picture of Babette, her tiny fingers working gold thread into the worn patches of brocade. More gypsy than peasant, she would probably hate every moment of it. Yet she wouldn't be quite certain how strong were her blackmailing propensities. She wouldn't quite know if she could hold Mrs. Cranmer to her promise of housing her without doing something to earn a roof over her head.

XIII

THE VILLAGE SHOP had managed to order for me the elastic bandage I needed for Marnie's foot. She would need support for it for some time to come. When I had collected it I walked to the farm through the woods rather than along the road.

On such a morning as this, dark and furtive things seemed alien, like bad dreams. On such a morning, I thought, rustling through the dry leaves and the brown bracken, a miracle could happen and I could come face to face, in these woods, with someone I sought —my mother, my father, my brother Anthony.

This was how I loved the country, a place of arabesques of light and shade, of gold and green and birds' songs.

I peered through the soft green light and saw a man coming towards me slowly, leaning on a shooting stick. As he drew nearer I recognized Monty.

He lifted his stick and waved it at me. I waved back.

"It's a lovely morning," he called.

I said that it was.

"I've come out here to cut some branches of beech for Gillian's two big blue-and-white vases. Did you notice them? They're rather fine specimens of Royal Delft." He spread the stick and perched on the small leather saddle. "Gillian was depressed this morning. I thought some of these golden branches would cheer her up."

He got out a clasp knife. "That's a lovely piece," he said and reached up to cut the branch. "She'll love this."

I thought, watching him, that a few sprays of bronze leaves wouldn't cure Gillian's depression. But Monty had the kind of perpetual immaturity that saw misery and offered a gift. "Please smile. Look. Pretty leaves." It must be pleasant to have such an uncomplicated child's mind.

"Gillian knows," I said, "about Claire's suitcase being found?"

"She must, but she hasn't talked about it. She doesn't say much about anything and I never ask her. It suits me, you see, to mind my own business," he added with a little chuckle.

"Why?"

He gave me his bland, gentle look.

"Gillian's good to me and there's no one else who would take in an old man without much money. Gillian is secretive and I've learned to let her be." With his arms laden with branches he looked a bit like a walking tree. He came towards me, the knife pointed ominously in my direction. "You're a nice, sympathetic sort of girl. I suppose that's because you're a nurse!"

"I don't know about that," I murmured.

"And I don't get many people to talk to." His old face peered through the bronze leaves. "It's nice meeting you like this, alone in the woods. We can talk, can't we?"

"Of . . . of course."

"I mean I've got something on my mind. I can't tell people in the village. Nothing's ever kept secret. But you, a stranger, and a nurse at that. I suppose you hear lots of confidences."

"I get my share," I said. "What's worrying you?"

"Miss Brant—" He leaned towards me, the knife still held wildly at the angle of my heart. "Gillian was the last person to see Claire alive."

"She was?" I exclaimed.

"Claire and Gillian had a violent quarrel that night after we came home from the party at the manor."

"How do you know?"

He gave me a sideways smile. "I never did have a head for drink. The second glass sends me dozing right off. Sarne ran Gillian and me home that night and put me to bed. But I wasn't drunk. I knew what was going on. I woke and slept and woke again. Downstairs I could hear Sarne and Gillian talking. Then they became very quiet." He gave me another of his little sly, sideways looks. "I got to wondering what they were up to. She's always been mad about him, you know. I remember once she'd got a book on the Medicis out of the library and she said she could understand anyone killing for love."

"We all say odd things at some time or other," I said a little impatiently.

He took up his story again.

"I heard Sarne go, eventually, and then I must have fallen asleep again, because the next thing I heard was shouting. I got up to get myself a drink of water. Claire was with Gillian, and I heard her accuse Gillian of scheming to get Sarne. I remember her saying, 'You always wanted him, didn't you? And if anything happened to me, you'd be the one to go ministering to his children, ingratiating yourself. Well, you needn't go on hoping, because if Sarne's ever alone, it'll be over my dead body.' And then she rushed out of the house. A minute or so after that Gillian left and I heard her running up the lane."

"She could have been going to patch up with Claire," I said. "After all, a quarrel between people living in an isolated village must be very awkward to maintain for long. Does Gillian know that you heard all this?"

"Oh, no." He was sawing off another golden branch. "She might throw me out if I told her I'd listened."

"How do you know you can trust me not to say anything?"

"Because," he said with his sweet open smile, "you nurses are like doctors and priests. You must hear so much and never tell."

I seemed to be fated to have confidences thrust on me. And I knew why. They had to tell someone and there I was: a stranger, an onlooker and reasonably sympathetic. No one in his right senses would believe that any of this affected me. Yet, had he only known, it affected me most of all. And I had no one I could confide in.

I dragged my mind back to what Monty had told me.

"Didn't Gillian tell the police she saw Claire that night?"

"No."

"But why not?"

"Perhaps she likes to let sleeping dogs lie." He eyed me. "After all, if the police knew this, she'd be a strong suspect, wouldn't she?"

"Not necessarily," I said. "People do quarrel, but that doesn't mean they resort to murder. The serious thing is that she lied to the police."

He looked a little scared.

"I shouldn't have told you what I did, should I?"

"It might have been wiser not to."

He sighed. "You're kind, my dear. You wouldn't tell on an old man, now would you?"

"The subject's closed," I said, looking at my watch. "And I must go. I'm on my way to see Marnie."

He patted my shoulder gently and his bearded face smiled wanly at me through the mass of golden leaves.

I continued along the narrow path across the woods. If what Monty had told me was true—and I had no reason to doubt it—Gillian must hate Deborah as she must secretly have always hated Claire. Mrs. Cranmer had been right—there were always many women to love a man.

Why hadn't Gillian told the police that she'd seen Claire that night? But placed in Gillian's position, would I?

Marnie was sitting in the patio, a rug over her knees and a blue Alice-band over her dark hair. She was painting a vase of michaelmas daisies someone had placed on the table. The painted vase was a little crooked and the daisies looked like purple roses. The picture pleased Marnie, however.

"Daddy's going to frame my picture for me when I've finished."

"Good," I said and removed the rug.

"One day I'll paint something terribly clever and people will come and pay me a lot of money to paint pictures for them like they did Uncle Tom."

I said, "And then you'll be a rich girl."

"And I won't have to marry."

"What *do* you mean?"

"Well, that's why girls marry, isn't it? So they can be rich?"

I laughed. "You mercenary little wretch. Who put that idea into your mind?"

"Martin—you know, the man who has the hut on the cliff—told me—"

"You'd better stick to fairy tales," I cut in quickly.

"Why?"

"Because in them, people marry for love and live happily ever after."

She stared away over to the orchard. Her eyes were sad. "Mummy didn't. She was always crying."

I put an arm around her and ran my hands up and down her soft hair.

"Some people cry easily, darling," I said gently, "from feelings that have nothing to do with being unhappy. Do you know once I went to Switzerland and I saw the dawn come up over the mountains. It was so beautiful that I cried."

She pulled away from me. "Mummy didn't cry that way," she said. "She cried as though she was hurt."

Quickly I picked up a fallen paintbrush and laid it across the box of paints.

"Let's have a look at that foot of yours," I said briskly.

"Will I be able to go back to school soon?"

"The doctor said next week, providing you keep the promise you'll have to make not to run and jump about for a while."

I saw Marnie look beyond me, and her eyes darkened. I knew who was standing behind me. Deborah seemed to materialize out of nowhere whenever I was with Marnie.

"Hello," I said.

Deborah flicked me an impatient glance. Her face had a vivid, burning look of fury.

"That damned gypsy girl has been here again," she exploded. "She's always around. She was caught stealing once and I'm not giving her a second chance. You saw her this morning, didn't you?" She addressed Marnie. "Why didn't you tell me at the time?"

"She r-ran away wh-when she saw me," Marnie whispered.

Deborah gripped the little girl's shoulder. "I've told you before, if ever you see that woman around here you're to come and tell me at once. Do you hear? *Do—you—hear?*"

"Sh-she's so l-little"—Marnie had tears on her voice—"and she only w-wanted a c-cabbage."

"I don't care if she wanted nothing at all. She has no right on our property."

Marnie raised her eyes to Deborah. "I d-don't think Daddy would m-mind if she t-took a cabbage," she said with a desperate defiance.

"But *I* do!"

"Mummy w-wouldn't have m-minded, either."

"Your mother isn't here to mind or not."

"But she w-will be. She will . . . she w-will. And then . . ."

"And then, what?" Deborah challenged.

"Th-then I'll be h-happy again."

Deborah turned to me.

"Why is it that there's always one impossible child in a family? But she'll be going to school soon. They'll knock some of the defiance out of her." She stood looking at me, and, as though suddenly remembering that she disliked me, said, "Thanks for all you've done. If you've finished I'll take Marnie down to the playroom to join the others."

I was dismissed. I hated having to disentangle the little girl's taut clinging fingers, but Deborah stood over us.

"I'll be here tomorrow," I promised Marnie, and kissed her.

I didn't glance back as I left them in the patio. I didn't dare in case I should see the child's longing look. I was troubled and unhappy about Marnie and there was nothing I could do about it.

I dawdled along the lane. The Sunday bells were soft and insistent across the moorland and I turned to look back at the village. As I did so, I saw Martin's green car drawn up under some trees. It was empty and I supposed that he had walked from here into the village to fetch his Sunday newspapers. I had only gone a few yards farther when I saw him down by the silver beech copse. Deborah was with him. He must have arrived almost simultaneously with my leaving.

Short of turning back, there was no way I could avoid them. And anyway, the lane was a public path. There was no reason why I should feel guilty at coming upon them. I wished I had the dogs with me so that I could pretend to give attention to something and not seem to be staring directly at them as I approached. I turned and picked three large ripe blackberries and rolled them in my hand. But I couldn't shut out those two people standing so closely together. I saw Martin make a movement, saw him draw Deborah to him quickly and kiss her. She didn't struggle. Nor, on the other hand, did she cling to him. I had a feeling that she was laughing, that they were both laughing.

I ate the blackberries slowly, lingering by the bush to look for more. When I glanced again towards the copse they were gone.

I had reached the main road when the green car caught up with me.

"I was hoping I'd see you," Martin called out to me. "Will you come and have a drink with me this evening?"

"I don't think so, thanks."

"But *I* think you will, because I have something to tell you and something in the hut you may find interesting." He held out his bag of sugared almonds. "Have one."

I turned my head away. "If you've anything to tell me you can say it now."

"Unfortunately I can't. You'll need proof and that's at the hut."

"Proof of what?"

"Oh, something to do with you." He smiled at me and let in the clutch, and the car began to crawl forward. "Will you come? Don't worry, I'm not a wolf."

I clung to the car door. "All right, I'll come this evening. About six."

He nodded. "And as proof of all the good intentions I have with regard to you, you can tell Deborah and Sarne that you're coming. There they are, just up the lane."

"I'll see you later," I called, and began walking quickly in the same direction as Sarne and Deborah.

I didn't want them to catch me, but all the way to the church I felt their presence behind me. It took all my will power not to turn around covertly and look to see if they held hands as they walked and if they laughed together.

I took the dogs and a flashlight with me that evening when I crossed the heath to Martin's hut.

There was a light inside and the door was open. The dogs

stopped and looked questioningly at me. I banged on the door with my knuckles. No one answered.

I took a few steps inside the door. By the light of the two oil lamps I saw that the room was empty.

"Martin?" I called, watching the two closed doors on the far side of the room. Nobody answered me.

There was a wine bottle on the roughly-made dresser and a single glass with red dregs in it. The bottle was empty.

If he had been sitting here drinking wine on his own, then he had probably gone out to clear his head. Anyway, I had no intention of waiting in this rather gloomy little room. I turned to go, and caught sight of something glinting in an open envelope lying on the low table. It looked like a golden stone. I bent down to look more closely, then took it out of the envelope.

It was my topaz with the phoenix engraving.

I held it in my hand and felt queerly moved. I had a feeling that finding it was an omen. This was why Martin had asked me here. I was curious to know where he had found it. But I was also annoyed that he hadn't bothered to be here on time for me. I found a pencil in my handbag and scribbled a note on the envelope.

"I've found what you obviously intended to give me," I scribbled. "I can't wait around. Perhaps you'll come up to the manor this evening and tell me where you found it and also tell me what it is you think would interest me."

I signed it "Loran," and, putting the topaz in my handbag, left the hut.

At first I thought how quiet everything was. Quiet? But it wasn't. There was a rustle of bushes on my left, too strong to be caused by the wind or a rabbit. I called to the dogs over-loudly. "Viola. Juliet."

Their black shapes paused and then bounded on. I began to run to catch up with them.

No one came after me. I crossed the heath, walking very quickly, and reached the manor grounds. I wondered if it had been Martin lurking in the bushes. But if so, why play hide-and-seek with me? Had he changed his mind about what he had to tell me? And did he think hiding easier than explanation?

Mrs. Cranmer called me from the kitchen when I entered the house. "You're back very soon."

"Martin wasn't there," I said, "but my topaz was." I held it out for her to see.

"I suppose he found it somewhere on the heath."

"I left a note and suggested he might call here tonight if he really had something to tell me. You don't mind?"

"Of course not, if it will help you." But there was caution in her voice.

I made a mental note not to bring him into the living room. But I couldn't stop my excited conviction that Martin really had something to tell me.

Sarne called immediately after dinner. He had an estimate for felling some diseased elms. I sat only half-listening to their talk about permits and the opinion of forestry experts on the lovely, noble line of elms at the far side of the estate.

I was waiting for Martin.

Sarne was standing by the mantelshelf, a whisky in his hand. His russet hair gleamed in the firelight; his brows were drawn together. He looked formidable and angry, but I knew he wasn't. He was merely discussing trees.

I stayed with them only a short while. I felt that Mrs. Cranmer wanted to talk to Sarne alone, and with a murmured excuse I slipped from the room. I went across the hall and into the dining room. I went to the window without turning on the light. Would Martin come? I stood looking out, my fingers playing with the tasseled cord that worked the curtains. I stood waiting for Martin for some minutes. There was no fire and I shivered in the stabs of cold wind seeping through the worn window frames.

When I heard the living room door open, I ran quickly across the dark room. I had to see Sarne. We came face to face in the hall. With so much to say to him, my voice wouldn't come. I stood dumbly. Then I managed a smile and pretended I was on my way upstairs.

He came towards me. "Forgive me," he said.

It was the last word I wanted to hear. It had finality.

"There's nothing to forgive and I *hate* the word," I said violently.

"Whether you hate it or not, it's a word you have to acknowledge in life."

"I'd have been happier if you hadn't said it. You ask forgiveness only for something you regret."

"That's right, you do."

I gripped the newel post and turned and took a step away from him. He gripped my hand and swung me around to that I nearly fell. I wrenched my hand away. I wanted to whip up temper in myself, to hurt, because he had hurt me.

"I'm going back to London next week," I said, "and then we can both forget. That's the way you want it, isn't it?"

"Yes."

I ought to have left him then, turned and marched up the stairs. I ought to have tried to understand that he had enough to cope with without my making scenes. But I didn't. My desperate unhappiness blotted out any consideration for him. I knew I was being unfair, flinging my own pain in his face, as I let myself go.

"*We'll* forget it all? *We'll* do no such thing. You will, but I won't. I'll remember how I met a man who had everything in his favor and yet who failed. A broken marriage, a complication with another woman, and on top of that an impulsive thwarted little affair with a third. I'll remember—" My voice broke and my teeth clicked sharply together. He had dragged me down the two stairs and was shaking me.

"What complication with another woman?"

"Why . . . Deborah," I said unsteadily.

"And a thwarted little affair with whom?"

"Me." He had stopped shaking me and I leaned trembling against the newel post.

"So that's what this is."

"Well, isn't it?"

Sarne was in no gentle mood. He seized me as though I were an antagonist and kissed me as though he were punishing me. Somewhere in some old story, I remembered the expression "to die upon a kiss." It had been sweetly sentimental. There was nothing sweet or sentimental about this. If I died at this moment it was because Sarne was giving me no chance to get my breath. You could murder someone this way. . . .

Somewhere behind us a door opened. Pinned against Sarne, unable to move my head, I saw Mrs. Cranmer out of the corner of my eye.

"Oh!" She put her hand to her mouth and stared at us.

Sarne released me slowly.

"Hello, Aunt Charlotte," he said as casually as if he had been lighting a cigarette.

I leaned back against the blessedly strong support of the newel post and took deep breaths of air into my stifled lungs.

Mrs. Cranmer didn't move.

"You're quite right in what you're thinking, Aunt Charlotte," Sarne said. "I love Loran."

You could . . . have told . . . me. . . .

It was only when I heard Mrs. Cranmer speak that I realized my voice could not have been more than a breath of sound, heard by neither of them.

"How long? I mean—you've known each other only two weeks."

"That's right," Sarne said.

"But how . . . ?"

"There's no 'how' or 'why' about it," he said harshly. "Loran's going back to London and she's going to take up her life again."

"Does she . . . love you?"

"I haven't asked her. I don't want to know."

"But you know all the same." This time he heard me.

"I know nothing about you," he almost shouted. His face was dark and drawn. He looked not at me but at Mrs. Cranmer. "I don't know a damn thing except that I love her. And the more I know about her the harder it will be to forget her, so if you don't mind, we won't discuss Loran again." He was discussing me as though I were invisible. I took a step towards him.

Sarne could move more quickly than anyone I knew. He was at the door and through it before I could collect myself and shout the words that were pounding in my brain. *"I'm here. Stop wanting to forget me. I love you."*

The front door slammed.

I turned and put my forehead against the cool wood of the post and curled my arms around it for comfort.

"It's cold out here, dear." Charlotte Cranmer's voice came from a great distance. I felt her arm go around me, and like a child I let her lead me into the living room. My knees were shaking; my heart thudded. I felt nervous and alarmed as though I were guilty of a crime. I stood by the settee, my hand resting on the soft down cushion and waited for her to say something, perhaps to vent anger on me that I'd dared to complicate Sarne's life further.

"Oh, Loran!"

Startled by the trembling tone, I lifted my head and saw that she was crying.

"It's too late," she whispered. "I would have wished this with all my heart, but it's . . . too . . . late. . . ."

She rushed past me with a soft swish of silk and out of the room.

I didn't see her again that night. I knew she couldn't bear to talk to me. But I knew, too, that she didn't condemn me for what she had seen.

XIV

I STOOD IN MY ROOM, the pale morning sunlight glinting on the topaz I held in my palm. I had got it back and it was unscratched. But where had Martin found it, and why hadn't he come last night?

I did remember vaguely that I had heard a car in the distance soon after Sarne had closed the front door. Few cars came up the lane, but I supposed it had been someone visiting the farm.

I laid the topaz in the little velvet zipper case in which I kept my few pieces of jewelry. I was glad that I had it back, but it solved nothing for me and its return could have no significance.

Suddenly, without any preliminary knock, my door opened.

I swung around. Ferry stepped quickly back, her large nose twitching in a way she had when she was surprised.

"I'm sorry, Miss Brant. I thought you had gone out."

"I've made my bed and if you like I'll vacuum my room," I said.

"Thank you, but I'll do it later."

I'd have liked to do it myself because she looked tired and old, but she was always too unapproachable to argue with. So I said pleasantly, "I'll be going out in about five minutes."

"To the farm?"

"Yes, but it won't be for much longer. Marnie's arm doesn't need any more attention and she can walk a little now. She'll be back at school next week."

Ferry might not have been listening to a word I said. She stood staring at me and I was so unused to her looking directly at me that I guessed she had something so important to say that she couldn't contain herself.

"You haven't heard the news?" she asked.

"What news?"

"Mr. Sarne telephoned to tell Mrs. Cranmer not ten minutes ago. She's gone to the farm to see him."

"What news?" I said again, sharply this time.

"That young man, Martin Cavall, has been found at the bottom of the cliffs. The fall had broken his neck. He's dead."

I had nothing to say. Every word I tried to form sounded too banal. I just stood and stared at her.

Ferry turned her face away. "I thought you'd better know, Miss Brant," she said. "And now I must get on with my work."

She stepped back into the hall and closed my door.

I wore a thick red tweed suit that morning. All I had to do was pick up my handbag and go to the farm, to Marnie. Instead, I stood at the window and stared down into the garden. It was too lovely a day to think of death, yet there it was. A young man with merry eyes and a liking for sugared almonds had died violently. I thought of my visit last night to the hut. Had he been lying there then, helpless on the rocks where the sea foamed? If I had looked over, could I perhaps have seen him and saved his life? But it had been too dark anyway.

I put my hands to my face and felt it ice cold. I'd been annoyed that he'd stood me up, and all the time he had been lying injured . . . or lying already dead—I hoped the latter. I hoped desperately that had I searched, I could not have saved him. It was too much to have on my conscience.

At some time while Ferry had been speaking I had picked up my comb. I ran it absently through my hair and my scalp felt sore. I threw the comb onto the dressing table and went on staring out of the window.

Suddenly Sarne came into the picture. I saw him standing in a distant field with his dog.

He's got his hut back, I thought. There'd be no car now to startle his Ayrshires and break his beloved peace.

Martin was dead. I had no real feeling for him except a queer, perverse liking. He had been so gay, and I liked gay people. I would never know now what he had to tell me. I picked up my bag and went down the stairs and out of the house.

Mrs. Cranmer was coming up the drive.

"I've just heard about Martin," I said. "Does anyone know yet how it happened?"

"It was an accident, of course," she said very quickly. "There were empty wine bottles in his room. He must have gone out for a walk while he was a little drunk, got dizzy and fallen."

"Where was he found?"

"Just this side of Falcon Point."

So I wouldn't have seen him if I'd looked over the edge of the cliff. He had been lying nearly half a mile to the west.

"The police don't think it was foul play?"

She stared at me in amazement. "Why on earth should they think that? I told you, he'd obviously been drinking."

"He didn't seem to me to be the type who drank too much."

"He probably wasn't in the ordinary course of things. But something could have been on his mind. Men drink to forget, very often."

"When do the police think he died?"

"Oh, some time last evening."

"And I was there some time last evening."

"Yes." She gave me a troubled look. "You went into the hut, didn't you?"

I nodded. "And left a note for him."

"You touched things, too?"

"The envelope which had my topaz in it," I began indifferently. Then I stared at her. "They wouldn't think that I was involved! Mrs. Cranmer, how could they? I was a stranger to him. Besides, you say it was an accident. . . ."

"Of course," she said soothingly. "Don't worry. But there's just a chance they could think that you and he had a quarrel last night."

"And he threw himself over the cliff for love of me?" My laugh touched on hysteria. "That's really . . . funny. Or no, it isn't. Martin's dead. . . ."

Her hand on my arm steadied me. "I wasn't going to say that. I was going to suggest that if you'd quarreled he might have been a little upset and drunk too much to forget and got dizzy and fallen!"

"But I didn't see him to quarrel with him," I cried.

"I know you didn't, Loran dear, and all you have to do is to tell the police that. There's nothing for you to worry about."

Nothing, except a haughty little note scrawled on an envelope and something relating to me that a young man with a laughing face would never now tell.

Mrs. Cranmer left me as the telephone bell rang. I wandered across the dew-wet lawn and breathed the cool sea air. But something in me was on fire. My restless mind took control. Thoughts whirled, stabbed and tore at me so that in the end I could bear my own company no longer. I left the golden garden and went back to the house.

Ferry was in the hall. She was reaching up, doing something to the face of the grandfather clock.

"Has it stopped?" I asked.

"No. The minute hand gets stuck."

I said, admiring the black-and-gold lacquer cabinet, "It's a beautiful old clock."

"It doesn't look its best here." She climbed down from the chair and dusted the seat carefully. "It used to stand at the head of the staircase to the west wing. And there was a lacquer chest up there, too, which matched it. But Mrs. Cranmer sold it at Sotheby's with a lot of other things."

It was the longest speech she had ever made to me and I wanted to encourage her.

"The house must have been lovely when it was all used."

"It was. But those days are gone. Only the house martins nest in the eaves there now. And that gypsy, Babette, with her disgusting camping habits."

So Mrs. Cranmer had told her that I now knew about Babette.

"She won't be staying long?" I asked.

Sunlight falling through the stained glass window of the hall shone onto Ferry's face, giving it a curious greenish hue.

"Madam must have been mad. Mad!"

"Babette was homeless."

"There's other ways to be kind to the homeless. Mrs. Cranmer isn't on committees in Arlesthorne without knowing that."

"But the whole wing of a house," I murmured, "lying empty."

"It would have been better to burn it down than have that . . . that witch living there."

I managed a laugh. "I doubt if she knows how to weave spells—" I began. And then I stopped. I remembered the crude and terrible little clay models with the pins stuck in their hearts.

Ferry was walking towards the kitchen. Suddenly I wanted to know if she was on Sarne's side.

"Just a minute," I said.

She stopped and turned, looking at me in cold surprise.

"Babette can't really harm anyone here, can she?" I asked. "After all, you can only hurt the guilty? And the police certainly wouldn't listen to any evidence of hers."

She regarded me rigidly. "What evidence are you talking about, Miss Brant?"

I'd gone too far to retract. "Babette believes that Sarne and Mrs. Millbrook are concerned in Mrs. Algar's disappearance," I said desperately.

Her eyes were like black almonds in her gray face.

"Indeed, Miss Brant, you seem to be well acquainted with a gypsy's gossip." She turned on her heel and let the kitchen door close behind her.

It was stupid of me to have said that and I'd asked for the snub.

I hung around the house and the garden for the next hour or so. I knew why I was waiting. At some time or other the police inspector would catch up with me and question me about my visit last night to Martin's hut. I was impatient for him to come and get the interview over.

From my room, which I had been tidying, I saw Mrs. Cranmer hurrying down the drive. I watched her until she turned the far corner.

At twelve o'clock she telephoned me. She was detained in the village, she said, but would I remind Ferry that Gillian and Monty were coming to lunch.

The dogs were mooning around the garden and Josh was shoveling rubble into the old well. I could hear in the stillness the scrape of his spade. A peacock screamed twice and then there was silence again.

I turned on the radio and heard a talk on weather. I gathered that we had had enough days without rain to constitute a state of drought in the South.

The clock had struck the half hour after twelve when Inspector Gray called. Ferry announced him, and I wondered what she thought of me. She had found me in Sarne's arms and now I was to be questioned about a dead man.

The inspector was charming, but I sat on a hard chair away from the fire and broke out into a cold sweat of fear. I didn't trust his gentleness. I could be so easily trapped by his slight diffidence into saying something that could trigger off another shaft of suspicion directed towards Sarne.

Had I been walking near Mr. Cavall's hut last evening? I couldn't drag my gaze from his deep Viking-blue eyes. Yes, I had. In fact I had actually called at the hut at Mr. Cavall's invitation. (As though you didn't know.) The inspector asked me the time I had called, and why. Did I go into the hut? What did I find? I explained. I told him about the note. . . . Oh, yes, there was a note. He looked almost apologetic for having to question me. *You're dangerous,* I thought.

By the door, the inspector's sergeant sat on a chair much too small for him and took notes. Suddenly I decided to become expansive. I had nothing to hide, and everything to gain by his knowing. So I told him the whole truth—why I was here in Saxon Magna and how I had tried to find my parents. I was sure he didn't want to hear the story, but I was determined that he should because I had an idea that in some oblique way he might be able to help me. At the end of my story I told him about finding my lost topaz at Martin's hut.

"So," I finished, "if you find my fingerprints on the dresser, you'll know why."

A trace of a smile lit his face. He was very patient. He repeated a question he had already asked me.

"And you didn't hear a sound, any sound, while you were there?"

"Only the sea. Was . . . was Martin already dead?"

"If you visited the hut at six o'clock, then yes, he was."

"So even if I'd gone to look for him I couldn't have saved his life."

"No."

"I suppose he went for a walk, felt dizzy and slipped."

"It could be."

The way he said it made me ask quickly, "It *was* an accident?"

His brilliant eyes sharpened into a question.

"Only," I rushed on, "I didn't think the police came around making inquiries in the case of an obvious accident."

"We always have to ask questions, Miss Brant," was his bland reply. Then he thanked me, picked up his hat and left.

I went out onto the terrace and leaned on the cold stone balustrade. I saw Mrs. Cranmer cross the lawn to meet the policeman. She must have returned while he was with me.

"We seem to meet, Inspector, only when there is trouble," I heard her say.

"That's the worst of my job, madam," he said gallantly. "I appear with bad news, never with good. By the way, just one thing, Mrs. Cranmer . . ."

She turned her head, as he paused, and saw me. I moved away and went back into the living room. From there I could just hear their voices but not what they said.

Mrs. Cranmer came into the room a few minutes later. She flung herself into a chair as though exhausted and passed her hand over her face as though to brush off some mask she had put there for the inspector's benefit.

"What did he want to ask you, Loran?"

"Only to inquire the time I called at the hut and what I found there."

She sighed. "Would you go and ask Ferry to make me some coffee, my dear? And have some with me, of course."

I went to the kitchen. I don't know whether Ferry was intrigued or not by the inspector's visit. She asked me nothing; she resorted to her usual way with me of neither looking at me nor showing the slightest interest.

"If you're busy," I said, "I'll come out and fetch the tray."

"Thank you, I can manage perfectly." Her words dismissed me.

I went back to the living room. On my way through the hall the thought that had all this time lurked as a possibility became a certainty. *Oh, no,* I thought. *No.* I shut my eyes. The knowledge turned into red letters dancing on the black background of my eyelids.

The police believed that Martin was murdered.

I pushed open the sitting room door and stood and looked across at Mrs. Cranmer.

"They believe Martin was murdered," I said very clearly.

She gave a sharp, high-pitched little cry. "Loran, don't for God's sake say that to anyone else. What makes you even think it?"

"I didn't," I said. "It isn't a thought at all; I just know that's what they think."

She had risen and was facing me. "Why should anyone want to kill him? He was a stranger here."

"Perhaps he wasn't, to someone," I said.

She laid her arms along the mantelshelf and put her forehead down on her hands. "I can't take much more," she whispered. "I'm tired . . . tired . . ."

I went swiftly to her side and put my arm around her. She was an upright, stocky little woman, but now her shoulders were bent so that she looked half her size, cowed and old.

"This has nothing to do with us," I said gently. "Martin probably had some enemy we know nothing about—he certainly managed to antagonize people, for all his gaiety. He could have chosen this unlikely place to live because he was hiding. And someone found him. And killed him."

"But we don't *know* that he didn't die accidentally."

"No. We don't know. I'm sorry. I shouldn't have blurted out what I did. Don't take any notice. I don't know any more than you—or anyone else in the village." I was trying hard to make amends for the shock my words must have been to her.

Ferry came in with a silver tray. Mrs. Cranmer went back to her chair and sat upright and white-faced while the coffee was set before her with Ferry's slow, meticulous ritual.

When Ferry had gone, she poured and handed me a cup, saying, "In the opinion of some in the village, Martin Cavall had been sent down here by Scotland Yard. If it's true, then he's been spying on us. It could have been he who found Claire's suitcase."

"I can't see him as a policeman," I said.

"Nor can I, but why was he here, a type of young man like that, intelligent, sophisticated, living in a remote hut?" Again she brushed her hand nervously across her forehead. "It doesn't really make sense, does it, Loran?"

I had to agree that it didn't. I took a swallow of scalding coffee. "Deborah knew him fairly well, didn't she?"

"Deborah is the type to get to know any presentable young man fairly well," she retorted.

"We're not doing any good, are we, conjecturing like this," I told her unhappily. "It just harrows us."

"Harrows you, too?" She let out a long unsteady breath. "But of course. Oh, Loran, for *your* sake, why do you have to love Sarne?"

I couldn't talk about it. I nibbled an unwanted biscuit and stared at a Victorian portrait on the far wall.

"Once," she continued, "I should have been gloriously happy about it. You're the kind of wife I would have loved for Sarne. Now, it's too late. It's eight years too late. . . ."

"Miss Gillian is on the telephone." Ferry put her head around the door. "She says she doesn't want to disturb you if you're busy, but shall she bring around that knitting pattern you like?"

The ordinariness of the message was almost ludicrous coming on top of our conversation. I began to laugh inside me. But as Mrs. Cranmer rose and went to the telephone the small hysterical outburst died. I had indeed come here eight years too late.

XV

AFTER LUNCH I went to the farm to see Marnie. She was in the patio disinterestedly winding a ball of scarlet wool. She didn't know where Simon and Nina had gone to, she said flatly, and I realized that she was almost in tears with the boredom of being left alone.

"Where's Daddy?" I asked her.

"One of the heifers is sick. The vet's there."

"And Deborah?"

"I don't know," she said, frowning.

"Well then, suppose you come out for a drive with me?"

"I'd love that." She dropped the ball of wool and it slid across the paving. I retrieved it. "We could go as far as Corfe."

"Oh." Her little face dropped disconsolately.

"Don't you want to go there?" I asked.

"I thought you meant to drive into Arlesthorne," she said plaintively. "I thought we could go and see Uncle Tom."

"But we couldn't just call without finding out if it's convenient for him."

"I *know* it is." Her face brightened. "He asked Deborah to bring me over this afternoon and she said she couldn't manage it. She didn't want to take me out; she doesn't like me."

"Oh, Marnie, don't say that."

"It's true," she said, her dark eyes lifted to me. "She'd like me to run away and never be found."

"What about this drive?" I steered her away from the dangerous subject.

"Wouldn't you like to see Uncle Tom's gorgeous paintings?" she said.

I laughed and gave in. I'd have done anything to wipe that sad look from her face. "But if, when we get there, it isn't convenient, it's understood we come away."

"Uncle Tom wouldn't ever let us stay if he didn't want us," she said wisely.

"Come on, then." I helped her hobble to the car. "I'd better tell someone where we're going."

"Chauncey's in the kitchen," she said. "She's making cakes."

I went through to the huge farm kitchen where the smell of baking coconut was so rich that I longed to be a child again and ask for a hot cake. Instead, I explained that I was taking Marnie into Arlesthorne and we might call on Mr. MacQueen.

Chauncey nodded her bright blonde head. "It'd do Marnie good to get out. She's been cooped up so long. Her father's tied up with the farm, and Mrs. Millbrook—well, she's pretty busy too," she added loyally.

"Well, Marnie will be mobile again by next week and back at school," I said brightly. "You won't forget to let them know that she's with me, will you?"

I went back to Marnie and found her carrying the book Tom MacQueen had given her with the little paintings in it.

"I'm going to take it with me," she said. "He forgot to write in it. He usually puts 'To Marnie with love from Uncle Tom.'"

"He's done all those lovely paintings," I said. "That's enough, isn't it?"

She shook her brown head vigorously. "It won't ever be my special book unless he writes in it."

When we reached Arlesthorne, Marnie had to direct me. I found, however, that whenever she had been taken by Deborah to Tom MacQueen's house she must have been looking at anything but the way. We spent half an hour trying to find the little cul-de-sac where his cottage stood.

When we stood outside the front door, Marnie insisted on ringing the bell.

"Simon and Nina and I ring it a very special way," she explained, "so that he knows it's us."

We had to ring twice before we heard footsteps. They were sharp and swift and high heels clicked on a wooden floor.

The door swung open and Deborah stood looking at us in amazement.

Marnie stepped forward. Deborah barred her way.

"What on earth brings you here?" Her tone was brisk and ungracious.

"We w-want to see Uncle T-Tom."

"I'm afraid you can't," Deborah snapped. "He's been taken ill suddenly. That's why I'm here."

"I'm so sorry," I said quickly. "Is there anything I can do?"

"No, thank you, Loran. He doesn't need a nurse; he needs a hospital. I'm afraid you'll have to excuse me."

"Have you sent for the doctor or can I go for one for you?" I asked.

"It's all taken care of, thanks." She was already shutting the door as she spoke.

"But, Deborah," Marnie began woefully. "I w-want to see him—j-just a peep. He s-says I make him laugh."

"Nothing you can do at the moment will make him laugh," Deborah retorted. "Now, please go. I don't want to leave him too long alone."

The door closed almost before we had turned away.

"Deborah said she couldn't take me to see Uncle Tom this afternoon." Marnie gave the house a mournful look as we got back into the car.

"Well, darling, if she was busy—"

"But she *did* go there."

"She has just told us that he was taken ill suddenly," I explained. "Come on, we'll go for a drive somewhere. Can you manage the car door?"

"But she didn't tell me Uncle Tom was ill," Marnie persisted.

I settled her in the car.

"She was out when I came to see you. She probably got home just as we left and Uncle Tom rang her then. We took rather a long time to get here. She probably arrived while we were still going around in circles."

"Daddy says I've only got a sense of direction when I'm on a horse and then it's the horse, not me, that finds his way. Simon's awfully good, though," she added generously. "He wants to be a racing driver when he grows up and have a car like Martin. Why did Martin die, Loran?"

I said it was an accident and it just showed that no one should walk too near unprotected cliff edges.

At the top of the road I found a shop and bought Marnie some toffees. The little bag in the glove compartment made me think of Martin. I felt I would never again really enjoy sugared almonds. I drove Marnie around for a while but it was cold and the sky was overcast. I felt that the golden autumn was over and the sad weather was with us at last.

We had tea at a little cottage where they gave us scones with cream and homemade raspberry jam. Marnie seemed to relax now that she was alone with me, to stop being a tight little scrap of poignant reserve. She became gay and talkative, forgetting to stammer, and when we reached home again she nearly fell over herself in her hurry to get out of the car and tell her news to Sarne, who saw us arrive.

"Uncle Tom's ill," she called, "and Deborah's there with him."

"I know. She had a phone call. Chauncey told me that you'd already set off and I thought you'd get there first."

"We took an awful long time. We went around and around."

I caught Sarne's amused eye.

"And I can guess whose fault that was."

"Yes, Daddy, it was m-mine. I never know whether you turn right or left at the inn c-called the Golden Goose."

"You do neither," he said. "You drive straight on."

We laughed and he sent her after Simon and Nina, who were in the basement playroom.

"Did Deborah say what was wrong with her father?" I asked.

He shook his head.

"Is it serious?"

"I don't know that, either. She's going to ring me after the doctor's called." Sarne looked from me to the car. "Would you like to take me for a run?"

"Why . . . why, yes, of course," I said, startled by this inconsistency with what had made him say only yesterday that he didn't want to see me again. But he slid an arm around me. "Come along, then. Let's go to a favorite place of mine. It's a valley of beeches and in the spring the ground is a carpet of bluebells. Sometimes I go there at night, by myself. I walk. But it's too far for you. Wait a minute." He called his dog. "You don't mind a threesome?" His laugh made him sound young.

"If Remus isn't jealous," I said gaily.

The dog leaped into the back seat of the car. I hesitated.

"Shouldn't we take your car?" I began.

But he was already in the passenger seat. "You can drive me. I promise not to lose you."

"But I'm lost already," I said.

He turned to me and laid his arm across the back of the car seat. I felt his fingers touch the nape of my neck.

"So am I, if it comes to that. Lost and wondering what the devil I'm going to do about it. Loran—"

"What?" I turned and faced him.

"This," he said, and kissed me.

I was suddenly very happy. Nothing mattered, nothing *was,* but this moment. Then, like an idiot, I became cautious.

"Sarne, not here! Someone will see . . ." I protested.

"Damn someone." His voice came muffled against my throat. "Let them see."

"Not here," I said again. "Let's go . . . quickly."

He never obeyed anyone. He didn't obey now. I gave up, closed my eyes and waited for him to say in tenderness what he had said so violently up at the manor. If he didn't, I would. I moved my lips from his, ready to say, "I love you." But the words never came. A car was heading towards us along the lane.

I wrenched myself away from him. He glanced lazily around. Then I felt his body grow tense.

"You were right, my darling. Why didn't we go while we could?"

"Is it someone for you?"

"Very definitely for me." He was sitting well away from me now, frowning ahead of him at the car's lights piercing the blue deepening evening. "It's Inspector Gray and his outsize sergeant," he said.

My heart gave a lurch. I swallowed and said weakly, "But they may not want you."

"No one comes up this lane except to see Aunt Charlotte or me. And it happens that this visit is for me."

"How do you know?" My hands gripped the wheel.

"Because," he said quietly, "before you went to see Martin last night, I was there at the hut. I ordered him to get off my estate. I threatened him, and someone from the village was walking by and heard."

"Oh, Sarne!"

He looked at me. "You see, you don't know me, Loran. Not the real me. That's why you're mad to stay here where there can be no peace and no real happiness for you."

I pressed my hand hard against myself to try to stop the claw of pain at my heart. I watched Inspector Gray get out of the car, saw him in the car's headlights pick up his trilby from the seat. What in the world did he want to carry that for, I thought irrelevantly, just walking into a house to question a man? Or was that battered old hat a badge of office? I realized that in the near-darkness the inspector didn't know Sarne was in the car with me. He might even have thought we were a courting couple, with the car drawn in hard to the hedge. A courting couple. It would have been heaven had it been that simple.

Sarne was making a move to get out of the car. I held on to his wrist. "No one can hold it against you for giving someone notice to leave."

From the back seat Remus's cold nose nuzzled our hands as they held. I jumped. I'd forgotten the dog.

"Oh, Loran." The cry burst from Sarne.

As I drew him near to me, I saw his face in the half light. It was exhausted and ravaged where it had so few minutes ago had laughter. "You take away my power of resistance," he whispered against my breast. "Let me go, darling. Let me go."

"To that policeman?"

"To whatever is there for me. You can't stop it, you know."

"Sarne—"

"It's too late, sweet."

I took his face in my hands and leaned forward and kissed him. "I love you," I said. "Whatever you are, I love you."

Just for one fleeting moment I saw the torment on his unguarded face and knew I was stronger than he. What he must be going through I could only faintly guess. All I knew was that he needed me desperately. We had no future, he and I. We only had this moment.

I wanted to start the car while the inspector was ringing the bell at the farm, and drive off to that valley he talked about. I wanted to be alone with Sarne, to let him make love to me. I wanted everything from him, in case circumstances, in the guise of a blue-eyed man with a battered trilby, took him away from me, from us all. Because how did I know, even now, that Sarne had not killed Claire? And even if he hadn't, there was a second woman to whom he had given a claim.

But I couldn't hold him. I watched him climb out of the car and walk away from me towards the house, without even a backward glance.

"Sarne!" I called his name, loudly and commandingly.

His dog heard me, and paused and looked around. Sarne just walked on.

I didn't attempt to turn the car in the narrow lane. Instead I drove around the estate and back to the manor, my mind bemused, not daring to think about the questions the inspector would be asking in that beautiful low farmhouse room.

It had been an evening almost without twilight. Just day and then night. I put the car in the garage and went around to the side of the house. The living room was in darkness and the only lights I could see from here were two in upstairs rooms. I knew now whose they were. Ferry's and Babette's.

While I stood hesitating, too restless to want to go indoors, I remembered that Mrs. Cranmer liked chocolate and that I'd been surprised to see a few attractive boxes in the little shop in the village. I would take a chance on the general shop's still being open. A walk to the village was at least better than this hell of inactivity.

The woman who served me wanted to talk. Wasn't it awful about Mr. Cavall? A smart young man like that. And Mrs. Algar's suitcase? There'd never been such things happening in the village. It was terrible, too terrible. . . . And she was loving it, I thought, as I came out of the shop with the black-and-gold chocolate box.

It was a very dark night, and an overhang of lime trees made a dark patch just before the turning that led to the manor. A car came speeding up behind me, the engine suddenly roaring over my shoulder. At the same time I leaped wildly backwards not knowing whether I was going to hit a wall or a ditch.

The blinding headlights were on me. I flung up my hand to screen my eyes. The car came within inches of me, swayed, careened crazily off the grass verge and plunged back onto the road. I kept my head sufficiently to stare at the number plate, but I couldn't read it, for the car was almost immediately out of range.

I glanced a little stupidly about me and groped in the dark for my handbag and the box of chocolates. I found my handbag first, and, feeling for matches, struck two together. The chocolate box lay in a few inches of muddy ditchwater. I left it there and struggled to my feet. I leaned for a moment against a tree, wiping my wet hands on some face tissues I'd had in my bag. My arms and neck were scratched with brambles, my shoulder burned where I had hit the ground. But I was whole, I was alive, and no thanks to a drunken driver.

The road was black and deserted. No one came by to ask me what had happened, to exclaim at someone's criminal driving.

No one had seemed to be around, either, when I had nearly fallen into the old well or been caught by the tide at Falcon Point. No witnesses, ever. . . . The thought roused me out of my shocked fury with the drunken driver. I knew perfectly well that whoever had driven at me had all his wits about him. It had been a deliberate attempt on my life—as deliberate as those other occasions. I knew it for certain now. I rubbed my shoulder. The pain wasn't bad; I'd been lucky. But I dare not push that luck too far.

Whoever wanted to harm me would try again. The thing for me to do was to get away before that happened. Because every "accident" would be as carefully arranged as these three, with no one around as a witness and in each case the clear possibility of my own carelessness.

I stepped out of the ditch and onto the road. A few yards farther on I saw the wall. So whoever had driven at me had misjudged my position in the dark. That was where I should have been, walking past the stone wall so that I could not have escaped by falling into the ditch.

I made my way quickly and warily to the manor, darting into the shadows at the sound of every approaching car. There was no further attack, but I didn't feel safe until I was standing outside the big door, feeling for my key. Even then, I paused and looked about me at the thick black bushes.

Mrs. Cranmer was in the sitting room. The daily paper lay in untidy sheets around her as though she had thrown down each page as she read it. She glanced up as I entered and her smile turned to alarm. She looked at me swiftly, up and down.

"My dear child, what on earth has happened? Your clothes . . ."

I met her gaze steadily. I knew that this time I would have to tell her the truth.

"Someone tried to run me down," I said. "He drove a car at me."

"Drove a car at you?" she repeated slowly and incredulously. "But I don't understand. You mean a drunken driver?"

"Oh, no. One with his wits very much about him."

"But, Loran, it couldn't be. I mean . . ."

"People do attempt murder that way," I said.

She was staring at me as if she thought me more than a little mad.

"It's quite true," I said more gently. "Someone drove a car at me just by that old mill wall outside the village. I fell into a ditch and it saved my life."

"You're hurt?"

"Oh, no, I've just jarred my shoulder a bit, that's all."

"Did you recognize the car?"

I shook my head. "He was careful to get away before I could even read the number plate. It was a medium-sized car and I think it was dark red. I saw a kind of glow of color as it passed a street light."

Mrs. Cranmer stood rigidly still, staring at me. Her face had become pinched and tight.

"Gillian's Hillman is dark red. Someone could have stolen it. We must phone the police."

"What's the use? Whoever drove at me will be miles away by now, or else quite near, sitting by the fire with the car nicely packed away in the garage."

Even as I spoke I saw the pinched look leave her face and color seep back.

"Loran, don't you see? This clears Sarne."

"I don't understand."

Her face, her voice, her whole being, became animated. "If there is a . . . a killer in the village, it isn't Sarne. He wouldn't attack you. He loves you. That's why we must tell Inspector Gray about this. He came to see Sarne earlier, but I saw his car leave the farm some time ago."

"Won't the morning do—" I began.

But she was already dialing the number of police headquarters in Arlesthorne.

Inspector Gray was out and Mrs. Cranmer refused to allow them to send anyone else. "Ask him if he could call here tomorrow morning," she said. "I have something important to tell him."

I went upstairs to my room and changed into a dress, sponged my skirt and hung it up to dry.

Mrs. Cranmer found me a bottle of aspirin spirit and I rubbed some on my shoulder. When I had washed the scratches on my arms and made up my face again, I felt better, though my hands still shook.

When I came downstairs again, Mrs. Cranmer had a brandy poured out for me.

"I tried to get in touch with Sarne," she said, "but he's out and Deborah tells me she doesn't expect him back until late."

"Deborah's home?" I asked in surprise. "She was at her father's house earlier." And then I told her about Tom MacQueen's illness. "I wonder if he's in the hospital?"

"I doubt it. Tom MacQueen has a perfectly capable housekeeper living in. But Sarne will know about it," she said. "We'll ask him."

"Don't tell him," I urged her. "Mrs. Cranmer, please don't tell him what happened to me tonight."

She shook her head. "I doubt if we'll see Sarne tonight, but we'll certainly tell him tomorrow after we've told Inspector Gray."

It was a long time since I had seen her smile so freely. And I knew why. If I could convince the police that someone had deliberately tried to kill me tonight, then Sarne would, through his love for me, be considered innocent of Martin's murder. There could not be two killers in Saxon Magna. And Charlotte Cranmer's anxiety for my danger was nothing in comparison with her love for Sarne.

XVI

GILLIAN HAD TOLD me once that she had to leave the house at half past eight every morning to be at the library by nine o'clock. Five minutes before the half hour I was at the top of the lane where it met the main Arlesthorne road, along which she would have to pass.

Mrs. Cranmer had exclaimed at my early rising but I'd merely explained that I was restless and wanted some air. It was a poor excuse but she accepted it.

I stood well back from the road, near a clump of rhododendron bushes and watched for the Hillman. Trucks made up the majority of the scanty traffic. Three times I looked at my watch. I had either missed her or she was going to be late. It was already nearly a quarter to nine. And then I saw the car. It wasn't going very fast and I stepped out into the road so that it had to slow down. Gillian's head shot out of the window.

"Of all the idiotic things . . . Oh, Loran! It's you! What were you trying to do, commit suicide?"

I grinned at her. "Sorry. I was daydreaming."

"Does it usually take you that way? Standing in the middle of the road?"

"No."

"You're out early."

"I . . . I've run out of cigarettes." I tried to make it sound convincing.

I glanced down at the right side of her car. It was certainly a little muddy. It was also scratched. But that didn't really prove anything. I wondered now what clue I had expected to find.

"Sorry to hold you up like that," I said brightly and glanced at my watch. "You're going to be late this morning, aren't you?"

Her eyes didn't leave my face. She had been watching my scrutiny of her car.

"I've got a good excuse for being late," she said. "At least I hope my boss will think it's good. My car was stolen last night. Monty and I were going to the doctor's house for drinks and when I went to get the car, it wasn't in the road. I reported it to the police and then we walked to Dr. Baines's house. When we came back the car was where I'd left it."

"You didn't hear it being driven away?"

She shook her head. "Our drive is a brute to turn in. So if I'm going to use the car later I leave it out in the road. Quite a bit of traffic goes by about six o'clock, so I wouldn't have noticed anyone starting it up. The police think it was used for a burglary, but none had been reported this morning."

"It's a bit scratched at the side."

"I know. It could have been driven too near a thorn hedge."

And it still could have been driven by you. . . .

I noticed how tight her hands were on the wheel and the dark shadows under her pale eyes. I didn't believe these signs of strain were caused by her car being stolen the night before. If, indeed, it had been.

She glanced at her wristwatch. "I really must be getting along."

"Yes, of course. I'm sorry I walked right out like that."

"You'd better not daydream any more." Her smile was empty. "It doesn't get anyone anywhere, does it?"

I agreed that it didn't and gave her a little wave as she drove on.

Inspector Gray called soon after I reached home, and I told him about my experience the night before. He didn't suggest, as I had supposed, that it had been a drunken driver. Instead he said that Miss Tasker's car had probably been used by some petty thief who wasn't an experienced car driver and had lost control of the steering wheel for a few moments.

"At the precise moment when he saw me?" I asked skeptically.

He gave me his brilliant, level look.

"That is what we'll have to find out, Miss Brant, when we catch him."

"You think you will?"

"Oh, yes."

I longed to ask him what other evidence he had to make him so certain, but I knew he wouldn't tell me—if, indeed, he had any.

Mrs. Cranmer had a very slight attack of angina early that morning. I had been expecting this to happen. Events were too much for her and when she was in bed and the doctor had gone, I left her, at her insistence, to Ferry.

When I rang through to the farm, Chauncey said that Sarne had come in very late the night before, long after she and Ned were in bed. He had left early this morning, riding over to a farm near Corfe in which he had an interest. Since Mrs. Cranmer was ill, I realized that he didn't yet know of the attack on me.

After I had seen Marnie and assured myself that she no longer needed me I took the car and went into Arlesthorne to change Mrs. Cranmer's library books.

There was a brightness and bustle about the main street that made me want to linger. I shopgazed and saw a dress I liked. It was gray with a thin silky white stripe in it. I went in and found that it only needed shortening. I bought it and then went and had some tea. By the time I reached the library it was getting dark. I collected two books for Mrs. Cranmer and then asked for Miss Tasker.

I was shown to a room off the reference library on the first floor. Gillian was alone there. She looked up from a list she was checking, and I obviously startled her.

"Why, Loran . . ."

"I thought you'd like to know why your car was stolen last night."

She waved me to a chair.

I shook my head. "I'm not stopping. I had a visit from Inspector Gray this morning. It was about your car."

She obviously found it difficult, or distasteful, to sit looking up at me. She rose and stood, arms folded.

"How are you involved with my car?"

"It nearly ran me down last night," I said.

Her gaze sharpened. "You didn't catch sight of the man who was driving? It was used for a burglary somewhere, you know."

"Well, that's the theory of the police." I took a deep breath. "Whoever nearly ran me down did it deliberately," I said slowly, making certain that she heard every word.

She didn't speak for a moment. Then her voice jerked at me. "For heaven's sake, Loran, why should anyone want to do such a thing?"

"That's what I'd like to know."

She leaned against her desk. "You're not really serious. You can't be." Her voice was husky. "Whoever stole my car didn't know how to drive, and lost control."

"It's the obvious explanation," I said. "And I have a feeling the police think it, too. But I know better. I was the one who was there."

"But why should anyone . . ." she began again, and broke off. Her eyes narrowed. "Unless there is a reason we know nothing about. Is there?"

"Why ask me?"

"It's so strange, all of it." She was considering me with suspicion. "Your reason for being here, for instance. You must know that it's almost impossible for someone to trace his real parents if he's adopted. So why *are* you here?"

"For the reason I thought everyone knew. The one you think is impossible."

"They're saying in the village that you came here to check on us, to find out what happened to Claire. Why? Are you some relative of hers or did the police send you?"

"They said the same about Martin. And he's . . . dead," I told her with more calm than I was feeling. "And someone is trying either to kill me or frighten me into going back to London."

"That's nonsense."

"Death isn't nonsense," I said shakenly.

She turned away from me and picked up some papers on her desk. She seemed unflatteringly uninterested in my near-escape from death. She wanted me to go. But I hadn't finished with her yet.

She was altogether too held in on herself, too evasive. I wanted to break through that.

"You're afraid, aren't you, that Claire is dead and that Sarne will be implicated?"

She looked up from the papers she had been fingering and her pale eyes hated me. "What gives you the right to come here and question me?"

"I'm sorry. But I'm obviously implicated as well. Somehow it's all linked up and I'm trying to find out why."

She made no comment.

"You were Claire's friend in the beginning, weren't you? So have you any idea—any at all—where she might have gone?"

"If I had I'd tell the police . . . or Sarne."

"Not if you had a good reason for not telling," I said. "There are already things you should have told them which you haven't. Like Claire's visit to you on the night she disappeared, for instance."

She raised her head. The flash of hatred was gone. She looked just plain and starkly miserable.

"I was never Claire's friend," she said, without asking me how I had found out something which the police didn't know. "How could I be? Claire married Sarne."

"You love him, don't you?"

I expected her to tell me to mind my own business. She said nothing.

"Gillian." I leaned forward, my palms spread flat on her desk. "Do *you* think Claire is still alive?"

"She's quite capable of being," she said in her flat, colorless voice. "Claire hated farm life; she didn't even love Sarne. She was possessive about him, and that's something quite different. I always knew one day there'd be a final, dreadful quarrel between them and she'd pack her things and leave." She paused and drew a long breath. "That's what I was waiting for—for her to leave him."

Suddenly she put her face in her hands. Watching, I felt a sudden, swift pity for her. I went around the desk and put my hands on her thin arms.

"You should get away," I said. "Go and find yourself an apartment in Arlesthorne. You don't meet enough people in the village, that's the trouble, and though you work here in a town, you rush home every evening to look after an old man. It's too narrow a life. Sarne isn't the only man in the world, you know."

She dragged her arms away from my touch as the door opened

and a girl carrying a load of art books came in. She crossed to a small desk and dumped the books.

"Let's get out of here," Gillian said in a low voice.

I followed her through the door and into a large, richly-furnished room adjoining her office. There was a long, highly-polished table running down the center of it and chairs arranged formally on either side.

"This is the committee room. No one will disturb us." She leaned up against the table and faced me. "Not that there's anything more we have to say to each other."

"You won't see, will you, that you're wasting your life? All right, so I'm interfering. But a village like Saxon Magna is rather like a secular convent, if you know what I mean. You can be shut away from the world, and unless you're careful your perspective gets all wrong."

"Thank you, Loran, but I don't need a lecture."

"I think you do. I think it's time someone told you to get out of the rut."

"It's all so familiar," she whispered. "It's a matter of belonging in Saxon. You wouldn't understand, but I . . . I'm afraid to leave it."

"If you don't break away now you'll soon find it too late."

"And if I stay." Little pinpoints of light gleamed in her eyes. "Don't you see? Deborah is no more suited for life on a farm than Claire. If she went . . ." She left the possibility in the air for me to grasp.

I wondered whether to tell her the truth that wishful thinking wouldn't let her face, to say to her, "Deborah isn't like Claire; Deborah knows what she wants. And farm or no farm, she wants Sarne." I didn't say it. I felt a deep sense of failure. I had tried to help her, but perhaps I'd gone about it the wrong way. For myself, nothing had been resolved. I still wasn't certain how she felt about me or what she was capable of if she thought I was here to watch Sarne. Such a circumscribed life as she had chosen for herself led to neurosis—it could even lead to violence.

I turned to leave her. The wild, rich colors of a painting over the mantelshelf drew me. I went and stood underneath it.

"That picture . . ." I began.

"It's one of Tom MacQueen's," she said. "It was presented to the library some years ago."

I scarcely heard her. I was staring at the lower right-hand corner of the picture. There, barely an inch high, was a little painted phoenix riding a spear.

"The bird . . ."

"Oh, that's Tom MacQueen's signature. That's how you know his paintings."

I went on staring at the little crowned, high-winged bird.

"It's identical with the engraving on my topaz! You didn't notice it, of course. I lost it on my second day here. Martin Cavall found it."

"So Mrs. Cranmer told me. Where do you think he found it?"

I didn't know and I didn't care.

"I've got to see Tom MacQueen," I said desperately. "I've got to see him now. The topaz was given me at my christening. It could have been a gift from my parents."

"You really did come down here to find your parents?"

"Of course. *I've* told you. *Mrs. Cranmer's* told you."

"I didn't believe . . ."

"I don't care what you believed." I was out of the room and racing down the stairs. And as I went I was saying Tom MacQueen's address wildly over and over again to myself.

Manx Cottage, Verry Road. Manx Cottage, Verry Road. . . .

I didn't stop to think that he might be in the hospital.

It took me ten minutes and many askings to find it. When I got there it was just a small, dark house in a very dark street. I rang and knocked and nobody came. Inside I could hear the telephone bell shrill. I went back to the car and sat and waited and watched. If he were in bed with whatever illness had summoned Deborah, his housekeeper must be looking after him. She could merely have gone out for a few minutes. Then I realized that Mrs. Cranmer might be worried about me if I stayed too long here. I drove off and found a public telephone booth and rang Ferry, telling her I would be home as soon as I could, but without explaining where I was.

Then I went back to the house. It was still in darkness but I rang the bell again. Somewhere inside I heard a sound. I stood with my eyes riveted on the door. It opened. I saw the beautiful cornelian-colored coat first.

"Come right in, dear," said Deborah.

"Is Mr. MacQueen in?"

"Come and see for yourself." The door opened wide and invitingly.

"There's something terribly important I have to ask him," I said and followed her into the living room. "Is he well enough to see me?"

She switched on the light without answering. The walls sprang to life. On every one I saw pictures, violent riotous color, fantastic form, restless and devastating to live with. Gauguin had painted the walls of his South Sea hut. Old Tom MacQueen had hung pictures on every square inch of his, and in the corner of each, as I looked slowly, as though in a dream, was painted the tiny phoenix bird.

Deborah laughed. "I know! You're stunned by it all. So is everyone who ever comes into this room. They think they've walked into either a nightmare or a heaven, according to their appreciation of Father's art."

I was only vaguely aware of the room itself. It was two knocked into one, furnished with a few curious pieces—one colossal settee covered in lime-green cloth, an enormous black carved chest, a lacquer screen. It was no room to feel cozy in. But I had no time to study it. I had to see Tom MacQueen.

"Please," I turned to Deborah, "may I talk to your father?"

"You'd better come with me."

I followed her into a back room.

On an outsize bed lay Tom MacQueen.

"You see?" she said, "he's sleeping."

I made a move towards the bed but she stopped me.

"You won't be able to wake him," she chuckled. "I've had to give him a nice strong sedative. Recalcitrant parents need something to keep them in order. Fortunately he can't walk. That makes it so much easier to handle him."

"He's ill. You told me so yesterday."

"Did I? Oh—oh it was nothing." Her eyes looked at me oddly as though not quite focusing; then she smiled and drew me out of the room. "Let's wait and see if he wakes naturally, shall we?

In the meantime, would you like to see his studio? It's right at the top of the house. He can only get up there now if he's carried. Kate, his housekeeper, gets help when he wants to go up there. But that's seldom, these days."

Actually, I was in a fever of impatience for Tom MacQueen to wake, to know if the similarity between the phoenix that was his signature and the one engraved on my topaz was mere coincidence.

I followed her reluctantly to the top of the old house. The studio stretched the width of it. One whole side was taken up by a vast wall of glass and on another there was an ordinary-sized window that opened onto a little semicircular Regency balcony. Against the other two walls were piles of canvases.

"All worth a great deal of money." Deborah waved towards them. She walked to the little window. "One day this house and everything in it will be mine. But I shall sell it, of course. If Sarne and I need a second home we'll probably have a London apartment."

"Sarne . . . and you? But there's Claire. . . ."

Deborah opened the window, stepped onto the little balcony, and leaned back against the low parapet, watching me. Her face was bright with color, and excitement sparked from her. She kept me waiting for my answer and when she spoke her voice had a throbbing, unnatural quality.

"Claire will never come back. She's dead."

"That's just village gossip."

"You think so?" She considered me, her head slightly on one side, the wind stirring her black hair. "Suppose I tell you that Sarne killed her."

"You can't know what you're saying."

She smiled slowly. "No one knows better," she said. "Sarne has a violent temper and he loves me. Add those two things together and you've a motive for killing."

You're quite wrong, he loves me. . . .

But even in my mind the words faltered before Deborah's strength and confidence. All I could be certain of was *my* love for *him.*

My legs began to tremble; I felt as though I were in a jungle of dread and doubt. I wondered for a moment whether Deborah was drunk, the whole situation seemed so beyond reality. But then that was how some things were . . . terrifying things that found their way into newspapers. I was tingling with an instinctive terror. The light from the room seemed to catch only Deborah's eyes as she stood on the shadowy balcony, and her steady gaze was like a cat's hypnotic stare.

I swung away from her and walked to the door and turned the handle. It didn't give. I turned it again and pushed. I put my shoulder against it.

"It's stuck."

"It's locked," she told me calmly.

My fear thrust deeper. But I gave that shadowy face on the balcony a level stare.

"Then unlock it and let me go."

She came into the room and stood by a mirror and combed her hair with her fingers.

"I can't, Loran. I just can't let you go." She spoke so simply, almost with a note of pleading in her voice.

"If you've got anything to say to me, say it later." I pretended impatience. "I want to see if your father is now awake. I must know why he chose that particular curious way of signing his paintings."

"There's nothing odd about it. Lots of artists have an individual mark that is entirely their own."

"I'm talking about the fact that his is an exact replica of the engraving on my topaz."

She looked at my reflection in the mirror.

"I've no intention of letting you talk to my father." Her voice was suddenly hostile.

"Oh, but all I've got to do when I get back to the manor is to pick up the telephone," I said.

She was shaking her head slowly, smiling that curious, brilliant smile. "It's too late. You see, I don't suppose my father will wake up."

I had been holding on tightly to the door handle. I let go. My lips felt very dry and I licked them.

"What have you done?"

"He was such a nuisance to me," she said, "so I've told you—I drugged him."

I could only think of one way to open that door and that was to smash it. I picked up a chair and turned to hurl it at the door. Deborah's hand came down on mine. She wrenched the chair away. "You can't get out until I choose. I'm very strong."

I didn't dare show I was afraid of her. I walked past her to the balcony and looked down. We were three stories up and immediately underneath was what looked in the darkness like a paved yard. I was still dazed by what was happening. As yet I was fighting an enemy without knowing why I was hated. Deborah was mad, of course.

Her voice came softly from behind me.

"It's quite a way down, isn't it?"

I knew that I was in danger on the balcony. As I pushed past her into the room I heard her heavy breathing.

"What have I done to you?" I whispered. "It isn't Sarne, is it, because you hated me before . . . before . . ."

She cut me short. "I'm not interested in your feelings for him," she said. "Sarne won't have any woman if the police find him guilty of Claire's death. He realizes that all I have to do is to give evidence, to tell what I know. I won't, of course, unless I'm forced to. He killed for *me*. I like that kind of ruthlessness in a man. But you see now, don't you, that his life is in my hands? I can save him or break him and a man values his life more than anything in the world. So I'm not afraid he'll ever leave me."

"I won't believe Sarne killed Claire—if she *is* dead," I said harshly.

"And what about Martin?" she asked softly.

I put my hand to my throat. I would have believed myself to be living in a nightmare had everything not been too sharply outlined for that, with too much reason underlying the madness. I backed instinctively from her.

"So now that you see what a predicament Sarne is in," Deborah said, "perhaps you'll get out of all our lives."

"Is this a form of blackmail?"

"You can call it what you like, but it's up to you whether I shall give evidence for or against him—should the police be able to prove that Claire was killed, that is."

"And if they can't?" I clenched my hands to tighten my control.

"Things have changed quite dramatically," she said. "This afternoon they searched the ruins at Falcon's Point again. And this time I think they found something. It's beginning to look bad, isn't it?"

I couldn't trust my voice.

"I've a proposition to make to you," Deborah said.

Still I stared, waiting.

"If you'll leave here tonight. Now. *Now,*" she repeated. "I'll give the kind of evidence that will exonerate Sarne. I've got it all worked out in my mind. It'll be perjury, but that doesn't matter to me. Will you do that? Will you go now?"

I couldn't meet her lovely, sleepy stare. I put my hands to my face and turned away.

"I'm leaving in a few days anyway," I murmured.

"That's too long to stay," she said impatiently. "I'll run you to the station now. You can write some note of explanation to Mrs. Cranmer—I don't care what excuse you give—and ask her to send your things on. And then . . ."

It was then that I saw the glint of a key in her left hand.

"For God's sake open that door. Your father could be dying."

"Give me your promise to leave now and I'll ring the doctor." She waited. Then as I didn't speak, she asked, "Is it so hard for you to tear yourself away from here?"

"I still don't know what all this is about. And for the moment I can't care. Just get that door open." I shouted at her and made a grab for the key she held.

"Uh-uh!" She shook her head, smiling as though it were a game, and put her hand behind her back.

"Give it to me."

Suddenly we were struggling. I tore at her hands, I heard her lovely coat rip at a seam. Her scent—Guerlain's Mitsouko which I'd always loved—was almost too powerful. She twisted and flung me away from her. I fell against the sharp corner of the dais. She watched me right myself and then she laughed.

"All right, since you're so obstinate, come and see Father. Perhaps you'll realize then that I mean it when I say I won't fetch a doctor until you promise to leave here and never contact any of us again. I'm sure you'll see, when you look at him, that Father will die if he doesn't have help at once. It could already be too late. We'll see. If it isn't, then it'll be up to you whether he lives or dies."

Her father—and Sarne. One life, certainly, and maybe two, had been made my responsibility.

She sauntered to the door and unlocked it.

I made a single wild dive past her and rushed and stumbled down the stairs. I was wearing low-heeled shoes. Deborah had high, thin heels which impeded her speed. I heard her clattering behind me down the three flights. I landed somehow on the parquet floor of the hall, raced into the living room and slammed the door and locked it. By a stroke of luck the telephone was in that room.

I dialed Sarne's number. Chauncey answered.

"It's Loran." I swallowed and gasped into the mouthpiece. "Get a doctor to come to Tom MacQueen's house. And the police. Quick . . . be quick. . . ."

The last words were drowned by Deborah calling out to me, "That isn't very clever. Other keys in the house fit that lock."

I didn't wait to replace the receiver. Nor did I dare now try to reach old Tom MacQueen. Deborah must have heard me call for the police. If I made a move in her father's direction, heaven knew what she'd do to ensure that he wouldn't wake, and that I wouldn't be alive to tell my story. She was too maddened by something . . . power, desire . . . to stop to consider her own danger.

I rushed to the nearest window, dragged it up and climbed up onto the ledge. The drop was easy. I jumped down into a courtyard. For a moment I stared around me.

XVII

My heart sank as I realized what I'd done. There were two windows in that room, one looking over the little garden and the street, the other into this well. I saw a wrought iron railing curving along area steps leading to cellars. High walls surrounded me on the other three sides. My ignorance of the layout of the house had trapped me.

Deborah's voice came from behind me. "When you open a window you should make less noise about it."

I turned and saw her tall, shadowy figure.

"The doctor's on his way . . ." I said hoarsely.

She was very still and her voice came softly. "It's a terrible thing to have your father take an overdose of drugs, and a girl you were trying to help kill herself before your eyes. Even the police will be moved by my story."

She began to slide almost imperceptibly towards me. At the bottom of the area steps loomed a deeper blackness. I clung with both hands to the iron railing that ran down to the cellar. Deborah stood between me and the window.

"You tried three times to kill me." My voice came jerkily, choked with terror. "First at the well; then you drugged the tea I drank at Falcon Point and . . . and then again last night. You stole Gillian's car, didn't you, and tried to run me down. Why?"

I braced myself as she took another step towards me. Had I been certain that the cellar door was unlocked, I would have made for it. But some instinct told me not to take that chance. If I ran down there and the door was locked, I was even more helplessly trapped.

"Poor Loran." Her voice came out of the darkness. "There was nothing I could do to save you. You were so overwrought because of your failure to find your parents and that brother—Anthony, did you say his name was? It was quite an obsession with you, wasn't it? And then when you learned that my father could help you, you rushed here only to find him dead. There was Sarne, too. You developed quite a thing about him, didn't you? Whereas to him you were just a—well—a pretty stranger. That was the last straw that broke your own little camel's back, wasn't it?"

I sensed rather than saw in the darkness her head turn towards the cellar steps.

I shot forward to try to get to the window. She was too quick for me. My gasp ended in a small scream.

"It's very isolated here," she said.

"Why do you hate me? You say it isn't because of Sarne. . . ."

Her short, harsh laugh checked me. I gathered all my strength. This wasn't the time to stop and question. The doctor was on his way, and perhaps Sarne. But Deborah was going to make certain they were too late. I was cornered whichever way I turned. I flung myself back towards the rail and my fingers caught and clutched the cold iron. Deborah was breathing deeply.

"You can . . . at least . . . tell me what I've done to you to make you want to kill me. . . ." I knew suddenly that I had to keep her talking to delay the final struggle between us.

"You came down here so full of fine hopes, didn't you?"

"Tell me!" I cried again.

"You still don't know?" She stopped abruptly and listened. I heard the sound, too. A car had stopped outside. I didn't dare relax my grip of the railing. She would have had me off-balance and lying with a broken neck at the foot of that twisted flight of steps before help could come.

A car door slammed. I began to shout. Deborah wheeled around. She hurled herself from the window towards me. I flung myself sideways, calling wildly to whoever was hammering on the door, "The window—try the window." I shouted so loudly that I hurt my throat.

Whether whoever knocked heard me or not I had no idea. I was fighting Deborah for my life. There were background sounds but I couldn't spare a moment to identify them. Deborah was strong.

Suddenly, as we struggled, a light came on in the room behind us. I had a swift sight of men rushing towards us. I heard someone cry my name:

"Loran!"

Deborah's grip on me relaxed. Free of her fighting hands, I swayed and staggered. Someone caught me and held me close.

"Sarne!" I cried, and then pushed him aside. "Her father! Get help for her father!"

Sarne steadied me. "Dr. Baines is with him. I brought him along."

"Tom MacQueen could be . . . dead. . . ."

Sarne didn't answer me. He half-lifted me back into the room, and as I blinked in the light I saw Inspector Gray and his huge sergeant in the hall.

Then I realized that the whole house seemed to thud with sound. I heard footsteps rushing up the stairs.

I broke away from Sarne and dragged open the door. The two policemen were pounding up the second flight. On the landing I saw a flash of cornelian color whirl through the air. Deborah had dragged off her coat and flung it at her pursuers. I stumbled over it as I reached the landing; there was a great tear down one sleeve.

"Loran, come back!"

I heard Sarne's voice but I took no notice. The cellar door must have been unlocked and Deborah had gone through it. Now she was ahead of us all, racing to the studio at the top of the house.

I was gasping for breath when I reached the great room. The inspector was on the little balcony, the sergeant stood just behind him. I could not see Deborah anywhere.

"Loran, come away!"

I took no notice of Sarne. I pushed past the sergeant. Deborah was crouched on the roof, just out of reach of us all.

"This is merely a delaying tactic, Mrs. Millbrook," the inspector was saying. "It's not helping you, you know."

In the light streaming from the room, I saw Deborah's face turned towards me.

"She's responsible," she said in a slurred voice. "She came here to find her father. She went looking all over the place, I'll give her that . . . she was thorough. But she didn't look near enough."

"We aren't talking about Miss Brant. We're talking of Mrs. Algar. You know where she is, don't you, Mrs. Millbrook?"

"Oh, yes, I know. And so does that half-gypsy creature Babette. She told you, only you wouldn't listen."

"She told us and we listened. But the police can't perform miracles," said Inspector Gray gently. "It took time. We found Mrs. Algar this afternoon. You know where, don't you?"

She remained crouched on the narrow ledge without speaking.

"We found Mrs. Algar's body at Falcon Point."

"It was careless of you not to have found her before, wasn't it?" she said still in that dreamy half-mesmerized voice. "We'd all have been saved so much, wouldn't we?"

"It was a thousand-to-one chance she was found at all," he said, as calmly as though we were sitting cozily around a fire. "The church that had been destroyed at the beginning of the century was medieval. It contained one of those rare old sounding urns that were used in olden days for acoustics. When the church crashed, the urn only partially broke. Mounds of soft earth falling at the same time must have saved it from being smashed to pieces. Mrs. Algar's body was drawn by the suction of the sea into it. That's why we didn't find her on those other searches."

"Sarne killed her," Deborah said. "He killed her for my sake. Why couldn't you leave things alone? I . . ."

"Sarne wouldn't kill," I shouted.

The inspector turned and put out a hand and waved me to silence. I felt Sarne's hand on my shoulder and looked at him.

"I'll never believe—" I heard my own harsh voice begin.

He gathered me to him without a word. I felt his strength enfold me and I felt safe. But I remained leaning against him, one hand gripping his lean, brown arm.

"There is just one thing about which you aren't quite correct, Mrs. Millbrook," the inspector was saying almost gently. "Mr. Algar didn't kill his wife. . . . You did."

She began to laugh. "Really, how could I? I was with my father. He had fallen and injured his spine. He was in Trenthide Hospital. I stayed the night with him—the night Mrs. Algar was killed."

"Not all night."

"What do you mean?" Her voice came sharply through the black night, each word like the crack of a whip.

"Suppose I try to tell you what I think happened?"

She said nothing. The inspector moved towards her.

"You'd better come inside first, Mrs. Millbrook. That coping doesn't look very safe."

"It's safe enough."

I watched the inspector, certain that he was not talking for talking's sake. I wondered who, or what, he was waiting for, playing for time with his story.

"I think your father regained consciousness and asked you to fetch some things for him from home. You went, though since he was in a private ward no one, apparently, saw you go. I suggest that when you passed through Saxon Magna on your way from the Trenthide Hospital to Arlesthorne late that night you saw Mrs. Algar. You already knew both her and her husband very well. You stopped the car and she, upset over a quarrel, got in. You let her talk; you drove her out to Falcon Point and then—you killed her."

"And am I supposed to have carried her body down to the cove and thrown it into the sea? Really, Inspector, you'll have to think up something more convincing than that."

"Oh, no. You had to get help. So you got Martin Cavall. Mrs. Millbrook, in another few minutes the fire ladders will be here and we'll have to bring you down by force. You don't want that, do you?"

"I'll jump."

"Oh, no, you won't. You're much too sensible. Tell me, was my deduction as to how you killed Mrs. Algar right?"

"You'll never know, will you?"

"We've been questioning the patients who were in Trenthide Hospital that night and we've traced one who is no longer living in England. The police in Switzerland have interviewed him. He saw you on the night in question pass the door of the ward where he lay. And that half-gypsy, Babette, saw you too, down at the point."

"You didn't believe her when she told you."

"We didn't at first, but her story tallies now."

"With whose? With someone lying in the hospital, probably half-alive?" she demanded in derision.

"No. With Martin Cavall's statement. You see, he didn't quite trust you, Mrs. Millbrook. So he wrote the full story. It was only to be opened and read by us in the event of his death. To be absolutely safe, he mailed the sealed envelope to his sister in Australia. We have just learned the contents."

"Oh, no . . . no. . . ." She gave a cry.

"If you were to be the cause of his death, he wanted you to pay the penalty. So in that letter is the whole story."

"What . . . story?" she asked in a queer, keening voice. "What . . . did he . . . tell you?"

"That you wanted Mrs. Algar's husband. That you killed her and then schemed to be taken on as his housekeeper. That you promised Cavall money, a lot of money, for the price of his help and his silence—you'd get that money by eventually selling your father's pictures, you said. You'd make Cavall comfortable for life on condition he helped you dispose of Mrs. Algar's body. The fact that if you married Mr. Algar you'd be committing bigamy didn't bother either of you, it seemed."

"Bigamy?"

"Of course. I wonder where Martin Millbrook found the name Cavall? He was your husband, wasn't he?"

XVIII

I HEARD the clang of the fire engine as it turned the corner of the road. Sarne heard it too, and said gently, "Come away, Loran."

The fire engine had stopped. I heard a wild, hysterical screaming. I wanted to cover my ears, to stop the impact of Deborah's trapped animal terror. On the landing I paused and faced Sarne.

"You got here very quickly after my call."

"Call?" He looked surprised. "If you rang I was already on my way here with the police."

"You must tell me." I stood a little back from him, not daring to touch him.

"Tell you what?" He was looking down at me and I had never before seen that look of sadness on his face.

"Deborah," I said. "You loved her, didn't you?"

"I knew her—Claire and I both knew her—and I liked her. She was beautiful and competent and intelligent. I was grateful to her for taking over when Claire went. I had three children to be looked after. But I didn't love her. She was only my housekeeper."

He didn't plead with me to believe him. He knew that I would.

I shut my eyes and for the first time since the beginning of that dreadful evening, I felt my body relax.

There were sounds coming from outside the house. Men's voices and Deborah's, high-pitched, protesting, still with that uncanny, keening, whining note. There was also a sound from the hall. I remembered suddenly.

"Tom MacQueen," I said and started to run down the stairs.

The cornelian coat was still there. I stepped over it. There was a man in the hall. He looked up. "I'm Dr. Baines," he said. "Are you Miss Brant?"

"Yes."

"Mr. MacQueen is asking for you."

"How is he?"

"Oh, he's all right," he said cheerfully. "I've telephoned for his housekeeper. She's on her way. I gather Mrs. Millbrook sent her to her daughter's for the night."

I went into the ground floor back room. Tom MacQueen was sitting in a chair by a large electric stove. He wore a brown monk's robe and his hair was all ways.

"What is happening?" he said to me. "Where is Debby?"

"Deborah is ill," Sarne said. "They're going to take care of her."

Tom MacQueen shook his head. "Don't save me a shock. I know. She's mad, isn't she? She didn't inherit it; she comes of very sane stock. Her own greed sent her mad; she wanted so much. You, Algar. My paintings and—" All the time he spoke he had been looking at me. Now his eyes deepened. "She wanted you out of the way, too."

"I still don't know what I've done," I said. "It wasn't because of Sarne; she told me so."

"No, it was because of what you are."

"What I am?" I stared at him, feeling that it was I who was drugged and stupid, not old Tom MacQueen.

He ran his fingers through his wild hair.

"Debby arrived here tonight as though devils were after her. For some time I'd watched her change, begin to crack under some strain—I didn't know what. Tonight the crack came. She couldn't even hide herself from me. She couldn't play-act any more. It's pretty awful when you suddenly realize that your own daughter would like you dead. That's the way she behaved tonight. I thought it odd when she became solicitous and poured me out a drink—she's always handed me the bottle before. She was in a ferment and she made a mistake. She put just too much water in my drink so that the strength of the whisky didn't hide the odd taste. I pretended to drink it. I swallowed some, but when she turned her back on me, I spat out most of it into my water jug. I'd have been dead if I hadn't. As it was, I went into a drugged sleep."

I drew back against Sarne and felt his arm around me. Outside I could hear men's voices and the start of a heavy engine. I wondered if they'd fetched Deborah's lovely coat from the landing and remembered how I'd torn it. I still ached with the violence of my fight with her and the marks of her nails were red and angry on my arms and face.

"I badly wanted to see you tonight," I said to Tom MacQueen. "But I'm afraid now isn't the time. . . ."

"The time for what?" he demanded as I hesitated.

"Perhaps if I could come tomorrow—" I began.

If I could ever have imagined Tom MacQueen being shy, I'd have said that that was what made him look at me in that odd, doubting way. For some incredible reason this wild old man was nervous of me.

"You'd like to know why Debby wanted you out of the way too, wouldn't you?"

"You mean you know?"

"Oh, she told me the truth after she thought I'd drunk that Scotch. She was so sure I'd never wake and it was a relief to tell someone, particularly someone who wouldn't live through the night."

The door behind us opened and Inspector Gray came in.

"Your daughter is accompanying us to headquarters, Mr. MacQueen."

"Of course she is," he snapped. "But you won't keep her there. She's mad."

The inspector looked at Sarne. "We'll want you there too, sir."

He nodded. "I'll come."

I watched the door close behind the inspector and then looked at Sarne. His face was gray. The accumulated strain of the past year had suddenly caught up with him. It was he who wanted comfort, not I. I longed for this meeting with Tom MacQueen to be over so that I could be alone with Sarne. But first there were things to be done.

"Deborah will want a suitcase packed with some of her things." The remark sounded irrelevant. As though her possessions, her lovely clothes, would ever matter now. She had tried to kill me, but I couldn't feel hatred, only a dreadful, weary compassion for her.

"Don't you know why Deborah wanted you out of the way?"

I shook my head at Tom MacQueen. "No."

"Did it occur to you that she went to great lengths to see that you and I didn't meet?"

"Yes, Mr. MacQueen, I suppose she did."

"Don't call me Mr. MacQueen," he interrupted me. "For Pete's sake, girl, don't you see now why all this happened?" He ran his hands again through his hair and kept them there. His face, framed in the wide monk sleeves, regarded me. "I'm your father," he said.

For a moment the words didn't quite register. Then I moved away from Sarne's arm and sat down weakly in a chair. I couldn't take my eyes from Tom MacQueen's face. *I came to find you. I came here to find you . . . and now it's happened, I can't believe it. . . .*

It could have been shock; it could have been partly because I was overwrought, or it could merely have been the irony of the whole situation, but I suddenly began to laugh. To my astonishment, so did old Tom MacQueen.

"At least," he said, "you're not a hypocrite, girl! You don't come running to my arms."

I stopped laughing abruptly. "I came here to look for my parents. Did you know that?"

"Of course I didn't. Except for that time at the library, you and I never had more than a glimpse of each other. Debby saw to that."

"You mean she knew all the time?"

He nodded. "From the moment you came here."

"But how could she?"

Behind me Sarne stirred. "I'll have to go down to police headquarters," he said. "Can you get yourself home, Loran?"

"Of course. I came in Mrs. Cranmer's car."

"If you like, I'll pick you up here when they've finished with me."

I shook my head. "I can get back all right. Although—" I looked across the room—"I oughtn't to leave you alone," I said to my father.

"Just because you turn out to be my daughter, you don't need to feel dutiful," he said. "Debby sent Katie off for the night. She's my housekeeper. The police have called her back. She'll arrive some time soon."

Sarne moved away from me. "I'll see you later, Loran."

I nodded. It was a matter of fact leavetaking.

When the door closed, Tom MacQueen said, "Your mother and I had damn little money, but she understood that I couldn't be anything else but an artist. You were our youngest child. When you were born your mother was too ill to look after you. She died only a few weeks after we gave you away. Soon after that, Debby and I went abroad."

"But how did you know me?"

"I didn't until Debby told me. I'd never have known, anyway. When you get a child adopted, no one tells you where it's going. But Deborah, always the little snooper, went to the doctor's one night to fetch some medicine for her mother. She was the only one in the waiting room and the patient with the doctor hadn't closed the door properly. So she listened. The man in there was your adopted father, Richard Brant. He was making arrangements with the doctor to adopt you—oh, all nice and legal, through an adoption society, of course. Because he was who he was, a surgeon, strings were pulled for him and his wife to jump the adoption line. I don't know whether it could happen these days. But this was just as war broke out. Anyway, that's what my dear little elder daughter heard. And she never told me she knew where you'd gone. So when you came to Saxon Magna and she learned your name and why you were here, she knew who you were. You could say that Deborah was mad with greed. My paintings will fetch a lot of money when I'm dead and they're put on the market. Debby didn't want to share that with anyone, least of all with a girl who'd been given away at birth."

"Did you give me the topaz with the phoenix on it?"

"Good God, have you got that?"

"I always felt it had been given me by one of my parents."

"That topaz had belonged to my grandmother—and an old Tartar she was. I took the phoenix as my trademark, as it were."

"One of your paintings hangs in Deborah's room. She showed it to me. But there was no phoenix in the corner. I now know why. She'd painted a little splodge of bluish-white to represent a pool of water there. Deborah must have recognized my topaz the day I went to the farm to lunch. A man named Martin found it, I don't know where. He probably managed to get into her room one day and take it. Did you know Martin was her husband?"

"Not until tonight. They married abroad. He was a nogood, too." My father looked at me and gave a little sigh. "I'm a louse, aren't I, giving you away?"

"I'll tell you when I've thought about it," I said, and went over and kissed his dry cheek.

Someone was entering the hall. I heard the sound of high heels, and then the door opened.

Katie was like the music-hall idea of a barmaid. She was a dyed blonde with cheeks rouged like a painted doll's. She came bustling in, beaming at my father in triumph.

"So you couldn't do without me."

"My daughter's in jail."

"What?" Her smile vanished. She dropped her handbag and let it lie on the floor while she stared at him. I picked the bag up, handed it to her and went to the door.

"Just one thing," I said. "I've got a brother, too, haven't I? An aunt of Richard Brant's said I had and that his name was Anthony."

"I'd have liked a son, that's why I gave Debby her first name. She hated it and always called herself Deborah."

"What was her first name?"

"Antonia," he said, "the nearest thing I could find to a boy's name that your mother would agree to." He leaned back and closed his eyes. His long white fingers were listless in his lap. I had a feeling he wanted to be alone, that as yet he felt no wild joy in having found me.

"I'll come and see you tomorrow," I promised, and walked out of the room and through the hall. I closed the front door quietly behind me.

I felt strange and not a bit as I'd imagined I would when I found a parent. I got into Mrs. Cranmer's car and sat for a minute or two, staring along the deserted street.

My meeting with my father, I decided, was in character. He'd have hated me to give him the prodigal father act. And for the life of me I couldn't feel warm towards him. That would take time.

I laid my arms across the steering wheel and rested my forehead against the cool metal.

Not a brother called Anthony, but a sister called Antonia. Antonia, Deborah MacQueen . . . Mrs. Millbrook. . . . And I? What Christian name would I have had, had they not given me away?

The little clock on the living room mantelshelf pointed to the half hour after ten.

"Go to bed, child," said Mrs. Cranmer. "You look worn out."

"I can't," I said. "I can't . . . yet."

"You're waiting for Sarne?"

I nodded, staring into the fire.

"Deborah had to take my topaz, didn't she, in case my father saw it? But I wonder why Martin took it from her."

"To give strength to his threats, I suppose," she said.

"Which means that at some time or other during their marriage she must have told him about me."

A ghost of a wry smile touched Mrs. Cranmer's face. "A very unwise move. But I suppose once she must have loved him, and confidences come easily then. I think you should have something to drink, Loran." Mrs. Cranmer was watching me anxiously. "Some coffee, perhaps, or a little brandy?"

I shook my head. "I'll be all right." I would keep awake all night, if need be, so long as Sarne came. I slid out of my shoes and curled up in the big chair. "I wonder if Deborah only meant to frighten me when she removed one of the planks at the well. I wonder if I was only really in danger when Marnie had her accident and I decided to stay."

"We'll probably never know."

"But Martin knew. He watched every move she made from the time she killed Claire," I said. "He must have been determined that whatever happened, she mustn't be suspected. She was his source of income for the rest of his life. I wonder what Martin had to tell me when he asked me to the hut."

"Certainly not the truth about yourself," Mrs. Cranmer said. "He could have had nothing to tell you and have invited you in order to scare Deborah."

I remembered that he had said, mockingly, "As a proof of all the good intentions I have with regard to you, you can tell Deborah and Sarne that you're coming." Deborah, and not Mrs. Cranmer, who was the obvious one to tell. He probably became greedy—or impatient. He could even have hinted to her that he was going to tell me the truth about myself. And so he had to die.

"Babette . . ." I began.

She nodded. "She must go, of course. But I shall see that she has a home. And she must be trained for some work."

"She pretended she knew who had killed Claire," I said. "She must have seen two people down at Falcon Point that night and recognized Deborah. I suppose she drew the conclusion that the man was Sarne."

Mrs. Cranmer said nothing. We sat so still in our strange new peace. In one terrible night fear had built up like a storm, had broken about us and was now gone. It was almost as though we didn't know what to do with the quiet.

"That afternoon on the beach," I said, "when I nearly drowned. Why did Deborah ring through to you to ask if I were home? She saved my life by doing that."

"Don't you realize? It was Marnie. Deborah was there when she told Sarne that you had promised her any very special shells you found on the beach. Deborah knew then that you'd be found. Sarne would wonder why you hadn't come and if she didn't ring through to me, then he would. She was safeguarding herself." Mrs. Cranmer rose stiffly. "She lost her head this afternoon when she heard they'd found Claire's body. She knew then that so much of the truth would come out . . . about you, for instance. The police are very thorough. They delve into seemingly irrelevant facts to get a complete picture of the truth. She had no time to work out a plan. She acted on impulse. This afternoon she rang through to ask if you were in. I said you weren't, that I wasn't well and you'd gone to the library for me. I think she must have gone there and seen you leave. She followed you to her father's house."

"My father, too. . . ."

"It's all over, Loran. I can't believe it." She stood and stared at her reflection in the mirror. "They used to say I didn't look my age. Dear God, I've added twenty years these past few weeks." She picked up her book from a side table. "I'm going to bed now. I'm so tired. But I won't sleep yet. Tell Sarne I'd like him to come and say goodnight to me before he goes." She bent and kissed me. "Goodnight, Loran. Love Sarne. . . ."

Yes, I would love Sarne.

I sat alone by the dying fire, my body aching with tiredness, my mind full of the fantastic jigsaw that had at last been completed. It was only half past ten and Sarne would come and, asleep on my feet, I'd wait for him.

When the door opened I sprang up.

But it was Ferry. Her little black eyes regarded me.

"Madam tells me that Mr. Sarne will be around later and that you will be waiting up for him."

"That's right," I said.

"Then if there's nothing you want, I'll go to bed."

"Thank you, Ferry, there's nothing. Good night."

She hesitated. "Madam told me what happened, about Mrs. Millbrook, and you being Mr. MacQueen's daughter, and about Mrs. Algar."

"It's all over," I said, "and I shall be going home in a few days."

She couldn't keep the joy out of her face. "You will, Miss Brant? You're really going back to London?"

"Of course! You didn't think I was here for good, did you?"

"I . . . I wondered."

"But I've got a job in London. I never intended to stay indefinitely."

"Madam seemed to like you being here. I thought maybe you'd change your mind and stay—for always, I mean. Goodnight, Miss Brant."

She closed the door quietly behind her and I was alone again.

So now I knew. She had been afraid that I'd usurp her position. She loved her life here and she couldn't conceive that I too wouldn't prefer it to my life in London. I'd been a threat to her security. Because of Mrs. Cranmer's affection for me, Ferry probably saw herself out of work and alone. Tonight, however, she realized that I would never take her place in the house and I had a feeling that in time she would even come to like me.

I rested my head on my arms and closed my eyes. Gillian would be the one to hate me now. I was perfectly prepared for it; I wouldn't even mind, if only it would force her out of her obsessed world. Let her get away, meet other men. Let her smash Sarne's photograph in that private room of hers and stop dancing to the phonograph with a cushion in her arms and girlhood dreams of Sarne in her mind.

Gillian . . . Ferry . . . Mrs. Cranmer . . . My thoughts see-sawed between them, mingled and lost their hold. . . .

I don't know how long I slept, but I was awakened by a tapping on the window.

I lifted my head, uncoiled myself and sprang to open the glass door. Sarne entered.

I looked into his drained, exhausted face.

"Was it very bad down there at the police station?"

"Pretty bad."

I put out my hand and drew him over to the fire.

He pushed me gently back into the chair, tossed my kicked-off slippers aside and knelt on the rug. I put out my arms and drew him to me. His head was heavy on my lap and his dark hair was untidy.

"I love you," he whispered. It was all he said.

We stayed like that until the clock struck eleven and he said he must go.

I sent him up to Mrs. Cranmer and when he came down again we kissed just once. Now that he knew we would be together, there was no longer despair and urgency. He had to recover, and it might take him some time. Too much had happened to him for him to be released into happiness all at once. I understood, although my joy had already begun. I stood watching him walk away from me down the drive. One day it would be different. I would walk between the tall elms with him. One day. When? Perhaps next spring . . . perhaps next summer.